At Close Quarters

EUGENIO FUENTES was born in Montehermoso, Cáceres, Spain. His novels include *The Battles of Breda*, *The Birth of Cupid* (winner of the San Fernando Luis Berenguer International Fiction Prize), *So Many Lies* (winner of the Extramadura Creative Novel Award), *Blood of the Angels*, *The Pianist's Hands* and *Depths of the Forest*, which won the Alba/Prensa Canaria Prize in 1999.

MARTIN SCHIFINO is a freelance writer and translator. His translations include Domingo Villar's *Water-Blue Eyes*, Eugenio Fuentes's *The Pianist's Hands* and Luis Leante's *See How Much I Love You*. He lives in Buenos Aires.

At Close Quarters

EUGENIO FUENTES

Translated from the Spanish by
Martin Schifino

Arcadia Books Ltd
15–16 Nassau Street
London W1W 7AB

www.arcadiabooks.co.uk

First published in the United Kingdom by EuroCrime, an imprint of Arcadia Books 2009
Originally published in Spanish by Tusquets Editores, Barcelona as *Cuerpo a Cuerpo* 2007

A catalogue record for this book is available from the British Library.

ISBN 978-1-906413-36-1

Typeset in Minion by MacGuru Ltd
Printed and bound in Finland by WS Bookwell

Arcadia Books gratefully acknowledges the financial support of the Spanish Ministry of Culture in
assisting with the translation of this novel.

Arcadia Books supports English PEN, the fellowship of writers who work together to promote
literature and its understanding. English PEN upholds writers' freedoms in Britain and around the
world, challenging political and cultural limits on free expression. To find out more, visit
www.englishpen.org or contact
English PEN, 6-8 Amwell Street, London EC1R 1UQ

Arcadia Books distributors are as follows:

in the UK and elsewhere in Europe:
Turnaround Publishers Services
Unit 3, Olympia Trading Estate
Coburg Road
London N22 6TZ

in the US and Canada:
Independent Publishers Group
814 N. Franklin Street
Chicago, IL 60610

in Australia:
Tower Books
PO Box 213
Brookvale, NSW 2100

in New Zealand:
Addenda
PO Box 78224
Grey Lynn
Auckland

in South Africa:
Jacana Media (Pty) Ltd
PO Box 291784,
Melville 2109
Johannesburg

Arcadia Books is the *Sunday Times* Small Publisher of the Year

Ophelia: Lord, we know what we are, but know not what we may be.
Shakespeare

1

The School Bus Stop

One morning as he was shaving, he heard children's voices on the other side of the fence outside his house. It was an unusual sound at that hour – ten past nine in the morning – in a quiet residential neighbourhood with wide streets, far from the city centre. He turned off the tap in order to hear better, and in the increasingly loud buzz he made out some adult voices. Razor in hand, his face still lathered with shaving foam, he walked over to the study and, unseen in the semi-darkness of the room, he observed, with surprise and curiosity, the group of children loitering on the broad pavement accompanied by their parents. The kids were all wearing the blue school uniform of the Marian Catholic School he himself had worn as a child. He'd just heard on the radio it was the beginning of term, and seven million Spanish children were returning to school after the summer holidays.

It all made perfect sense when he saw a shiny school bus appear at the end of the street. His house was on a corner, and the stop for a new bus route had been situated there. He realised he was smiling, pleased at the sight which stirred a peaceful but rather boring neighbourhood, in which any novelty – the annual pruning of trees, a change in the traffic system – almost felt like an event. There was too much quietness in the area, too much reserve, as people stayed in their houses and patios, seldom going out into the streets. And so, the sounds of the local children gathering at his doorstep as they set off for school would be like a fresh breeze each morning.

The bus, bearing the name of the school on its windscreen, stopped at the corner. Samuel saw an assistant help the little ones get through the front door and settle in their seats. The parents kissed their children goodbye and then waved at them through the windows, with excessively broad smiles and much movement of the arms.

The last of the children had boarded the bus when he saw a young woman hurrying along the pavement with two children – the elder, who must have been four or five, hanging onto the stroller in which the smaller was sitting. The woman hastily raised an arm to stop the bus from pulling off, and Samuel almost leaned out of the window and shouted at them to wait up, but he checked himself on realising he was still holding his razor and his face was covered in foam. The driver seemed about to shut the doors when he saw the woman crossing the road. She then stopped the stroller, and helped the boy up, giving him a quick kiss.

She breathed out in relief when the bus drove off. Since the other mothers were already walking away, she stayed alone on the pavement – Samuel saw her clearly from his windowed balcony – catching her breath while she tried to make her small child more comfortable in its chair. Then she turned round and checked the number of the house, as if she'd never been there before and wanted to make sure she wouldn't forget the address. When, with a touch of curiosity, she lifted her eyes to the balcony windows, Samuel instinctively stepped back, into the shadows, fearing that she might see him and think he was spying on her. Her eyes lingered for a couple of seconds on the glass, and even though he knew the reflection of the sun and the darkness of the interior prevented her from seeing him, he withdrew a little further, though not to the point of being unable to observe her. The woman was very beautiful. She didn't look weak or fragile, but there was a grace to her movements that she had not lost even when she'd been hurried and agitated, running towards the bus along the pavement.

Then she slowly walked away, her steps undulating slightly under a hemline that stopped just below her knees. He kept his eyes on her until she turned the corner at the second junction, where the detached houses ended and the three-storey blocks began. Samuel was not experienced enough with women not to be moved by visions such as this. When she disappeared from view, he noticed the foam had dried on his face.

That morning, while Samuel was having a coffee in his local bar, the waiter confirmed what he already suspected. The old Marian school had outgrown its small, antiquated premises, a damp dark building in the heart of the run-down city centre, from where the new bourgeoisie had fled over the last decade, preferring the recently developed suburbs. The Marians had acquired vast plots of land on the outskirts, where they had built a modern educational compound with sports facilities, an indoor swimming pool, state-of-the-art installations, and easy access for vehicles, hoping to attract the children and grandchildren of those who had already been educated with them and who refused to take their offspring to the old place, where the cold and draughty classrooms with their high ceilings were now obsolete, and never big enough to take in the teeming crowds of immigrant children whose families had, little by little, taken possession of the dilapidated big houses of the city centre.

He felt gladdened by the news when he left the café. There seemed to be more people in the streets, and he noticed a kind of first-day-of-school excitement affecting even adults without children. This small event would allow him to see the woman the following day, and the one after that, and after that, perhaps for a long time.

Five years previously, Irene and he had bought the house off the plans as its proposed size had closely matched what they were looking for: a place comfortable enough to raise the three children they hoped to have. Although it was a bit far from the beach and the promenade around which the city was laid out, they liked the new area which turned its back to the hustle and bustle of summer tourism, with houses of two storeys at most that by law had to be set back at least three metres from the pavement. Besides, it was near the industrial area where his small company was situated. They had it all planned, and yet, fifteen months after signing the deeds to the house, when it was almost ready, Irene had left him for a frantic web designer whose visual montages were nauseating. They reached an agreement. He bought her out, and settled into a house too large for a single man.

It wasn't an easy period of his life. He thought that as far as women were concerned there were two kinds of men: hard, sarcastic, tough-skinned ones incapable of love and immune to pain; and men capable of pleasure and tenderness and passion, and as a consequence prone to suffering from a lack of the same. He was among the latter. Not that he complained. On the contrary, he was convinced that, in the long run, in the final reckoning of a life, no feelings of love counted as a loss, even if one had given one's love to someone who did not deserve it.

For a few weeks following the separation, he walked about in a daze. One morning, after a restless night of insomnia, he got up wishing Irene all the worst. This surprised him, as he couldn't remember ever feeling so resentful. He searched for an explanation and said to himself: 'Because I loved her so much then, I hate her so much now. Because, for her sake, I gave up meeting other women, instead putting in more hours at work and having fun with no strings attached.' He felt that Irene had planted that small, painful amount of malice within him when she left, and later he had watered it, fertilised it and made it grow by forgetting her.

As time passed, he did start to forget her. He rarely went out, and when he did he avoided places where he might meet her. A couple of times he had seen her from the car, and on one occasion they'd run into each other at the cinema, but they exchanged little more than a greeting and a couple of polite questions that left a bitter aftertaste.

Later on he learned that she wasn't happy. She had separated from her techie boyfriend and now lived alone. It surprised him how little he was affected by the news. What business was it of his whether she was happy or not? Either way his life would not change, because he didn't want a second chance or a fresh start. He no longer missed her, although at times he remembered her, calmly and non-dramatically, in a spirit of gentle disillusionment. The memory of her had stopped hurting, and he was left only with a mild feeling of disappointment.

He had already shaved and was buttoning his shirt in the semi-darkness of the study when he saw the woman walking down the pavement, pushing the stroller and holding the elder boy by the hand, this time in no hurry because she was in good time. She was wearing a light-coloured shirt and quite faded jeans, and perhaps the clothes made her look younger, less of a mum, to the point that he started having doubts about his previous assumption. He even wondered whether the two children were hers. She might well be an au pair hired by working parents. But when he saw her kiss the elder boy goodbye his doubts disappeared. The gesture, halfway between vigilance and tenderness, oblivious to the eyes of others, was an unquestionable indicator of motherhood.

Now he had another reason – a small, but a constant and pleasant reason – to get up in the morning. In good and bad weather, whether it was cold, hot, sunny or foggy, she would come to the corner, and he, from his high window, would be able to observe her way of walking, her dark hair sometimes tied up in a ponytail, her attractive form, her impatient movements when the bus was late, her way of rubbing her hands as if they were always cold, her smile and her farewell wave at the boy on the other side of the bus window. It was like a ritual – a small daily gift that had fallen in his lap by chance, due to a simple change in a bus route, a secret he couldn't share with anyone, because even if it felt like nothing of the sort to him, the outside world might see something obscene in the fact that he was spying on an unknown woman from the anonymity of a dark room; they would call furtiveness what he called reserve, and would find guilt where there was only harmless voyeurism. Not even the fact that he was home and she was outside, in a public place, would be considered a mitigating factor, because that was a legal technicality that did not apply to the general notion of chivalry.

Sometimes, while waiting for the bus, she would cast curious glances at the house, at the pointed cypress growing by the entrance, the saplings with yellowing leaves on the branches over-hanging the fence, the windowed balcony with its three-metre wide window box, where he had planted geraniums that spilled down the lower wall.

Samuel loved plants and their inability to hide their needs and grievances, the shameless innocence with which they displayed their genitals on top of their stems, as he'd read somewhere. At weekends, he spent several hours looking after the rose bushes, the vigorous wisteria, the hydrangea, the lantanas, the bougainvillea, the jasmine, and the begonia, which, with its explosion of flowers, seemed to want to escape its destiny as creeper but was hindered by the muscular branches which coiled between the metal bars of the fence making it warp. He was not put off by the constant atten-tion they demanded: watering, pruning, fertilising, cleaning them of plant lice, slugs and snails, replanting and grafting in order to keep a balance that they often broke by growing or wilting unex-pectedly. When the gardener's away, it was said, nature finds a way.

He came to suspect that she too liked flowers, because one morning he saw her approach the bougainvillea that hung over the fence and caress its dark petals; another day she stopped off to smell the jasmine, and yet another smiled in front of the explosion of fuchsia bellflowers arching over the door.

One evening, Samuel placed a flowerpot containing a spectac-ular rhododendron in full bloom on the cornice of the balcony windows. She quickly discovered it the next morning and stood a few seconds admiring it. Then her eyes slid slowly along the rest of the façade, as if wondering who might live in that house where she'd never seen any sign of life, where no one came in or went out, where no noises gave anything away as to the movements of its inhabitants, but where obviously there lived someone who treated plants with great skill and knowledge. Another day, Samuel added the bursting flowers of a hibiscus, making the window box look like a frieze which contrasted with – and made more mysterious – the darkness reigning on the other side. He left flowers there, beneath the place from where he spied on her, until they lost their splendour, and in a way he felt he was sending secret declarations of love and affection to the woman, who seemed to have grown used to appraising the changes offered each morning by the mysterious, anonymous occupant of the house.

He knew her well, and yet didn't know a thing about her. People, it was said, discuss others a lot; they tell each other details and gossip, murmur about men and women they've never seen, cast and recast anecdotes about prestige and infamy, accept apocryphal biographies without questioning their veracity. Yet he did know the way she walked, flicked her hair, stirred to keep warm in the cold, caressed her children, hung her head when she seemed worried or pensive, or smiled luminously when remembering something. One day he discovered that what seemed peculiar about her movements was the fact that she was left-handed. It was the left hand that she used to help her son up the high steps of the bus; the left hand that did up a loose button of her shirt; and the left hand that first waved at a known face. Samuel would have recognised her shadow without having seen her body, and yet he didn't know anything else about her. What was her name? Did she live alone? Was she in a relationship? Did she have a job or did she stay at home until it was time to pick up the elder son at half past five, as he'd noticed one afternoon he hadn't gone to work? Why did the children's father never bring them to the bus stop?

At other times his thoughts were not so chaste, and he would catch himself aroused at the thought of the texture of her thighs, or the slight weight of her breasts, or of how hard her nipples would feel if one day he got to kiss or bite them. He imagined his tongue knifing through her lips in search of hers; he pictured the peculiar way in which she would fondle his stomach with her left hand; and a few minutes later, with eyes closed, he would smile at remembering all the things he imagined doing with her. He would invent pick-up lines he knew he'd never use, as he'd never been very decisive with women.

More than a month had passed since the first time he'd seen her when, one morning, after the bus had left, he installed a tripod with a camera in a corner of the study. For unknown reasons – perhaps a child being ill, or a journey – the left-handed woman had not appeared for three days, and Samuel had suddenly feared she would never return, that she would vanish without a trace, like a bird that darts through the clear blue sky and doesn't leave behind anything but a memory of its shape and elegant flight. He imagined dozens of reasons why such a catastrophe could occur at any time: her child might not have adapted to the new school and he might need to go to one in the centre; her husband, if she had one, might be transferred to another town, taking all the family with him; she might move to another, more central area of the city; or she might get a job whose hours didn't allow her to take the kids there: no doubt she could do that, as she looked like quite a capable woman. These stolen – that was the word that sprung to mind – images of her would then be like mementos she would not know she'd left him.

At ten o'clock he took three test shots and checked the framing. He double-checked that the flash was off, opened the wide-angled lens even if that meant losing resolution, and programmed the camera to take one picture every sixty seconds for half an hour, starting at five twenty. Then he left for work, but all that day experienced a crushing feeling of unlawfulness, like the poacher who sets a trap in private property at sunset and later, during the night, cannot sleep for fear that, in spite of all his safety measures, something unforeseen might happen and the trap might snap shut its iron teeth on innocent ankles.

Against his habit, he let his employees close the shop and went back home before half past seven. As he was parking the car in the garage he saw three men across the street staring at the ground. One of them was explaining something with emphatic gestures as he pointed to the fence of the house they were standing by. The pavement was wet, and some water was trickling down into the gutter, as if they had just washed away a stain. Impatient to see the photographs he'd programmed, Samuel did not attach much importance to the scene, and went up to the study without even taking his jacket off. Before switching the lights on, he picked up the tripod and the camera, sighing in relief. He would never do it again, not once, not ever, he said to himself trying to control his shaking hands. Although it wasn't forbidden to photograph a thoroughfare, he could not help feeling that foul play, fraud or immorality were involved. It was astonishing how many ways there were of acting disgracefully without breaking any article of the law, but he had always tried to do the right, ethical thing and did not expect the penal code to make provisions for every rule of conduct.

He connected the camera to the computer, downloaded the files and started looking at the pictures. At twenty past five a few mothers were already waiting for the bus. Since the wide lens took in all of the corner and the junction, the figures looked distant and small, as if they'd been captured from a much greater height. The left-handed woman appeared in the fourth picture, walking down the pavement, turning to look at a car that had no doubt gone past at great speed, leaving a fuzzy trail behind it. The picture at five twenty-five showed her looking up to the windowed balcony, and Samuel had such a vivid impression that she was staring straight at the camera, to have her photograph taken, that he jumped back in his chair, startled for a moment. It was as if she knew, as if she had guessed everything.

The bus had arrived a little earlier than expected, and the photographs showed the children getting off and walking away with their parents until the street was deserted.

He clicked through the uninteresting images quickly, until one of them caught his attention. Three boys, of about fourteen or fifteen, were walking down the street in front, passing a football around. Their outlines, distant and slightly blurred, suggested a confident, perhaps rowdy attitude, and one could guess they were being noisy. They were wearing trainers and the kind of sports clothes that looked two sizes too big and which Samuel never knew whether to call modern or downright sloppy. Then something seemed to give them a scare at the fourth house on the street, and without looking Samuel knew what it was: the fearsome pit bull that barked furiously when anyone touched the fence, ready to defend its territory. He too had been caught unawares a few times, and preferred to walk down the opposite pavement. Once the postman had told him he was afraid of dropping post into the letter box of that house.

The boys, however, had no doubt quickly recovered from the fright, and later appeared shooting the ball against the fence, an adolescent display of bravery in response to the barking. The quiet emptiness of the street was interrupted in the next image, in which a woman who was passing by looked at the scene with a disapproving face. Obviously, there was no one at home to reprimand the boys and calm the dog, which sixty seconds later was seen with its front paws on the metal edge of the fence, its threatening, toothy jaws wide open.

And then, all of a sudden, the time between one take and the next seemed to have condensed into horror. The pit bull was on the outside, biting one staggering boy in the arm, while the two others ran away in terror. Shaken, Samuel clicked 'next': the ferocious tenacity of the dog that would not let go of its prey, not even when faced with some passers-by who either fled the scene or cautiously, fearfully, approached it, trying to help; the pit bull sinking its teeth between the fallen boy's shoulder and neck while a woman, visible through a window, spoke on a mobile phone, her face a mask of despair as blood stained the ground ... At last, two policemen had shot the animal, which lay on the pavement by the boy, one of the officers crouching down beside him.

The headlights of the ambulance took up the centre of the last shot, before the sequence came to an end. It had all taken barely fifteen minutes, but when it was finished Samuel was shaking. He had tried to capture some images of harmony, of the woman he liked so much, and had ended up with a horror scene.

For several days he didn't know what to do, although he couldn't stop thinking about the pictures. He put away the tripod and the camera in a cupboard as if they were dangerous, even harmful, just as he would have hidden a bear trap or a gun. On the one hand, he wanted to delete the pictures from the hard drive without printing them, as though they had never existed. What did he want them for? What use were some images in which one saw a completely unknown adolescent die? Only the boy's initials, MGS, had appeared in the papers the following day, next to a picture of the pit bull looking at the camera with a peaceful, innocent expression which belied any streak of aggression. But then, he imagined an inquiry would be conducted, and if the law required it, he was in a position to provide evidence that would cast light on what had happened, so that everyone could face up to their legal responsibilities. Keeping the images could help avoid a miscarriage of justice.

The house had remained locked since then, and he heard a neighbour say that its owners, distressed by the tragedy, had moved away. One morning a bunch of flowers appeared on the pavement against the fence; no one touched it, and it wilted until another morning it was gone, without anyone knowing who had brought it or taken it away.

After two weeks, however, the street returned to normal. The tragedy was fading in people's minds and they resumed walking down the pavement they had at first avoided, the street cleaner swept the fallen leaves where the boy had lain, the postman put letters through the letter box, unafraid now the dog had disappeared.

Until he decided what to do with the photographs, he separated the ones of the left-handed woman, created a file called 'Dog' and embedded it in a folder called 'Various', among other subfolders, committing the order to memory. Never again, he vouched, would he take furtive pictures of the woman who brought her child to the bus stop. Yet neither would he stop watching her from behind the window.

At the end of October, when it had all become a habit, a pleasant, secret rendezvous, something happened that altered that routine. The bus had already taken the children away, but the woman remained a few seconds on the wide pavement straightening the small child in its pram. And when she stood up, Samuel saw a glittering something fall to the ground. She didn't notice, though, and walked off and across the street leaving the small object lying on the flagstones.

Samuel acted on such a quick impulse that it was only when he was opening the gate that he realised how risky it was to pick up the object and run after the woman to return it. She would thank him, surely, but some inevitable questions would also arise: how did he know it was hers? Where had he been at the moment she had dropped it, seeing that the street was deserted? Why was he returning it, supposing it was valuable? And, above all, who was he, what was his name, who should she thank for that unusual gesture of decency and kindness? And at that point he wouldn't know what to reply, wouldn't be able to speak without lying, without concealing from her that he was a solitary man who, hidden behind a window, watched a woman whose name he didn't even know any more than her occupation, address, or civil status, but whom he could safely say he liked a lot, in a naive, almost adolescent way.

He slowly opened the gate and walked out onto the empty pavement. He saw her for a few seconds at the end of the street, before she turned the second corner, pushing the stroller in that peculiar way of hers, without leaning forward much but neither completely straight, halfway between the heaviness that goes with great effort and the lightness of excessive energy. He took a few steps and, sure enough, found the shiny object. He quickly picked it up and went back inside.

It was a slim gold bracelet with small flattened links and delicate oval charms. The clasp had come undone, perhaps having caught a snag on the stroller. In between the links was a plaque of about two centimetres with a filigree engraving on its flipside which read *Marina*.

'Marina,' he said out loud. 'Marina. It's a nice name. Like placing a grain of salt on your tongue and listening to the crystals dissolve.'

He had to find a way of giving it back; he couldn't keep it. Besides, it was the perfect excuse he needed.

Samuel put away the bracelet in a drawer and left for work. He was in a daze all day, swinging between the joy of a suitor who presents his beloved with a jewel and the caution of someone who fears he will be accused of stealing it. On coming home that evening he took another look at the bracelet and imagined the moment he would approach her and the words he would say. He supposed she would be grateful, given that he was returning an object of value. There was only one thing that worried him: she might ask him how he knew it was hers, and then he would have to hide the fact that he spied on her from the window balcony, and claim that, purely by chance, he had seen her drop the bracelet and that she had vanished by the time he came down to pick it up. If that part of the story sounded convincing enough, the rest might hold.

By the time parents and children started arriving the following morning, he'd been waiting for a while behind the window. He had the jewel between his fingers. Marina – he had no doubt that was her name – was among the first to arrive, and for a second she studied the ground, no doubt looking for the bracelet but without much conviction, as if she imagined that if she had lost it there someone else must have found it by then. A little later the bus appeared and took the children away. Samuel waited until the mothers too had left, and only then went out. Marina was already walking across the street, and he quickened his pace to catch up with her before she turned the corner. He had to hurry, but at the same time didn't want to look clumsy or say something silly in haste. His hesitation made him walk more slowly. It had always been the same with women, he ran after them fighting an impulse to retreat. Instinct and feelings pushed him towards them, but he never entirely cast off the suspicion that everything would be easier if he closed his eyes to the mysterious feminine world and spent his free time cultivating his garden, sitting at his computer, or hanging out with friends.

Marina disappeared round the corner before he had a chance to catch up with her. Fearing he would lose sight of her, he ran to the junction and was relieved to see her only ten or twelve metres ahead. If he was going to approach her, now was the time, he couldn't take any longer without further complications. He walked faster and, bracelet in hand, almost came level with her, but then she abruptly stopped at a doorway and started looking for her keys in the bag hanging from the stroller.

Samuel stopped too, surprised that, although she lived so close by, he'd never seen her around except at the bus stop. Marina looked at him questioningly, perhaps thinking he too wanted to go into the building. A delicate scent, which reminded him of the lilacs in his garden, wafted from her or perhaps from the boy who was staring at him from the stroller with a sort of neutral curiosity.

'Excuse me,' he said.

'Yes?'

He put out his hand with the bracelet before he could find the words to explain himself.

'Yesterday, by chance, I thought I saw you drop it and ...'

'My bracelet! Where did you find it?'

'Yesterday, by chance,' he repeated, handing it to her, 'at the school bus stop. I thought I saw you drop it, and came down to get it, but by the time I picked it up you'd already left.'

'You came down?' she asked, not knowing what he meant.

'Yes, I live in the house on the corner and I was ... looking out the window when I thought I saw something shiny fall off the stroller,' he cautiously explained, fearing he would trip himself up. He realised that he was striking up a conversation by deceiving her, but told himself that, if he was granted another opportunity to speak to her, it would be the last time he would do such thing. 'I thought it was a toy or something, but then, when I picked it up, I saw it was a bracelet. This morning I was waiting for you to give it back. And so I came out and managed to catch up with you. Only just,' he added with a smile, pointing to the door.

'So you own the house on the corner?' she asked, as if the rest of the story was barely interesting.

'Yes.'

'It's very pretty. I've often noticed the plants.'

'The plants, yes. I have some free time and I find it relaxing to look after them. It's not hard. Do you like plants?'

'I do. But here in the flat, you know, I have no room. A few flowerpots on the terrace …'

'If you like, you can drop by the house one day. I can give you a few seeds, perhaps some cuttings,' he dared to suggest.

'That's very kind,' she said, without suggesting she would take him up on the offer. 'And thanks for the bracelet. Not everyone would have taken the trouble to give it back.'

'Oh, no problem. On the contrary,' he replied, surprised at how easy it all felt, how quickly he was loosening up.

'The clasp is ruined,' she suddenly said, putting the bracelet for a moment over her left wrist. 'But if I change it, I'm sure …'

'May I?' he interrupted her, taking a look at the jewel and regretting not having thought of it before. 'It's very easy, actually; you just need to tighten up one of the links. If you like, I …' he was about to say he could take it home and bring it back in a few minutes but she interrupted him, pointing to her flat.

'Could you do it now?'

'Yes, if you have a small pliers.'

'Come on up,' she said after a moment's hesitation. 'And I can make you some coffee to thank you. If you're not in a hurry, that is.'

'Work can wait.'

They took the lift to the second floor. It was a recently built flat, like everything else in that neighbourhood, medium-sized and nice-looking, though Samuel got the impression that it was not fully decorated yet, that there was room on the walls awaiting the right painting, empty surfaces on the furniture lacking picture frames or books, pegs in the coat rack at the entrance without any clothes on them. It suddenly occurred to him that the emptiness was due to an absence of masculine objects. On a table he saw a framed photograph in which a man smiled next to her and the children, but he looked over fifty, and his attitude did not seem that of a partner but rather of a relative.

Marina took her son out of the stroller and put him in a playpen. From there the child, unconcerned at his mother's absence, observed with curiosity Samuel's not entirely convincing smiles. She presently came back with a toolbox.

'He's very calm,' said Samuel.

'Yes, he gets on well with everybody.'

As he straightened the open, twisted link, the smell of freshly made coffee wafted in from the kitchen. He had fixed the bracelet by the time she returned with a tray.

'We're having coffee and I don't even know your name,' she said. When she smiled, her upper lip rose almost excessively, up to the edge of the gums, and her cheeks stretched out slightly.

'I'm Samuel.'

'I'm …'

'Marina,' he interrupted, pointing to the small plaque of the bracelet.

'Of course. Now we're on a first-name basis. It'll be easier.'

'Indeed.'

'Earlier you said work could wait. What's work?' she asked.

'A small company that collects paper for recycling,' he replied vaguely, as he suspected she wouldn't be interested in that kind of subject. He would have preferred to hear about her, her children, the school bus the elder one took every morning, or for her to make a comment that explained why he had never seen a man by her side.

'I don't know a lot about that. But it sounds like environmentalism.'

'It is too. But if it didn't make any money …' he trailed off. 'I don't think environmentalism would be reason enough to do it. Anyway, it's simple: we leave some large boxes in offices, schools, colleges, printers' offices and so on. Then, when they're full of scrap paper we come round to empty them and we sell the contents to a processing plant. It's a small business, with an office, three staff and a couple of vans.'

'Is much paper thrown away?'

'You wouldn't believe how much.'

'And you're the boss?'

'The owner,' he gently corrected her.

'I remember seeing those boxes you mention somewhere, but I never paused to think who was behind all that.'

'Now you know. We're behind it.'

'I think I'll look at them differently from now on.'

Her manners were a little flirtatious, but casually so, and he didn't feel uncomfortable. He was shy, but her way of asking question after question, of showing an interest in things she didn't know, led him to believe she was not aware of his shyness, or that, if she was, she didn't mind. Marina's confidence did not highlight his own deficiency in that department.

Often, when he found himself at a party in front of extroverted, excited, radiant women, who attracted everyone's attention with their wit and outgoingness, he felt suspicious, almost afraid of their expansiveness, and strangely vulnerable, as though he were out in the rain in spite of the waterproof ceilings. Perhaps that was why he still lived alone, because he was not skilful or daring enough to approach the kind of woman who might respond to a gesture from him, and he himself had not responded to those who approached him with too much familiarity, on occasion even with boldness. His complicated relationship with the feminine world could not be called a failure, but rather a tepid abstinence, and he knew he was of an age, thirty-six, when one is more risk-averse and finds it harder to deal with rejection. Once, someone had told him he was prematurely aged, but if that were true, he was sure he had not acquired the defects and funny ways of old people, and he could still boast that his relatives and friends needed him. The fact that Irene had left him, on the other hand, had heightened his natural carefulness, and he now mistrusted any kind of brashness in other people's looks or behaviour. He'd come to believe that being flamboyant is the same as being frivolous, and that vehemence by necessity courts danger – and although he wouldn't have forbidden anything to others, he preferred to steer clear of both frivolity and danger. He was a calm man, perhaps excessively so, but one at peace with his character, and he was no longer prepared to lose this advantage, no matter how disquieting the yearnings of the heart might prove. He lived alone, to be sure, but was far from that point where loneliness turns into anxiety.

During the days that he had spied on Marina from the darkness of his study he had wondered what she might be like. He thought her very attractive, and liked the way she smiled when she said goodbye to her elder son, and how she walked on her way back home. Now, while he downed the last sip of coffee, he thanked chance for making her drop her bracelet, as this gave him the opportunity to get to know her.

'I think I owe you a coffee. Drop by the house if you like. Anytime,' he said, standing up. And thinking his invitation a bit too vague, he added: 'Weekends I'm usually in.'

'All right. I will,' she said.

He stooped slightly to touch the child's head, but the boy barely looked at him, engrossed as he was in an electronic device which emitted strangely high-pitched animal noises, as if it were a transmitter receiving calls from animals that were about to be put down in a slaughterhouse. Samuel said goodbye. As he walked back home to get the car and drive off to work, he went over the encounter. He seemed to have taken a step in the right direction, and one with enough momentum. It had all started well, slowly, and at the right moment. He hadn't lost the sense of calm that made him feel comfortable, and nor had she suggested that, in order to seduce her, he had to turn into an adventurer overflowing with anecdotes and wit who is also ready to run physical and emotional risks.

From an early age, Samuel had lived among old paper. His father amassed and sold cardboard in a plot in an alleyway near the city centre, where bales of it were piled until a truck came round to pick them up. His father did not actually collect the material in the street; those who needed the money did that at night, rummaging through rubbish bins and bringing their finds round in the morning. These were weighed on large, dark scales, and his father would pay instantly, with scrupulous accuracy, neither haggling nor bargaining. Samuel remembered some of the people who brought round small quantities of material: old timers who had accumulated newspapers for a month; children who collected cardboard and other materials – his father also bought copper, bulb holders, bottles – and got a few coins for the cinema; shopkeepers who kept packing materials and paid their staff a short holiday by selling them at the end of the year.

As with any activity that deals with waste, it was a bit of a dirty job, and not very lucrative at that, given the effort, the hours and the vast storage space required; but Samuel's father, a world-weary, premature widower, didn't know any other trade, and at least he earned enough for Samuel and his two brothers to live relatively well.

The biggest downside was the complete lack of prestige attached to the job. In a way, Samuel, being the owner's son, was part of the business world. And the family did not collect paper or cardboard in the street, but limited themselves to purchasing what others brought them. But at school, and later in college, he had always been the son of the rag and bone man. Not that they called him that, but sometimes in a fight, or when a classmate wanted to mock him or insult him, the words would roll out of someone's mouth: 'Hey you, rag and bone boy,' and he had to give in and accept it if the name-caller was older or more aggressive. That label made him weaker, more fragile, pushed him to try and be kind to everyone, even his nasty classmates, as he was aware that, at the slightest sign of conflict, his opponents had a very effective weapon against him. He often wondered how that had contributed to his later shyness, his apathetic way of carrying himself, as though he were always on the defensive.

Now it all seemed forgotten. His father was dead, the old warehouse had been sold and knocked down to build flats, and he lived far from the city centre. Yet deep down he was still that spineless, insecure adolescent who tried to hide the family business. In fact, his own business was an extension of his father's, even if adapted to modern times: nowadays no one took a load of old paper to be weighed on scales for a few coins in return. In any case, that was his occupation and his patrimony, and with that he intended to live in peace and comfort. As he drove, the more obscure details of his work vanished before the intense satisfaction of the half hour he'd spent with Marina.

2

Barracks Without Soldiers

He hadn't left the house in uniform for over ten years, because that was what security regulations recommended – and he was obsessive about regulations – but also because the military leadership had restricted the presence of army personnel on the streets and among civilians, confining it to the barracks and only allowing uniforms outside on days of patriotic celebrations. In any case, he still found civilian clothes awkward, and would fumble for the pockets of his army jacket while wearing a coat, or would take an extra fraction of a second to recognise himself in the mirror of the vestibule without his greenish clothes on, or would step in a puddle on the pavement shod in moccasins and, only when the cold water soaked his foot, realise that he was not wearing the army boots he'd always liked so much, from the first time he put them on and felt the firm hold on his heel, making him walk more energetically and emphasising the strength of his legs. But today was an exception, and he was wearing a uniform because the importance of his meeting warranted it.

How he loved his job! To be an officer! An officer among civilians! Whenever he walked into a bank to withdraw cash, or into a shop to buy anything, his uniform turned him into the centre of attention and gave rise to admiration or negative responses, but never indifference. He was treated with courtesy and respect, too, of course, especially since the disappearance of the last residual Francoist cliques – fallen from favour even within the barracks – who had thought the army should take the place of the legislature, because they didn't accept that the first obligation of a soldier is not to write laws, or to seek supporters, or to indoctrinate people, but actually to obey the law as it stands.

Yet neither public esteem nor public rejection altered his conduct. Just as the former didn't reassure him the latter didn't alarm him; if anything, both tickled his pride. Pride, he knew, was his weakness and his obsession. He was positive that, if there was a cardinal virtue in a military man, it wasn't courage, strategic intelligence, ambition or equitableness, but pride, and that all other qualities depended on it. He took pride in his name and surname, Camilo Olmedo, and in representing a lineage of soldiers that harked back to the first Carlist war; pride in his medals and unblemished professional record; pride in the fact that no one would be able to name a single country where Spanish troops had been deployed in recent years and where he hadn't been present. And so he didn't mean to do without pride; he would just validate it by doing his job well. Besides, that trait of his character had never been an obstacle in the path of his career. On the one hand, the sovereign peacefulness with which he embodied it separated him from boastful types, like Bramante, who mistook conceitedness for pride, and were constantly bragging about their muscles and courage; on the other, pride had helped him at difficult moments to alleviate feelings of insecurity such as those experienced by Ucha – to name only two of the colleagues whose criticisms he'd have to deal with over the next few hours.

He put on the peaked cap and looked in the mirror. Not bad: he was still young enough not to feel crushed under its weight. The peak shaded his eyes, but did not extinguish the two hard sparks, clean and devoid of malice, of his pupils. His thin lips and clenched jaw made him look more serious than he really was, and a large chin which refused to retreat bolstered the impression of inflexibility. He turned his head slightly to observe his profile and saw a calm, elegant man who still wondered how it was possible that three square metres of green cloth, a dozen golden buttons, some two-toned ribbons and tin stars wrapped and dotted around his body had the power to predispose him to being punctual, daring and good at his job. Irrespective of his decision in a few weeks' time – whether to continue on active service or ask to pass to the reserve – he would still wear his uniform one last time, even if he wouldn't notice, as he would be dead. He had stipulated in his will that he wanted to be dressed in his uniform at the moment of entering into the eternity of nothingness, and he knew his daughter would carry out his wishes.

He made sure all the documents pertaining to the report were in his briefcase. Then he put the small Star in the holster under his armpit and buttoned up his jacket. He always carried a gun. Although he had no intention of using it, it gave him a feeling of security and confidence, because even if a gun is not fired it could always well be.

Carrying a gun had become a habit during the three months he'd been stationed in Afghanistan, as part of NATO, in a peace-keeping mission that also worked towards the disarmament of extremist groups linked with Taliban guerrillas. Back there, a pistol on one's hip was as necessary and natural as the boots, cap or trousers. And once in the habit of carrying a gun for protection, he felt more vulnerable without it than someone who'd never held one. Over the last few years, the Mediterranean coast had become the scene of terrorist attacks, and although he knew it was unlikely that someone dressed in trainers, jeans and a hoodie might attack him at close quarters, putting a bullet in the back of his head, he could not forget that his name had appeared on a list of terrorists' targets after an interview he'd given some years previously, on his return from the Balkans. If he were the victim of an attack, it would probably involve explosives, and his gun would be useless, but neither did he forget that a colleague from the academy had been riddled with bullets in the garage of his house as he was parking his car, and that, perhaps he would have been able to defend himself if he'd had a gun.

His time in Afghanistan, his discipline, and his rigorous and efficient compliance with procedure had earned him a promotion to major, and on returning home he enjoyed a solid prestige both among the rank and file and his superiors. In Madrid they had praised his firmness when dismantling installations, disarming guerrilla groups without humiliating them, and restructuring his own units. His reputation as a courageous, intelligent soldier had influenced his superiors' decision to commission from him a report on the advisability and difficulty of closing down the San Marcial base. Abolishing obligatory military service, turning the army into a professional institution and introducing new technology had rendered obsolete the old idea of efficient, mighty armed forces. Squadrons, companies and battalions were no longer discussed so much as warfare technology. A country's defence budget could no longer be wasted on dressing, feeding, housing, disciplining and instructing a host of recruits by making them do archaic exercises, more aesthetic than tactical, when they would hardly get the chance to engage in hand-to-hand combat. By necessity, the modern army based its power of deterrence on technology, not on the number of its troops; the function of the latter was a thing of the past, just as the cavalry had superseded the infantry and motored vehicles had superseded the cavalry.

He had been among the first to understand and accept that premise, often disagreeing with nostalgic colleagues from the old school, which was already in decline. Those fanciful, outdated ideas about the honour of old military families; the allegiance to a crown or an empire; the clicking of spurs on the marble floor of palaces; the swords forming arches outside a church when a soldier was united in holy matrimony; hierarchy and words of honour; recruits who never lie, even when they keep silent – that was all very well in films and novels which, indeed, he found moving as much as the next guy, but they had no place in the third millennium.

'All right, all right,' he had half-conceded in more than one argument with his colleagues. 'A laser-guided bomb will never confer on the person who releases it the same prestige earned by a soldier who's always right on target with his rifle; the clunky clumsiness of a tank unit on the move will never become as legendary or as romantic as a cavalry charge; the general who relies on a satellite for a plan of attack will never attain the glory of the old-time leaders; a lieutenant equipped with GPS and a night visor will never look as elegant as an imperial cadet with his sabre and tall polished boots … But we'll have to give up all those points of aesthetics if we want to be more efficient. It's not the beauty of a regiment that wins wars,' he concluded.

The report that he'd written in accordance with those convictions left no option but to close down the base in San Marcial. The city was not in a strategic location. Given that there was an airfield and a naval base a hundred kilometres to the south, and that a branch of the General Headquarters of the Third Military Region was situated a hundred kilometres to the north, its maintenance was superfluous as well as costly. The vast land it occupied on the outskirts of town would be very valuable on the real estate market, and its sale would bring considerable revenues to the coffers of the Ministry of Defence. It was neither strategically nor economically viable to preserve the place. It had to be closed down, and that was what he had written, citing numbers and arguments, for the eyes of his superiors in Madrid, who would ultimately take the decision.

The hardest problem would be to relocate the staff, who would be professionally affected and perhaps even personally offended by the closure. Olmedo knew all too well that, faced with an unpleasant demand, the first impulse of an official is to oppose it and lodge a complaint with the Administration that pays him; but although army men were no different, their particular sense of obedience and discipline would trump their reservations. The majority, used to transfers, would accept this one without putting up much resistance. And some would even benefit from it, as it would allow them to reach their desired destination.

But a certain sector was adamant against the closure. In the survey he had conducted, which was included in the report, two officers had strongly rejected it: Captain Bramante and Captain

Ucha. The old colonel, too, had voiced his opposition, even if less radically, and almost for sentimental reasons. Colonel Castroviejo regarded the barracks as his own creation and often referred to it as 'my home'. He'd kept it running and improved it during the four decades he'd served there, and he expected that they would reward his service with the courtesy of postponing the final liquidation. He would probably be more painfully affected than anyone else if the base was closed down.

At times Olmedo suspected that the decision had already been taken in Madrid, and that his report was only a sheaf of papers they would barely read, a way to keep up appearances, to comply with administrative procedures while the certainty of the closure settled among the officers. By commissioning a report they designated a scapegoat. Everyone would see Olmedo as the one whose hand had pressed the button. In spite of his discretion, news of the commission had begun to spread a little after his return from Afghanistan, and soon he started feeling the hostility of those who were against change. He'd pretended not to notice the reproachful looks, and once he even heard someone say they wished he'd been blown up by one of those bombs the Taliban planted by the side of the road and detonated at the passage of military vehicles.

But he hadn't been blown up, and this morning, in one hour and a half from now, he would conduct the last part of his job: the meeting with the bosses and officers where he would present the final conclusions of his analysis. Hence the uniform, for it would lend its presentation greater solemnity and authority.

Before going to the headquarters he had to drop by his daughter's house, to get her to sign some bank documents, and Marina didn't mind seeing him dressed like that. One the contrary, she always said that in uniform he looked younger, more handsome, and that it reminded her of when she was a child.

He went down to the garage, opened the gate with the remote control and started the car. Going out into the street as carefully as always, he saw Rosco, the road sweeper, cleaning the street with the large wire brush he always used. The effort showed in his face.

'Good morning, Rosco,' said Olmedo through the window.

'Morning.'

'Lots of work, right?'

'Lots. These plane trees are always making a mess. In autumn, it's the leaves. In spring, it's the seed fluff blowing everywhere and clogging the drains. Too much work. Should cut them down.'

'But the shade is nice,' he said as he reached the street.

The clock in the car read half past nine. He had more than enough time – the meeting was not supposed to start until eleven, after the officers had given instructions for the daily routines. Fifteen minutes later he parked by his daughter's building and went upstairs.

'I've been waiting for you,' said Marina with the smile that had returned to her face in the last few months, since she'd started seeing Samuel. She'd already taken her elder child to the bus stop, and the little one, in his playpen, was chewing on a biscuit as he watched cartoons on the TV. 'Coffee?'

'Yes, please.'

When she returned with a tray he'd already laid the application to change the titleholder of an investment fund on the table. Two hundred thousand euros, while not a fortune that would allow anyone to retire, was a considerable sum nonetheless, which needed looking after and might tempt greedy people. Before leaving for Afghanistan he'd put everything under both their names, so that if anything should happen to him, Marina could have direct access to the money without paying any inheritance tax. Back then, she was still married to Jaime, and that piece of information was in the files at the bank and might pose a problem. He hadn't taken action in the last year, but now that Marina was getting divorced he needed to become the sole titleholder once again. For a few months at least only he would have access to that fund.

'Do you think it's necessary?' she asked, sitting beside him.

'It's advisable.'

'You and your military mind,' she joked. 'Always seeing problems where there aren't any. Jaime would never dare claim any of that money. He knows it's not his,' she said, and further explained. 'He knows it's yours.'

'Well, tomorrow when I take these papers to the bank there will be no point in speculating whether he'd claim it or not. He simply won't be able to. Has he paid this month's alimony, by the way?'

'No. I've told you he's had some trouble at the company.'

'You not demanding what your children are entitled to won't solve his problems.'

'Your never liked Jaime, Dad,' she said. The sweetness of her tone softened the harshness of the comment. 'You've always thought badly of him. I don't mean to say he didn't disappoint me either, but I know him …'

'Better than me, I admit,' he interrupted.

'And I know he'd never do such a thing. But for your peace of mind, I'll sign those papers right now. Give them here.'

As he passed her the printed papers marked with crosses where she should sign, he remembered the conversation they'd had when she'd told him she was going to marry Jaime. He'd warned her that he didn't like him and didn't think it was a very good idea. Jaime struck him as immature, silly, volatile, very well suited to that company of his, Vertical Mediterranean, but not calm enough for the stability a marriage requires. He admitted women might find Jaime very seductive when he put on his harness and clipped himself to a safety rope and climbed up to carry out one of those jobs he did: putting up an advertising poster on top of a building or fixing a satellite dish or an aerial. Up there, all lightness and confidence, he might look like a sleepwalking angel, a bird or a feline moving along the parapets, oblivious to vertigo and fear. But back on the ground he suddenly looked smaller, as if he wasn't the same person that had been silhouetted against the sky, and his comments sounded vain and trivial when he responded to the praise of those who had seen him at work. Time had proved Olmedo right, but he'd never been cruel to his daughter, had never said, 'I told you so, I did tell you he was only a peacock. I said he wouldn't make you happy, and you didn't listen, didn't take my advice. So now take responsibility for your actions and deal with the consequences on your own.' On the contrary, when she confessed her failure, he opened his arms and gave her his full support.

'Here,' she said, handing him the signed papers.

'I don't care whether I was right or wrong. I only want for you to be happy.' He was pleased to see his daughter smile before she gave him a hug.

'I am, Dad. I'm pretty sure I am.'

'It's the only thing that matters.'

'I know.'

'What time did you tell Gabriela?' said Olmedo, and cast a glance at the clock ticking on the wall.

'In five minutes. She'll be here any moment. You know how punctual she is.'

She cleared the cups and took them to the kitchen.

Olmedo was about to take the boy out to play in the garden when he discovered his grandson needed a diaper change. He told his daughter, who picked him up and went to take care of it. One minute after ten the doorbell rang.

'Can you get that?' shouted Marina from the bathroom.

But he had already lifted the receiver of the intercom, and when he heard, 'It's me, Gabriela,' he buzzed her in. Then he opened the door and waited in the doorway with a strange feeling of novelty. It was the first time Gabriela had visited his daughter's house; whenever all three had met before, to go shopping or share a meal, it had been in a public place or in his flat. But the fact that Gabriela was now coming to the house where father and daughter – the family – were waiting added to their closeness, as if she were saying she did not only accept him, Camilo Olmedo, but also the circumstances surrounding him.

But there was a further dimension to her visit. For someone who had lost her son so violently, to the jaws of a dog, any reference to children could only bring to mind her own loss. The imbalance between his own general well-being and Gabriela's situation seem terribly unfair to Olmedo; her suffering was such that she spent whole afternoons in her flat, thinking of her son, looking at pictures of him, fighting back an enormous amount of pain. And so he felt he was beholden to her, and wanted to spend time with her not only for the sake of passion, as would have been the case twenty or thirty years before, but also to impart something of his own serenity and try to assuage her sorrow.

The lift stopped and out came Gabriela, tall and fragile, looking around as if searching for something, a gesture that was characteristic of her. She greeted him with that calm smile which was never entirely free of affliction, and at times she seemed to be on the brink of bursting into tears. She'd gathered her blonde hair into a ponytail, and this gave her an air of youthfulness. Her face, clear and clean, only looked troubled in its lifeless eyes and in the deep, M-shaped wrinkle that had formed between her eyebrows, as if Manuel himself, in dying, had engraved it there so as to make his presence felt every time she looked in the mirror. Olmedo admired how beautiful she still was. Only a woman with an upright neck and straight nape can carry off a ponytail like that. In a few years it would suggest stiffness and harshness.

'Have you been waiting here long?' she asked.

'One minute,' he replied as he approached to kiss her lightly on her thin, cold lips. They were the same height.

They went inside, and while his daughter showed Gabriela around, he sat in the living room with the child, who was now changed, and smelled fresh and clean. The boy started passing him all the toys he had in his playpen, as if that disorderly exchange of pieces were the most fun thing in the world. Olmedo heard the women in the other room, his daughter chatting about colours, furniture, decoration. They seemed relaxed when they returned, and he thought he could go to his meeting now, as they didn't appear to need him at all. They had planned to drop by Samuel's together, to pick up some plants he had promised them.

'We'll ransack his garden, you'll see,' joked Marina as she carried a huge wicker basket and a roll of plastic bags. 'I've bought a dozen flowerpots,' she said, pointing to the balcony where one could see the empty containers of all sizes, 'and we'll get enough plants to open a botanical garden.'

'Poor Samuel!' said Gabriela.

'I wish I could come with you, not to help you carry anything, but to stop you carrying so much. I really should be going, though. The meeting starts at eleven.'

He put the printed papers in his briefcase, picked up the car keys and walked to the door with Gabriela.

'Shall I stop by tonight?' he asked.

'Better tomorrow. I've got several things to do at home.'

'All right. Tomorrow then,' he said, respectful of the reserve she often showed him.

They'd been seeing each other for four months, and he knew that patience was needed to solve a contradiction in their relationship: he sought Gabriela's company more than she did his, and yet he was sure that, of the two, she was the one who needed the other more. But Gabriela would have to arrive at that conclusion on her own. In the meantime, he would stick around, and only when she opened the door would he step in, never trying to force the lock before that moment. He wasn't a man who liked talking about himself, nor did he have enough mastery of the complex vocabulary of feelings to persuade her of all he could do for her. He felt awkward with sentimental words, perhaps because of his profession, in a time when the military had left behind the art of gallantry. If one day Gabriela looked him in the eye and asked: 'Who are you? What are you like inside? Why do you take such pains with me and show me such kindness?' it wouldn't be easy to reply to her. He needed time and facts, more than words, to explain things.

Now it was Gabriela who approached to kiss him, as if with that kind gesture she meant to compensate him for her refusal to see him that night. But when she placed her hand near his left armpit she must have felt the bulk of the gun, because she withdrew it quickly. Olmedo knew how much she disliked it when he was armed.

'I'll call you tomorrow then,' he said.

'Tomorrow, yes. Good luck at the meeting.'

'I think it'll be fine,' he replied.

Fifteen minutes later he walked into his office in the main wing of the San Marcial base. He sat at his desk and went through the points of the report he would discuss in a few minutes. He remembered all facts and figures, all useful and redundant details. Nobody would put forth an argument he couldn't firmly refute. It was a foregone conclusion. He was closing the folder when there was a knock on his door.

'Come in.'

'Do I have your permission, sir?'

It was one of the Latin American soldiers who, over the past few years, had enlisted in the Spanish army in order to get Spanish nationality. His accent sounded incongruous in someone wearing the same uniform as him. At first, Olmedo too had looked down on them and demanded from them double the effort, but he had ended up getting used to these dark-skinned guys with their strong teeth, stiff black hair, and short statures who, when they eventually swore allegiance to the flag, shouted the patriotic slogans with as much fervour as the natives.

'Come in,' he repeated.

'The colonel would like a word with you.'

'I'm coming right over.'

Colonel Castroviejo's spacious corner office, at the end of the hall, was lit by two large windows; one gave on to the entrance of the base and the other to the training field where parades, ceremonies and official acts took place, an esplanade closed off on one side by cement stands which made it look a bit like a football stadium.

'May I come in, sir?'

'Please do, Olmedo.'

The colonel did not move to greet him. He stayed with his back turned, looking out of the window at a company of soldiers doing exercises on the pitch. With his hands behind his back, he stooped forward slightly, appearing older than he was. Olmedo knew how much the colonel was disconcerted by the tremendous speed of the modern world, its confusing international conflicts without defined combat lines, and the new wars against invisible enemies hidden among civilians. He suspected that, in some way, the colonel blamed him for being complicit in those changes. On his desk was one of the two copies Olmedo had made of the report. The other was in Madrid.

'I've reread your papers carefully,' said the colonel.

Olmedo noticed the scornful nuance.

'I should congratulate you on a job well done,' continued the colonel, 'except that your conclusions are not to my liking.'

'I'm afraid there was no other ...'

'I know, I know,' he interrupted sharply. 'I know you were following orders. And orders are given to be obeyed; the army is not a democracy. It's not me you'll have to convince of simply having carried out a technical commission. I don't agree with your premises, but, at least in public, I won't oppose them. Don't worry, I won't raise any objections at the meeting.' He paused and then, as though he'd thought it through, but wasn't too sure how appropriate it was to say it, added: 'Today no one can say that the Spanish military is not disciplined. Not once have we spoken out in protest, in spite of the victims we've had in the last few years ... as a consequence of the civilians' deficient administrations. I won't speak out now about a matter of lesser importance.'

'Thank you, sir.'

'You're aware you'll make enemies?' the colonel asked, turning to look fixedly at Olmedo, his eyes slightly blanched by age.

'I am, but I have them already, sir.'

'But this won't just be professional rivalry. Some will be personally affected, and will see your report as an offence. Others will even think of the word humiliation. And all of them will feel like a band of veterans sent away from the city walls on the basis that they will be better defended by new weapons mounted on the tower keep,' he added, using one of those examples of old military strategy that he liked to quote in public.

'But no one's leaving them outside the walls,' argued Olmedo. 'They only need to accept a transfer. Or take early retirement.'

'You know well that for some neither is a very honourable possibility. But they too will obey ... they all will. I know them, they are disciplined, as I said. And discipline is best shown by obeying orders we don't like.'

'I would never question that.'

The colonel, who had not moved from his place, once again turned his back to him and looked out of the window. The soldiers were leaving the training field three abreast and presently the place was empty. There was no one walking along the clean streets in front of the pavilions with manicured areas of grass and straight paths flanked by whitewashed stones. At one end of the pitch one could see the deserted stands and, beyond, the high brick wall complete with barbed wire surrounding the compound and enforcing a dual purpose: to keep soldiers in, and to keep people out. The barracks, usually aflutter with activity, were at that moment in the deepest calm, the officers waiting in the meeting room, anxious to learn the results of his report. There was none of the shouting or clicking of heels normally heard during instruction, and nor did one hear vehicles or everyday noises generated by cleaning or pruning trees. For Olmedo all that solitude and emptiness heralded the final closure. The colonel must have thought something along the same lines, because he asked, again without looking at him:

'Do you realise? This is all going to disappear. Everything we established with a view to remaining here will be reduced to transient, useless work.'

Olmedo didn't reply. He just nodded briefly, even though the colonel couldn't see him.

'It had to happen, it was inevitable since they abolished compulsory military service. At the end of the day, there's no better reason to knock down barracks than the fact that they're empty of soldiers. And I seem to remember you agreed with that measure too,' he added recalling an old grievance which was more bitter that Olmedo had thought.

The colonel had looked at him when uttering the last phrase, and now he was expecting an answer – an austere, hardened old man silhouetted against the large window, scornful of luxury and super-fluity, who would retire from active service in a few months' time with neither pomp nor circumstance, just as he had lived his life.

'Yes, I did agree,' Olmedo replied. 'We no longer needed hun-dreds of thousands of men …' – he paused before saying 'wasting time in the barracks' and chose a more positive expression – 'to fight for their country.'

'It wasn't all about fighting, Olmedo, and you know it. The mili-tary service was a good way of getting to know one's country, and for getting to love it,' he added.

Olmedo did not agree with that either, but he didn't contradict the colonel. 'I think that, all in all, we have as many men as we need. And whenever the quota has not been met, we've received enough applications from foreign soldiers. Such as your own orderly,' he said, knowing the colonel held him in high esteem.

'Make no mistake about them, Olmedo, make no mistake. I remember that, a few years ago, when we almost went to war with Morocco over Perejil Island, we were putting together a squadron to take part in a rescue operation. The officer of the Legion asked volunteers to step forward, and you know how many foreigners took that step?'

'I don't.'

'Not one! None that were not Spanish. And by Spanish I mean those like you and me, not those who wear the uniform in order to obtain Spanish citizenship and because six hundred euros a month is a fortune in the countries they come from.'

When he finished, the colonel turned again towards the window, as if he wanted to hide his face as he added, in a voice so low that Olmedo had difficulty understanding him:

'All too often those who make greater sacrifices for their country end up being neglected by their superiors.'

It was a remark Olmedo could not answer without expressing his disagreement, and so he remained silent, waiting for his orders, as the meeting should have started five minutes ago. Castroviejo must have noticed too and approached the table to pick up the documents.

'Let's go over, and persuade them of the accuracy of your report,' he said. 'I won't be affected by any of it. In six months, before the excavators tear down the walls of these pavilions, I'll be retired.'

3

Soldiers Without Barracks

Castroviejo and Olmedo walked down the corridor, as soldiers stood to attention, clicking their heels and saluting them with a quick, exact movement of the hand. They went into the meeting room where the officers were already waiting, standing round a long oval table the two ends of which were noticeably empty. The oak of the wall panels and the table and chairs might once have been clear, but time had darkened the wood and its drab patches showed where it hadn't aged well. By one of the windowless walls were two cabinets which kept symbols and trophies that told the history of the base under lock and key; in between the two pieces of furniture, under the motto 'All for one's country', a Spanish flag enjoyed pride of place, its flagpole a little splintered and the cloth frayed in one corner. It had been recovered from the enemy by the San Marcial soldiers who, in 1898, had taken part in a battle somewhere in the Philippines. Olmedo could never remember the exact name of the place. Behind the glass, each in its frame, were pictures of the last three Spanish monarchs – and of Franco – visiting the premises or presiding over a ceremony or parade in one of the courts that would soon be turned into flats, gardens or streets. At the back of the room, in a corner, was another cabinet containing unique treasures: certificates of victories in combat; two old swords stained with urine, which was said to be Moorish blood; and a bunch of medals with hard, resounding declarations of honour which purported to prove that the prestige of an army rests on how much enemy blood it spills. Those symbols of sacrifice, strictness and toughness did not greatly appeal to Olmedo, reminding him that the army was the only place he'd known where one could be issued the death penalty just for idle talk.

The room was the most solemn one in the base and was seldom used. Olmedo understood the colonel had chosen it because the meeting would be a kind of farewell, a declaration that San Marcial was being demolished, and few things could be more important to him.

Olmedo stood at one end of the table and the colonel at the other. Olmedo would have preferred to have had him by his side, but he guessed what the seating plan actually meant: Castroviejo was leaving him on his own, standing as far away from him as possible. He would not contradict his report, as he'd said a few minutes before, but neither would he encourage the suggestion that he supported or shared its conclusions.

Olmedo waited for the colonel to be seated before sitting down himself. All eyes were on him, following with curiosity and excessive tension – as if he were handling explosive material – the movement of his hands as he opened his briefcase and took out the report, which was bound in black – not the most appropriate colour, he realised at that moment.

The colonel spoke first:

'You've all heard, even though a final decision hasn't been taken yet, that San Marcial will be closed down … suppressed,' he corrected himself. 'As you know, the Ministry of Defence had commissioned Major Olmedo to write a report on the strategic and economic viability of the base. He will tell you his conclusions now. Major?'

'Thank you, colonel,' said Olmedo, thinking that, even though the tone had been kind and the introduction neutral, the colonel had chosen his words very carefully to hint at his disagreement and dissociate himself from the report, thereby throwing Olmedo to the lions, one would have said. The major could almost feel some of the officers running after him, in hot pursuit, tongues hanging out, trying to bite his heels and waiting for him to stumble and fall to tear him to pieces.

He devoted the first twenty minutes to presenting facts, figures and performance indexes, while not forgetting to acknowledge all the hard work that had been carried out at the base, its historical importance and the integrity of those who had run it. He then spoke of the increasingly empty pavilions, that some premises seemed underused and others obsolete. He knew that figures are incontrovertible, and he cited them to counter the hostility he saw in some faces. His interpretation would follow, and that would require eloquence.

No one interrupted him as he presented his conclusions, but when he finished, several officers raised their hands. The lieutenant who was taking down the minutes next to the colonel established the order in which they'd have permission to speak. It would not be easy. But Olmedo didn't feel guilty about the report and was not cowardly about defending it. He was not there to impose a new order, but neither would he exempt anyone from duties long ago contracted. So he turned his gaze to the officer who was about to say a few words.

His full name was José García Bramante, but many did not know it, calling him only by the second surname, which he preferred. He'd recently been promoted to captain. He was forty-one but, thanks to his enthusiasm for physical exercise, was in very good shape; at the end of the long nocturnal marches with his Cetme slung on his shoulder and a backpack loaded with fifteen kilos of rocks, or on the hard running track, he was usually the first on the finish line, leaving behind a couple of hundred exhausted twenty-somethings. He seemed pleased when the other officers or soldiers congratulated him for those exploits. Every now and again he asked for a couple of days' leave of absence in order to run marathons. Olmedo had known others like him: army men obsessed with physical strength who, in time, ended up looking like those gym-equipment salesmen who appear on TV very late at night. Even the muscles of his cheeks and forehead appeared buff from so much effortful contraction. A few days previously Olmedo had watched him in the shooting gallery, as he was the officer in charge of armaments. Bramante held the Cetme so firmly and so close to his body that it seemed a continuation of his arms, so much so that the bullets appeared to be issuing from his fingers. And yet, Olmedo was not sure he was a great soldier. Perhaps his cunning might be useful in guerrilla warfare, where it was fundamental to react quickly, but he wasn't very efficient when it came to modern tactics. Unlike sportsmen, soldiers did not always get results in direct proportion to the dedication and intensity they put into their training, and often those who best deported themselves at parade and respected the rules and repeated the lessons about strategy performed less well under real-life fire than those who neglected their training in times of peace. Olmedo had seen, in Bramante's service record, that the captain had never asked to take part in missions abroad that might entail risk. He had the impression that, underneath the hardness, the need for admiration and recognition, was a hidden fault, a degree of insecurity, which had always reminded him of the modern version of the Roman *Miles Gloriosus* who defended his privileges while the barbarians were pushing the borders of the empire.

'Major, I agree with you that the army needs to be modernised, equipped with better technology and housed in better premises, and that we need to train enth-enthusiastic professionals instead of a bunch of ap-apathetic recruits,' he said, uttering some words with difficulty, perhaps because he talked too fast fearing that, if he stopped, he'd forget what he had prepared. 'Where I don't agree is when you say that that can't be done here, in San Marcial. We've got all the necessary inf-infrastructure.'

'I may not have clearly explained what Madrid wants in terms of strategic reorganisation on a national scale,' he conceded. 'The idea is to concentrate resources, which are now too spread out, in a few highly operative centres.' He chose abstract words that might contribute to dispelling disagreement.

'No, you have, you have. But, if I may say so, your explanation does not answer my question,' he replied looking at the colonel, seeking in vain his support, as Castroviejo remained silent, apparently less interested in what was being said than in the reactions it gave rise to in those who were listening to it.

'I'm afraid that, in that case, only someone in charge of making decisions can answer you. My powers do not go beyond the writing up of the report.'

Olmedo noticed how irritated Bramante was by his answer, and how coldly the colonel leaned over the agenda of the lieutenant to check the list of those wishing to speak.

'Captain Ucha,' he said.

'I think you'll be able to answer my question.'

'I'll try.'

'I've listened attentively to your conclusions and, although you didn't put it this way, what you've come to tell us is that the better the weaponry of an army the less necessary the men who are in charge of it. I don't agree with that, but this is not the place to argue the point. I only wish to ask you: what are they going to do with us? Not with the rank and file, but with us, the officers. Some will perhaps choose to pass to the reserve. But, the rest, where will they send us? Ceuta, Melilla? The Balkans? An Arab country, under UN or USA supervision? Where will they send us? What will they do with us?'

'It's not the first time an army base has been closed down, and the rights of all affected parties have always been respected, and many requests have been granted. It is safe to assume that our superiors will be generous and will respect our choices.'

'Except the choice of staying here, in San Marcial.'

'Except staying here, yes.'

'But that's the only thing many of us want.'

Ucha was sitting very near him. In spite of the man's calm tone, Olmedo thought he might be the officer less inclined to accept a transfer, and one who would never forget who had written the report. Among the military caste, there were always types like Ucha – quiet, patient and tenacious, men who knew that good things come to those who wait. He was an unsociable man, chose night shifts, and always appeared distant, not because he was afraid of anything, but because he wanted no responsibility.

Other officers spoke against the report, but their opposition was less staunch. They mentioned what the city would lose with the closure of the base, the sources of revenue and jobs that would disappear, such as cleaners and food providers, maintenance and transport technicians, bars and restaurants patronised by the troops. Or they expressed blanket complaints about how politicians marginalised everything to do with the army. But then a commander agreed with Olmedo's report and the fears dissipated into arguments among the officers. For a few minutes neither Castroviejo nor Olmedo said a word, while the assistants commented or discussed the likely consequences of the closure. One of the younger captains raised his voice in support of Olmedo and attracted everyone's attention when he described the changing times with a futuristic vision that was in sharp contrast with that image of old wood, bloodstained spoils and photographs of deceased soldiers:

'I do see the need to substitute these damp, colourless barracks with modern, functional buildings of steel and glass, with a computer on each desk, fast lifts and concealed staircases, with automatic doors that don't need to be guarded as they would be accessed via a keypad and code.'

An hour later the colonel was about to bring the meeting to a close when Ucha asked one last question:

'And you, sir, what will you do?'

'When?' replied Olmedo.

'When they close San Marcial, as we all know will happen. Where will you go? Because you're a part of this too,' he added leaning back in his chair, well aware that he had lost the battle but, also, that he could still inflict some pain.

That was the only question Olmedo had feared, because it was the only one he didn't have an answer to. The people from Madrid had suggested that, if he so wished, he could be destined for the central offices of the Ministry. The last few missions he'd been involved in had not been easy and they wanted to compensate him for his good work. Apart from a likely promotion in due course, he would not want for new special commissions, as there were many aspects of the army that needed reorganising. And if he did not want to be far from his homeland, the Mediterranean he was so attached to, they could post him to Valencia. But in both cases he'd have to leave the city, and doing that meant being away from Gabriela, as she would not follow him. He could always ask for an extended leave of absence, or even take early retirement, but he didn't really want to. Although he sometimes felt tired and worried, he was too young to be inactive. He knew he was good at his job, and early retirement would make him miserable, miserable like someone who, trained to fly planes, is reduced to driving horse carts. Besides, he loved his profession, the army life, the camaraderie shared in effort, the closed world of the barracks, the respect of honour, courage and loyalty, even the harsh, terse language, provided it didn't get too crude. He felt at ease as a part of a solid, enduring organisation that extended from King Don Juan Carlos I down to the last soldier in San Marcial – a brotherhood that would come to his help whenever he might need it. He liked all that, even if some people might question it upon hearing his report. Indeed, he would find it very hard to devise or invent for himself a satisfactory life outside that of the military. And so, fully aware of the attention everyone was paying to him at that moment, from the colonel to the lieutenant in charge of the minutes, he replied:

'I don't know, I don't know what I'll do if they close down San Marcial.'

He noticed everyone went quiet as he walked into the canteen. Bramante, Ucha and three or four other officers who appeared to be conspiring in a small circle near the bar stopped talking when they saw him. He drank a beer near other officers and promptly left, unable to stay there to eat in their company.

He drove towards the promenade. With the arrival of April the wind had changed and carried a slight warmth that encouraged tourists to walk along the beach, with the bottoms of their trousers rolled up, and their shoes in their hands, like pioneers braving the cold water. To the west, the mountains were wearing their new green suit, having cast off the grey heavy coat of clouds with which they robed themselves in winter.

Olmedo sat on the terrace of the restaurant of the navy headquarters – his uniform did not look out of place there – and chose a tastier dish than those available at the canteen. Alone, facing the wide beach, he searched for a response to the only question he had not known how to answer. What would he do when they closed down San Marcial?

He asked for only one glass of Rioja, but the waiter, who recognised him and was grateful for his tips, left the bottle on the table for him to refill his glass at will while he nibbled some delicious tomato-topped bread and waited for the fish.

He had to make a decision, could no longer postpone it. No matter how the details came to be arranged, there were two possible roads ahead of him: one looked easy and clear and would take him to professional success, quite likely towards a promotion, prestige and the satisfaction of a job well done. The other was a winding road, but at the same time a fascinating one, because it meant entering virgin territory, without tracks or signs or bridges, where he'd have to clear his own path. It led to Gabriela, but he could not be sure that, on arrival, she would welcome him as openly as a new office would. He knew that she liked him, that things worked out when they saw each other, when they made love, or when they occasionally travelled together. But her commitment went only so far. Gabriela still kept things back, did not share the embers of grief that awakened her in the middle of the night, the pain that singed her heart at any recollection of her son's death. Her feelings of loss had prevented him from suggesting they live together or, if she wanted, even get married. Olmedo had finally understood their relationship would not move forward before his capacity for consolation improved. There might be a degree of pain, he thought, that encourages other feelings, enhances one's sensibility, nourishes the hope to find the kind of happiness that will cure one's wounds. But too much suffering is sterile, searing the heart and scorching the ground of feelings with the salt of tears. Gabriela was very close to being in that position, and he wouldn't be able to pull her out if he was too far away.

A little later he realised the bottle was half empty and he'd finished the fish without tasting or even noticing what he was eating. Surprised, he put down his knife and fork, and looked at the beach where at that moment, the onset of the afternoon, more and more strollers and sunbathers were arriving and spreading out their towels on the sand. He felt a strong desire to take off his uniform for a few hours, put on a bathing suit, and swim to the point of exhaustion. Suddenly, with absolute clarity, he saw what his life without Gabriela would be like: a job in which it would not be easy for him to befriend new people; a separation from his daughter now she seemed so happy with her quiet boyfriend, who was so different from her ex-husband; quick solitary meals which he would wolf down rather than savour; the odd cultural event in which he would confirm that men of the past had created enduring works of art to relieve themselves of anxieties not unlike the one he was experiencing.

At first, when he met Gabriela, he thought it was loneliness that had brought them together; they satisfied each other's need for company, tenderness, and the spice of sex. Gabriela was attractive, but he soon realised that, even if that were not the case, it would not have made any difference. At his age canonical female beauty didn't matter so much. All women are equal, he'd once thought; if there's anything that distinguishes one from the other it is what each might be prepared to give. It is generosity, affection, sweetness and intelligence that establish the enormous gap between one and the other, what makes them vulgar or magnificent. In only a few weeks he had realised that his feelings were not just a form of pleasure. He'd fallen in love with her when he was getting used to living alone and now she was as essential to him as the wind to the flag. Now he had hopes for the future, he didn't know how much solitude he could bear. Since his wife had died in those ridiculous circumstances – at an operating theatre, as she underwent aesthetic surgery – he had not felt like this. He liked to compare his love for Gabriela to the grains of wheat that archaeologists, digging into a pyramid, had found in a three-thousand-year-old vase, left there to feed the deceased pharaoh in his new life. Brought back to light, the grain had germinated. Gabriela, he told himself, had made him flower again, awakened him from his sentimental apathy. In return he was prepared to be generous and would try to make up for all she had suffered.

He pushed the full glass away and made up his mind, although he was aware that his decision implied renouncing some advantages. But he had an answer now. That very afternoon he intended to buy a ring and everything he needed for an intimate dinner the next day. He would ask her to move in with him. If she said yes, he would ask for an extended leave of absence of at least two years, even if that would not help his career. If she said no, well, he'd rather not think about that possibility...

4

Cupido Listens

One morning, as he was walking out of the flat he had rented, a journalist and a photographer from the local paper, armed with a microphone and a camera, waylaid him to ask him a few questions about a case known as 'Bling', which, touching as it did on the intimate conflicts of some well-known families of the city, had whetted the already voracious appetite of the tabloid press. Cupido had pushed away the camera without saying a word. Such stories evoked in him the worst memories of the rural world he was from: unhealthy gossip, the dictatorship of appearances, the shady complacency that some people felt at the disgrace of others. In a Shakespeare play he'd read: "What great ones do, the less will prattle of." Now he watched in astonishment how that petty curiosity percolated down to all levels of society. No doubt other detectives would have seen in this an opportunity to satisfy their vain glory, publicise their services and raise their fees, but Cupido had always stayed away from the public eye. He liked anonymity and tried to remain unknown and escape people's notice. Besides, he knew that being unknown, if possible invisible, was essential in his line of work.

And then he was in a city that wasn't his own. He'd first visited it the previous July – a sojourn motivated not by a desire for a holiday but the need to accompany his mother. She had liked the climate and the seabathing so much that they had decided to return in the middle of March for a stay at the same guesthouse catering for elderly customers. Cupido had rented a flat for the period and had invited Alkalino, as he knew how few opportunities his friend had to do the things he enjoyed most: travelling, visiting cities and places that differed from the provincial, rural Breda he knew so well, and observing – with astonishment and scepticism, but never outrage – habits and beliefs that were sometimes opposed to his own. Alkalino was very grateful for it and had planned to stay for two or three weeks, not wanting to make a nuisance of himself. But a month had gone by and he was still there. Which actually suited Cupido just fine; he was amused by Alkalino's comments and witticisms, and interested in his moralistic yet compassionate view of the human condition. Besides, Alkalino visited his mother now and again at the guesthouse. The place was nice, they answered the phone promptly, and there always seemed to be an employee cleaning the corridors, the windows or the toilets. Alkalino, who felt at ease with old people, already knew some of the guests. One afternoon, Cupido could not help but laugh out loud on seeing him dressed in a track suit, with a label still attached to his trousers, ready to go to an aerobics session for the old timers.

Cupido didn't know how he'd started getting commissions, as he hadn't advertised his services anywhere. He guessed it had to do with the nature of his job – a lot of people wanted to clear up something disquieting, or shady, or shameful – and his discretion in previous jobs attracted customers who were looking precisely for someone who solved cases inconspicuously.

He'd accepted a first commission just to please his mother. An old man from the guesthouse engaged him to help his daughter. She'd been unlawfully dismissed from work, without any severance pay, accused of an obscure cyber crime, when in fact they had sacked her for other reasons. They had withdrawn all disciplinary sanctions and had paid her compensation when Cupido appeared at the owner's office and threw on his desk an envelope containing a dozen pictures showing him entering and leaving a hotel with his new employee, his arm around her waist.

A little later he was asked to work on relatively uncomplicated cases; he accepted them because he was extending his stay in the coastal town and it would be good for his finances, which were suffering considerably although he couldn't quite tell what he spent his money on. He looked into an insurance claim by someone who was pretending he'd sustained an injury; searched for a girl who had run away from home, never finding her; investigated yet another case of adultery, which made him think that it's impossible to be a private eye without encountering deception and lies, passion and jealousy. The saddest part was the discovery that the people who hired him were almost always right, their suspicions astonishingly accurate.

But he had always been discreet. He never divulged anything a client told him in confidence, and only when the law was broken did he encourage the intervention of the police. He guessed it was his reserve, as well as the fact that he was a stranger in town, that had driven the dead colonel's daughter to approach him to see if he could uncover the truth behind her father's death.

As she waited for an answer at the other end of the phone line, Cupido remembered what he'd read in the local press a few days before. The story appeared on the front page, and he'd been surprised that a military man had committed suicide, because although suicides were not rare among troops who were under pressure, Cupido had the impression they were infrequent among officers. The paper spoke of 'puzzling circumstances', the usual euphemism when something illegal was suspected, but also reported that a note had been found suggesting it was suicide. Cupido half remembered the picture of a man in his early fifties, dressed in uniform, with cropped hair and that air of energy so common among army men on active service.

'You'll take the case, won't you?' she'd asked after a few seconds of silence, only to add: 'I'd like to speak with you.'

Cupido gave her the address and they arranged to meet in an hour.

Alkalino came back from the street, from one of his solitary and slightly mysterious walks, and when he saw Cupido underlining a piece of news in an old newspaper, he asked:

'More work?'

'Yes.'

'What member of the family hired you?'

'How do you know it's a family member?'

'Because I doubt it's a colleague. I can't imagine a soldier hiring a private detective. Soldiers don't usually like civilians and prefer to solve their problems within the walls of their own institutions. To ask for help would be like admitting professional incompetence.'

'Sometimes I think you should be the detective and I your assistant,' said Cupido, smiling at Alkalino's sagacity.

But Alkalino wasn't smiling. On the contrary, his expression suggested that this was one of those days on which he surrendered to apathy and tiredness – he whose nickname referred to his resistance to fatigue and his inability to stay quiet – and terribly missed the drink, the old feeling of oblivion and the pleasure of the cognac bathing his tongue, the velvety heat going down his throat and swaying in his stomach. In those moments he was torn between his thirst and the guilty desire of quenching it, and none of his dialectical ingenuity could get him to break out of it: it was painful to hear the loud call of booze, but he knew he would feel even worse if he answered it. A few months before, in Breda, he had succumbed: every night he vowed not to drink the following day, and every morning he cursed himself after taking the first sip. But he'd managed to overcome it, and since then his sympathy for the weak seemed to have increased, as had his scepticism towards those who boasted of their virtue and strength of will.

'That would be as ridiculous as teaching a frog to catch flies,' replied Alkalino. 'I mean, you're already very good at what you do, and you don't need any help.'

'No, that's not true. You know how much I appreciate your contribution. You know I value your words, and not simply as ingenious or eccentric speculations.'

Alkalino looked doubtful.

'Sometimes I do get that impression, but there are moments when I'm not so sure my opinions are worth much.'

'You've known me long enough not to doubt it.'

'Well, I don't know much about you,' he said, still serious.

'What do you mean?'

'You're in the business of knowing. You're the one who asks and listens and thinks things over and knows. The rest of us are what is known. I haven't heard you talk about yourself for a long time, Cupido.'

The detective looked at him in silence, weighing up the words Alkalino had used to describe him. It was true. He'd never been someone given to confidences or talking about himself, but with the passage of time he was becoming even more secretive. He hid from everyone his disappointments, his loneliness, his fears and how fed up he was with his job, the profession that led him to believe that no person can love another forever. He kept those impressions to himself, where no one might see them and point out their painful harshness. Looking back, he realised he'd been able to salvage very few things from the wreckage of time, that the wealth of his youthful dreams had rotted before they could come true. He no longer hoped to have children. Nor did it seem likely that he would have for a woman feelings as intense as when he had first loved. He no longer believed that an ideology could make the world a better place; and as for the human condition, well, he'd seen his fair share of evil and misery, and had concluded that some men can only do harm. He'd seen people die and people kill. It was true that, when he thought of the future, the moral landscape he identified in himself was not lacking in dignity, but it wasn't the kind best shared with anyone else. He was over forty and knew that, unless he did something about it, he'd get lonelier as each year passed. Up to this age, he often told himself, most of the people one has met and known are alive, but from now on the balance will start to even out, until the presence of the living weighs as much as the memories of the dead. And a little later everyone would start dying around him, if his number didn't come up first. Nowadays, all he felt was a sort of pity towards innocent victims, filial love for his mother, and friendly affection for half a dozen people. Alkalino took pride of place among them, and Cupido didn't want him to feel scorned, or that he was someone who didn't matter, someone one doesn't count on, and whose opinion is not consulted because one's indifferent to it.

'You may be right in part,' admitted Cupido.

'I am, Cupido, I am.'

'Some day I might talk about myself.'

Alkalino still looked doubtful.

'I'm not so sure. You're very self-sufficient. You've become isolated, and … and …' He looked at the furniture, searching for an inexistent bottle of something, and made a vague gesture, as if he suddenly didn't know where he was or whether his words meant anything. Nor did he seem to be expecting a reply. 'I think I'd better go back to Breda,' he said, leaving the previous sentence unfinished.

'What, now? When summer is coming and the city fills up with all those tourists you like to watch so much?'

'Precisely now that the first ones are arriving. I've come back from the beach, and people have already started sunbathing. The girls were coming out of the water in their wet, almost see-through bikinis, cold and trembling, as if they were waiting for someone to come and wrap them up in a towel.'

'And what's wrong with that?'

'Wrong? Nothing wrong if it was me they were waiting for. No,' he said, serious again. 'I'd better get away from all this fun. I'm beginning to miss Breda, the Casino Bar, my routines, even the landscape … And I've been living off you for a few weeks now.'

'Nonsense,' protested Cupido. 'On the contrary, I'd still owe you money if you were not so pig-headed and refused payment for the help you give me when I need it. At least wait a couple of days before making a decision. Any time now the daughter of the man who died from a gunshot will be here,' he said, pointing to the paper. 'A family member, as you said. Don't tell me you're not curious.'

'All right, all right,' he accepted. 'It's impossible not to be whenever someone comes round to ask you to help them put together again what someone else has shattered. But I don't know if curiosity is as powerful as that ...'

'If I take this job here, in a city where I barely know anyone, I'll definitely need your assistance.'

Although he was able to handle the investigation on his own and bring it to a successful conclusion – as he'd done many other times – he wanted Alkalino to feel needed.

The entry phone rang at that moment, as if bearing news. Cupido walked over to the door and stopped for a few seconds in front of the small screen to look at the woman waiting at the door.

'She's pretty,' whispered Alkalino, who'd followed him.

The detective buzzed her in without a word. A minute later the lift stopped on his floor, and the woman came out trailing a delicate lilac perfume. They shook hands and introduced themselves.

She's left-handed, thought Cupido as he watched her sit in the armchair he'd offered her. Although she was wearing dark clothes, a soft clarity emanated from her – a sort of troubled serenity.

Alkalino had disappeared before she came in, and was hiding in his room so as not to meddle in the interview, but he'd left the door ajar. Better that way. The woman could just talk directly to Cupido, wouldn't have to worry about someone else listening to her words. The conversation was bound to include confidential information about the victim, and a third party, watching, listening and saying nothing, would only inspire nervousness.

'I don't entirely understand what you expect from me,' said Cupido. 'With a death like this, a judge always commissions an inquiry. And since your father was a high-ranking officer, I don't think the police will be inclined to shelve the case before it's solved. Your father was, in a way, one of them.'

'The judge has ruled, perhaps too soon, that it was suicide. But my father didn't kill himself. I know the circumstances would appear to indicate he did. The note he left seems to prove it. But I know it's not true, it cannot be true.'

'From what I've read, the post-mortem doesn't rule it out either.'

'I know, I've got the report. But then I don't think anyone's interested in proving the contrary.'

'What do you mean?'

Marina took a deep breath. Her face registered an expression of tiredness and defeat.

'Do you know the San Marcial base, here in the city?'

'Yes.'

'My father had just written a report, commissioned by the Ministry of Defence, suggesting it should be closed. On the morning of the day he died he presented his results to his colleagues. As you can imagine, some of them will be affected if the base disappears. I mean, he made himself enemies.'

'Who?'

'That morning he mentioned two names: Bramante and Ucha,' she said, and then continued explaining. 'But the last thing the army wants is for public opinion or the press to suspect that one of its own men killed him out of revenge or because of internal conflicts. To them ... murder,' the word sounded strange in her mouth, as if she'd just discovered it and was uttering it for the first time, 'is worse than suicide. It would damage an institution whose public image is always fragile. They'd want to stick to the suicide version even if it weren't true.'

'And you don't believe it is?'

'No, I don't. I spoke to my father that morning, before he went to the base. He stopped by my house, as he wanted me to sign some documents he needed to take to the bank; he was changing the account holder's name. All seemed normal, like any other day. He wasn't depressed or ill. I can't imagine him putting a gun to his chest and pulling the trigger,' she said in a broken voice. She searched through her bag and took out a tissue to wipe her eyes. On her left wrist a beautiful bracelet made of gold links shone for a moment.

Cupido waited a few moments. He understood her reluctance to accept that version. He sometimes thought of assisted death and imagined himself in old age, alone and tormented by an incurable disease, asking someone to leave some painless poison at hand, maybe on his night table. But everything about suicide seemed more problematic. Suicide contaminates everyone close to the victim, family and friends, with a dose of remorse. It makes them ask themselves what they could have done to avoid the rope, or the gas, or the water, or the gunshot in the chest. And no one wants to take the blame: 'Someone else killed him, I had nothing to do with his death, there was nothing I could have done to avoid it,' were always the most comforting answers.

'Had he received any threats?'

'Not personally. He knew his work wasn't to everyone's liking, but he didn't seem worried about that, he considered it a natural consequence of his profession. The only precaution he took … the only thing he was afraid of was an attack. Some time ago, his name had appeared on a terrorist organisation's target list, and for that reason he always carried a gun. But personal enemies, no, he was not afraid of them. Or of any other kind of aggression. I mean, a soldier knows how to defend himself from a common thief. But there's something else that's not quite clear,' she said, screwing her eyes.

'Yes?'

'The weapon he … it wasn't his regulation gun.'

'Tell me slowly, from the beginning. Tell me all you can remember, in detail,' he asked. He knew recollection could be capricious, and that memories don't surface in the same way when one speaks of a recent event or of something that took place a while ago. With time details may be forgotten, but previously unnoticed patterns appear.

Cupido picked up a pencil and opened a simple spiral notebook. He used a new one for every investigation. He jotted down the known events and whatever facts he came to find, and also all kinds of details and circumstances – weather, place and landscape, anecdotes, professions and so on – which didn't immediately fit into the investigation. Yet he was very careful not to run ahead of himself with a hypothesis. He disliked rushing things, preferred ideas to settle bit by bit, so he could slowly interpret the meaning of every piece of information. By hurrying one risked overlooking what was important, or destroying evidence without finding anything useful, like the treasure hunter who, assuming the beeping of the metal detector signals gold, digs into the ground damaging valuable material, only to find a rusty horseshoe. From the moment an investigation started, patience was of the essence, patience to analyse what the victim was like, and who his enemies might be; to deduce at what moment the word 'murder' had rolled off someone's tongue and in what way that person had savoured its bittersweet taste, their lips no longer refusing to utter it; to imagine the hand that later searched for the appropriate weapon, and held it, while a pair of eyes looked at the clock and measured time; to find the place where the murderer hid and retraced his steps as he fled the scene. Cupido saved a page for each of those involved, and slowly filled it with information about their personalities and emotions, the way they looked and what their relationship with the victim was. It was there, in those pages, in the way each person acted, in their feelings of love, hatred or indifference, in the reactions to simple facts that eventually Cupido found the key to the mystery. Experience had taught him that only when he had managed to define those portraits which emerged from the shadows did the narrative hang together; moreover, he could never understand it unless he understood the protagonists, so that both elements – narrative and characters – cast light on one another, and in the end both truths converged: the objective, incontrovertible truth of facts, and that other truth, no less untameable, of feelings. When that hadn't been the case, when he had only scratched the surface of places, actions, and people's movements, the investigation ended in failure, in an absurd, hectic segue of comings and goings, routine questions and fruitless answers. To centre oneself on alibis was like coming into possession of tools and then being incapable of building anything with them. Such tools were essential, yes, but useless if not used correctly. That's why Cupido asked about a person's relationship with the victim rather than where he was on such and such a day at such and such a time.

'That evening I rang my father up, like any other day,' the woman started saying. 'It was half past eight. I checked it several times in the phone memory, and the time fits with what forensics have established: that he died between eight and nine. The phone rang a few times before he picked it up. He said he couldn't speak to me at that moment, as there was someone with him, though he didn't say who. Then he said he'd call me back later. When he didn't, I rang him back at eleven. He didn't answer and I thought he might have gone out, on his own or with a colleague, as in the morning he'd had that meeting I told you about.'

'Yes.'

'I wasn't worried yet. But the next day, after taking my son to the bus stop, I tried again. As he wasn't answering I rang his mobile. It was turned off or out of reach, and I imagined he must still be busy with that business of closing down the base. I began to get worried at noon, when I still couldn't reach him. I called his office and they told me he hadn't come to work, they assumed he was ill. It was then that I began to suspect that something was wrong, as he didn't normally miss a day of work, not even to be with Gabriela.'

'Who's Gabriela?' interrupted Cupido.

'The woman he'd been seeing for a few months.'

The detective wrote down the name in his notebook, but before he could ask, she answered his next question.

'My mother died four years ago, while she was undergoing plastic surgery. In theory, it should have been a simple operation, but there were complications with the anaesthetic and she never came round. Since then, my father had barely shown any interest in a woman, until he met Gabriela. He fell in love with her. He never told me so in so many words, but he couldn't hide how much he wanted to make her happy. I mean, in that respect, he didn't have any reason to take his own life either. I don't think he felt lonely.'

Cupido nodded slightly as he looked at her hands: she was wearing a ring on each, but neither was a wedding ring. That didn't mean he should assume anything about her marital status, as he knew some married people who didn't wear rings, but then he remembered that, when she had rung and they arranged to meet an hour later, she'd mentioned something about needing to get someone to mind her children. He'd have to ask her about that too.

'I think Gabriela reminded my father of what he went through four years ago: the same grief and emptiness when you unexpectedly lose someone in your family.'

'Did she lose her husband?'

'No, much worse – her son. Her only son, a teenager. My father suffered a lot when he lost my mother, but one day, talking about Gabriela, he told me her experience was the more painful, the wound deeper, more difficult to come to terms with. Because, in a way, he said, you can find a substitute for your partner, someone who might compensate for the person you've lost. But not for a son, a son can never be replaced. I asked him, jokingly, if he loved me more than my mother. He refused to compare us and simply answered that he had really loved her, but now he also loved Gabriela.'

'How did he die, her son?'

'In a terrible, absurd accident. He was fifteen. It seems it was the result of teenage bravado. He and two friends were walking down the street and started goading one of those dangerous dogs, a pit bull, I think, that was behind a fence. The owners were out, and the dog got furious and ended up jumping over the fence and attacking them. By the time the police got there and shot it, the boy was already dead.'

'I see. Back to your father's case, did you call Gabriela that morning to see if he was with her?'

'I did, although I knew the previous night they hadn't seen each other. They had both been at my place in the morning and I heard them say they wouldn't meet that evening. Then my father left for work. And Gabriela and I went over to Samuel's.'

'Samuel?'

'My boyfriend. The previous day he had invited Gabriela and me to his house to pick up some plants and cuttings he'd prepared for us. He has a small garden, but a very pretty one. And in the evening I rang Gabriela to discuss how we'd arranged the plants. Samuel had been to her house to give her a hand. That's how I also know my father did not go out with her that night.'

'You were saying before that, by noon the following day, you started feeling something must be wrong,' said Cupido, putting her narrative in order.

'Yes, and I decided to go over to his house. I've got a set of keys. So I opened the door ...'

'Sorry to interrupt again.'

'No, please.'

'Has anyone else got a set of keys?'

'Aurora, only Aurora.'

'And she is?'

'The cleaning lady. She has my complete trust. My father had hired her for both houses, as she's Rosco's wife, and Rosco is a street-sweeper form his neighbourhood. My father liked to know the people around him, needed to feel in control of his surroundings. I used to tell him it was a military obsession, seeing danger where there isn't any. In any case, Aurora didn't have her keys that day.'

'How do you know?'

'Because I had them. She works two days a week for us, Mondays and Thursdays. First she cleans my father's house, and when she's done she comes to mine. It's a good arrangement, because she organises herself and splits her time according to what she needs to do at one place or the other. That Monday she was at his house first and then came to mine. She keeps all the keys on the same key ring, and when she finished cleaning, she closed the door behind her and left them inside. She collected them the following Thursday. So no one could have used her keys on Monday afternoon to go into my father's house.'

'All right. Please go on.'

'I was saying I opened the door and called out "Dad, Dad" because the house looked strange. Everything was tidy, but too tidy. Once in the living room I started noticing the details: the remote control was on top of the TV, where Aurora always leaves it, as if it hadn't been touched the day before, and the cushions were perfectly arranged. I went into the kitchen and saw only one coffee cup in the sink. Just one cup, although the previous evening my father had had a visitor. And if he'd had dinner or breakfast at home, there should at least have been a plate, a knife. The door to the bedroom was open, and I could see the bed was made, not simply with the covers pulled up as he sometimes did when he was in a hurry. It seemed that he had spent the night out, hadn't been back since the previous evening, when we'd spoken on the phone and he'd told me he'd call back later. I opened the door to his study and it was then that I saw him. He was sitting in his chair, slumped over his desk. I remember thinking he'd suffered a heart attack or something like that, but then I saw a large bloodstain at his feet, on the light-coloured carpet. I ran to help him, although I already knew he was dead. The way he stayed still – it was too heavy, too silent. From that moment on I don't remember precisely what I did, but I do know I lifted him slightly to feel his chest for a heartbeat, thinking about doing resuscitation as I've seen it done so many times on TV, and that's where the wound was, the blood already darkened and dry. At the centre of the desk, by his hand, was one of his cards with only two words written on it. Here,' she said, showing him an ivory-coloured card.

CAMILO OLMEDO

Forgive me

Cupido picked it up carefully, as if no one had analysed it yet. On the top left-hand corner he read the printed name, unaccompanied by any profession or contact details. On the centre were the two handwritten words.

'They gave it back to me yesterday, after they officially ruled it was suicide.'

'Is it his hand?'

'Yes, his handwriting was unmistakeable, tilted forward slightly, firm, solid and large. Graphologists have confirmed it was he who wrote the note, although they add he must have been under great stress, as the lines are a bit shaky. But of course he was under great stress!'

She stopped for a moment, as if she needed to catch her breath before continuing with the story in the right order, without leaving out any details, as the detective had asked her.

'I went to the phone at once to call an ambulance, and I stepped on something. On the bloodstained carpet was the gun with which they shot him … or he shot himself … I don't know what to think anymore. Right now, going over everything, I wonder if I should really be here. Perhaps my father did commit suicide, and it would be best for me and for everyone to accept it and leave well alone. Anyway, the ambulance arrived quickly. They saw the body, but didn't want to touch anything before the police and judge checked the scene.'

'They did the right thing,' said Cupido.

'Yes, I don't doubt it. They asked me to step out of the study and one of the nurses gave me a bottle of water so I could drink without touching anything in the kitchen either. Until then I hadn't realised how thirsty I was, my mouth felt dry and acrid, a taste I identified only later and which reminded me of what it used to feel like, as a child, to touch a battery with my tongue.'

'Yes,' said Cupido, thinking of the taste of gunpowder.

'It was later, once everyone accepted the hypothesis of the suicide, that I began thinking about that gun I stepped on.'

'And that's what you don't understand,' said Cupido.

'I don't understand it, no. I don't understand why my father, who was so scrupulous about the law, chose that gun, whose sole possession was illegal, to shoot himself, if that was indeed the case. Why not use his regulation gun, which he always had to hand? Because the other pistol had a silencer? I don't think so. What did he care, if he was about to die, whether someone might hear the noise? I've tried to find a satisfactory explanation before I decided to come and talk to you, but nothing seems conclusive, and perhaps there isn't one. I even told myself that, faced with the other, deeper mystery of why he committed suicide, any other details were irrelevant. If I cannot understand the main thing, everything else will remain inexplicable.'

'How come he had an illegal gun?'

Marina looked at him as if she didn't understand the question, still engrossed in her thoughts. She took a few seconds to reply:

'As I said, my father was worried he might be attacked and wanted to feel safe. And, less than a year ago, there was an unpleasant incident at the base. One day, during shooting practice, his gun accidentally fired and hit an assistant, a rank and file soldier, in the thigh. The boy didn't lodge a complaint, as it clearly was one of those mishaps that are inevitable when you handle weapons. But an inquiry was carried out all the same, and the officer in charge of armaments, García Bramante, who didn't see eye to eye with my father, asked for a formal investigation to determine whether he was guilty of negligence. This upset my father, who was proud of his brilliant, impeccable service record, and scrupulously adhered to very rule. Still, he didn't worry too much; obviously it had not been deliberate, and he knew they just wanted to introduce a little blemish onto his CV. However, once the inquiry started, disciplinary measures took their course, and in those cases they take away the regulation gun as a precautionary measure. It was only for a couple of months. But he didn't want to go about unarmed, because he felt unsafe, and so he got another gun, which is not difficult if you're in the army. Once he told me that that had been his only infringement of the law, a small, secret one, in thirty-five years of service. Fortunately, no one ever knew, and he didn't need to use it, which would have led to serious disciplinary measures. And then, when the inquiry was closed, and he got back his own gun, he put the other one in a drawer and never touched it again … if it was he who pulled the trigger … until …'

'Until that day,' said Cupido.

'That's right.'

The detective was quiet for a few seconds, going over the first pieces of information. Then he asked:

'Do you know what this all means?'

'No,' she replied, disconcerted.

'It means that, if it was homicide, it could only have been someone he knew, someone he asked in, whom he didn't expect would attack him. Otherwise, since he was a soldier who'd fore-seen the possibility of danger, he wouldn't have just stayed seated in his chair, without attempting to defend himself.'

'Yes, he would have done that.'

'The previous evening, when you spoke to him, and he said he was with someone, did you get the impression it was a stranger?'

'I don't know, why?'

'If it had been someone you both knew, would your father have mentioned he was there with that person?'

'Yes, I think he would have,' she replied after thinking it over for a few seconds. 'Yes, we were very close.'

Those two details didn't quite fit together, but no doubt there had been some logic to Olmedo's acts. If he had shot himself, he could have perfectly used the unregistered gun, as if even in death he didn't want to tarnish that service record he was so proud of. If it hadn't been him, well, that was the mystery Cupido had to solve. As a civilian, he wasn't sure he understood what impulses, fears and interests drove a military man. Why would someone keep a gun that's not legally his when it may occasion problems? An illegal pistol – you either used it at once or threw it into a deep swamp. To keep it was to court risk. And yet, soldiers are familiar with them, and no doubt careful and deft in handling them, aware that they represent danger.

Marina took a photograph out of her bag and passed it to the detective.

'My father,' she said.

Either the picture had been taken from a slight overhead angle or Olmedo had tilted his head forwards, but as he stared at the lens his eyebrows appeared slightly curved into a quizzical look, giving the strange impression that he had just asked a question to the photographer and was expecting an answer. His hair – cropped, abundant, and combed back – and a coarse, open-necked shirt of a greenish colour accentuated a look that was so stern it seemed almost scornful. Cupido decided to take the job, but now he would have to *find* the man, get to know him, investigate his world until the human being behind the face became familiar. The mystery was hiding in Olmedo; in Cupido's experience, the keys to the truth did not turn up when investigating the suspects but the victim. He mistrusted that old adage, 'Find the motive and you'll find the culprit', as he had come across murderers who had futile motives to kill and, conversely, innocent people with powerful reasons not to be so.

'The funeral took place this morning. Forensics had finished their work. Right now he's being cremated. I'm talking to you as the body of my father burns. The foreign woman at the beach, the one who rents hammocks, knows you well and told me I can trust you, precisely because you're not from this city, not even this region,' she said, and Cupido imagined that the Nordic woman must have told Marina that he came from inland, where some people have never seen the sea, 'and that you solved your previous case very efficiently. I'm interested in the fact that you're a stranger, someone who owes no favours and knows no one here. A local detective might get swayed by the military class, which has so much influence in this city. Will you accept the job? Will you help me? I don't know how much you charge, I've never had to hire a detective before, but I don't think money will be a problem. Will you take the job?' she repeated.

'Yes,' replied Cupido. 'I'll need access to your father's flat, his diary, documents, things, and I'll need to talk to you again. You'll also have to give me some phone numbers. And it would be nice to arrange a meeting with the top officer at the base.'

'That won't be a problem.'

Marina thanked him. They discussed the financial details, and as soon as she left Alkalino reappeared in the living room.

'I think I'll accept your invitation and stay for a while. I won't leave you alone in this city against an entire army,' he joked. His tone had changed after hearing the conversation with Marina.

'I didn't expect anything less from you,' he answered with a smile, glad that he had aroused his friend's interest. 'And I don't think it'll be an easy job.'

'No, it won't,' replied Alkalino. 'But you'll find out the truth. Sometimes I wonder how you do it.'

Cupido shrugged his shoulders and said, 'By talking. You ask a suspect about the victim and then, in a bizarre shift, the suspect starts talking about himself, even if he didn't intend to.'

'If that's the case, I'll be able to help you. You know there are few things I enjoy more than talking. But then with soldiers, those hermetic, proud and corporate people, you might need more than words. A word may sometimes move a mountain, but it's often useless. The simultaneous shout of all the spectators at a Champions' League Match at the Bernabú Stadium wouldn't produce enough energy to warm up a cup of coffee.'

'All right, but even if we cannot move a mountain, we'll try and dig a tunnel into it to see what lies beneath.'

'Beneath you'll find pain, or the kind of hatred aroused by three or four elementary passions: power, greed, revenge, and sex, of course, sex and that sublimation we've invented to justify it. Any of those can be an excuse to kill,' said Alkalino, and after a few seconds of silence repeated: 'Of course it won't be easy. People seem to get smarter the more they hate. Hatred keeps them awake, sharpens their minds, which are tame and drowsy when they're in love, when they're enjoying things and feeling good. Hatred wakes you up, love stuns you. That's why hatred is better at carrying out its purposes than justice is at preventing them, and most crimes would go unpunished if chance didn't play a part, if we didn't use a good share of the national budget to avoid them, and if we didn't have a few judges and detectives like yourself, who know that appearances can be deceptive.'

'You mean you believe Olmedo didn't …?'

'I believe her, Cupido. I don't think her father committed suicide, although …' he hesitated.

'Say it.'

'Although the way he died fits the theory.'

'How do you mean?'

'How would a soldier kill himself?' replied Alkalino.

'By shooting himself,' said Cupido. 'No pills, ropes, or jumping out of a window. A soldier would shoot himself in the heart or the head. They've got the guns, know how to use them and where to aim to avoid mistakes.'

'That's right. The way he died fits in with suicide. But there's something I don't get.'

'What?'

'The way she described her father, he didn't sound like the kind of man who would sit quietly at home and then shoot himself in the chest, leaving a card saying "Forgive me". I'd say someone else shot him, someone he let into his house and his study. But you're the one that is going to have to find out who. Well, with my help,' he concluded with a crooked smile.

5

Empty House

He went into the flat using the keys Marina had given him, closed the door behind him and walked into the living room. He stood there a few seconds, alert and still, looking at the premises in the dim light that came in through the blinds, which were only half open.

Not knowing quite what he was looking for, he just expected to find material for further speculation. The police had gone through the rubbish, had dusted for fingerprints, searched for DNA, and checked the call register of the day in question. They had checked his computer files, and studied the movements of his bank accounts and credit cards. It was unlikely, though, that they had found anything out of the ordinary, because they accepted the theory of suicide.

He went from room to room without touching anything. There was none of the lonely-male atmosphere he had seen in similar places, a sort of stale stuffiness redolent of raw materials: the smell of animal wool that unwashed clothes acquire, the autumn smell of old furniture, the mineral smell of metallic decorations. He didn't see a flat unaired as if no oxygen were left in it, or poorly cleaned, or with smudged glasses of every shape and form lying everywhere, or remains of plates, or bits of scrap paper with phone numbers but no names on them, or fast food brochures piled up in the kitchen, or clocks with their hands still because no one had bothered to change the batteries. On the contrary, everything was meticulously tidy, in a way that couldn't be just the work of the cleaning lady, Aurora – the name Marina had given him. The doors of the bedroom and cupboards did not creak when they were opened, and the suits on the hangers were protected with plastic covers, the trousers ironed with a crease down the middle, the shirts missing no buttons.

He went back to the living room and searched the flat systematically, checking every corner, opening all drawers, inspecting the diary and the margins of the telephone directory. Fortunately, the decor was not too ornate. There were few things, but all were of good quality, solid, authentic: the carpet made of thick wool, the table and the cupboards of wood, and the coat rack at the entrance of stainless steel. Not a hoarder's house, but a house made to last.

Seeing a picture of Olmedo with his wife and a teenage Marina, Cupido noticed there weren't many signs of the woman who had lived in that flat until her death in an operating theatre: barely one or two photographs, ceramic knick-knacks, and some clothes he couldn't imagine the major had bought himself. Cupido wondered why houses empty little by little when a woman dies or leaves, and why they fill with furniture and paintings and decorations when it is the man who passes on.

He checked the medicines in the bathroom cabinet: painkillers, antibiotics, digestion tablets, a cream for haemorrhoids and several kinds of vitamins typical of a man who likes to stay sharp. That was all, no peculiar drug that might indicate depression or insomnia.

Cupido tackled the study last. The parquet was lighter under the desk, from where the bloodstained carpet had been removed. It took a while to check every drawer and every shelf. Two dozen insubstantial novels indicated Olmedo was not too keen on fiction. However, there were numerous books on history, biography, monographs on armament, military strategy, and recent armed conflicts. They had been obviously studied with attention, as some passages were underlined in pencil and annotated in the margins.

On the desk were the bank documents needed to change the name of the account holder on an investment fund, which Marina had mentioned in their interview. They were signed by her, but not by the major, the other account holder. In a small cupboard Cupido found a wooden box with medals and decorations, the oldest ones dating from as far back as Olmedo's time in the Academia de Zaragoza. Next to the box were several folders with old bank statements, income tax returns, and the title deeds to the house and a small farm in the countryside. The last folder he checked contained the dossier of a trial. Cupido sat on the floor – he didn't dare sit down in the chair where Olmedo had died – and carefully perused the report: the judge found an anaesthetist called Lesmes Beltrán Villa guilty of criminal negligence at work during an operation which had resulted in the death of a patient called Pilar Rodríguez Pando. The lawsuit had been initiated by the victim's husband, Camilo Olmedo, and the anaesthetist had been barred from practising for four years and sentenced to pay a hundred and fifty thousand euros in compensation to the family of the woman.

Cupido wrote it all down in his notebook for discussion later with Marina.

Over three hours had gone by when he went down to the garage. Even here, everything was impeccably tidy, with the tools in order and two old tyres placed on the back wall as buffers. A racing bicycle in perfect condition hung from a hook and made the detective want to take it down and go for a ride for a couple of hours, pedalling until he was exhausted. The car was open and he went through the glove compartment and looked under the floor mats without finding anything important.

He left the building with the feeling that the man who had lived there had no secrets. The surface of his life looked like a hilly landscape, with the inevitable accidents created by time, but it didn't hide pits inhabited by unknown monsters, or caves full of bones and bats, or frozen, inaccessible mountains whose very existence was a mystery. Olmedo seemed to have led a sensible life, and on that evidence the theory of his suicide seemed strange and incongruous. Cupido now better understood Marina's refusal to accept it and her need to find another explanation. She could only rest if she came to understand Olmedo's death just as she'd been able to understand his life.

At his request, Marina had arranged for him to meet with the colonel in charge at San Marcial. The appointment was for five p.m. but ten minutes earlier Cupido was already at the entrance to the base, showing his ID to the corporal on guard duty, well aware that military men appreciate punctuality, which they consider another daughter of discipline. At five o'clock, the colonel's orderly, a soldier with South American features and accent, opened the door of the office and led him in.

Cupido had not set foot in an army base since the day he finished his compulsory military service, and for a moment he was taken aback by the air of authority emanating from the elderly colonel, who was looking at him from across his desk at the back of the enormous room, flanked by a Spanish flag and a picture of the king. Cupido was surprised to realise he hesitated between using the form of address employed in the army – 'Colonel' – which was more rooted in his memory than he'd suspected, and a more neutral kind of expression.

'Good afternoon,' he said eventually, standing still at the start of the long, emphatic and solemn carpet that led to the desk.

'Come closer,' ordered the colonel, pointing to one of the two upholstered chairs in front of the desk.

Barely rising, he offered a hand which was small and lively, like a mouse. It was accompanied by a faint smell of ripe apples, as if someone had just eaten fruit in the office. The colonel fixed his gaze on Cupido, his blue eyes slightly veiled with that milky white that hints at the onset of cataracts. Around them, on his nose and cheeks, fine thread veins gave the impression that minute red-legged spiders were running under his skin. Yet the colonel appeared to have left behind that age when sudden death is a risk, and to have settled into a state of enduring good health.

'I must say I don't understand why you'd like to speak with me,' he said before Cupido had a chance to ask him even one question. 'I think everything is clear enough. But Marina Olmedo rang me and I don't have the heart to refuse anything to the daughter of a dead colleague, considering the circumstances.'

'Do you believe it was suicide?'

'I do better than believe. One believes when there's no evidence, but everything indicates that Olmedo died by his own hand.'

'And yet, he gave no warnings. No one ever heard him mention that possibility. And his character was the opposite of a suicide's.'

'Warnings? Character? Do you know how many people commit suicide in the army without giving any warnings? And tell me, what's a suicide's character like?'

Cupido was surprised by the hard, terse, almost hostile tone. He searched for an answer that wasn't too vague, but when he hit on an adjective to define someone who would take his own life he also found the exception; when he tried to circumscribe an age group or a cluster of reasons, he remembered a case that contradicted them.

'In all my years in the army,' continued the colonel, 'I've signed several suicide dossiers, and I can assure you they all have the word "unexpected" in them. Olmedo was a well-balanced man, indeed, but he was under a lot of pressure because of his last mission and the responsibility it carried. Marina must have mentioned the report he had written about the base.'

'Yes, and I've read everything the newspapers published. I guess that commission earned him the hatred of a few colleagues.'

'I don't know if "hatred" is the right word,' qualified the colonel.

'Why not? In his report he recommended the closure of San Marcial. Which would affect the interests of many people. Some people would be made redundant.'

'Reduce us to unemployment? No … detective,' he said after a pause, as if he'd tried in vain to remember his name, 'make no mistake about it. There will never be unemployment in the army. Reforms, changes, recycling, yes. But before the army disappears, man himself will have to disappear, along with his desire to take over his neighbouring country. The army will always exist,' he repeated without looking at Cupido.

Although stiff and short, he stood up without any apparent effort, neither sighing nor emitting one of those faint whimpers which usually accompany the movements of people his age, and walked to the large window commanding a panoramic view of the base.

'No,' he explained from there, his back turned to Cupido, 'it wasn't the disappearance of the army that Olmedo wanted. I think no one will say that he wasn't a true soldier. And a soldier endeavours to make the army more efficient, not weaker. However, his methods were so daring that some people found them upsetting. I won't deny it: I myself thought he was acting too precipitously. He wanted to replace things that, at least for now, cannot be replaced.'

'Such as?'

Castroviejo turned to look at him as if he were a dim pupil, perhaps wondering if an explanation was worth the effort.

'Armies are designed to kill, even if Olmedo had helped in Bosnia and Afghanistan to keep people from killing each other. Olmedo, and others like him, following the directives from the civilian government in Madrid, hope to create an army that's mainly a peace corps, which is a contradiction in terms,' he explained, raising his eyebrows in bewilderment, as if he couldn't believe that something so simple was so hard to understand. However, the next moment he tempered his words. 'In any case, they want a small, versatile army, trained to fight outside Europe, as if war could never again break out in this continent. I frequently heard him say that, in an armed conflict, victory no longer depends on having a greater number of soldiers and how well they adapt to the climate and the scene, but on better technology, more digital screens and men who are half soldier and half computer.'

'And isn't that the case?'

'No, not really. Technology wins wars, but it doesn't maintain peace,' he explained with slight irritation. 'The faster and bigger the capacity of an army to obliterate an enemy's war structures, the more difficult the post-war period will be, because the teams of enemy experts will not have been touched.'

'As in Iraq,' said Cupido.

'As in Iraq,' he echoed. 'To control a defeated enemy you always need additional troops. And not fewer of them! That's what Olmedo refused to accept.'

'And do you think those arguments may have triggered a crisis that led him to kill himself?'

'Trigger? I don't think so. But perhaps it added to his confusion. I don't know, and nobody can know, what went through his mind after he left the base once the meeting was over. But he surely was aware that he'd affected some officers' lives. And then, Olmedo had lived alone since the absurd death of his wife, and lonely people sometimes react in strange, extreme ways, which others may find puzzling.'

The detective passed over this last comment – he himself lived alone and didn't feel he fitted that category – and said:

'You mentioned officers whose lives might be affected.'

The old colonel's eyes turned to look at him with a brief glint of suspicion, and then he raised one eyebrow. Cupido remembered something he'd heard in the military service. They said that that little expression, which occurred in tense or upsetting conversations, gave away a real soldier, one who was so used to taking aim that the grimace became second nature.

'I never cease to be amazed by the false ideas civilians have of the army. In moments of conflict, a soldier might become a hero, but the rest of the time we're only civil servants. Perhaps a bit special because of the nature of our job, but civil servants nonetheless, who are used to the monotonous succession of three-year posts, the slow climb up the hierarchy, the fear of being posted far away or somewhere unpleasant. How could there not be affected colleagues?'

'Bramante, Ucha?' said Cupido, repeating the surnames Marina had mentioned, and whose first names and rank he did not know. The colonel raised his right eyebrow slightly once again, as if he was surprised that the detective was in possession of that information.

'There wasn't a unanimous consensus,' said the colonel dodging the question, and he turned around to look out of the window. But then, like the athlete who thinks he's left his rival far behind but a few minutes later hears someone's breathing at his back, he turned to reply with annoyance at the detective's stubborn remark. 'That's why, when Olmedo left, the idea emerged of calling a meeting for everyone concerned, in order to adopt a common stance in the face of what we thought was the inevitable closure of the base.'

'At what time?'

'Eight o'clock. The meeting carried on till ten,' he specified, while Cupido wondered why he was giving him such precise information, leading him to another question.

'Did everyone turn up?'

'No, not everyone. The two officers you've just mentioned didn't. The purpose of the meeting was to negotiate the rendition, so to speak, and they didn't even entertain that possibility.'

'Were you there?'

'No, I wasn't there either. I won't be affected by the disruption that Olmedo created. I'll be retiring in a few months.'

Cupido was surprised to note the change in the colonel's tone, as if the questions, which seemed to irritate him one by one, together proved the detective highly skilled and had an internal logic that was in the colonel's best interest to answer. Because Castroviejo surely knew Cupido was inquiring into the alibis that people may have, and perhaps suspected the case was not definitively closed, so by replying he swept away any possible accusations of covering up.

'Marina asked me to talk to you and make things easy for you. I promised her I would.'

'Thank you.'

'No, don't thank me. The sooner she understands she's wrong, the sooner we'll all be able to put the matter to rest. Olmedo's death has been painful for many of us. I don't want to leave open wounds behind me when I retire. There's something else I'd like to do,' he said, without clarifying what. 'On Sunday I will officiate for the last time at the soldiers' pledge of allegiance to the flag.' He returned to his desk, and when he walked past, Cupido noticed again that faint smell of ripe apples. The colonel sat down and picked up a card which read, in block capitals, INVITATION.

'I forgot your name,' he said.

'Ricardo Cupido.'

'Ricardo Cupido,' he repeated as he handwrote it and appended a long, old-fashioned, baroque signature underneath. 'Come and see us on Sunday. It'll be my last official ceremony at San Marcial. I think you'll understand us better afterwards. And you'll be able to appreciate everything Olmedo was going to take away from us.'

He hadn't thought of it for a long time. The workings of recollection are strange and awkward, he told himself, and there seems to be neither rhyme nor reason as to why a small detail might unleash a barrage of memories, just as it is impossible to know why the whole machinery of mental cranes, pulleys and pistons, asked to bring back a piece of information buried in time, sometimes only digs up incoherent fragments. Perhaps he hadn't thought of it because he'd always refused to talk about that period of his life and found it tedious whenever an occasional interlocutor, whether with nostalgia or contempt, told anecdotes of his military service. But just now, as he was leaving the pavilion after the soldier saluted him at the door, and he looked at the training grounds where a company of recruits could be seen, some clear notes tore through the afternoon and his memory was jogged by the sound of a bugle. He suddenly pictured his twenty-year-old self wearing a uniform: a rather lanky soldier who, because of his height, was one of the first in line, and who followed instructions during training with ease. As soon as he'd arrived at the barracks in the Madrid sierras, on a cold autumn morning, after a long journey on a crowded train, he'd been taken to the barber's, where several veterans, armed with clippers, unceremoniously cropped his hair. When he glanced in the mirror to see how he looked, his head shorn of the hair he'd always worn long, he knew that this would not be a period of 'useful experience', as he'd heard it described. It took only a few days before he understood how true the bit about *military* was, what with all the rules and regulations that bore no resemblance to those of the civilian world outside, and to what degree the word *service* was inexact, as there was precious little one could do to serve one's country in there, living for a year at its expense, being required only to learn some callisthenics and how to operate a Cetme, and now and then shoot a few bullets without even trying to hit the bull's eye. Time was punctuated by stints on reserve guard and on duty, receiving lessons on strategy which he had absolutely forgotten and getting passes to go out to a club where there was only one girl for every ten soldiers. Other nights he would get quickly and thoroughly drunk on an acrid, flinty wine that one of the veterans bought wholesale and resold by the bottle, smuggling it into the barracks in the same sixteen-litre cylinders in which they transported diesel, and whose narcotic effects wore off only after the second day, following much vomiting in the toilets and urinating a dark yellow liquid – all silently condoned by the high-ranking officers, as if intoxication were another subject in the virile military curriculum. The rest of the time was devoted to skiving, searching for a secluded spot to escape anyone's notice, or pretending to be busy when an NCO walked by. Skiving was the utmost goal, on it the sharpest strategies were honed, and through it the mystique of honour and effort was exchanged for the mystique of the picaresque, so that whoever was better at making himself invisible was also the most admired among his peers.

It had been a hollow, sterile and, to all intents and purposes, lost year, always being shouted at by disconcerted officers who resented the changing times and the accusations of having been complicit in Franco's regime, which had ended only a few years before and for which they felt profoundly nostalgic almost to a man. At the age of twenty, Cupido learned how far he was from sharing the values and certainties of the army, their codes and traditions, their arbitrariness and harshness when it came down to exerting punishment for infringing a norm, no matter the reasons that might explain the infraction.

For all this he thought he understood why Major Olmedo wished for a more professional army.

6

Loose Ends

On Sunday he would attend the ceremony, and he'd be able to talk with some officers and observe them in their element, but it was still Thursday, and Cupido decided to use the time to talk to Aurora and Samuel to double-check the information that Marina had given him about them. He also needed to look into two items that had caught his attention in the major's flat: the lawsuit against the anaesthetist, and the bank documents.

He rang Marina up, and she asked him to meet her half an hour later at her house. Alkalino said he would like to come along, and Cupido had no problem with that.

Marina was waiting for him. A simple black T-shirt and dark trousers gave her a discreet air of mourning.

'Did you speak to the colonel?' asked Marina sitting in front of them, her back turned to a window that opened onto a terrace where one could see colourfully lush plants.

'Yes. He's convinced your father committed suicide, but he answered my questions politely. He also invited me to attend a pledge-of-allegiance ceremony next Sunday.'

'Are you going?'

'Yes. I'll get a chance to speak to some of your father's colleagues. Did you know that at the time he died there was an informal meeting at the base to discuss the consequences of his report?'

'No, I didn't.'

'Not everyone was there. At least two officers were missing, Bramante and Ucha. And the colonel himself.'

'Does that mean that …?'

Marina trailed off, hesitating cautiously, as if she were afraid to look into the abyss of suspicion that the investigation was already opening.

'It means it narrows down the number of possible suspects, if your father did not commit suicide,' explained Cupido in a first step towards clarity, striving to find his bearings in the dense fog that would only clear once the investigation advanced.

'He didn't,' said Marina, with greater certainty than the day before.

Alkalino, sitting slightly to one side, stared at her, in the same way that a painter stares at his model before the first brushstroke, still unable to choose the traits that best define her.

'I found two things in the flat I'd like to ask you about.'

'Yes?'

'The first is an application to change the titleholder of that investment fund you told me about. It is signed by yourself, but not by your father.'

'He asked me to do it. I never worried about those things. My father took care of them. Anyway, he wanted to be the only person with legal access to that money, at least for a while. We both were titleholders and he wanted to avoid the possibility that, during the divorce, Jaime might raise some trouble about our common assets. My father told me he'd take everything to the bank himself.'

'But he didn't. He didn't even sign the papers. So the change is not official.'

'No, it isn't,' she said, sitting back in the armchair.

'So, if your father died before signing, your ex-husband could claim some of that money.'

'I'm sure that won't be a problem. I said so to my father and I'll say the same to you now. I'm sure Jaime won't create trouble between us for a matter of money.'

'I'd like to talk to him.'

Marina picked up the cordless telephone lying on the table and dialled a number with her left hand. In the quietness of the room, and since the volume was high enough, Cupido clearly heard at the other end the convivial voice of a man who readily agreed to an interview. He would help in any way he could, he said.

'You can go over right now. He's waiting for you at his office,' said Marina after hanging up. Then she added: 'You mentioned a second thing.'

'Yes, among your father's papers I found a lawsuit against an anaesthetist, Lesmes Beltrán. He was sentenced to pay compensation and disqualified from practising for four years.'

'Because of my mother's death,' she explained. 'But that was a long time ago. I haven't heard of him since then, and I wouldn't like to find myself face to face with him either. It was all very unpleasant.'

'Can you tell me about it?'

Marina looked at him, her tiredness tinged with sadness, not sharing his interest.

'We don't have many leads,' insisted Cupido, 'and we cannot overlook any possibilities.'

'My mother was obsessed with her looks,' she said, sighing. 'In that she was the opposite of my father. He liked to stay in shape, sure, but I think it was for health reasons. He was an austere man, of simple tastes, who didn't ask for elaborate, exquisite food, and did not demand great comforts. My mother was different. She wouldn't go out unless her hair was neatly done up, her clothes well ironed and colour-coordinated. She wouldn't go to an important party in the same dress she'd worn to another one. She might not sleep if a hotel bed was not comfortable enough, or if it was noisy outside. If she saw so much as a mosquito flying over a dish, she wouldn't touch it,' she said, as Alkalino looked at her, puzzled. 'Well, I may be exaggerating a little, but she was like that, she wanted everything to look impeccable. And though my father would sometimes mock her, deep down he too liked the fact that she made sure he was clean-shaven and wore polished shoes. It was five years ago that she decided to undergo plastic surgery. Apparently, it was a simple procedure: to lift the skin of her cheekbones to eliminate some wrinkles or bags that only she could see. She used to say, exaggerating, that every time she looked in the mirror she saw a dromedary. Anyway, something went wrong during the operation and she never woke up, even though she wasn't allergic to anything and didn't have a difficult medical history. She died five days later. My father filed a lawsuit and had to fight to arrive at the truth; it wasn't easy to break through the clannishness uniting the doctors at the clinic. It emerged that the anaesthetist, due to negligence, impatience, human error, who knows, had applied a strong enough dose to put an elephant to sleep. He was said to be an unstable man, an overworked one at that, and perhaps he shouldn't have been doing such a delicate job. Later came the sentence, the payout and his temporary disqualification.'

'Where's he now?'

'I don't know, though I guess he must have gone back to work. It's been a long time.'

'Did your father ever hear of him again? Did he ever mention anything?'

'Not that I remember. It was a subject we tried to avoid. I liked to talk about my mother and to remember her when she was alive. But it wasn't pleasant to remember her death.'

Soon afterwards they said goodbye and walked to the address where Jaime, her ex-husband, awaited them. The company was on the ground floor in a complex of buildings surrounding a piazza. Two offices open to the public were separated from the rest of the premises by large windows with venetian blinds, through which one could see the adjoining warehouse; it was full of aluminium ladders, rope, brackets, hooks, harnesses, metal bars and also housed two vans with the name of the company, Mediterráneo Vertical, written on them in large blue capitals.

A secretary looked up from a sheaf of papers and, when they introduced themselves, stood up to lead them into the other office.

'He's waiting for you. This way.'

Cupido had the impression that Jaime closed a window on his computer with a quick click of the mouse. He then stood up, walked around the desk and, smiling, shook their hands too warmly, as if they were old friends he was happy to see. The detective struggled to picture him as the father of two children. He knew looks were not the reason, as no appearance is characteristic of paternity, but Jaime's excessively youthful, restless style made it difficult to imagine him at weekends changing diapers, mashing vegetables for baby food or sterilising bottles, staying up all night when a child was ill or playing with them in a sandpit. Everything in the office was shiny and aseptic, and had that kind of mechanical neatness in which any tool that's not equipped with an electrical engine seems out of place.

'Sit down, sit down,' he said pulling out two chairs of such stylish design that Alkalino looked at them with suspicion, fearing that, if he sat down on one of them, it might collapse under his weight. 'I don't know what I can do to help clarify Camilo's death ... if anything needs to be clarified. In fact, I don't understand why Marina won't accept what's happened. I think there's no use going through all this over and over. For her sake and the children's. That's how it happened, and there's nothing we can do about it.'

'She's convinced it wasn't suicide.'

'But that's a very serious thought. She seems to be implying someone out there is a murderer.'

'Marina's aware of that.'

'And would she be prepared to accuse someone?'

'Yes, I think so.'

For a second the kindness disappeared from his eyes – those big, gentle, attractive eyes – giving way to a glint of jealousy and distrust, a malaise born of the fact that a stranger could introduce the purulence of suspicion into his shiny, aseptic office – the fact that a detective who operated on the dodgiest fringes of society might meddle in Marina's private affairs and come to know more about her than someone who'd been a member of her family. A moment later a smile returned to his lips, and once again his face became round and kind, concealing the thought it had just revealed: *Get out of here. Are you trying to come between her and me? Get out of here.*

'It's a mistake to think that,' he said. 'I've already told her, it's a mistake, and she should accept it.'

'How can you be so sure?'

'Because if not it'll cause her a lot of worry.'

'I meant, sure it was suicide.'

'All the evidence points that way. He was on his own. He was holding the gun in his hand. He wrote that note. And then, I can't believe that anyone would dare try to kill him.'

'Perhaps someone he knew, whom he may have let in, whom he trusted and therefore took him by surprise.'

'I don't think Camilo would have let anyone take him by surprise.'

'Why do you think that?'

'Because I knew him. He was always on guard, never relaxed. Before he drove out of the garage, he looked both ways. Whenever we went to a restaurant, he chose a spot where his back was against a wall. I guess it's a military mentality.'

'Were you on good terms?'

'As good as an ex-son and father-in-law can be … Although I don't like those words,' he concluded, as if what the question suggested were so absurd that no further explanations were necessary.

'As good as …' repeated Cupido.

'Yes, that's right. Perhaps because Marina and I are on good terms too. We had an amicable separation and we had an understanding on everything: the kids, the house, the alimony.'

Cupido thought of the documents Olmedo had not managed to take to the bank, but didn't say anything. Perhaps Jaime didn't know. And it was up to Marina to tell him.

'We both fulfil our obligations with our children, and never interfere with visiting rights,' he continued. 'She kept the flat and I kept the company. So I can't say there's any trouble between us.

We're not like those ex-couples who shout insults at each another. Apparently Camilo found this hard to understand.'

'Why?'

'One day, a long time ago, I heard him say that in every separation there's an aggrieved party. And he couldn't get his head round the fact that you could take a separation in your stride. Army mentality!' he exclaimed with a conciliatory smile, without apparent rancour. His expression changed when he looked at Alkalino and saw his puzzled expression. 'I think that, deep down, Camilo would have liked us to hate each other, so we could break up for good. As if he feared that one day we might get back together.'

'Did you like him?' insisted Cupido, in a quiet voice.

'Well, whenever I saw him I didn't think of killing him, if you know what I mean,' he replied jokingly, his mouth stretched into a fake smile, friendliness hiding the scorn on his face like so much make-up. Then he added: 'Seriously now … He never liked me. I guess he would have wanted a different kind of husband for his daughter. A high-ranking officer, like himself, or a civil servant with a good job – I don't know, someone more stable, closer to his ideas. He often repeated the phrase: "One should have one's feet on the ground".'

'He didn't like what you did for a living,' said Cupido looking around.

'He didn't. He said I ran excessive risks for too little financial return. Camilo had a farm not far from here, a few kilometres inland, which he leased out to sharecroppers. Once he tried to convince me of the finer points of nature. He wanted me to take care of the land.'

'And you refused?'

'Of course! I have nothing against the countryside, but I am a man of the city. Can you imagine? Working from morning till night, putting up with storms, pests, sweat mixed with dirt, the smell of cows and sheep, grimy fingernails. I've been doing my job for the last fifteen years, and it's going from strength to strength.'

Cupido heard Alkalino's almost imperceptible sigh of annoyance, and wondered how he managed to stay quiet, he who had an opinion about everything, who went on talking when everyone else had nothing left to say. Surely he did not agree with that disdain of the rural world where he was from.

'May I ask you one more question?' said Cupido.

'Yes, go ahead, yes,' he repeated, as if impatient to hear it, his expression still friendly and composed, a slight hint of anger in his voice.

'Where were you the afternoon the major died?'

Jaime sat back and sighed, as though the moment he'd been expecting had finally arrived. However, he said:

'If that's the best question a detective can ask, then that detective won't go very far.'

'It may not be, but you'll help Marina by answering it.'

'There are lots of people in this city who know me and like me enough to declare I was with them that evening,' he said. 'But I don't need anyone to lie for me. I was here, in this office, on my own, trying to catch up with the paperwork. Some figures shouldn't be seen by even the best secretary. I think that answers your question?'

'Yes.'

'Allow me to tell you something, then,' he added, serene, dignified, yet almost vindictive. 'I think Marina could think of a thousand better ways to spend her money than trying to find out what people were doing when her father shot himself in the heart.'

'These smiley guys, I can't stand them,' murmured Alkalino as soon as they'd left the office. 'Such readiness to smile at strangers, such friendliness, so much smiling, as if they needed to prove how happy they are! What's with the chumminess? It's not like he was trying to sell us something.'

Alkalino was shorter than the detective, and he was walking one metre ahead of him with quick, offended steps, almost bumping into passers-by when he turned his head.

'Did you take a look at him?' he went on. 'One of those

muscular, good-looking, stupid players who cannot appreciate the worth of their victims, so full of themselves that any woman they call comes running after them. So fake and … and …'

Cupido was amused by the indignation in his friend's dark face, and guessed what Alkalino didn't dare utter: 'And yet a magnet for gorgeous women who'll never love us.'

'Come on,' he replied instead. 'Women can always say no. They can always resist.'

'Resist? As soon as a woman utters the word resist she is lost.'

'Okay, okay,' protested Cupido.

'And those chairs! So much design in everything around him, so much modernity, so much gloss!'

'The place was spotless.'

'The poles are spotless too, and you'd die from the cold there. And also …'

'What?'

'That patronising manner, that scorn towards the country-side, as if we didn't all come from there, as if our first job hadn't been to attach a sharpened rock to a stick and chase any edible animal to smash its brains, as if the first time someone thought of settling somewhere and building a roof over his head it hadn't been because he counted on the wheat he'd planted nearby. When you think that some people have been forced to spend centuries feeding and serving townies, and then a superficial guy like him comes and says that …'

'Now, now,' said Cupido.

'As if our forefathers had not been shepherds and farmers …'

'One of whom killed the other,' he put in.

Alkalino suddenly stopped walking and stared at Cupido with a puzzled expression in his sharp dark face, which looked as if it were made of harder materials than flesh and bone, a bit like wood before it turned into charcoal.

'You mean you believe him? You accept he spent that spring afternoon sitting in there, behind the blinds, doctoring the accounts and figuring out the best way to cheat the taxman?'

'Not yet. I don't like to assume anything. Not even that he was not telling the truth.'

Alkalino was soon walking by his side, calm and thoughtful, his short, harsh steps more leisurely, the tips of his feet slightly curved in. He advanced with his head lowered, lost in thought, oblivious to the noise of the doors and shutters of the shops that were closing; the passers-by on their way home planning some rest and a quiet dinner; the girls who'd been waiting for the warm weather to show off their bellies, their skins smooth and sweet, their navels like a delicate buttonhole; the doves that lived in the belfry of a church and, at that hour, were defending their territory from the swifts.

'At least he was right about one thing,' said Alkalino suddenly.

'He who, Olmedo?'

'His ex-son-in-law, whatever his name is.'

'What was he right about?'

'About the fact that most acts of bloodshed usually involve the family, or those strangers who become a part of it. He doesn't like words like son-in-law, brother-in-law, stepmother, stepbrother and so on. Have you noticed how cruel the jokes about these relations are? What bad press the names have? Have you noticed? There's something pejorative about them, a bit scornful, as if the relationship was conceded out of courtesy to one's brother's choice, but not out of one's own free will. And it's there, in that periphery, where hatred and bad blood usually arise. Remember all the family conflicts in the Bible, and in Greek tragedy, and between those two Russian brothers who were worse than wolves.'

7

Work at Height

He hadn't slept well. Dreams came and went randomly, featuring phantom figures that stood at the foot of his bed and watched him sleep: Camilo, Marina, a naked woman whose face he couldn't identify, the detective and that grouchy, dark-skinned assistant of his. It hadn't been a nightmare that he could have banished by getting up to drink a glass of water, but a constant whirl of elusive images and isolated, shameless words that he couldn't quite remember.

He got in the shower and stayed a long time with the water washing over his head, eyes closed and hands hanging by the sides of his body, before picking up the soap and shampoo. Later he threw the towel on the bed and looked at himself naked in the wardrobe mirror. He didn't yet dislike what he saw. In a few years his pectoral muscles, now firm, would climb down the ladder of his ribcage, his waist would thicken, and the hairs on his legs would become greyer and scarcer. Wrinkles, liver spots and stretch marks would show. But for now he was in great shape: he hadn't yet reached that age when a man only looks elegant in a jacket. He was thirty-four, and had no intention of wasting the good years he had left.

For breakfast he had tea, two pieces of thinly buttered toast, and orange juice. That day two employees would clean the glass façade of an office tower. He and a third guy would install the clasps needed to hold the new drainpipes in a refurbished block of flats. It was a quick and energetic task, unlike the monotonous jobs of cleaning or painting. He put on his work clothes, a chequered shirt, a pair of sailcloth trousers with lots of pockets, and hard boots. Mediterráneo Vertical – a small competitive company, dynamic and efficient, devoted to work at heights, which had required little investment in infrastructure, and of which he hoped to open a branch in Valencia – was doing well, in no small part, because he took an active role in the work and always kept an eye on how his workers were getting on.

When he reached the premises, his employees had loaded all they needed into the vans and were waiting for him. He himself drove one of the vans to the block of flats. He rang the number he'd been given, flat eight, and a woman asked them to come in. She was the president of the neighbours' association. Once upstairs she offered them coffee, and he accepted a cup while his employee climbed onto the terrace to secure the ropes from which they would hang.

'A coffee is always good to gather one's strength,' said the woman with a smile as she carried a tray in from the kitchen. She sat in front of him to pour him a cup and Jaime looked at her: a woman in her early forties, married to the man with a moustache and glasses, a photo of whom – he had a startled, mistrustful look, as if even at the moment it had been taken he knew what was coming – rested on a bookshelf against another picture frame with the portraits of two girls, aged eight or ten. The woman's chest was abundant, her hips and arms a bit heavy-set, and her fingers slightly thicker than the kind of fingers that would make a beautiful hand; her armpits were stained by sweat. She was an attractive mature woman, without a job outside the house, a little bored and perhaps a little unhappy, but kind or canny enough to hide it.

'Mind you, it hasn't been easy to reach a consensus among all the neighbours in the community,' she was now saying. 'I'm sure you've come across such cases. Imagine, forty-eight landlords who all have to agree with one another without anyone feeling they're the worst hit. And some of them! The ones that don't pay their membership fees and yet do nothing but complain and make demands! Those who want to raise the fees to carry out improvements! They come to the meetings and don't contribute anything at all! Well, you can't count on people. I'm very tired of being the president, always trying to appease everybody. Thank God that, in a few months ...' she said, trying to draw his attention to her capacity for self-sacrifice and her contribution to universal concord. 'You know, the world is full of spiteful people. And it would be so easy to have an exchange of ideas, be kind to one another, love each other! Right?' she asked, as if she'd suddenly realised she was doing all the talking, in fact talking too much.

'Of course!' he replied with a smile, almost touched by how naively she tried to gain him for her cause – her desire for fraternity.

That was what he liked best: to please. It happened often enough that, at a bar, or a shop, or on the beach, a woman would cast him a kind smile. If circumstances were favourable, he soon approached her, was courteous and funny but also made it clear he was up for anything, was ready to put into practice all that he'd learned in twenty years of loving women. And why the hell not, since it was so easy and enjoyable? Why not make those mature women happy for a few hours, given that they felt they were as capable of seducing him and arousing his desire now as they had been fifteen or twenty years before? They would embrace him, clasp him with both hands, kiss him with passionate, open mouths while he distilled into their ears the lie that real beauty is eternal, love never dies and time does not pass.

And he too was happy embracing them, consoling their nostalgia for that which they would never be again, holding breasts that sagged a bit like ripe fruit, caressing stomachs slightly cushioned by age and thighs made smooth by firming creams. The only way not to offend a woman who asks you for an embrace, he'd tell himself, was by embracing her, even if that hurt another man. Faithfulness might be good for some people, but for him it was absurd, didn't make any sense, not even with a woman like Marina. In spite of his numerous adventures, he had loved Marina, still loved her, and for her sake he would have cut down on his escapades and restricted them to some faraway area where they wouldn't upset her. All would have been fine, and they would still be together if it hadn't been for Camilo's meddling. From the beginning, his had not been a frontal opposition, but a constant campaign of resistance that, because of its very moderation, seemed never to exhaust itself. Oh, that sarcastic look in Camilo's face, the way he never had a kind word for what Jaime did but, on the contrary, kept repeating that annoying line of his, 'Feet on the ground!', as though suggesting he had his head in the clouds. Needless to say, the old man didn't mean his work, or not just his work. He must have heard rumours: a handsome guy who worked at the top of buildings and seduced women who stared at him with a frisson of excitement and fear and, when he came down, took him in their arms as they would a good and beautiful angel who needed rest and tenderness – kind, torn hostesses who'd tremble at the touch of his fire and later caress his shoulder blades as if they were the feathery wings of a bird … Well, of course, people talked. But Camilo only interfered when Marina found that message on his mobile, those affectionately obscene words sent by his latest conquest. At that point he did raise his voice to defend his daughter, and you would have thought the major was more hurt and offended than she was. In all his life Camilo had loved only one woman – the tall woman he'd been seeing these last weeks had not appeared yet – and couldn't understand how Jaime could cheat on his daughter like that. Because, really, he had no reason to. Marina had always been cheerful, sweet, loyal to him, had never pressured him, never refused him anything. And so, Camilo came to tell him, if she is there for you, smiles at you and hugs you, how can you not love her? How could you look at others if she offered you everything you needed? Who do you think you are to hurt her like that?

He took one last sip of coffee and got up to go to the terrace. The woman accompanied him to the door.

'Be very careful, please. Yours is a dangerous occupation. Twelve floors! I don't think I'll be able to watch. Vertigo, you know,' she explained. 'My legs start to shake and I feel a kind of shiver when I climb onto high places.'

His assistant had everything ready. He had tied the ropes to the anchoring hooks and had set the plumb line. The smells of fresh coffee, gas burners, and laundry softeners wafted up the internal patio. Outside many windows were clotheslines, but the area where they had to secure the clasps was free of encumbrances.

He put on his helmet and tied his harness, passing the rope through the rings. With his cleat shoes on, and the power drill and clasps in his belt, he climbed onto the ledge and started descending slowly. Forty metres below was the hard cement of the ground floor. Although he had barely slept that night, he felt good up there, safe, almost weightless, while he swung slightly in the void.

He had to fix the clasps at every floor, so that all that was left for the plumbers was to screw on the drainpipes. The plumb line marked the vertical line near the row of windows.

Legs apart and feet firm on the wall, he started drilling. The bit went in with ease, into the plaster first and then into the brick. He secured the first set of clasps and, when he descended to the next floor, saw that many onlookers were by the windows, attracted by the noise of the drill: not only women and old men, but also young and middle-aged men. How come they were not at work that morning? he wondered. What were they doing at home? Some leaned out to look at him with curiosity, with apprehension, or simply amusement. Others disappeared all of a sudden and came back with another person in tow in pyjamas. A cleaning lady, feather duster in hand, rested against the window, waiting to watch the show. A teenager appeared with a mobile phone and took several pictures of him before walking off to make a call.

Jaime liked to create a buzz of expectancy, to be the centre of attention in front of men who would silently consider his job and compare it to their own; of trembling women who would stare at him with a bejewelled hand to their mouths, and then look at the ropes he was hanging from as if they feared they might snap at any moment; of children who screamed in excitement while pointing their fingers at him. He had the feeling that up there he expanded, became larger, but also that he was lighter and more powerful, because he saw others from a point of view inaccessible to themselves. Through the windows he could see bedrooms with unmade beds, or even with someone asleep in them, too tired or lazy to respond to the alarm of the noise, and the chaotic, higgledy-piggledy lairs of adolescents, and the tidy offices of technicians or professors, and the humble secrets strewn in bathrooms or hung out on clothes-racks.

Once again he bored into the brick with firm, precise movements, his legs resting on the wall as if he was holding it up, his hands on the drill, and a screw between his teeth. On the eighth floor he saw the woman leaning out of the window near to him, and once more she said something about his courage, and vertigo and danger, showing her concern and responsibility in front of her neighbours; then she looked at the tense rope that held him, cast an anxious glance downwards, and withdrew from the window with her eyes closed, as if the glare from the bottom of the patio had dazzled her.

As he proceeded downwards, the number of spectators dwindled. His work became less interesting the nearer the ground he was, as if, deep down, everybody expected him to fall into the void. Little by little people disappeared from the windows, some to reappear a short while later to check on his progress or to make sure that he hadn't fallen. The woman too had leaned out again and was staring at him from above.

When at last he finished and treaded on the patio there was barely anyone left at the windows. He went back to the rooftop, where his employee was putting away the equipment.

'Take everything in the car,' he said. 'I'll follow you later.'

'Later, eh?' repeated the employee with a slimy, complicit smile that he refused to acknowledge.

'Yes, wait for me at the warehouse, while you tidy things up. I'll get the invoice signed and collect the cheque.'

He took the lift to the eighth floor. When the woman opened

the door, he noticed her strong, almost aggressive, perfume, which she had not been wearing earlier, and a new hairdo with every lock in place. She had also changed into a dress that was too elegant for that time of the morning, one of those flimsy numbers that always made him think that, the more you pay for them, the easier they are to take off.

'Please sit down. You must be tired after all that work, and the rope looked like it wouldn't hold! You must have been scared up there.'

'Scared, well,' he said, 'who isn't? But everything worth doing is kind of risky, isn't it?'

'Would you like anything to drink? A beer?'

'Thanks. Perhaps a Coke?'

'Right away.'

He saw her leave and return with the drink and a bowl of almonds, which she seemed to have prepared beforehand. He took a long sip, not rushing things, took the invoice out of his shirt pocket and slid it across the table towards the woman.

'It's what we agreed. You can sign the copy.'

'Right,' she said, barely looking at the amount. 'You've done a good job. And a dangerous one.' Anxious, nervous, she got up to get a pen, and opened a big drawer in the cupboard, under the photograph of the man with the moustache and glasses. She rummaged through it and finally came back and sat down beside him on the sofa.

'One must sign,' she said, and wrote her name in round, uneven letters because her hands were shaking, as she added: 'It's what I always say at meetings. If we want the association to run smoothly and the work to get done, we all need to pay on time. You cannot imagine the problems we have with debtors … Let me get the cheque.' She stood up again and went towards the corridor connecting the living room with the bedrooms.

'Do you mind if I wash?' he said, showing her his dirty hands.

'Not at all. Come with me.'

He followed her down the corridor, and she opened the door

to a bathroom. The wall tiles were decorated with flowers of such lurid pinks and greens that her perfume seemed to issue from them. He turned on the tap, filled his palms with water, and buried his face in them, rubbing energetically. While he towelled off, he saw the woman in the opposite room, the bedroom, sitting on one side of the bed. She took her chequebook out of a drawer in her night table, wrote one out, tore it off carefully, put back the chequebook in its place and, without getting up, left the cheque there on the quilt. That piece of official paper on the bed suddenly turned her into a different woman, without children, husband, home, community – just the eternal feminine flesh asserting its right to exist over and above modesty and social rules.

Jaime felt that that simple gesture abolished the distance between them. The woman was staring at him again, with a look full of trepidation and yearning. He dried his hands slowly, put back the towel on the rack and crossed the corridor into the bedroom.

The cheque was lying next to her hips, which he pictured round and warm like bread, the kind of bread that's no longer crispy and fresh but still tender. He took a few steps with a feeling of desire and affection, and thought: 'Don't worry now, stop shaking. The fact that you're so fragile and so afraid of what you're doing makes you all the more charming. Stop shaking. For two hours we'll be happy.'

8

Anaesthesia

He had just buttoned up his white coat when his pager buzzed and a message flashed annoyingly on the screen: 'Dr Beltrán, urgently needed at the operating theatre.'

He almost slammed shut the door of his office, which had a plaque that read Dr L. Beltrán, Anaesthetist, and quickly strode down the corridor towards the wide staircase. He'd been back at work for less than a month after his four-year suspension, and was still feeling the weight of responsibility, though not the apprehension of the beginner. He'd always felt at ease at the hospital; it was his home, and for him the word 'hospital' signified healing, not pain. In the few days he'd been back, he had reacquainted himself with the nurses' shoes swishing along the corridors; the smell of disinfectant; the blue and red reflections that came in through the windows of dark rooms, indicating that an ambulance was bringing in another patient; the air of anxiety and hope on the faces of patients' relatives; the procedures involved in operations; the fear with which patients touched their faces when they came round, checking if their beard had grown so as to gauge how long they'd been under the effects of the anaesthetics, as if they feared it had been years. When he reached the ground floor he almost bumped into Dr Añil, the chief surgeon, also in a hurry as she flicked through a report covered in handwritten notes.

'What is it?' he asked her.

'A boy. Sixteen years old. Crashed his motorcycle into the

fence of a roundabout and flew over the handlebars. What's the world coming to?' she added with a tone of disappointment and complaint.

'Teenagers!'

'Teenagers, and their parents! The admissions people fear he's on drugs or something. We'll have the test results in a minute, but it could be one of those new drugs that the lab has problems analysing. What's the world coming to?' she repeated.

They pushed the swinging doors open and walked into the prep room. A nurse was waiting for them, and handed the doctor an X-ray of the patient's neck and chest, an electrocardiogram and some initial test results.

'There's no cranioencephalic trauma. Fortunately he was wearing a helmet. Quite a blow and first-degree burns on his left leg. The neck seems to be okay,' she said looking at the X-ray on the viewer. 'But it would seem the spleen is burst,' she said reading the chart. 'And another thing. He had these in his pocket.' She showed them two capsules, one of them open. 'Speed.'

'Speed?' said Beltrán.

'Ketamine pills, if it's not cut with something else. Will you be able to get him off to sleep? Is it compatible with the anaesthetic?'

Dr Añil eyed him over her glasses and he guessed she was remembering what had happened four years earlier and wondering whether his present apprehension and caution might not affect the normal course of his work. The inquisitive gaze brought back with painful clarity the image of the woman's bandaged head during the five days she'd been in a coma. He feared that, on his reinstatement, he'd become an awkward colleague, who would hesitate too much before making a decision and get alarmed at the appearance of any anomalous symptoms. And in ER there was no room for fear. Quick and clear decisions had to be made, and the reasoning behind them defended later no matter what the result might be. Fear widened the margin of error.

'I don't know,' he replied. 'If he hasn't taken a high dose, I think I can manage. But we'll need to keep a closer eye on hemodynamics.'

'I'll see you inside then,' said Dr Añil, as she saw two orderlies bring in the patient on a gurney. They left him with the boy and the nurse.

'What's your name?' he asked.

'Iago,' the boy replied with a whimper. 'Santiago.'

His face looked extremely pale and sweaty; his hair was cropped in bizarre furrows. When the nurse held up his arm to take his blood pressure, he resisted with an expression of pain.

'Easy now,' he said, 'easy. I'll examine your stomach now.'

He pulled up the boy's shirt and palpated him. The abdomen was swollen, tense like a drumhead, pulsating. According to the tests, his haemoglobin levels had been pretty stable on admission, but his condition seemed to be worsening and he needed to be operated on straight away.

'Five eight,' said the nurse.

'Are you going to operate on me?' asked the boy, almost in tears.

'Calm down. Yes, we are, but stay calm. It's not serious.'

'Will it hurt?'

The boy looked him straight in the eye. Patients usually did that. When they spoke to the surgeon who was going to operate on them, they paid attention to his hands, hoping that they were clean and delicate, that they not shake, did no more harm than necessary. But they looked him in the eye in silent prayer, as if imploring him to control the pain, to alleviate the suffering. 'Please don't let me suffer. Please.'

'No, it won't hurt. A little when you wake up, maybe. It'll only take a few minutes,' he lied.

'Have you told my family?'

'Of course. They're on their way. When you wake up they'll be waiting for you. Don't worry.'

'My mother ...'

'Yes, don't worry now. She'll be the first person you'll see when you wake up.'

The boy shut his eyes to fight back the tears that, nevertheless, seemed to seep through his thin eyelids and slide down his temples, between two furrows of hair. The anaesthetist waited a couple of seconds before asking:

'Did you take anything tonight?'

'Take anything?' the boy echoed, opening his eyes with suspicion, ready to deny everything even before he'd fully understood the question.

'Have you had dinner? Drunk anything?'

'Yes, I did have dinner.'

'How long ago?'

'What time is it?' he asked, disconcerted.

Lesmes looked at the clock.

'Three o'clock.'

The boy shut his eyes, calculating the time and the best way to lie, still putting up a hard front over his pain and his fear.

'I had dinner at nine.'

'And later, did you take anything? Did you have anything to drink?'

'A little,' he replied, pale, aloof, hostile, with that annoyed attitude typical of adolescents who believe they're owed something, that the world is always asking them questions and never giving them satisfactory answers.

'Have you taken anything else?'

'No.'

'Pills?'

'No!'

'Fine. Calm down,' he said, and then whispered to the nurse: 'We'll have to pump his stomach. Get the catheter ready.' Then he told the boy: 'Open your mouth.'

Ignoring the smell of Coca-Cola and cheap wine he exhaled, Lesmes helped him take off his braces, which were in the way.

He left the boy in the nurse's hands and went into the operating theatre to check everything, well aware that there was no room for improvisation and that preparation was as important as the execution itself. The nurse had already laid out the catheter, the laryngoscope and the seven-and-a-half inch tube on the kidney-shaped tray.

'Is the blood ready?'

'Yes,' she said, pointing to the two bags that shone, fat and dark, on the work surface to one side.

A few moments later Dr Añil walked in, followed by an attending and a resident, all wearing caps and gloves, their masks hanging from their necks.

'We're ready.'

Lesmes went back out. The nurse had already emptied the boy's stomach; he looked paler, almost waxen now.

'We're going in. Don't worry. It'll only take a few minutes.'

'Doctor,' the boy called out. Fear had reappeared on his face and his hostility was directed only at himself.

'Yes?'

'No, nothing ...'

They went into the operating theatre, and the boy shut his eyes when they placed him under the intense glare of the lights. Lesmes fixed the electrodes on him and checked that his arterial blood pressure and heartbeat were fine on the screen. He ensured the capnographer was working properly, as the memory of the woman, her face all bandaged up except for her eyes, once again flooded his thoughts. The heart of an anaesthetised patient goes on functioning, but not his lungs – the machine does the breathing. If the machine stops working and it doesn't alert them ... He blinked away the memories and applied an analgesic. Then, thinking of the empty ketamine capsule, he measured the dose of hypnotic and let it slowly penetrate into the vein; he felt the eyes of his three colleagues studying his every movement.

'Don't worry,' he said one last time, 'now you're going to fall asleep,' he said, as if he wasn't a doctor telling his patient about the process but a hypnotist ordering him to withdraw into unconsciousness.

Half a minute later he touched the boy's eye with his thumb. It was unresponsive, the boy was asleep. Once he had intubated him, the graphs of the respirator indicated everything was all right, and it was only then that, without raising his eyes to his colleagues, he said:

'Whenever you're ready.'

Several gloved hands – precise, efficient – made contact with the body of the boy as soon as the nurse disinfected his chest and stomach.

Lesmes sat by the boy's head, in that station he'd feared he'd lost forever, checking his vitals on the screens as the scalpel cut through his skin. He saw the inverted sleeping face, strangely serene now, oblivious to the pain and anxiety that a few metres away, out in the corridor, was no doubt taking hold of his relatives, who must all be arriving now, after having been awakened in the middle of the night by a distressing phone call, and who must be asking what had happened, where he was, why they couldn't see him. Sixteen years old, barely two years younger than Lesmes's own children: an age when they seem to be always on the move, even if they don't know why, or where they're going, or for how long; an age when they're uneasy about having lost the graciousness and charm of childhood and have not yet picked any of the fruits born of an adult character. The strong lights brought out the boy's strange haircut: he had fine shaven furrows on his scalp, front to back, so that his head looked like a field sown with tiny black plants. Lesmes wondered whether girls his age found that repellent or terribly attractive, but he had no way of knowing. The world of teenagers was incomprehensible to him. He didn't find it easy to communicate with them; at times they spoke like parrots and at others barely used one-syllable words. He was disconcerted by their sudden oscillations between apathy and excess, the enthusiasm with which they embraced some fashion and the scorn with which they later rejected it, their nearly violent sulkiness and their occasional, impulsive displays of affection, the sincerity of their promises and the ease with which they broke them, their lack of appetite and their feeding frenzies, when they used the knife like a saw and the fork like a shovel. They seemed to him half-formed beings, and he couldn't imagine the outcome of their jumpy growth, their teeth imprisoned in braces, their eyes outgrowing their glasses, their skin riddled with acne – all that imbalance of gangling legs and childlike torsos.

He had two children, Ana, who was nineteen, and Lesmes, eighteen. Both had gone to study in Madrid. At least, now that he was back at work, he wouldn't find it so hard to pay for their life away from home, their costly university fees and accommodation. They'd never said as much, but he'd suspected that their choice of courses answered less a real calling than a need to distance themselves from home, to avoid the sad, oppressive atmosphere that had surrounded them during the years he'd been out of work. They were good children, though, in spite of their move, which he didn't want to view as an escape in the strictest sense, but rather as the kind of need that makes a diver return to the surface in a moment of tension, not because his tank is short on oxygen, but because he has to see the light, the sky, the clean air. They phoned often enough, got good marks and did not seem prone to excesses.

On one occasion, two or three years previously, he'd overheard a conversation between Lesmes and a friend. Both were in his son's room, allegedly doing homework but actually talking about girls.

'Have you ever been happy?' he heard his son ask.

'Yes,' replied his friend after a couple of seconds' hesitation. 'I'm pretty happy. Aren't you?'

'I've been happy this week. And it's great! I can't believe how good it is!'

He stood still in the corridor, near the doorway, and retraced his steps without making a noise, overwhelmed by anxiety.

When the judge ruled against him and he was suspended, family life became very complicated. He still got up in the morning at the usual time, as if he had work to do, but only to face a day that was eminently empty, hollow even, of all that had filled it before. He would make breakfast for his children and Carolina, who got up a bit later when she smelled the freshly made coffee. The children left for school and the two of them stayed alone. Unhurried, they would drink a second cup of coffee in the kitchen, smoke too many cigarettes, and listen to the news and the talk shows on the radio, sometimes to a programme for job hunters. Carolina had left her office job at a laboratory when she'd got pregnant and had never worked again outside the home. It was unthinkable for her to look for work after twenty years, to catch up with so many new techniques. However, four years was a long time, and he had to do something. He knew that once the period of suspension was over it wouldn't be hard to return to work: the present world had become too hedonistic and couldn't stand any pain. Professionals who eased its suffering would always be needed.

His professional insurance policy had barely covered the one hundred and fifty thousand euros established as compensation. As it happened they had some savings put aside for a beach house, a dream that would never materialise. That gave them a measure of financial security, but not for long. They soon discovered that money doesn't last long, flows like water, dries out; it was astonishing how quickly one's bank balance decreased when no wages replenished it at the end of every month.

'You have to find something,' she would say, encouraging him out of the apathy he'd sunk into. 'He has really hurt us, but we cannot let him destroy our lives completely.'

He started asking around in pharmaceutical laboratories and health companies, offering his services as sales representative or external collaborator, willing to take any replacement jobs, any hours. He applied for a position in a private ambulance company which no one wanted because it was unrewarding and tiring, and risky to drive at high speed. Nothing but rejections. In a medium-sized city, people knew of his suspension and no one wanted to put their image on the line. They preferred young, obedient people with clean track records.

But it wasn't just unemployment that created tension in the house. Carolina, who'd been used to being alone during the day doing the household chores in her own time, couldn't wholly adapt to the new situation. Now they were together twenty-four hours a day and they realised that they got in each other's way, and small everyday conflicts arose easily: when she was vacuuming in the living room and made him lift his feet for too long; when one of them was watching a certain programme on TV and the other had to resort to the small set in the kitchen to watch a different channel; or when they had to go to the toilet and the other was locked in there, and took forever bathing or depilating. He suspected that Carolina was discovering that a stay-at-home husband, who shuffled around in his bathrobe far too long before shaving and getting dressed, who invaded areas that she had previously had all to herself, was less interesting than a working husband.

They hadn't had any serious problems before, had always got along fine. If on occasion they had hurt each other, it hadn't been intentional. And, besides, what true lover has never tasted the blood of the person they love, and then, feeling remorse for what they've done, licked the tears they have caused only minutes earlier? Yet now it was different. They frequently had arguments, raised their voices for stupid reasons, carried out exhausting discussions for days on end until they couldn't even remember why they had started. When the children came back from school, they often found them in different rooms, not talking to each other, no dinner made, the ashtrays full of cigarette butts, the air stuffy with smoke and tension. Brother and sister seemed to come together at such times, finding shelter in each other, claiming they were not hungry, and patiently, silently waiting for peace to be re-established. This situation not being propitious for romance, he and Carolina seldom made love. There was something incongruous about looking for sex at nightfall when they hadn't touched, hadn't kissed, hadn't shown any affection for each other during the day.

It was during those bad times – they were thinking of a separation – that, one morning, a small unexpected event came to alleviate their financial difficulties. One of their neighbours, an old man who suffered from diabetes, asked him if, being a doctor, he gave injections. Nurses were on strike and the man didn't know where to go. He accepted that small job, and then another, and another, and a little later he had a satisfied clientele, mostly elderly people from his neighbourhood, who appreciated his technical skill, his familiarity with needles, and his pleasant, discreet manner. On top of that, his medical knowledge allowed him to anticipate a few diagnoses, and give advice that was later confirmed by specialists. His reputation grew among those he gave injections to, and he started taking their blood pressure. He visited them at home, some periodically, some whenever they needed it, so that they didn't have to wait for medical visitors and could avoid queues at public hospitals. He didn't make much money, but enough to live on, considering that he didn't declare any earnings or pay income tax. The fear of being reported to the police for practising clandestinely made him very careful, but he never encountered any problems.

And yet, he couldn't forget his professional degradation: he, a doctor with one of the best track records of his class, had been reduced overnight to burying the needle in flaccid, often unclean buttocks, or in arms that were either emaciated or rippling with obesity. These were supposed to be the best years of his life, and yet he saw with astonishment and despair that his dreams and projects had been cut short. What was left of him, that young, brilliant anaesthetist whose graceful hands everyone trusted, who was sought after by his colleagues when they had to undergo an operation? What was left of that specialist of whose patients it was said that they only experienced one small, fleeting discomfort: the first prick of the needle going into the vein or the muscle? Once, in those days that now seemed far gone, someone had called him Dr God. It was a joke at the basins, as everyone took off their gloves and washed under the taps, but it had a good ring to it and the nickname caught on. Someone else explained that Dr Lesmes Beltrán possessed a gift that had so far been the privilege of the gods: he could eliminate pain without taking away consciousness. Hadn't paradise been like that before the fall? What greater dream of happiness might man achieve?

His task was indeed complex, delicate, with small margins of error between efficiency and grave danger – a specialism in which the words pain, critical state, coma, and death resonated more frequently than in other areas of the hospital. Someone suffering from flu or having a wart removed was not given a general anaesthetic.

At times, seeing that he was not given credit for surgical successes but was the first to raise suspicions when it came to failure, he had regretted his choice of specialism, but it had always been a fleeting impression, and he'd soon felt proud of it again. Perhaps it was he, along with the intensive-care doctor, who best knew the secrets of the body, who had the most complete vision of what it was made of and how it worked in real time, precisely at the most serious times, when its suffering was at its most intense and its activity clearly observable: the energetic beating of the heart or the lustrous density of the liver, the hardness of the femur or the smooth texture of the thyroid, the elasticity of the vagina in childbirth or the prodigiously long labyrinth of the intestines tidily tucked away. His colleagues might well be experts in one organ or one function of the admirable body mechanism, but as an anaesthetist he worked with all. Besides, his colleagues might work on the flesh, but he also worked on the spirit. They cared about the wound, he cared about the pain. He alone had the power to soothe it and put patients to sleep, in various degrees and for different durations of time, depending on the rhythm with which he administered the drugs. From one minute to the next the ill were in his hands: living but dead, their blood coursing through their veins but their brains unaware of it. He was the god of sleep and shadows who took them to limbo and brought them back to reality, who looked at their nakedness or covered them with a sheet, who could make a child come into the world amid his mother's conscious happiness or through a tunnel contracted by pain and blood. He pulled the strings, could control them like puppets. Other doctors might be able to rummage through their guts, or drain their lungs, or transplant their organs, but only he had the key to consciousness. Others could widen the roads for the blood and dig alternative tunnels in the heart, but only he could light or extinguish the flame in the cave of the soul. Others could sew up the skin without leaving any scars or screw bones together with titanium plates, but only he opened or closed the lungs to insufflate life into them. Even the patients acknowledged that enormous power of his, as when they were informed of the risks of the operation, they were always less afraid of the scalpel or the frequent infections than of the negligible possibility of not coming round from the anaesthetic. Negligible? Well, yes, at least in his hands, even if that woman had floated away into nothingness. Because it wasn't he who had failed during the operation, he'd been alert to everything that was happening on the surgical front. The capnographer had simply broken down, no longer giving the information he needed to act on. When he saw the other dials flicker, it was already too late, and a pulmonary embolism had sent her into cardiac arrest.

He now cast away those memories and fixed his attention on the pulsioxymeter and the capnographer, alert to any anomaly. Everything was fine. If the boy had taken any ketamine, the stomach-pumping had got rid of it.

'Doctor Beltrán?'

'Yes?'

'How's it going? Everything in order?' Doctor Añil glanced at him before clamping the blood vessels.

'Yes, everything under control.'

'Fine, we're going to extirpate then.'

Once they drained all the blood spilled by the broken spleen into the abdominal cavity, the surgeon sank her arms up to her elbows in the boy's belly to cut and extract the inflamed, spongy organ, its pulp palpitating between the stomach and the kidneys. In a low voice she ordered a nurse to transfuse a new bag of blood and make sure his blood pressure remained stable. The most complicated part was over. It was then, as they prepared to close him up, that Lesmes, enveloped in the smells of blood and disinfectant under the bright lights, sitting in the place he'd feared he'd lost for ever, watching over a boy who would recover without serious after effects, once again felt good about his profession, calm, more satisfied that he had been in years.

'I think we're done,' said the doctor soon afterwards.

Half an hour later they left the boy in the observation room, in the hands of the intensive care doctor. When he went back to the washroom he saw that Dr Añil was still there, as though she had been waiting for him. He took off his stained gown and turned the tap on with his elbow.

'How's everything?' asked the doctor.

'Fine, fine,' he replied. 'His vitals are up. He'll come round in an hour or so.'

'How are you feeling?' she clarified.

Lesmes was a bit puzzled by her question; he was not the kind of person who aroused sympathy in others. It was the first time a colleague had taken a personal interest in him since he'd come back to work.

'Fine, fine,' he repeated.

'I couldn't help observing you during the operation, and, well, I got the impression you're still a little nervous.'

'No, no. I'm calm. Don't worry,' he replied, struggling to keep his voice steady. Yet his hands shook slightly under the tap. When he raised his eyes he saw she was looking at them.

'We work as a team,' she said, 'even if I'm responsible to the directors for all that happens here. It's not my role to punish people if anything goes wrong, but rather to see how we can avoid it.'

'It's an important difference.'

'It is. I mean, there's nothing to be afraid of. All that business … it's in the past,' she said, adding: 'Don't get me wrong. If I bring it up, it's actually because I don't think it matters now.'

'It was an accident. A tragic accident. Nobody's fault.'

'I know, I've read the report. From now on, the only thing that matters is for you to do your job well. And since, tense and all, you've done it perfectly well in the last few weeks, there's no reason to think you won't under normal circumstances.'

'I'm glad you think that,' he said. He didn't need to continue drying his hands with the towel. They were no longer shaking.

Dr Añil offered her hand, and he shook it briefly and cordially, before she left in a hurry as bosses do.

'I'm going to speak to the family,' she said from the door. 'They'll be glad to know he's come out of it.'

He went back to the observation room. The boy was breathing calmly and all his vitals were adequate. He was returning to consciousness. The nurse was writing down the facts in a chart.

'Everything all right?'

'Yes, shall we take him to his room, doctor?'

He hesitated for a moment, but caution won.

'Give it fifteen minutes. Better for the family to see him a bit more recovered. I'll check on him later.'

He left the area through the back door to avoid bumping into anyone. He wanted to be in his small office and slowly, comfortably smoke a cigarette on his own, without anyone turning their head or looking at him reprovingly while making a fuss about the smoke.

'Do you think they'll let us in?' asked Alkalino.

Walking on, Cupido studied their appearance.

'We don't look like we're ill, but we'll try our best.'

They walked into the spacious waiting room of the hospital. Fifteen or twenty people sat on hard plastic chairs near which were a couple of vending machines. At the back, under a sign that read Information, two receptionists took care of admissions, handing out entry passes that were then checked by an orderly sitting at a desk at the entrance to a wide corridor. To one side stood a security guard, his arms crossed.

'Come on,' said Cupido. 'Be quiet for a change and follow me.'

They walked to the corridor and were stopped by the orderly.

'May I see your passes, please?'

Cupido took out his wallet and showed his donor card.

'We're here to give blood,' he said.

The man studied the card, which had a dozen stamps certifying his donations, and returned it.

'What about him?' he asked pointing to Alkalino, who was a little behind Cupido.

'I've managed to convince him to do it.'

The orderly looked him up and down, as if doubting that the

blood of a guy like that – Alkalino was unshaven, his clothes crumpled – would be healthy enough for transfusions.

'But he's a bit scared of the needle, and I fear that if we make it difficult for him he'll run away at the smallest opportunity.'

'Fine. You can go in.'

'Do I look so bad?' asked Alkalino as soon as they took a few steps down the corridor.

'No, why?'

'Did you see the way he looked at me? As if he was looking at someone who's very ill, and was only letting me in because when they analyse my blood they might discover some new virus.'

'You may not be in very good health,' joked Cupido, 'but one cannot say you're not doing well for that.'

The corridor led to a hallway with signs hanging from the ceiling that pointed in every direction. They followed the one indicating the operating theatres and, after wandering around for a few minutes and walking up and down different staircases, they found a door with a plaque that read Dr L. Beltrán, Anaesthetist. It was in a narrow, silent corridor, and a sign forbade the entrance of unauthorised personnel. No one replied when they gently knocked on the door.

'I rang and they said he was working today. Let's wait for a while,' said Cupido.

Fifteen minutes later they saw a small slim man walking towards them. He looked emaciated, as though he were about to faint, like someone who's been ill for a long time and has not fully recovered. They would have mistaken him for a patient had they not seen his ID badge clipped over the pocket of his coat. The man looked at them with suspicion before inserting the key in the lock.

'Dr Lesmes Beltrán?' asked Cupido.

'Yes.'

'Could we have a word?'

He finished turning the key but didn't open the door, as if he wanted to hide something. Then he turned towards them and looked at them for few seconds.

'What's it about?'

'Someone who's died.'

'In this place,' – he made an ample gesture – 'we prefer to talk about how to prevent people from dying.'

'But it's not always the case, right? Sometimes there's nothing you can do for them. Sometimes they come in when it's too late, when they're terminally ill and you can only ease their final suffering. And sometimes there are accidents.'

'What do you mean?' he asked with a strange expression, as if he feared that bad luck would strike him at any moment. 'Who are you?'

Cupido said his name and profession.

'Police?'

'No, private detective,' he corrected.

'Isn't it the same?'

'No. A private detective is not even a kind of police officer.'

'What's the difference?' he asked in a dry, incurious tone, as if he were indifferent to the answer.

'It's not you who pays me, it's my client. I can't arrest anyone. Nor have I taken an oath, and so I'm free to choose which job I accept. Marina Olmedo has hired me to clarify some doubts she has about the death of her father. She doesn't believe it was suicide.'

'And does she think I can help her with that?'

'No, she didn't mention your name. On the contrary, she'd rather not talk about this business. But among Olmedo's papers I found the file of the lawsuit concerning his wife's death.'

'It was an accident. No matter what sentence was passed, it was a tragic accident,' he said in a low voice, barely moving his lips, as if it weren't he who was talking.

'I see no reason to doubt that,' conceded Cupido. 'But that's precisely what I'd like to discuss with you.'

'I don't follow.'

'If it was an unjust sentence, anyone might think you're glad Olmedo is dead.'

The next door along opened, and a doctor came out into the

corridor. As she walked past, she looked at them with curiosity.

Cupido's direct, almost impertinent words made the anaesthetist want to turn his back on the two of them, go into his office and close the door behind him. He was under no obligation to discuss all that with a man who had no authority to interrogate him. When Olmedo died, he'd feared the police would come to talk to him, even though according to the press everything indicated it had been suicide. After ten days he'd stopped worrying about a possible visit from the police. And yet this private detective appeared, at the very door of his office, making compromising statements within earshot of the passing doctor. He could call a security guard and have them thrown out from the area reserved for medical staff, but he held back. If he didn't answer his questions, the detective might make things difficult, bring about loud, annoying complications. Lesmes pictured this tall fellow and his small dark sidekick scuttling about all the corridors and asking his colleagues whether they remembered seeing him in the hospital on the evening Olmedo had died, or whether they'd ever heard him talking about revenge. He imagined them digging up what had happened with the woman, rummaging through the clinical files and even stealing the dossier. And that was the last thing he needed now that he was back at work and starting to feel his presence was appreciated, now that the chief surgeon had complimented him on his work, now that he was on his way to regaining his old pride in being Lesmes Beltrán, the best anaesthetist in the city, the master of pain, Doctor God come back from the dead. So he opened the door and said:

'Come in. We'll talk inside.'

The window in the small office was open, but there lingered a faint smell of tobacco. Beltrán went to the other side of the desk while he invited them to take two chairs. From a drawer, he took out a pack of cigarettes, matches and an ashtray full of water for the butt ends.

'You smoke?'

'No,' they replied.

The doctor took out a cigarette, caressed the golden end as if it were more than just cotton and paper, put it in his mouth and lit up. Although he looked hungry for nicotine, once he gave in he seemed to feel guilty. After a few seconds the smoke streamed out of his lungs in a long, sustained exhalation, more grey than bluish, which softened his expression and appeared to have a calming effect on him.

'So you think I'm glad Olmedo died?' He recapped on the last words they had exchanged in the corridor and for a few seconds of silence he seemed to study the burning tip of his cigarette. 'Well, yes, I think I am,' he said and continued gently, without anger or defiance. 'There's no loss when some kinds of people die. In fact, nothing would've been lost if they hadn't been born.'

He saw the two men were listening intently. He knew that, when he described his work, many people wished to ask: 'Did any of your patients ever die on the operating table? What happened? What was it like?' But they very rarely dared to. However, he had just offered the detective that opportunity, so he wasn't surprised to hear:

'What really happened during the operation after which Olmedo's wife died? What was it like?'

'An accident, like I told you. I didn't do anything I hadn't done hundreds of times. In the prep-room we didn't detect anything. She was given the indicated dosage for her age, weight and the kind of procedure she was undergoing. However, during the operation the capnographer, the machine which monitors the concentration of carbon dioxide leaving the lungs, broke down,' he explained. 'Yes, I know it sounds strange, exceptionally unlikely perhaps. We've become used to believing that it's always the human element that's responsible for most accidents, and that machines never fail, but in this case it did. It stopped working without turning itself off, so the monitor wasn't giving any information about what was happening inside her lungs and, therefore, we weren't able to react. Without such devices, an anaesthetist is blind before the patient. The woman had a pulmonary embolism and went into cardiac arrest.' He went through the details quickly, in a professional, clipped manner, with the kind of clarity and consistency that disappeared as he continued: 'Olmedo wouldn't believe it … Or perhaps he did, but he accused me of negligence anyway. I guess when the pain is unbearable it's inevitable to think about revenge. And you need to take revenge on someone; you cannot just accept the work of chance or fate. Olmedo looked around for a culprit and he found me: I was the one most directly involved in his wife's death. He hired a good lawyer and obtained medical testimonies claiming that other symptoms could have indicated that something was wrong … And then, the jury … In cases like these, we doctors always look guilty. Inspiring pity is very easy for the family of someone who dies in a hospital where everything is arranged precisely to prevent people from dying. A prosecutor utters the words heart attack, coma, agony, pain, while pointing to the relatives in mourning, and he has every chance of winning the case. Which was, indeed, what happened.'

'Did you ever speak to him again?'

'Never. What about? What could we discuss? The operation, once again? The fact that he ruined my career? What, really?'

He took one last furious drag, blew the smoke out and threw the butt in the water-filled ashtray, where it expired with a hiss.

'Can you remember where you were the evening of his death?'

Beltran made a face, annoyed that his previous explanation had not been at all useful.

'Isn't it your job to find an answer to that question?'

Cupido was tempted to reply that it wasn't, or at least it wasn't entirely. Each suspect – and the doctor was one – was for him more than just coordinates in space and time, for although such considerations were complex and necessary, they weren't always definitive, and no accusation could be mounted on the basis that someone lacked an alibi. What Cupido regarded as a challenge and a mystery was the suspect as a subject, his motives, his feelings for the victim, precisely everything that wasn't coordinates in space and time.

'Let's say finding out those answers is only half my job,' he conceded.

'And the other half?'

'To ask the best questions.'

Beltrán looked at him rather disconcerted.

'Why should I answer? The police already have all the detectives they need to do their job properly.'

'Do their job properly? But they haven't come round to ask you anything'

'No, they haven't. I guess it didn't occur to them. They take it for granted it was suicide.'

'And you don't?'

'I find it hard to believe,' he said. 'People who do others harm don't usually harm themselves,' he added in a hoarse voice which contained the hint of a cough.

'In that case, you shouldn't be surprised that I asked you where you were that evening.'

The doctor nodded several times, very slowly, as if he finally recognised that Cupido thought faster than he did. Still, he said:

'Do you think his daughter will believe me even if I tell the truth? Will she be any different from her father?'

'That will depend on how convincing your answer might be.'

'Then there won't be a problem. I was here in the hospital, delivering a baby. They can confirm that.'

9

Pledge of Allegiance

It was hard to find a space in the car park at the base, which was as packed as that of a supermarket or a football pitch on a weekend afternoon: long rows of cars and buses, and lots of disorientated people who talked a little louder than usual. The women were wearing party dresses, while the men, no less smart, were animated by the promise of nostalgia and renewed vows of patriotism.

Cupido showed his invitation and identity card to the lieutenant at the entrance. Further down, several corporals wearing white belts and bandoliers directed people to different gates to access the compound. After one of them showed him the way, Cupido went up a staircase and emerged through a gangway onto the stands.

The place was like a football pitch, but one in which the spectators sat only on one of the sides. The red-carpeted stands for the authorities were on one of the shorter sides, still empty. On the pitch, however, the five companies of soldiers about to pledge allegiance to the flag were already standing in formation, in order of height. Officers and NCOs kept watch at the front. It was a geometric, harmonic, resplendent whole. The green of the uniforms complemented the red and yellow of the flags martially flapping in the wind. From the east, in a sky sparsely dotted with the kinds of horse-shaped clouds that seem so suited to a military scene, groups of fat cirri scudded across the blue space, casting waves of shadow over the pitch as they escaped from the sea, still ignorant of the brutal collision that, only a few kilometres inland, a chain of grey deserted mountains had in store for them, blocking their passage onto a plateau that was always in need of water. On the horizon one could see some rocky outcrops, which appeared to have been erected by the land itself near the coast, against invaders. Eagles often flew from their tops towards the shore, less with the purpose of finding food than of observing in disbelief the massive flood of tourists lying in the sun. Through the loudspeakers, the chords of 'Soldadito español' lent a Castilian flavour to a not quite successful heroic scene.

Fifteen minutes later people were still arriving, but the stands had still not filled. The gaps on the cement seats were a sign of the growing public indifference toward army ceremonies ever since the military service had ceased to be compulsory. At one point murmurs were heard, and all eyes looked to the stands where the military authorities and a few civilians were beginning to take their places. From his seat, very near them, Cupido saw Colonel Castroviejo accompanied by a general, to whom he was indicating the company of recruits on the pitch. Then the bugle sounded and all the soldiers, clicking their heels and holding their rifles by the butt, stood to attention and presented arms.

After a few words of welcome from the captain who acted as the masters of ceremonies, the band launched into the first chords of the Spanish national anthem. Everyone stood up, and Cupido noticed that some people on the stands sang the Francoist lyrics, the old words with which someone had tried in vain to strengthen the bland music. For a moment, Cupido thought that the troubled identity of his country showed through in its confused symbols: a flag without patriotism, an anthem without lyrics and a coat of arms without a history.

When the music ended, the officer introduced the general, who would give the speech before the pledge.

'Soldiers!' the latter exclaimed from his lectern.

Cupido was near enough to see that the general was a youngish man, at least young for a general, and his youth increased everyone's expectations. The detective too was interested in hearing the speech, and he wondered to what degree the recent death of Olmedo would temper criticism and accusations against the person who had been directly responsible for the closure of San Marcial. After a brief greeting, the general sighed unashamedly through the loudspeakers, looked at the soldiers standing to attention and then at the spectators, as if he wanted to encompass both groups with his words, and said:

'As you all know, this will be the last time we pledge allegiance to the flag here, at this square that you have washed with your sweat. The San Marcial base is being closed down!' he exclaimed. In the pause that followed, his words echoed in the absolute silence of the compound. His voice was deep, trained not to lose authority even when it sounded confidential, as if he was about to tell something that no one but this audience must hear. 'The government of our country have decided to close down this base for the greater efficiency of our army, in order to centralise our forces and improve their operational capacity. And we who obey must accept that decision, because, I suppose, they must have their reasons for this decision. But I wouldn't want you to worry!' he continued, in a more peaceful tone, 'not you, the soldiers, and not you, the civilians who are concerned about how convenient that measure might be. Because they may close this and other bases in Spain, they may empty these barracks and training grounds, they may take down our fences and build houses or gardens here, but I can assure you that the Spanish army will never disappear!'

He made a theatrical pause that would have been filled with applause had he been in a less solemn place. The general was eloquent, and treated those present as patriots who loved Spain as much as he did himself. His tone of voice, his magniloquent yet emotive phrases, and the fact that he adopted the role of victim moved an audience that was attentive and prone to effusion.

'It will never disappear because the spirit of the army resides less in a physical place than in our souls, less in the buildings of the base, however much we love them, than in our hearts. I know,' he said, lowering the tone to favour complicity, as if he feared that the loudspeakers would fling his words beyond the compound, over the barbed wire on its walls, 'I've heard it myself, that in some quarters people criticise us, question our very existence, or, at best, tolerate us as a necessary evil best kept to one side, where we don't give anyone any trouble. They ask us to do the dirty work and later refuse to shake our hands because they're dirty! But let me tell you, soldiers, you who are at the beginning of your military career, that nowhere else shall you find the protection you find here. Here there will always be someone near you to tell you where you belong, in what corps, company or patrol, and which way to go if you get lost, and what to aspire to when they try to confuse you. The army will welcome you into a group of peers where camaraderie is the norm, and you will share your thirst and sweat, yes, but also water and bread, and you will see day by day that you are not alone, and that another soldier is your best companion and his company your best society. The army will always offer you a lesson in order, support you if you ever stumble. In return, soldiers, you will have to obey your superiors with discipline and diligence. If we do this, every-thing will be well, even if a base is closed down now and again. This glorious country in which we live, Spain, where does it come from if not from the intimate union of its people and its military leaders? Where indeed? Do not believe those who say otherwise, who try to tear down this country which has a history that goes back more than a thousand years.'

Just like a rally, thought Cupido. *After twenty years I had forgot-ten it, but I think that, in essence, nothing has changed much since I was the same age as those lads down there who seem touched by this rough, repetitive harangue, put together with the detritus of the pompous rhetoric of the past. The only difference is that we were forced to attend and didn't believe in anything that smacked of the army, and found speeches the more false and creepy the higher the rank of the person giving them, while these kids here enrolled vol-untarily and seem to have blind faith in what the general tells them.*

Enthusiastic applause broke out on the stands. And presently the bugle sounded again and the ceremony continued. The captain stepped forward holding a luxurious golden book in his hands, placed it on the lectern and opened it on a marked page before taking a few steps back. Then the general began reading in a loud, solemn voice:

'Soldiers! Do you swear under God and on your honour and conscience to fulfil your military obligations, to defend and enforce the Constitution as the fundamental law of the State, to obey and respect the King and your superiors, never abandon them and, if it is demanded of you, give your lives in defence of Spain?'

What did that formula resemble? What did that stiff pledge remind him of with its demands of eternal fidelity and no provision made for any possible future reasons to reject it? But of course... Cupido took a few seconds to associate it with something he'd often heard but had never been asked directly. What had started as a rally ended as a sacrament, the open-air grounds falling silent like a temple, the officers' stands turning into the priests' altar, the promise of a festivity culminating in an oath.

'Yes, we do!' answered several hundreds of voices, in a confident, unanimous shout.

'If you fulfil your pledge and your promise, the country will thank and reward you, and if not, you'll deserve its scorn and punishment, like unworthy children,' replied the general, no longer reading from the book. Then, raising his voice, he continued: 'Soldiers, long live the San Marcial base!'

'Long live San Marcial!'

'Long live the King!'

'Long live the King!'

'Long live Spain!'

'Long live Spain!'

Not only the soldiers answered the call. Patriotic voices could be heard coming from the civilians' stands, while the detective remained in stony silence, alone and removed from everyone around him. He was no longer touched by stories that weren't intimate and individual. Any collective outburst to do with politics, religion or one's homeland left him cold.

The band launched into the chords of 'Himno de Infantería'

and the companies started parading under the flag. One by one, armed with a Cetme, the soldiers walked up to the two-coloured banner and kissed the cloth swiftly before moving on.

An hour and a half later, when the ceremony was over, Cupido asked a corporal where the cocktail party was taking place. He showed his invitation again to access a large room where a couple of hundred people – army men in uniform, civilians in suits and women in radiant party dresses, too much make-up for daytime and hair carefully dyed in all shades of blonde, the roots not allowed to give away their age – were consuming the drinks and canapés that were laid out on a table and being replenished by soldiers doubling up as waiters. He grabbed a glass of beer and took a look around, feeling quite awkward in those surroundings that represented everything he was not. To one side, a group of NCOs were heatedly discussing the army and the civilians' patriotic obligations. Somebody said something and the others laughed, pleased in the knowledge that they believed in the same leaders and the same ideals. Behind Cupido two women were chatting, and one of them praised the general's speech.

'Where is he staying tonight?' he heard one ask.

'I don't know, why?'

'He's got such a beautiful voice! I wouldn't mind spending the whole night listening to it.'

Cupido stepped aside to let two elderly officers, who were no doubt retired by now but still in uniform, their white hair neatly combed back and thin moustaches over their top lips, approach the trays of croquettes, cheese, salmon and caviar canapés, which they instantly started grabbing with trembling, avid fingers. Cupido wandered around towards the back of the room – where Castoviejo was talking to the young general – hoping in vain to catch one or the other of those two names Marina had mentioned, Ucha and Bramante. Nor did he hear Olmedo's, as if in two weeks he'd been forgotten or everyone wished to cast aside his uncomfortable memory, either because they suspected someone had killed him, or because they thought suicide was an act of cowardice, and a coward was an unworthy officer. The conversations revolved around what measures should be taken to fix the sorry state of the national affairs, and included the frequent cursing of politicians, nostalgic anecdotes about San Marcial, and reveries about the more heroic times of exploits, rowdiness and beautiful women. He overheard some gruesome and malicious innuendo that went over his head, and such detailed and explicit gossip as he could hardly believe an officer capable of uttering. When he left the glass on a table and tried to catch a waiter's eye, he saw the colonel was looking at him and beckoning him over.

'I see you were not able to overcome your curiosity,' he said, shaking his hand. He seemed more affable, less worried than when Cupido had seen him in his office.

'I've succumbed to it.'

'And what did you think?'

'I've already attended one ceremony like this. My own. Back then, from the other side, I didn't find it that pleasant,' he dared confess with a smile.

'And now?'

'Now I have to say I didn't dislike it. The order, the perfect formation, the synchronised movements. And then ...' he hesitated.

'Then?'

The detective was surprised to see the degree to which military men are pleased to hear civilians praise their work. But then they were used to being regarded with suspicion by a society that still hadn't forgiven them their participation in the dictatorship, so any sign of recognition, any word of praise, must be doubly valuable to them.

'There was an instant when I told myself: so many soldiers and officers bearing arms, and not even one shot? For a moment I was inclined to believe Olmedo's idea that modern European armies should not be there to kill, but to stop people from killing each other.'

The mention of Olmedo ignited a spark of alertness in the colonel's slightly veiled eyes.

'A pity he's no longer among us to hear your comment. I'm sure he would have liked it.'

'May I, colonel?' An officer with the rank of captain interrupted them apologetically.

'Yes, of course. You've saved me from having to send for you. The detective, Ricardo Cupido, would like to have a word with you ... and with Ucha, if he's around. This is Captain Bramante,' he said.

'How do you do?' the man said, shaking Cupido's hand with the same brief energy with which he would have saluted. 'I thought it was you. The colonel told us he'd invited you,' he said in a dry, monotonous voice, as if he had some difficulty putting sentences together.

'Yes,' said Cupido. It didn't escape his notice that Bramante had come to talk to him before being summoned by the colonel, as if he were boasting he had nothing to hide.

Castroviejo called his orderly, said something in a low voice and presently another officer, who was introduced as Ucha, joined them.

'The detective would like to talk to you, if you don't mind.'

'Now?' asked Ucha.

'Yes,' jumped in Bramante, 'it's as good a moment as any.'

The colonel left them alone, and went back to join the general, who was surrounded by several women. All three remained silent, standing a little to one side by the wall, waiting for the waiter carrying a tray to move along. Ucha exchanged his empty glass for a full one of white wine. Bramante chose mineral water.

As far as Cupido knew, both officers had been dead against Olmedo's project. But how different they were! Whereas Bramante seemed to show off his strength, energy and health in every gesture, Ucha was his exact opposite. His back had immediately sought out the wall to lean against it, as if the mere fact of standing tired him. His facial features appeared weighed down by gravity, dripping towards the lower half of his face. His forehead was broad, and tilted slightly backwards, as if his eyebrows had descended from their normal place and pushed his eyes down. His cheeks pulled the cheekbones downwards too, so that his nose, mouth and chin were concentrated in a small space, which gave him a strangely frail, gluttonous and lecherous appearance, but also made him look incapable of satisfying those appetites.

'I find it curious that the colonel should ask us to help in a private investigation when he hasn't ordered a military inquiry. He has no doubts about what happened,' he said.

'And what about yourselves? Do you think Olmedo committed suicide?'

'I haven't formed an opinion on the matter,' said Bramante, avoiding a compromising answer.

'No,' said Ucha.

'Except for the colonel, no one thinks that Olmedo shot himself, and yet no one does anything about it.'

'Right now we have enough problems at the base as it is, mostly as a result of that report that Olmedo wrote, so we don't need further speculation,' said Ucha. 'And we are officers, not detectives. We're not as curious about the particulars as you might be.'

'Were you not surprised by his death?' insisted Cupido, ignoring the scorn in his tone.

'I was, yes,' said Ucha. 'The untimely or violent death of people I know is always a surprise. After a few days, though, when you think about it, you begin to see that there's a certain logic to it, either because the dead person did not take care of his health, or was reckless, or attracted too much hatred. And yet, I still find Olmedo's death surprising, even after two weeks. I would've said he'd be the last person to die from a shot that … in any case, doesn't look like it was an accident.'

'What did you think of him?'

'As an officer?' asked Bramante.

'As an officer and a person.'

'I'm not sure you can separate them. I'm not sure a bad person can be a good officer,' said Ucha.

The names of a few strategists who had applied their skills

to infamous causes popped into the detective's mind, but he didn't contradict him, limiting himself to ask, in the direction of Bramante:

'Was he a good officer?'

'He was in Bosnia and Afghanistan. But he stopped being one when he devoted himself to administrative work and recommended closing down San Marcial. He shouldn't have collaborated with the politicians who make such decisions,' he explained with some difficulty. 'He was not one of us. It's as if he'd gone over to the enemy.'

'Do you mean that ...?'

'That it seems inevitable that in any army there will be a traitor,' interrupted Ucha. He looked around, fearing that someone might have overheard his comment, which wasn't exactly appropriate when two hours earlier several hundred soldiers had solemnly pledged their allegiance to the army.

But the party went on around them, and the guests continued talking and laughing as they consumed drinks and canapés. On the tables were empty bottles and glasses, some with lipstick traces, crumpled napkins, little plates with leftover food.

'I guess we shouldn't speak badly of him now he's dead,' put in Ucha. 'But I'm sure the colonel hasn't invited you just to hear us sing Olmedo's praises, but also so we can tell how much unease his report had generated. Isn't that what you expect of us?'

'Yes.'

'No one liked him much. And anyone who says anything to the contrary is lying,' he affirmed. 'Olmedo was the kind of person you make friends with not because he's like you, or because you admire his intelligence, humour or wit, but because you're afraid that otherwise he might become your enemy. When he returned from Afghanistan, we all knew he had kudos, influence and prestige in Madrid and with the colonel, and so it was convenient to be on good terms with him. But there's a difference between that and liking him.'

'No one really liked him,' confirmed Bramante.

'But I don't think, either, that one of us killed him,' insisted Ucha. 'I really don't. Shooting an equal is a serious thing, but if you were part of the army you'd realise that it is really unthinkable to shoot someone of a higher rank. To respect and obey a superior is the first rule one learns when putting on a uniform. You've just heard it in the general's speech.'

'Yes.'

'And it is so engraved in our minds that even in, say, mortal danger we wouldn't dare break that rule. You don't think, do you, that because we're familiar with guns we go around shooting those who get in our way or threaten our interests.'

'But you yourselves think someone shot him. You don't believe he committed suicide,' he insisted.

'Shooting is easy,' replied Bramante. 'You don't have to be a soldier to know how to do it.'

'That evening there was an informal meeting here, held to consider the consequences of the likely closure. Everyone attended, except the colonel and the two of you.'

'That sounds like suspicion,' said Ucha.

'Which anyone who could prove they were far from Olmedo's house would be above.'

'In that case, you can rest assured about me. I was at the Vigour and Beauty Gym. The owner, and perhaps some member, can confirm it,' said Bramante.

'I think I'd find it easier to say where I wasn't than where I was,' said Ucha before the detective had addressed him.

'Where?'

'I was driving along the old road inland. But, of course, I couldn't say exactly where I was at a given hour.'

'Were you alone?' asked Cupido.

'Yes. It's an old habit. A way to relax when I'm worried or have to make an important decision. I really like driving. I get in the car, fill up the tank at the first station, and drive off without a schedule or a planned route. And that evening I particularly felt like it, after the meeting with Olmedo. The closure of the base will change everyone's professional situation here. I'd be able to think better about all this while driving alone and in silence than at a meeting where we'd talk a lot and nothing would be solved. I know what those meetings are like. And so I drove, but as I didn't get a fine, or have an accident, or stop anywhere to buy something with my card, I don't think there would be anyone who can confirm they saw me driving along small roads.'

He broke off brusquely, as if he considered that with that he had already obeyed the colonel's orders to answer the detective's questions. Then he looked around impatiently.

'I think that should be enough,' said Ucha.

The officers started walking away, but Bramante stopped and retraced his steps.

'If someone shot Olmedo, if there's a culprit, you won't find him in the army,' he said tersely and dryly.

Cupido thought for a moment, trying to make sense of his words.

'Do you mean to say that, if that were a possibility, people would cover for him?'

'Cover? No, I mean we don't admit that possibility,' he concluded.

'Who was that?' asked Carmen getting in the car, once the general had left the cocktail party – by then drinks with English names had appeared – thus giving everyone implicit permission to do the same.

'Who?' he asked in turn, although he knew who she meant.

'The tall guy, the one talking to you and Ucha,' she said, feigning indifference as she lowered her sun shade to check her make-up in the little mirror and stop him seeing the interest in her eyes, the curiosity with which she was awaiting an answer.

Of course she meant him, thought Bramante, recalling a distant incident, trying to remember the first time she had lied to him. Of course she would have noticed a civilian like him, with his hair longer than anyone wearing a uniform could ever wear it, the only one dressed in casual clothes, without a suit or a tie, who scorned the solemnity of the ceremony. One of those attractive guys who know there will always be a woman who remembers them at the end of a party. A guy oblivious to the military euphoria of that day, but who had listened intently, with suspicious concentration, to what he and Ucha had told him, as if they could only be the bearers of bad news.

'The tall guy,' he repeated, as if he didn't remember him well, 'was a private detective.'

'How interesting!' she exclaimed. She finished applying lipstick quickly and deftly, careful not to smudge the edges. 'I would never have guessed. It was about Olmedo, wasn't it?'

'Yes. Marina's hired him. She doesn't think her father …'

'Does anyone?'

He furiously sounded his horn at a driver who cut in at a roundabout without giving right of way. He saw his face, a young man with long hair tied in a ponytail, and through the window he uttered his favourite insult, wishing the lad would see him, stop the car and give him the chance to confront him, burst a soft part of his body, feel the blood running on his face. He thought of turning the wheel and making as if to ram his car into the other's, to wipe off the scornful expression that appeared on the lad's face on seeing his uniform.

'No, no one does. And yet no one does anything to prove it's not true,' he said, surprised to be repeating the detective's words.

'It's better that way, isn't it?'

'Better?'

He turned his head and saw she was looking directly at him, with a faint expression of defiance on her painted mouth, a hint of mockery that did not match the seriousness of the suggestion.

'I don't understand.'

'If that detective goes around asking everyone questions …' she trailed off.

'Things can get a bit sticky for Ucha,' he replied after a few seconds. 'He told him he spent several hours driving down small roads that evening, but that he doesn't think anyone can confirm it.'

'That ridiculous habit of his. One day he'll get into trouble for it. And you?'

'I have nothing to worry about. I told him I'd been at the gym, as you know,' he said, trying to eliminate from his words any trace of defensiveness or even concern.

'I never know where you are when you're not home,' replied Carmen. Her sarcasm had turned into a hint of reproach.

Bramante saw her head turn towards the window. Her blonde hair hid her face. What was she really thinking, he wondered. What was she suspicious of? Impatiently, almost anxiously, he searched for the right reply, but the words that would have made her look at him did not materialise, or they fled before he could catch them. Why did he find it so difficult to talk, to persuade someone who disagreed with him, to make himself understood, even in front of the soldiers, when he gave them the simplest orders? There were so many people who used language deftly! He'd always been astonished and disgusted by people's ability to fight him verbally. Words in their mouths were like quick, invisible weapons which left him defeated and dumb. And he always ended up feeling a violent desire to shout, to address a subordinate only to utter an order or a punishment, nothing in between. He ended up feeling a desire to cut off the tongues of those smart-arsed civilians who would quiver if he but unclasped his holster.

They parked the car in the garage and went up to their flat in silence. He hung his jacket in the wardrobe and looked at the clock on his night table. Five, a stupid, hot hour, still too early to sit in front of the TV and too late to start any task, what with the mixture of excitement and exhaustion after the ceremony. He sat at the foot of the bed and untied his smart shoes, which he'd never broken in.

'Have you noticed?' he heard Carmen say in the bathroom, over the noise of running water. 'I put on a new blouse and Loreto spilled wine all over it! She's terrible! She took a whole bottle from the waiter. She drank half of it and the other half she splashed all around her. You wouldn't believe what she dared say to the general.'

'What?'

'That his voice sounded so interesting that she wouldn't mind staying up all night listening to him. You should've seen him run!'

He moved along the bed to see her in the bathroom, excited at the ability of feminine flesh to embody mystery and arouse desire and make men run after it like a hungry dog, mouth watering, whimpering to be allowed a few minutes inside it. She had her skirt on, but had taken off the stained blouse and was washing it by hand, leaning over the basin. The delicate cloth of her bra contained her breasts, which swung gently in their cups, big and round.

He saw her almost whole now, half naked, only concerned about her wine-stained garment, oblivious to him and his gaze, to the way her breasts awakened in him a painful ardour. He left his shoes at the foot of the bed, stood up and, without saying a word, held her by the waist from behind as he looked at her in the mirror.

'Not now,' she protested, 'I've got to finish this.'

'You can do that later,' he whispered in her ear.

'No, really. If it dries, the stain won't come off.'

'You're splashing water all over yourself,' he said.

Ignoring her protestations, he unclasped her bra. He touched the garment to his lips and nose, smelling the warmth of perfume, creams, and a hint of sweat. He was always moved by lingerie, by the refined harmony of skin and silk. When he returned from the base, whether from manoeuvres or a twenty-four-hour guard duty, the contrast between the coarse army blankets, the hard bunks, the belts and sweated canvas, on the one side, and, on the other, the delicateness of silk or cotton quickened his breath in an uncontrollable manner. Hence his opposition to allowing women in the army, another of those ridiculous ideas dreamed up by guys like Olmedo which threatened an order so painfully gained over centuries. The women at the base disconcerted him; he never managed to give them precise orders and didn't know whether to treat them the same as men. He either patronised them, which on second thoughts seemed absurd in the army, or unleashed against them a kind of mocking, scornful severity, as if he hated them, sometimes demanding of them greater efforts than of male recruits. Because he couldn't not think of the flesh underneath their uniforms, of the canvas hardened by the sweat of their tender skin, of the sharp smell of power mixed with perfume, of the image of a female soldier who, out on manoeuvres, against regulations, holds a machine gun in a hand with nails all painted a different colour.

One day on coming home, dazed by all those thoughts, he implored Carmen to take off all of her clothes and put on just the coarse belts he threw on the bed, a peaked cap over her blonde hair, and his shiny army boots. And she accepted, curious and excited by the game, indulging him as he tried to guess from her movements and initial caresses how she would satisfy him. But that was a long time ago. Now, seeing how cold she'd been with him over the last few months, he wondered whether she might not be hiding something shady and secret, and feared that she might confirm the saying whereby in every barracks there is a captain's wife in love with a soldier.

'Not now.'

She attempted to move away but he held her securely by the hips, doubting the firmness of her 'no', and recalling the ambiguity of other times, in which 'no' had cunningly meant 'yes'.

'Not now, I'm telling you, I'm not in the mood,' her hands covered in soap pushing away his.

'But I am, I really am.'

He pressed his tongue against her neck as she stood still, withstanding the awkward pressure against the washbasin, and the wet whisper of his lips on her neck. When he opened his eyes he saw her in the mirror, looking at him with a gesture hardened by patience, her hands once again sunk in the washbasin, not even resisting or despising him, but completely indifferent. His eyes slid down the mirror towards the hands that fondled her breasts, her nipples like dark small flowers emerging in the crack between his thumb and palm.

He moved away without saying a word and sat in front of the TV in the living room, quickly changing channels, not caring what he saw, disturbed by the difference between his life at the base and his life at home. At the base, at the sound of his voice, even if it was a confused voice, the three hundred men and women of a company would obey and stand to attention, clicking their heels in unison, sticking out their chests and chins for inspection, fearful of the possibility of a missing button or insufficient polishing of their boots, and they would salute when they passed him, and take off their caps and shout, 'Yes, captain!' or 'No, captain!' every time he expressed a wish or a prohibition – and it was all respect and discipline, and they would obey his orders without questioning him. However, in his own home, his wife often made sarcastic comments about his patriotism, and he didn't know what to say and searched in vain for something he'd done that day that he was proud of, but felt dazed and angry, so close to uttering an insult, and then she would say 'no' to him and reject him when he … when he …

How things had changed in a short time! How he missed those years, not so long ago, when being a soldier was the highest destiny a man could aspire to, to be someone who renounces easy gains and is prepared to give his life to defend his people, someone who values honour above all else! How he missed the noble, noisy, drunk camaraderie of his days as a cadet, the tumultuous elation when they were allowed to break ranks and several hundred men in uniform hurried towards the gates of the base, even if, on reaching the street, they looked around in bewilderment, not knowing which direction to take! What wouldn't he give now to relive the days of taverns in whose toilets you changed into civilian clothes that fooled no one, bars with cheap wine and gin, giant servings of *patatas bravas* and huge sandwiches of spicy cold cuts! The time of sunsets spent in parks with nannies of nimble, wide hands, who indulged them on their days off, and always worried about grass stains on their white shirts and trousers! That time when there was always a brothel near the base where the whores had ten-centimetre-long tongues … Ah, all that was so far in the past now!

She appeared in the doorway dressed in the soft dressing gown she wore at home.

'Come here,' she said, extending a hand towards him, trying to be kind in a way that covered her previous rejection, that concealed it with a sudden offer.

He saw her smile joylessly and, for a second, thought about not accepting the offer of reconciliation. Then, weakened by desire and her outstretched hand, he stood up, accepted her hand and followed her down the corridor back into the bedroom.

'Come here,' she said when it was no longer necessary, when he was lying down and she was on top of him.

He felt his previous irritation dissolve among the kisses, the caresses, the hands moving slowly, in preparation, as they whispered in each other's ears the most submissive and daring offers.

'Wait, not yet, can't we do something else first?' he asked, gently pushing her by the shoulders.

Carmen remonstrated for a moment but then slid down and, with one hand, seemed to weigh up his scrotum, elastic with fullness, deftly fondling the smooth skin, as if she could calculate the intensity of his desire. Satisfied, she traced with the tip of her finger the line that snaked up the shaft. She studied with curiosity its shape, its palpitations, and then closed her eyes and took him in her mouth.

'Enough,' he said a little later, strangely lucid and distant, without having reached the expected climax. He missed the intense happiness which those same gestures would have provoked a few years earlier, when both gave themselves with the blind desire to be immortal, when their lovemaking had not lost its emotional content and was not yet reduced to the pleasant satisfaction of a physical need.

'Have you been out today?'
'No.'

His father looked him up and down, trying to find fault with his uniform. Not finding it, he turned round and put a yellow tack next to Baghdad on an enormous map, three metres by one and half, which was mounted on a cork plank on the wall. For several years, with rigorous punctuality, he'd been sticking into it coloured drawing pins flagging the cities where terrorist attacks had taken place: yellow for Islamist attacks; red for nationalist attacks; blue for unclaimed attacks and attacks by strange unclassifiable organisations. There were tacks everywhere.

'You have to go for a walk, as the doctor said.'

'I'm not in the mood to go for a stroll with that Indian. She can't even talk. Or maybe she pretends she doesn't understand when I give her an order. I don't trust her. Any time she could push me down an embankment. Or drown me.'

'That's absurd.'

'It's not absurd. If you want me to go out, come for a walk with me,' he complained from the armchair he liked to sink into, in front of the television and the terrorism map, proud of his stubbornness, happy to be able to still impose his own rules.'

'You know I can't, I've got a lot of work.'

'But they'd give you the time off. Since when does a soldier not cover for a colleague who needs to get out for a couple of hours to take a walk with his elderly father?'

'Time off? No one would give me a hand.'

'In that case, at least find me a Spanish servant, not that Indian. I don't trust her.'

'Let me remind you that you didn't trust the Spanish ones either. And Evangelina is the most trustworthy and careful one you've had. The problem is she doesn't let you get away with anything.'

His father turned his face to the TV, annoyed at his comment. Evangelina was the best maid he'd had in years: tidy, indefatigable, patient with his old man's whims, even with his latest, dirty habit of rolling up pellets of bread and dropping them all over the dining room. She was also a good cook, something that the two men, living on their own, especially valued. His father didn't like her because she wouldn't humour him and his funny little ways, which were those of a former officer used to giving orders; because she didn't pamper him or let him stay in bed till noon in an unaired room; didn't buy him wine or any food not allowed by the doctor; and didn't have that servile attitude with which previous cleaners had, in fact, appeased him, so that he would not make trouble while they watched the soaps. Evangelina woke him up at the right time, made him take his medicines punctually, took him by the arm to go for a walk, shook him out of his laziness.

'All right, all right,' Ucha conceded. 'It's half past five now. I'll lie down for an hour. I was on guard duty last night, and it's the same tonight. We'll go out for a walk at seven.'

He went to his room and took off his uniform before lying down, tired and nervous, and a little tipsy from the white wine. He thought of the last pledge of allegiance at the San Marcial base, of his professional insecurity, of Olmedo's death and the detective's questions at the cocktail party. His near future looked very uncertain; with eyes closed, he went over the things he could salvage.

An hour later he awoke violently, in a daze, lying in the same position in which he'd fallen asleep. The sun slanted in through the window like a hard, shiny bar of warmth, and he had to face the wall to let his eyes adapt. Then, when he moved, he felt it. The pain was there, as if a skewer passed through his head from temple to temple and his head was being roasted over acid flames, causing him the kind of confusion and pain that grew with any activity. It suddenly spread from his temple to his neck, and he tried to stand in order to stop it cold. The more he let it settle in him, the greater his efforts to expel it.

Very slowly he put his feet on the carpet, wishing there were someone by his side to lower the blinds, put a fresh hand on his forehead, and fetch a glass of water and a couple of painkillers from the kitchen – not because he had asked them to but simply because they cared about him and wanted to alleviate his agony. Head lowered, he slowly opened his eyes and saw his bare feet on the carpet, his sad weak knees, and the white thighs that put him in mind of a different, older kind of man. Stooping as if he were about to be beaten, he stood up and walked towards the kitchen. He took two pills from the bottle and, without waiting for them to dissolve completely, drank the effervescent liquid and waited for it to take effect.

'Are we going now?'

His father was by the door, fully dressed, impatient to go out, sure he wouldn't refuse. Ucha thought of telling him he would not come out after all, that the white wine, or the stress he'd been under, had given him a headache. But he imagined his father listening in silence and disbelief, turning his back to go and sit in front of the TV, imagined his reproaches later on, and he just couldn't do it.

In a quiet voice, resigned, he accepted:

'Let me get dressed and then we'll go.'

10

Marina and Samuel

As he approached his house, he saw the woman, an old lady, who had been stealing flowers from the plants by his fence for a few weeks. She'd just torn off some purple begonias and delicately gathered them into a beautiful bunch with the white flowers of the solanum and a red branch of bougainvillea.

He'd noticed the small thefts – the flowers cut gently and surreptitiously, without cruelty – and wanted to put a stop to it. Yet now, seeing the old lady, he didn't much mind; he thought that what she might do with the flowers was no worse than what he did by leaving them there as decoration to be seen by only a limited number of people: Marina when she brought her children to the bus stop every day, neighbours, friends who visited him, and a few passers-by.

He slowed down to make time for the woman to leave before he arrived at the entrance and only then went in. It was Saturday. He would devote most of the afternoon to working in the garden, which looked rather abandoned. He'd been forced to drive one of the company vans all week, as one of his staff was in hospital with appendicitis, and he preferred not to hire a replacement.

The garden was like a shield against chaos: in it, nature's wildest impulses were tamed into harmonic wholes of colours and shapes. He sometimes told himself that as long as he managed to keep it tidy and beautiful his life would be under control. He'd seen that the garden is the first thing to deteriorate in an abandoned house, the first place invaded by confusion and ruin before windowpanes get broken, roofs start leaking and woodworm ruin the carpentry. A garden, like a musical instrument, shines brighter the more you use it. Unlike utensils, furniture and electrical appliances, which wear out with use and the passage of time, a garden improves with the years, and the seasons gather in its trees and bushes, provided there's a hand to guide its drive to endure. A garden, he concluded, is like a stage where, in the course of the year, a theatre company, that may not be very disciplined but has ample improvisation skills, floral dresses and vegetable props, puts on the wide-ranging theatre of nature, from the Victorian melodrama of autumn to the *commedia dell'arte* of spring, from the Scandinavian tragedies of winter to the fantasies of colours and smells, water and dreams that take place on midsummer nights.

He changed his clothes and shoes and went out onto the patio with a very clear idea of what he should do and in what order.

When he'd bought the house, he planted a cherry tree and a lemon tree next to each other pretty much at the same time, and now they grew together, like two good friends, still in their youth, of different build and breadth, vying with one another in height and fruit-bearing. But they got along well, did not steal the sunlight from each other, and nor did their roots fight in the soil for nutrients or water. The cherry tree did not boast about its greater height, or of its small red succulent fruit, or the changing colours of its perennial leaves, or of its docility when children climbed on it. For its part, the lemon tree didn't brag about the sweet fragrance of its monthly flowers, or about its cleanness or that its fruits remained on the branches for a long time once they matured, neither dropping nor rotting.

A couple of years ago, he'd tied a branch with a piece of twine to alter its direction, because it was growing horizontally and got in the way. One day, when the branch had already accepted the new direction, he cut the twine, forgetting however to untie the knot round the branch. And as it grew the twine had cut into it, as a small ring would around a girl's finger if she never took it off. The branch appeared weaker than the others. Samuel picked up the knife and prised the twine from inside the bark. A deep, circular mark remained where it had been, and it seemed the branch would snap along the indentation as soon as the first gust of wind hit it.

'Maybe I should prune it,' he mumbled to himself, convinced that the tree would not recover from the deep scar caused by the twine and his forgetfulness. But on closer inspection he saw that the spring leaves on the branch were no smaller than the others, and neither did the flowers seem scarcer, so with the profound feeling of sympathy one has for the wounded whose scars are healing yet they carry on without complaining, he decided to give it a chance.

However, the maple tree wouldn't make it, also because of his negligence. A few months back, in early November, he was spraying the soil with nitrates when the phone rang. It was Marina with something or other to tell him, but the conversation went on for longer than expected, and he had forgotten the bag of nitrates leaning against the trunk. That night and the following days it rained, and the water carried an enormous amount of acid into the roots of the tree, scorching it. When the leaves fell off, Samuel hoped that that would be it, and that the toxins would not reach into the heart of the wood. But little by little the roots too dried up, from their extremities all the way up to the trunk.

He put on his gloves and started digging energetically around the basin, cutting the roots he found as he dug deeper. He took a break as he wondered how many men and women had died like that, from an excess of acid that someone, out of negligence, had spilled near them. By the time he finally managed to pull it out he was covered in sweat and had dug a deep hole in the ground, where nothing would grow for a while. Scorched earth. He would leave it to air out before deciding what to plant in it.

He still needed to prune and pull out some weeds, but he'd run out of time. He put his tools away and went in to wash before going to Marina's.

There was a patent sadness in the way Jaime looked at the flat – the new pictures in which he was no longer present, the plants on the balcony with lots of pots where the calm green of the leaves contrasted with the intense colours of the flowers, the new arrangement of the furniture, with the highchair in between the chairs at the table, the sofa where they'd made love so many times – as if he were suddenly discovering that it was a good place to live, but he had been locked out for ever. For a moment his face registered the kind of regret an exile feels when he understands the intensity of his longing and, at the same time, the tenuousness of the reasons that made him leave in the first place.

'Have you got any diapers at home?' Marina asked from the children's bedroom.

'Yes,' he lied.

'You sure?'

'Throw in a couple just in case.'

He went to the room and saw her filling the travel bag with clothes, diapers, bibs and several toys. How easily she packed everything, how decisively she chose the right garment, whereas he, when he had the children every other weekend, had to gauge, calculate, go over what they needed, only to realise that he was always missing something essential.

'Well, that's it,' she exclaimed, doing up the zip. 'I don't think I've forgotten anything.'

The children were in the living room, and Jaime thought this was a good moment to broach the subject.

'I got a letter from the bank this morning. About the investment fund.'

Marina listened without much interest. She had received it too, being the joint account holder. But she had hardly paid it any attention; there had been another, upsetting letter that day.

'And what does it say?'

'It offers two possibilities.'

'Which ones?' she asked impatiently. She suddenly remembered her father and feared that his predictions about Jaime would come true. Perhaps he was mean by nature, and not even she could alter his character.

'One. It can be renewed for another three years, on the same conditions. Two. We can get the money now, along with the interest.'

He'd said it. The plural could not be a simple slip of the tongue, as they'd been separated too long for it to be a speech habit.

'*We* can?' she asked while folding some clothes, avoiding his eyes, as she could no longer look at him. 'But that's not your money, Jaime,' she said, ashamed of having to say it, of proving her father right.

'Legally it is. It says so in the letter.'

'But it's not about what the bank says, but what we say. You know that money … I don't want to argue about it. It's very unpleasant,' she said, refusing to continue.

'No arguing,' he accepted. 'But we need to clarify it.'

'Fine. You know that that money is not a joint asset. It was my father's and he put it in my name when he was sent to Afghanistan. Just in case.'

'But back then we were married, and so …'

'Of course we were married! But that doesn't change anything, Jaime, not a thing. That money is my father's business and mine. I never would have thought of claiming half of any inheritance money of yours.'

She hesitated for a moment, almost telling him that her father had anticipated his reaction and, a few hours before his death, had made her sign some papers that never made it to the bank, in which case they would not be having this unpleasant conversation.

'I'm not claiming it for myself! It's for the children. I'd like to open a branch in Valencia and, in the long run, they will benefit from that.'

Marina had not expected such a reply and looked at him as if she didn't recognise him. Starting at his mouth, the anxiety was spreading over his whole face, which when he got angry became ugly and looked older, contrasting with his athletic, youthful body. The angel turned into a vulgar, irate, miserable mortal. In spite of the financial reasons he put forward, she suspected his problem was not so much greed as bitter spite born out of jealousy: perhaps he suspected that the money would make things easier for everyone including Samuel, or he imagined that the children would associate the trips, gifts and little luxuries with the appearance of the man who had replaced him. 'That's what it is,' she told herself. 'His resistance to let go of the place he once belonged to; his absence from the pictures of birthdays and anniversaries, which will now be counted back up from zero; his absence, too, from that bed in which, if he hasn't lied to me, at one point he was happy.' So she wasn't surprised at the turn the conversation took.

'Did you ever really love me?'

It was the first time she'd heard him say that. Jaime had asked the question as if he'd suddenly realised the feeling existed, as if everything that had been spoken of in those terms had been a lie. He then took his fingers to his eyes and seemed to look in astonishment at their wet tips, as if he'd never cried and suddenly wondered what that moisture in his eyes was.

'Yes, I did,' she replied.

'And do you think you'd be able to again?' he said after a few seconds.

'I don't think so.'

'Not even if I told you that ... not even if I assured you that ... if I swore to you that never again ...'

'No, Jaime,' she interrupted, unwilling to listen to him any longer, and refusing him the manipulations of nostalgia. No, he was like a kid who's not funny any more. She'd heard enough, and his desire to be absolved struck her as artificial and sentimental. There was nothing for her to forgive, because the past no longer hurt her. She only wanted him to leave, and leave her alone in the knowledge that there comes a time when a man and woman can no longer live together, and not even children, compassion, or the most profound religious conviction about sacred vows can remedy the sad failure. Besides, she doubted his sincerity. He'd lied so many times he was no longer trustworthy.

Jaime must have noticed her impatience and the way she avoided his eyes, because he got up from his chair and picked up the bag. In the living room the children were playing with an electronic gadget that made strange clicking noises. He put the baby in the stroller, picked up the elder one and opened the door. On entering the lift, as if choosing that moment not to give her the chance to reply, he turned round and said:

'I'll think about the fund. I'll let you know my decision.'

Marina went back in and lay down on the sofa. Without the children, the house felt strangely silent, empty, hollow. She was very tired of all the conflicts surrounding her father's death: her own inability to explain it to her elder son when he asked about his grandfather; the depressive indifference Gabriela had sunk into; Jaime's attitude, halfway between complaint and threat; the tense expectations about the conclusions of the detective's investigation; the fear that someone might threaten her at her door or leave another evil, dirty note in her letterbox. Samuel was about to arrive, but she would have preferred not to see him, however kind and calming he always was. If she could, if she were brave enough, she'd go away for a few days on her own, without the children. She'd travel somewhere in the north, in a cold, arid landscape, where no one would know her, and where they spoke a language in which she couldn't communicate.

The bell rang, surprising her. Samuel had keys, and anyone else would have rung the intercom first. She got up and noiselessly approached the door. Through the peephole she saw a stranger and Samuel, who was about to put his key in the lock. She opened first and looked at them wonderingly, until she understood it was all a coincidence. The man was coming to see her, he'd entered by chance behind Samuel and had rung the bell right before Samuel got his keys out. And then she recognised him: he was the police inspector who, along with the judge, had told her that her father's death had been a suicide. There, in the corridor, the man looked greyer and blander than at the station: the kind of person that never gets noticed, of medium height and medium build, and so entrenched in middle age that she couldn't tell if he was nearer thirty or fifty.

'Marina Olmedo?' he said.

'Yes.'

'I hope you remember me. Inspector Mejías,' he said as he showed her the badge in his leather wallet.

'Yes, I remember you. Is anything wrong?'

'Nothing important, don't worry,' he clarified. 'Just a small detail we need to tell you about. It'll only take a few minutes of your time.'

'Come in.'

She let him in and then gestured towards Samuel, who seemed as surprised as she was. The inspector accepted a chair, but before speaking he cast a glance towards Samuel. Marina told him who he was.

'This morning someone paid us a visit at the station,' he explained, using a plural that somehow seemed to refer only to himself. 'Something to do with your father.'

'What?' she asked anxiously.

'Don't worry. It's nothing that might affect what the judge wrote down in the file. The owner of a jewellery shop came to show us his commissions, and to give us a wedding ring.'

The inspector took a small velvet-covered case out of his jacket.

'Here,' he said, opening it with great care, as if fearing that he might drop its contents on the floor.

The ring was sitting in a groove in the box; it was gold, simple, perfect, with no adornment or stone to distort the purity of the metal. It reflected the light from the lamp and shone disturbingly.

'Your father bought it. We've checked his signature. He paid cash. We thought we should bring it to you as soon as possible.'

'But why was it still at the jeweller's?'

'Your father bought it the day of his death, in the early afternoon. When you purchase a ring of this sort, you have the option of having something engraved on the inside at no extra cost. We've spoken to the employee who served him, and she remembers that when she suggested it, your father hesitated, not knowing what to answer just then. He asked her to wait till the following day, when he'd phone with a decision. The employee put the ring aside, but the call was never made. And then the owner, going through his books, recognised your father's name. He didn't know who to contact and called us to tell us what had happened. And to give us the ring.'

The policeman left the case on the table and pushed it towards Marina before brusquely sitting back in his chair, which seemed to imply that his business with her was concluded.

Marina picked up the case, took out the ring and studied it carefully, as if she might guess from its weight, style and material, the intensity of her father's feelings. She thought of the finger it was destined for.

'So my father had doubts about engraving her name,' she said, still unable to identify what that might mean.

'But that doesn't change anything,' the inspector said. 'Of course, we consulted with the judge before coming here. It doesn't either eliminate or confirm any theories,' he added tactfully, avoiding any words that might suggest a form of death. He took out of the pocket of his jacket a pen and a receipt for the jewel and slid them towards Marina.

'Please, if you could sign here.'

With her left hand, almost without looking, she drew a quick flourish at the bottom of the piece of paper.

When the inspector left, both remained silent, looking at the ring she'd put back in its case, on the table.

'You should tell Gabriela,' he suggested.

'Gabriela?' she asked, lost in thought. Then she looked at the chair where the policeman had sat.

'Who else?' he replied kindly, trying to take things easy. 'You know how much he loved her. He must have bought this as a gift to make their relationship official. And maybe he wanted to know whether she agreed with him before having her name engraved on it. Gabriela can be so hesitant, so complicated.'

'So, if she didn't …'

'You mean if she didn't agree? If her "no" pushed him to a decision? That might explain what we don't understand,' he dared suggest.

'I don't know, Samuel, I don't know what to think.' She shook her head, and pressed her eyes with the tips of her index and ring fingers. 'If my father had asked her formally and she had refused, she would have told me straight away. But then, if she didn't, and now thinks her refusal may have influenced him …'

'She wouldn't say it. Maybe she wouldn't say it,' qualified Samuel.

'I don't know, I really don't,' she repeated. 'I'm so confused, so tired of all this. I just want it to end. A few days ago I wanted above all, to find out the truth, what happened there in my father's study. But not anymore. I'm not strong enough to deal with all this anxiety. And if it means that in order to live in peace, without cops knocking on my door, without suspecting that people I care about may be keeping things from me, without anonymous, nasty notes in my letter box, that I have to do without finding out the truth, then I'll accept that.'

She had started crying quietly, without sobbing. Two slow, fat, difficult tears ran from her eyes to her chin before she took out a handkerchief to wipe them away. Samuel had never seen her cry and felt strangely moved. He could never tell why, but he'd come across women whose crying irritated him with its ease, its slight credibility, and others whose tears moved him to the point that he would do anything to prevent them. It was the same result, but some tears seem born of sorrow and others of some kind of slyness.

'What's that about anonymous notes? Did you get one?'

'This morning.'

She went to the bedroom and came back with a letter which she placed on the table, near the case containing the ring. Samuel leaned over it, not daring to touch it.

'Open it, don't worry, I've touched it a dozen times. If it had any fingerprints, they're probably useless by now, ruined by mine. But then whoever wrote it, whoever was miserable enough to write and send such a letter, must have thought of a way of doing it without leaving any traces.'

Samuel picked up the white envelope with two fingers and looked at it carefully before opening it and reading the message:

HOW DOES IT FEAL NOW YOU SON OF A BITCH?
WHO ARE YOU GIVING ORDERS TO?
WHO ARE YOU GOING TO ARREST IN HELL?

'When I collected the mail, I found that envelope among the other letters, no sender's name, nothing but the address and Olmedo in capitals. I opened it first; I don't know why I thought it might be important. Inside there was only that page, in those big letters, as if to make sure that no one missed the point. I had to lean on the wall for support and I dropped the other letters. I gathered them together and came up, sat down and put the letter in front of me, trying to think. If I tear it into a thousand pieces, I thought, maybe I'll be able to forget it. '"How does it feal now you son of a bitch? Who are you giving orders to? Who are you going to arrest in hell?"' She repeated the lines in a voice that didn't sound like her own, rather a hoarse sound that filled the room with the hatred of someone else's words. 'But I didn't dare. The envelope or the page, I thought, might have a print or give us a clue as to who could have sent it and from where. I don't know why, but when I thought about all that, I didn't think of turning it over to the police but to the detective, Cupido, as if he'd be able to reach better conclusions, although I'm sure he doesn't have the equipment or a lab for that kind of thing. Maybe because I thought that what mattered was not the fingerprints but the intention, and that he'd get it at once and would guess the identity of the author. Because whoever planned this, whoever chose and wrote the words, wanted to hurt *me*, not my dead father. Me! That's why there wasn't a name on the envelope, but just a surname, Olmedo, and although the questions are addressed to him, I'm the one that's supposed to be reading them. They want to hurt me with this letter.'

'It doesn't matter. An anonymous note!' said Samuel. 'There's plenty of people who have nothing better to do! This ...' He leaned forward to read the unfolded page, but didn't touch it. 'The third question suggests it may have been a recruit, or in any case a subordinate your father must have arrested at some point. Someone who thinks that he's getting his revenge by writing this. Really, don't worry about it,' he insisted, calm and musingly, searching for more convincing words. Then, as if he'd suddenly found them, he added: 'Someone who doesn't regard the pain of a violent death as punishment enough. You can't let someone like that influence your acts or your decisions.'

'That's why I didn't show the note to the policeman a few minutes ago. He would only have asked me lots of questions only to reach a similar conclusion.'

'And the detective? Are you going to show it to him?'

'Not him, either.'

'You sure?'

'No, I'm not,' she said after a few seconds. 'I only want this to end. Besides, I find him quite puzzling.'

'Cupido?'

'Yes. Whenever I'm talking to him, when he's in front of me, I feel I can trust him. And yet, today I've been having doubts.'

'Why?'

'His job. What kind of person do you have to be to become a private detective? What happened to him that he chose such a profession?'

'I don't know. It used to be said they were all ex cops ... fired from their jobs because of drinking problems.'

'I can't imagine him drinking. His assistant, perhaps. But I can't imagine him making a spectacle of himself, as drunk men do. On the contrary, I'd say he hides things from others, doesn't want to be known.'

Marina got another tissue and blew her nose. Samuel went to sit next to her and hold her. He closed his eyes when Marina nestled her head on his chest, calmer now, and said in a low voice:

'I don't want to go on with all this, Samuel. I know I am beholden to the memory of my father, and, if I were one of those tragic heroines, I would not rest until I settled this. But I'm not that strong and I need to rest. Because I have other obligations too: towards my children's happiness, towards myself, towards you,' she added after a brief pause.

Samuel listened in silence, but held her a little tighter. It was the first time she'd included him among her priorities. Not only did she accept him as someone kind, good and uncomplicated, she also valued him enough to be able to make an effort for him, even sacrifices if it came to that.

They were alone in the flat, without the children or anyone that might stop them from giving and receiving consolation and oblivion, and escaping from all that hurts. They kissed and caressed in silence, and a little later went into the bedroom. They didn't turn the lights on, instead they opened the blinds to let the spring air in along with the gleam of the city and the Saturday-night enthusiasm of some adolescent voices who trusted their wishes would be fulfilled. But the walls protected their intimacy, their nakedness, in the warm semi-darkness of the room. Samuel thought that right then they were like two pearls inside one shell, sheltered inside a wet, sweet darkness. They didn't need anyone else. He only feared that the greedy, callused hand of a fisherman, armed with a knife, might come and disturb their well-being.

They made love tenderly. Later, Samuel went on tracing his fingers along her back, still surprised that desire and its satisfaction had fitted so perfectly. Marina stirred a bit and then she lay on her side, with her back turned to him, while he caressed her buttocks, one fuller than the other because of her position, with a feeling of plenitude.

11

Cycling

Cupido arrived at the house at eleven in the morning, as arranged with Marina on the phone the previous day. She'd said she had something important to discuss, and the detective imagined she was referring to delicate news of the kind that shouldn't be divulged on the phone. He had not expected to hear what she was now saying:

'I don't want you to go on with the investigation.'

'May I ask why?'

'It's not you. I've no complaints about your work, and I don't think anyone else could have done it any better. It's not that. I'll pay you for your time and expenses so far. I'm sorry if you had to turn down other cases to take this one. If I have to compensate you, I'll do that too.'

She talked with stubborn firmness, and Cupido knew that nothing he said would alter her decision. He wouldn't insist. People hired him to find things out – although once he had been hired to not find out something – because that was what he had to offer: his efficiency, perhaps his talent, to solve mysteries. If someone changed their mind, well, all he could do was go back the way he'd come.

'Why do you want me to stop, then?' he asked, neither insistently nor impatiently, just out of curiosity.

Marina hesitated and then picked up an envelope from the table and handed it over, unopened.

'Read it.'

The detective studied the lines written in capitals, no return address, a sheet of paper like a million others, the typeface an Arial 20 font that any printer could turn out, the ink injected on the paper like poison in a vein, and those three hatred-filled phrases with a spelling mistake.

'An anonymous letter,' she said. 'I don't think it's very important. It's so easy to send something like that!'

Marina started telling him the reasons for her decision. It wasn't just the letter, but also the visit of the policeman who'd given her the ring which her father had bought and on which he had not had time to engrave Gabriela's name. She would pass it on to her, as that was what her father would have wanted, but she wouldn't ask her any questions as to whether he'd proposed and she'd rejected him; or whether anything had happened between them that might have pushed her father to kill himself. Gabriela had been through enough with the death of her son not to have to suffer further with that of Camilo.

Marina talked with downcast eyes. She would glance at him every few seconds, but her gaze returned to the table, the letter and the case containing the ring; it appeared as if she had nowhere else to put them in the flat and they had to remain there until someone came along to take them away or destroy them.

'And Jaime!' she added unexpectedly. 'He came to see me. He wants part of my father's money, from the fund I told you about.'

She raised her eyes and looked directly at Cupido, breathing with difficulty, as if the words she'd uttered were nails sunk in a piece of wood and she'd had to extract them one by one to form sentences. Then, speaking slowly, she said:

'It's all too much. I rushed to believe what no one believed. But my father does not need to be avenged by a doubtful, tormented orphan, because, no matter what I thought at first, he wasn't poisoned in his sleep. It just can't be that everyone is wrong when they advise me to forget and I'm the only one who's right. I give up,' she said.

Cupido understood her reasons, her weakness, her mistake in

underestimating the pressure she'd be exposing herself to by hiring him. But when he said goodbye he still wondered whether something else might have happened which Marina hadn't mentioned. There might be new information behind such a sudden change of heart, or a suspicion that pushed her to lie and call weariness what was in fact fear.

Disconcerted by the sudden cessation of the intense physical and mental activity that any investigation demanded, he went back to his flat, ate something, put on sports clothes and walked over to Olmedo's place. He hadn't returned the bunch of keys to Marina yet, and he was able to access the garage using the remote control. He was no longer employed, but he told himself that surely Marina wouldn't mind if he used her father's bike just once. He took it down from the hook and adjusted the seat to his height. The tyres had the right pressure, and everything was in perfect working order. It was a sober, efficient model, just like its owner had been, without fancy handlebars or any of the latest features.

Out in the street, he pedalled towards the city centre. Ten minutes later, after crossing a bridge over some rail tracks that fanned out in the direction of the station, he took the old small road that led out of town towards the west: the same one Ucha had been driving along on the evening of Olmedo's death.

He shifted to the highest gear and, ready for a workout, stood on the pedals and picked up pace. It was a splendid day – clear, windless. Up in the blue sky hung some shreds of harmless, clean clouds, and a few birds flew by slowly and peacefully. The narrow road wound its way parallel to a brook on whose banks a group of poplars watched over the narrow stream. Beyond extended fields of orange and lemon trees, small orchards, and a few hillsides planted with cereal where poppies grew taller than ears of wheat. And then, twelve or thirteen kilometres further down, rose the steep sierras that did so little for the good of the region, preventing the humidity of the sea from reaching inland and so creating a hot, dry, harsh interior, where fire was prone to break out. He knew that without the adequate training he wouldn't be able to climb any hard incline. He'd barely cycled in the last few months and felt heavy, fat, with toneless muscles – characteristic of the amateur cyclist he'd once been. He looked at the sunflowers and thought of the times when he was so used to pedalling uphill that no mountain looked difficult enough, provided he had a few hours to tackle it at the right pace. Back then, he cycled three thousand kilometres every year, and his legs felt as hard as his bike. And when he'd pedalled on level ground using the large chainring and the small cog he felt as wild horses must feel when galloping on the prairies.

He hadn't heard a thing when, all of a sudden, he saw a slim silent form appear beside him, to his left. He swerved towards the hard shoulder, almost off the asphalt, in surprise. Another cyclist apologised for having startled him and overtook him with strength and ease. The man was soon two hundred metres ahead, and Cupido decided to try and keep up with him from a distance.

He held on for fifteen or twenty minutes, using the big chainring, but slowed down as the road became steeper, for fear of finding himself exhausted, in the middle of nowhere. Now and again cars and large lorries drove by, taking the bends on the outer side of the road, their engines reverberating, but he wasn't scared. He was enjoying the swish of the warm tyres and wasn't in a hurry to get anywhere.

Then, pedalling slowly, he grew oblivious to the physical effort and went over the information he had gathered so far. 'In fact,' he told himself, 'I know nothing of what happened that evening, I haven't been able to offer Marina any piece of information or clue that might encourage her not to give up.' From what he'd learned about Olmedo's character, he too refused to believe he'd committed suicide. Gabriela's hypothetical rejection didn't seem reason enough. Olmedo was one of those men who see difficulties as challenges. But what about that note in his own hand with so clear a message? *Forgive me*. It was confusing, inexplicable. If, for whatever reason, he had been shot in his own house after he'd let someone in, it had to be someone he knew.

He went over the names and placed their faces next to Olmedo's, hoping that from that visual contrast an image might come to light that words and conversations had missed, an indication of a lie, a revelation that was so obvious that he had initially overlooked it. He discarded Samuel, who'd been with Gabriela on that evening. But there were others who'd had the chance to approach the house and had said they'd been either alone or with someone that would back up their lies.

He thought of Lesmes Beltrán, of his tired eyes on coming back from the operating theatre, his smell of tobacco and anaesthetics, the unconcealed, untempered hatred he had for Olmedo, the satisfaction he'd derived from his death. He thought of Jaime and his disdain for his ex-wife's father, whom he blamed for the failure of his marriage, the airs of winged horse he gave himself, as if Olmedo had tried to tie him to an earthly yoke. He thought of Castroviejo, and wondered whether scorn decreases with the passage of time, as do strength, health, memory, ambition and the intensity of love, or whether the old colonel held Olmedo in such contempt as to shoot him when he had the chance, because he had written that pernicious report that brought down what he had striven to build. He thought of Ucha, driving alone along the same narrow, silent road on which he was now pedalling, and he was not free of suspicion either: on the contrary, Cupido found it easy to picture him pointing a gun at the major's chest, with a dark desire to get even over an offence that seemed to go beyond his professional life. He thought of Bramante, picturing him strong and solid, full of muscles, sweating, panting after some athletic exercise or perhaps a tough march, sitting on a barricade with a Cetme between his legs while he waited for the others to catch up, hiding under his vigour and boastful bravery an ambiguous insecurity. Or perhaps you shouldn't call it bravery. Looking back, Cupido noticed how much his idea of courageous acts had changed: it used to mean a violent adolescent fight against someone stronger than yourself, or participation in political demonstrations during the transition to democracy against a brutal police. Now, however, actions that he would have previously considered pusillanimous seemed to him unquestionably courageous.

The meter registered thirty-six kilometres and eighty minutes when he turned around and started on his return. He'd missed one person, Gabriela, and he realised he knew next to nothing about her: he hadn't talked to her, didn't even know what she looked like. From the start he had considered her a collateral victim of the death, someone close to Marina and impervious to suspicion because of Samuel's alibi. No one questioned that Olmedo had bought the ring for her, even if he hadn't decided to engrave it with her name when he bought it. What did he need to confirm? What doubts did he have? He definitely had to talk to her and fill in that blank he'd left unexamined. Perhaps Olmedo had revealed things to her, projects or feelings of the kind one might discuss with a partner but not necessarily with a daughter.

The death of Olmedo was still a mystery, and the detective was by nature allergic to unsolved mysteries. They haunted him. He decided that, even if no longer officially on that case, he'd do one last thing: talk to Gabriela. If after that he didn't see more clearly, he would abandon the investigation for good, even if new leads – the ring, Jaime's claim on the money, the anonymous letter – had turned up that morning.

It was often like that. An investigation stopped at a dead end; he didn't see a way to proceed and then, all of a sudden, he encountered a barrage of information he needed to analyse. Too bad it had arrived so late, when Marina had decided not to go on.

He entered the city but didn't return to the garage straight away. He drank some water from a spring in a park and washed his hands and face. Then he got back on the bike and pedalled very slowly to Marina and Samuel's neighbourhood. He studied the broad, silent streets, with large trees on the pavements, a few blocks dotted with three-storey buildings, then mostly detached houses. It was half past six and the few passers-by he saw didn't look hurried, were not running errands or rushing to the shops before they closed. Not even the vehicles sped by as in the crowded main roads of the centre, as there were no traffic lights here, and thus none of the anxiety they engendered. A few speed bumps did all the work. It was a pleasant neighbourhood – although the same could not be said of all of its inhabitants – with large, silent, detached houses, which cost a lot to acquire and to maintain; they had several lamps on the external walls, signs stating they were protected by private alarm companies, and motion sensors which triggered lights when anyone walked by. Behind the iron fences set up on top of low walls were hedges and saplings, and behind those it wasn't difficult to imagine someone looking at him – he who was openly prying around as he pedalled slowly – entrenched between four walls, protected by alarms or dogs like the one that had killed Gabriela's son.

Cupido pictured the kind of people living there: a slightly pretentious middle class, so used to comfort, security and consumerism that they would get anxious if, of a morning, they didn't find at least three menu options in their capacious fridges. An urban middle class, well adapted to their times, who regarded the past century as deep in the past, who had barely any recollections of the countryside, the fields which seemed to them an exotic place one could never return to. A satisfied middle class, not necessarily conservative, for whom luxury did not consist of jewels, dresses, aristocratic circles, owning land, founding big companies, or consolidating lineages of prestigious surnames whose scions achieved more than the parents, but a sceptical, well-meaning middle class who often had children rather late in life and did not expect them to be heroes or landowners or millionaires or geniuses, but were concerned only with their well-being, people who were happy for their children to have a professional future like their own present, untouched by uncertainty, conflicts and global instability.

Soon afterwards he cycled off to Olmedo's house. He stopped at the garage gate and, as he fumbled in his pocket for the remote, he saw a man looking at him intently and with suspicion. He was wearing grey and green overalls with the logo of a cleaning company and was leaning on a wide brush which he used to sweep the dirt off the pavement before scooping it up into a small bin on wheels. Judging from his attitude, he seemed to have recognised Olmedo's bike and must be wondering who it was that was using it after his death.

Cupido took a few steps towards him.

'Do you usually work in this street?' he asked the man.

'In the neighbourhood,' the other replied, studying the bike.

'Yes, it's Camilo Olmedo's. His daughter, Marina, hired me to investigate his death,' explained Cupido, avoiding any lies. 'Did you know the major?' he asked, although he knew the answer. In his first interview with Marina, she had told him that Olmedo's cleaning lady was the wife of the neighbourhood road sweeper. He remembered his name: Rosco.

'Yes, I often bumped into him in the morning, when he left for work. And in the afternoon, when he came back.'

'Long hours,' observed the detective.

'Hours? I haven't got working hours, I have streets to sweep. And these trees,' he said, disdainfully pointing upwards, towards the plane trees whose branches stretched out over the street lamps, 'never stop shedding dirt.'

'The major,' insisted Cupido, 'died two weeks ago.'

'Yes.'

'It was a Monday. Were you at work on that evening?'

'Morning and evening.'

'Do you remember seeing anything out of the ordinary, or someone who asked for Olmedo or visited him?'

'What do you mean, out of the ordinary?' He looked to the ground, at his pile of dirt, as if he was considering picking it up in order to avoid further questions. 'Why should I remember?'

'Because few people are better placed than yourself to know who is from the neighbourhood and who isn't. Perhaps those who aren't regard the street as not theirs, and throw more litter.'

Rosco looked at him in silence, pensive, as if the detective was asking questions at greater speed than he could keep track of.

'The ones from here are no better,' he said. 'Some people seem to be waiting to go out to spit their gum, throw cigarette butts or tear any piece of paper into a thousand smaller pieces.'

'That evening someone visited the major. When his daughter rang him, he said he'd talk to her later, because at that moment he was with someone. But he never did ring her.'

The road sweeper started shaking his head even before hearing the last words. He shrugged his shoulders and pursed his lips quickly, signalling that he knew nothing. Then, seeing that the detective was still waiting for an answer, wiped the sweat off his forehead with his forearm and looked away.

'I'm not saying no one came round. Just that I didn't see anyone. No one asked me about him.'

'I understand. A lot of people come and go round here.'

The detective pressed the button of the remote control and waited for the garage to open. Rosco turned his back on him and picked up the dirt with quick, deft movements of the brush, his gaze fixed on the ground, as if he meant to imply that in the posture demanded by his job there wasn't much he could notice in his surroundings. Cupido wheeled the bike in. He hung it on its hook and took one last look at the car, the tyres and the tools. He had the impression that the road sweeper had seen something, but knew it would be pointless to insist, given his stubborn suspicions. And he had no authority to lean on the man. All he had left was Gabriela, and a few questions that perhaps she could not help answering: who was she, who was Olmedo, and where were they headed before, all of a sudden, the major was stopped in his tracks.

12

Gabriela's Height

When Cupido rang her up early the following morning, Gabriela agreed to see him an hour later, no doubt because Marina had not yet spoken to her. Her voice, at the other end of the line, betrayed the slowness and tiredness of someone who's been suddenly awakened after a bad night. The detective felt awkward, as if there were something indecent in hearing her first words of the day while imagining the person uttering them: a woman still in bed, wrapped up in the warmth of the sheets, perhaps delicately wiping her eye with her index finger, unaware of how long she'd slept.

He let an hour go by and went to her place, which turned out to be a medium-sized flat, full of objects and adornments, lamps, clocks, paintings, rugs, heavy furniture and chairs which no one seemed to sit on, placed in strange spots. It was a flat marooned in a time that admitted no alteration, a house cumulatively decorated with remnants of the past and memories, and enough clutter to make anyone feel uncomfortable in it. With the blinds almost down, it seemed not so much a home as a hideout, and put the visitor on the alert: in the semi-darkness, one couldn't walk without bumping into this or that.

A greenish rug, wide as a prairie, was spread out under the table, the armchairs and the sofa where he was invited to sit as Gabriela raised one of the blinds a few centimetres. In better light, Cupido noticed that the dead child's face appeared everywhere; his pictures seemed to have been taken from family albums and put in frames to catch the viewer's eye from any direction. It was impossible not to find his face frozen in the most varied expressions, not always of joy.

Gabriela took a few seconds to sit down, as if she were expecting a few questions or doubted whether she should offer him anything. She was quite tall, though her almost six-foot frame did not give an impression of strength, power, or arrogance. On the contrary, her height intensified her still attractive and fragile femininity. Under her light blonde hair she had that sad, puzzled gaze characteristic of beautiful women who reach maturity without achieving happiness. But her tempered beauty was still there, in the graceful movements of her body, and in her face, despite the fine wrinkles on her skin, the M engraved in the space between her eyebrows, and her slightly low eyelids, which looked sleepy or weighed down by invisible tears. No wonder Olmedo had fallen in love with her: a strong man would be moved by her air of vulnerability.

When she crossed her hands, Cupido recognised the ring Marina had shown him the previous day. She had put it where she would have done if Olmedo were still alive. She's surrounded by the dead, thought Cupido with a shudder. But he saw what that meant: if she had the ring it was because Marina had spoken to her and, in that case, she must know he was no longer hired to go on investigating.

'She gave it to me last night,' she explained, seeing his eyes. 'She asked me to take it. It was the gift her father had meant to give me. What's left of Camilo to remember him by.'

The ring looked the right size. Olmedo had calculated well the width of her fingers, thin and long like her body. She was turning it around and around with her other hand, as if it burned her skin.

'Marina also told me that she didn't want you to go on investigating, that she accepts her father's death was suicide. But I don't mind talking to you. On the contrary, sometimes I'm surprised at how much I like talking about them,' she said, including among the dead, with an unequivocal look, the boy smiling in a picture on a small table by the sofa. 'My friends, the few friends I have left, insist that I should not think about them so much, that I need to forget them and find consolation in other things, go out more, talk to people, read, listen to music instead of staying in here on my own ... But then, others expect me not to go out, to be in mourning, because they think it's the appropriate thing to do, and would be scandalised if I went around having fun ... Fun! As if that were possible! As if you could smile when you're torn inside! I know what suffering is,' she added with the plangent pride of those who regard pain as their prerogative. 'I don't want to forget them. I like to remember the dead, it's the only thing I can do for them. For Camilo, and above all for my son Manuel.'

'What happened to him?'

'He was killed by a dog,' she said calmly, in a low voice.

'It sounds unbelievable,' commented Cupido.

'Doesn't it? You hear a fifteen-year-old has died and you think of a traffic accident, or of a terminal illness. But you don't think another living creature could have killed him. It was a pit bull. A beast.'

'I know those dogs,' said Cupido, who remembered an acquaintance who had a couple of them guarding a warehouse. Two quiet, discreet animals, tame when with their master but prone to biting. They'd been bred to bite, and locked their jaws until their teeth pierced through the flesh they'd bitten.

'I don't know how anyone can keep them,' said Gabriela. 'I wonder whether when you buy a dog of that breed you don't half think that one day you'll use it. It's like someone who buys a gun. They might say they appreciate it as an object, and are amused to shoot bottles on top of a rock. But deep down they never forget that they have it and that, if it should be necessary, they'll be able to use it.'

Cupido nodded gently. Most of the dogs he'd come across were harmless animals, loyal, charming and affectionate, even too affectionate in their way of slobbering over any stranger who patted them on the head and dirtying their jackets with their paws. But there were also cold-eyed, evil dogs, with big jaws ready to bite, dogs that did not look like dogs but like mutant wolves, bulls or hyenas. Their owners sharpened their teeth for fights and trained them to endure suffering. Cupido didn't trust those breeds. When he was a child, dogs didn't live indoors. They were bred to shepherd cattle, hunt or help in some task or other. And they were also good to teach the kids of the countryside the facts of life, and show them that when one dog mounted another – he and his friends had sometimes interrupted them brutally – there were consequences a few months later: a mass of blind puppies in a basket. It was dangerous to approach the mothers protecting their litters, and the kids thought of their parents and felt safer knowing that, in case of danger, they'd be protected with as much fierceness. Dogs were good for things like that, not to be tended to, and cleaned and combed and dressed and taken to a psychologist or the dentist for their teeth to be brushed. Their work and company was valued, their loyalty and sacrifice too, but no one forgot they were a different species.

'They were coming back from a football match. They'd lost and were angry. You know teenagers. They think they're adults but are still children, and see games as a battle and defeat as failure. People told me later they were making a lot of noise in the neighbourhood, they were shouting and kicking the ball against the fences. When they reached that house, the dog spooked them with its barks, and instead of ignoring it they provoked it, made it so angry that the pit bull jumped over the fence and attacked them. There was no one in and the dog was very agitated. It caught my son and never let go. A few people went by and a couple of neighbours tried to calm it. Someone called the police, but by the time they arrived and shot the dog it was too late.'

Although her breathing was shallow, she'd spoken slowly, for the detective to follow her memories step by step; then she looked at him to confirm that he had not lagged behind somewhere along the difficult, stony road she was revisiting.

'My son was happy ... He shouldn't have died,' she added, as if that statement bore a logical relation to the previous one. 'I wasn't,

I was not happy at his age, and so I always made sure that he wasn't unhappy himself. I think children with an unhappy adolescence, kids that are not lucky to feel loved, admired, popular, later in life have a constant need of affection that makes them cling to anyone who might whisper a few sweet words in their ears, even someone unsuitable. But that wasn't Manuel's case,' she explained. Each time she uttered his name, her mouth shed some of its sadness, her brow relaxed and her face lightened. 'He was a bit of a rebel, but he was full of laughter, health, strength, curiosity. He'd just started seeing someone.'

'Was she there when …?'

'Violeta? No, no, only the boys. They'd been playing football.'

'And the owner of the dog? What's happened?'

'It all went to court and the judge ruled they were not guilty. The dog was inside the fence and the boys provoked it. I learned through my lawyer that they were devastated and offered to do anything they could for me. But what could they do? They could not bring back Manuel. They moved away. Now the house is for sale, but no one wants it. It's all locked up and the bushes have grown over the fence, which is beginning to rust over. Sometimes I walk by and I stop across the road and try to imagine how it all happened.'

Gabriela looked at the pictures again, and Cupido respected her silence. He tried to find a link between the death of the child and Olmedo's but couldn't think of anything except Gabriela herself. They hadn't even met. They belonged to different worlds: a military world with a rigid sense of duty, and that of a teenager interested in sports, girls, and no doubt in the latest technology. Both were alien to Cupido, but, more so than by the military, he was disconcerted by this generation of kids he saw in the street dressed in trainers without shoelaces and baggy clothes, who started having sex very early, and many of whom smoked, drank, and took pills, and some of whom were crippled after they crashed their motorcycles into walls at high speed. He wanted to know more about the boy, Manuel, to complete the picture. He remembered the name of the girl he'd dated, Violeta.

'Did you already know Olmedo when your son died?'

'No, not yet. I met him later.'

'How?'

'I went out with a friend one day and we bumped into Camilo in the street. She introduced us. The conversation went on and he invited us to have a coffee in a bar. From the beginning he was very kind to me, even more so when he learned how my child had died. He was a military man, but he found violence in any form repellent. And there had also been a tragedy in his family.'

'Yes, his wife had died after what should have been a simple procedure,' said Cupido.

'Because of negligence,' she corrected him. 'I think that fact moved him, and he offered to help me in anything I might need. I gave him my number and he called two days later. Then, well, we were both single and started going out. I didn't really want to, I didn't want to do anything, but he was patient and more persistent than me. He managed to help me overcome my suspicions.'

'Suspicions?'

'Not everybody spoke well of him,' she explained. 'When I got to know him I found it strange that he had a reputation as a tough, intransigent man, because he wasn't like that at all, at least with those he loved. There were rumours that he wanted to close down San Marcial and people said he did it out of personal ambition. Rumours, you know – idiots believe them, and rascals spread them even if they know they're not true. I didn't mind his reputation, but I didn't like his profession, as I'd never had anything to do with that milieu. I imagined that soldiers were always evaluating possible dangers from the outside and forgetting to take care of what's closest to them. And I thought them irascible. But I was surprised by Camilo's kindness, his good manners.'

'That reputation you mentioned, did he have any enemies who might think badly of him?'

'I guess he did, but I didn't know him well enough to be familiar with the details. He sometimes spoke of colleagues whom he had trouble with, but he was vague about it, I don't remember any names.' She paused for a few seconds and then added: 'Once … once he told me he had plenty of enemies. But neither did he worry about them nor was he willing to change in order to avoid them. He was one of those self-sufficient people who are dead set against political chicanery, who don't take refuge in group mentality, who don't grovel.'

'So would you say there were people who hated him?' he insisted, hoping a name would pop up.

'Of course there were. It's so easy for one person to hate another. We all know what no one wants to hear about themselves. It's enough to whisper in someone's ear something another has said, and there's hatred forever. It's that easy! Hatred is a plant that grows quickly and in every terrain, with barely any need for water and fertiliser. A very small seed is enough.'

'Did he tell you if he'd ever received any threats?'

'No, but he was always very careful. Always carried a gun, as if he was afraid he might be attacked.'

'Did Olmedo speak to you that evening? Did he ring you?'

'No, I was at home, on my own, until eight, and he didn't call. Neither did I. Then Samuel came round to help me re-pot some plants. Marina and I had been to his place in the morning to pick up a few.' She looked around as if trying to find them and pointed to a rubber plant at the end of the corridor by the door, and some green blurs on the balcony. 'Then we had some coffee and chatted till about nine.'

'And yet,' said Cupido, pointing to the ring on her finger, 'Olmedo told the people at the jewellery shop that he would confirm the following day whether they ought to engrave the ring. One might think he would have asked you if you would accept it.'

'What are you implying?'

'That if you had rejected him, it might be motive for what everyone believes happened.'

'Everyone?'

'Marina too. She seems to have accepted that her father killed himself, but she doesn't understand why.'

'Well, he didn't speak to me on that evening,' she repeated with a touch of defiance, rejecting the possible reproach in the detective's words. 'Camilo didn't kill himself because of me. You can tell everybody.'

'Would you have accepted?' asked Cupido in a calm voice.

'To have my name engraved?'

'And what something like that meant.'

'I think I would have,' she replied.

'From your knowledge of him, you don't seem to believe that he committed suicide.'

'But I do. Didn't he himself write that word asking her forgiveness?'

'Her forgiveness?'

'His daughter's, Marina's. She'd be the worst hit. She's the one who has the right to forgive him. Who are the rest of us to say what anyone can do with his life?'

Her reply was pregnant with something that made Cupido insist:

'Did you ever think he might do a thing like that?'

'Yes,' she replied, and seeing his surprised face she added: 'Is there anyone who hasn't thought of it at some point or another? Who hasn't, even for a few seconds, thought of disappearing, of ending everything? Haven't you?'

'No, never,' replied Cupido.

'Maybe because you've been happy,' she said, without malice or envy, but with a hard, rigid, resigned sadness, in a quiet voice, almost a whisper, as if seven months after the event she was still mourning her son's torn body. There she was, the mother of a dead child, the fiancée of a dead man, seemingly close to death herself.

Still, Cupido was disconcerted by her reply. Among the epithets that people who knew him might use to describe him, perhaps no one would have chosen the one Gabriela had just used. Lonely, compassionate, tenacious, loyal to a few friends, intelligent, odd at times, resigned most of them, tall, proud, yes, but happy? No, not happy. You're not happy just because you haven't considered the possibility of killing yourself; you're happy when you're terrified that death might come looking for you, he thought.

He said goodbye and left the house where Gabriela spent her time staring at the pictures of Manuel. The more painful the present, the more one thinks of the past as a paradise lost, he told himself, overcome with a mixture of compassion and disquiet. Coming into contact with other people's misery always caused in him a hard, uncomfortable melancholy; for a long time he'd been able to manage it, but now it weighed down on him.

He wasn't in the mood to go back to his flat, so he took a walk along the seafront, without noticing much, until he realised he'd walked to the outskirts, where the town turned into industrial depots and dirty warehouses, many of them without a sign to indicate their activity.

At the end of the pavement were six boys of fifteen or sixteen, roughly Manuel's age if he had lived, sitting on the parapet that separated the street from the rocks of the beach. Two of them had their hands flat on the cement and two others held magnifying glasses a few centimetres away from them, so that the rays of the April sun concentrated on a part of their hands. The game was to see who could endure the heat for longer. The two contestants made faces, gnashed their teeth and studied their adversary's reactions, calculating their own pain threshold, while the other ones egged them on:

'Hang in there!'

'Don't give up, come on!'

Cupido stopped to watch them and found himself rubbing his hands together as he imagined the burning sensation. He stared at their frenzied buffoonery, their shouts, the way they communicated with insults, shoves and loud laughter. He too had played rough games at their age, but now they seemed distant, and he would have thought no one engaged in this kind of thing anymore.

Many seconds went by until one of them, his face dotted with pimples as if a rain of fire had fallen on it, brusquely moved away his hand, spat on the burn and stepped off amidst mocking shouts and congratulations for the winner.

The detective walked back towards the town centre and, when he reached the beachfront, took off his shoes and proceeded along the almost depopulated sand. The weather was unpleasant, one of those April days that seem a leftover from winter and, like a trembling beggar dressed in rags, has come to crash the splendid party of spring. The sky was a mixture of blue patches and dirty-grey clouds of the kind that neither produce rain nor make the landscape attractive, but scud past, shapeless, frayed, unable to organise themselves into forms. Seagulls flitted about in the cold breeze. And above them, higher up, a bird of prey, an eagle or a hawk, tore across the grey mantle. A few rays of sunshine, piercing through the clouds, reached the waves and the sand where a few bathers awaited them. Most of these were foreigners visibly eager for sunshine – the women blonde, wide-shouldered, with long legs and narrow hips, the men Nordic types with light hair and pink skin, all fleeing the frozen-over, medieval winter of the Baltic.

When Marina had asked him to stop, Cupido told himself that his meeting with Gabriela would be his last if no new information came to light. They hadn't, but instead he had another name, Violeta, the girl who had dated Manuel. He quickened his step, hesitating, fighting back his desire to find out the truth. 'No one's paying you anymore,' he told himself. And yet, by the time he'd reached the town centre he'd decided he'd search for the girl and speak to her. After that, he would see.

He put his shoes on and walked to the home where his mother was staying. Although he'd talked to her on the phone, he hadn't been to see her since the beginning of the investigation. She would go back to Breda as soon as the summer season started and her present residence was turned into a hotel for holidaymakers.

When he went through the automatic doors he saw the doctor that supervised the patients' health, administered drugs, and often joked about how they were doing, saying he would like to have half the energy and spirit of many of the pensioners there. Cupido's mother usually spoke highly of him. He remembered the man's name was Fuentes; perhaps because he never wore a coat or a badge, he didn't look like a doctor at all. With his shabby clothes, his stubble, his smudged glasses which he surely wiped with his shirt, he looked in fact like a rural schoolteacher or a vet. His body was thinner than his face suggested, he had a deeply receding hairline with a few eternal hairs hanging onto his scalp, and seemed to find it so difficult to talk to strangers that one imagined him with only a few faithful friends sliding into lonely old age, provided sudden death didn't find him earlier, without anyone near him to shut his eyes. He had about him, in short, an air of calm acceptance which seemed born of past sadness.

'Good afternoon,' said Cupido.

'Good afternoon,' replied the doctor. He looked at him for a few seconds and then added. 'Your mother was on her way to her room. I passed her in the corridor.'

'How is she today?'

'Angry,' he replied with a mischievous smile.

'Why?'

'Because her time here is running out. She doesn't want to leave.'

'Which proves she's well looked after.'

'It's not us but the weather, the water, the leisure.'

Cupido couldn't help smiling about his mother's love of bathing ever since she'd started hydrotherapy after her hip accident.

'I'll have to find her another spa,' he joked.

'Let me warn you she's found it already.'

'She hasn't mentioned it to me.'

'On the internet,' the doctor added.

'On the internet? But she's never touched a computer.'

'Maybe she never had, until two weeks ago. As they have a lot of free time here, she signed up for a course and, well, she sits in front of the screen and doesn't let go of the mouse until her hour is up,' he said before shaking his hand and saying goodbye.

When Cupido went into her room, he was surprised to find her lying on the bed, as it was only half past twelve. He always thought of his parents on their feet, could barely call up an image of them lying down. As a child, when he awoke they were already up, and when he went to bed, they were still awake. Now, seeing her sit up with effort, he thought of the tiredness accumulated over the years and also of the threat of illness.

'Are you tired?'

'A little. I didn't sleep well last night.'

'Why?'

'I couldn't get yesterday's accident out of my head.'

'What happened?'

'Luis, one of the guests, was taken to hospital with a ruptured stomach. He'd been disorientated in the past, but nothing serious. Until yesterday. At siesta time he left his room and went to urinate – in the cleaning closet. Then he drank some detergent thinking it was water.'

'An accident,' said Cupido, as he thought of the inevitable mental decline, the misfiring connections in the brain which wipe out everything one has learned over a lifetime. 'He'll recover.'

'Yes, they got there in time.'

As the doctor had said, on top of the night table he saw several printouts from the internet on spas and thermal-water pro-grammes, with lists of treatments, dates and prices. There was also an application form.

'So,' he said to change the subject, 'you're thinking of checking into a spa for a few days?'

'I'll apply for it, but I don't think I'll get lucky. There isn't room for everyone. Can't you see the world is filling up with old people?'

'Then they won't take you,' he said with mock seriousness.

'No? Why?'

'Because you're not old yet.'

She smiled and waved her hand to indicate how long ago her youth had passed. Then she started talking about what she'd read on the internet about the benefits of thermal waters.

'It's not just the water but the heat, the iodine, the minerals and also the mud. I'm sure your father, who was such a good swimmer, would have loved it.'

He stayed a while with her, chatting about the spa, her fellow guests, Fuentes and the coming of summer, but his thoughts kept returning to the unsolved investigation.

'I think I'll stay for a few days,' he said.

'You do your job. I'll be fine at home. There are always people there.'

On his way out, Cupido looked about for the doctor to thank him, but Fuentes was nowhere to be seen. Cupido walked back home quickly and once there, tired and famished, he wolfed down a dish of rice and chicken that Alkalino had had delivered to the flat. Alkalino had already eaten half of it and was lying down on the sofa, reading Schopenhauer.

'I'll need your help once again,' said Cupido.

'You're still at it?'

'Yes.'

'I knew it. I knew you wouldn't give up, leave a job unfinished, even if they fired you. What should I do?'

'Seek out a girl. I only have a name.'

'Seek out a girl?' he asked, echoing Cupido's words as he always did when he found them strange or disconcerting. He shut the book and sat up on the sofa.

'She's sixteen.'

'Seek out a sixteen-year-old girl? Me? A guy who looks like a child molester?!' he exclaimed rubbing his thick stubble, which pierced through his skin and blackened his face as soon as he'd finished shaving.

'Indeed.'

'A guy that even women twice his age flee from?'

'That's what I'm asking. It's something you know how to do better than me.'

Alkalino breathed in, held it for a few seconds, and breathed out slowly through his half closed lips.

'Who is she?'

'The girlfriend, if that is the word, of Gabriela's son.'

'The dead lad's?'

'Yes.'

'Anything to do with Olmedo?'

'That's what I'd like to rule out.'

'What do you know about her?'

'Very little, almost nothing, as I say. Her name's Violeta. She's sixteen. She lives in this city.'

'Great,' he joked, standing up, 'the perfect job for me.'

13

Ashes

It was a consolation to think that she could end it at any time, that no one could take away from her that privilege. The decision was hers to make, and no one would be hurt if one day she swallowed a bottle of sleeping pills or disappeared in a violent way leaving behind no ashes or bones or dust, without releasing the nauseating smell that, in the course of a few days, infuses the flats of those who die alone. Everyone she'd loved had died, and she didn't care about the rest of the world. True, she was fond of a few friends, and of Marina, who was charming, and of Samuel, who was always in a good mood and said thank you to any kind gesture. She was sure they would be saddened by her death, but also that they would forget her before long. And so she could say that the world was as indifferent to her as she was to it.

She'd been defeated. Ever since her son's death, she had lost her strength, her will, her beauty. Her height, which she had always been proud of, seemed to have decreased a few centimetres, so often did she slouch and hang her head. Tragedy had tarnished the beautiful expressiveness of her face. Whenever she looked in the mirror now she saw, under that deep M engraved between her eyebrows, a pair of empty, watery eyes, a gaze that was vacant and contained nothing, not even the bitterness that might have given her the necessary will to live. During the first few days she couldn't quite understand what was happening to her, dazed by pain and the drugs she took to deaden it. She didn't remember, but they told her that, when they let her see the body, after they had disguised the damage done by the pit bull, she'd exclaimed: 'He's asleep! He looks so handsome!', unable to admit what had happened. She'd taken a few days to accept his death, like the small child who, when he falls and hurts himself, takes a few seconds to wonder what is that unknown sensation and, only on seeing blood, acknowledges the pain and bursts into inconsolable tears.

The dead had defeated her, and she often wondered whether it wouldn't be better to turn into a handful of ashes with them than to stay like a shadow among the living. Groggy from tranquilisers, she closed her eyes and imagined Manuel welcoming her with a calming smile and, a few seconds later, with the characteristic fickleness of his age, telling her off for taking so long. Behind him, over his shoulder, she could make out Camilo's face, ascetic, kind, compassionate, and he offered his hand while her son turned around to look at him in surprise, wondering who that man he'd never seen might be, perhaps the father he'd never had. In that place which was not Earth, which had neither corners nor rooms, but was not heaven either, everyone moved very slowly, gliding along and talking in low voices. Beside her, in silence, motionless, never touching each other, were shadows clearer and more compact than the bodies that generated them, alien to the drives, desires and dissatisfactions of the flesh.

She would then open her eyes and once again identify the darkness of the flat where she spent so much time on her own, bathing in the gazes of the photographs, their different expressions, while outside the clamour of the world seemed colder and more distant every day. Lost in remembrance, she went over memories, evoked her son at different ages, from the calculated moment of his conception with a passing man – she was not looking for love, or even pleasure, only his seed, that energetic, blind, untameable minute white fish – who never knew he'd been used for that purpose, until the moment of his death. After a while she returned to the present and discovered herself short of breath. Her mouth dry, she would stand to go get some water or a black coffee that she didn't even bother to warm up. She barely ate, lived on pain. It seemed pointless to spend two hours in the kitchen preparing a succulent dish that only she would taste. When she entered the bathroom, she passed with indifference the mirrors in which no one looked, and then returned to the living room, whiling away the hours of the Saturday and the Sunday until Monday rolled around with its routine, her job at the office offering a measure of solace and forgetting.

When she went back to work after her initial depression, they transferred her to a different department. At least she was no longer in customer services, did not strive to pretend she was alive when she was dead, that she had come through destruction unscathed when she was destroyed. Sitting in front of her computer screen, she confined herself to filling forms and updating files, pleased that it was others who gave information about laws, dealt with pleas or complaints and talked, thus allowing her to stay silent. Her new task was easy, but it required enough concentration for her not to have much time for other thoughts. Work finished at three and she went back home. It was as if she led two lives, one in the world, one outside; in one she didn't wish to talk to anyone, in the other she didn't have anyone to talk to; both were sad, but in the latter she found a certain voluptuousness in her sadness.

She got up from the armchair and turned on the light. The detective's smell was still in the air, a hint of shaving lotion or deodorant – something masculine, no doubt, though different from the smell Camilo left in her bed when he went off to work. The detective's questions had not made her ill at ease but, in a strange way, had calmed her, as if with his request for concrete answers he had made her come back to earth from her cloud of affliction. He had asked kindly, not nervously, as if he knew every one of them – Camilo, Marina, Samuel, herself – better than they knew themselves, and wished not so much to glean new information as to confirm the information he had. His calm, resolute manner reminded her of Olmedo, and now she wondered whether she shouldn't pull herself together, get her life back on track and put the ghosts to rest in a place where she could visit them but not live with them. Camilo, with his firmness and his conviction that life is always hard, but almost always endurable, had told her several times:

'Put it to one side, Gabriela. It doesn't mean that you'll forget him. It means you need your own space to live. He's always so present that I can feel him here between us. And that's not good for me, Gabriela, and neither is it for you. Especially not for you.'

The small urn where she kept his ashes was very light. She'd instantly decided to cremate him. Although the idea of a tomb and a granite gravestone with the words "I HAVE DIED. I ONLY LIVED FIFTEEN YEARS. REMEMBER ME" crossed her mind, she soon discarded that possibility, terrified to imagine the decomposing body. She took the urn with her back to the living room, put it on the table and sat down to think, telling herself that her decision would have nothing to do with the word oblivion. But she had to do something with the ashes if she wanted to shake herself out of the somnolent, morbid and depressive state she was in.

She had often wondered where she might scatter them, but had never found a place worthy of her son. One afternoon, she went out for a walk to the lighthouse at the end of the pier, where fishermen gathered with their rods. She looked at the horizon for a while and, when she was about to go back, saw a hundred or so people at the end of the pier walking in her direction. The sun had just set and the people, all dressed in dark clothes, were silhouetted against the yellowish glow of the twilight. With the water on both sides, they looked motionless for a minute or so, even though their feet moved towards the lighthouse. When they finally arrived, the fishermen, who had understood before she did, as if it wasn't the first time a thing like that had happened, reeled in their fishing lines, respectfully lowered their rods and laid them down on the huge rocks of the pier, in complete silence, as in one of those military parades in which soldiers surrender their spears as a general walks down the corridor they form. On stopping by the lighthouse, a woman separated herself from the cortège – some were crying and many had flowers in their hands – and walked to the edge of the last rock carrying a small blue ceramic urn.

'His sister,' whispered one of the fishermen.

She realised it was the funeral of the boy who had drowned nearby a few days before. The sister lifted the lid of the urn, tipped it forwards and, very slowly, poured its contents into the sea. The ashes floated for a few seconds. Then, as they began to sink, people threw flowers, whose intense reds, yellows and whites bobbed up and down in the waves while handkerchiefs wiped away tears.

A short silence was observed for anyone who so wished to say a prayer. Then the sister blew a kiss towards the water. She turned around and the cortège parted to let her through and return home. All left at the same time the way they'd come, putting away their wet handkerchiefs, comforted by one another's company, and with expressions on their faces that seemed to indicate they intended to be happy, reasonably happy, as if the ashes and the flowers slowly carried away by the tide reminded them how fragile life is.

She stayed by the lighthouse until everyone disappeared and then, only a few minutes later, saw the fishermen bait their hooks, raise their fishing rods and throw the lines into the water. She may have been wrong, but she had the impression that more fish started to bite then. And when, right beside her, a man pulled out a gilthead, the mineral sheen of its body lashing in the air, it occurred to her that they were catching fish which minutes before had eaten the ashes, and which in turn would be eaten by the fishermen's families. She thought of her son and, shuddering, walked away quickly.

No, she didn't have anywhere to scatter the ashes, neither a piece of land that was her own, nor a special spot that Manuel would have liked, nor a clear, fast flowing river where he had bathed. The whole earth was too rough, too bloody to take in his remains. If she could, she would send his ashes into space for them to float in the void like star dust, until at some point far in the future they came across a comet that swallowed them and carried them even further away, burning them in a luminous tail before they disappeared for ever.

When she lifted the lid, a slight smell of burning wafted up.

Very slowly, she took her ring off, held it for a few seconds in the air, and then dropped it in. It sank without a noise into the ashes, leaving a round mark bigger than itself. Now the two people who had loved her the most were together. If she was going to disappear, she would not leave behind their traces, would not allow anyone to throw the ashes into a bin with a face of disgust, and no woman would wear that ring.

Again she though of a place to hide them and, all of a sudden, the combination of metal and dust called up an old tungsten mine near her parents' town, where she had gone on holidays until she was sixteen. It was a deep shaft, with an entrance four or five metres in diameter, fenced off with crude planks and a sign saying 'danger', even then almost illegible, with which the owners of that dry, deserted piece of land exempted themselves from all responsibility if an animal should fall in, or, even worse, one of those trekkers who, in the spring, walked about in search of truffles or wild asparagus. Death was certain. As a child, she had gone near it many times with her band of friends. From a distance, they would fling a stone into the shaft and listen in silence as it went down knocking about the rocks, reverberating with a deep, fearsome echo, before plopping into a bed of subterranean water. That was the ideal place to hide them; no one would profane them there. One of these weekends, she would go back to that town she'd never revisited.

Suddenly she noticed a tiny mark on the back of the hand resting on the urn. Surprised, she looked at the tear that stopped for a moment, as if it were hesitating, before sliding down her skin and falling into the ashes. Only then did she realise that she was crying. It had been so long since she had pitied herself. In the solitude of the house, she abandoned herself to the sobs which shook her whole body and in which she found, for the first time in seven months, a strange kind of consolation.

14

Rosco and the Dogs

Thanks goodness for weekends, when you could rest your stiff bones and muscles! It was wonderful to have a few hours to put up his feet or do whatever he liked. During the autumn the company asked them to work on Sundays to pick up fallen leaves, but it was now spring and there was no need to do extra time. Saturday mornings were enough for his expert, furious broom to clean the streets of cigarette butts, pieces of paper, the shiny wrappers of children's sweets, and dog excrement. He was good at his job. His boss had never had any complaints. On the contrary, once he had set him as an example to his colleagues.

'You should learn from Rosco,' his boss had said. 'The streets in his area are cleaner than the floors of the houses of some people I know.'

It was true, and yet the man was wrong to say that. How could anyone feel like polishing the surfaces in their homes after sweeping rich neighbourhoods all day, enduring the back and shoulder ache caused by the heavy metal broom, dragging the bin which by the end of his shift weighed a ton. In those fancy areas they planted big, ostentatious trees, with deciduous leaves, which needed pruning and were always shedding bits, much as the people who lived near them threw stuff away. Luxury generated an enormous amount of rubbish. Things were different in the poorer areas; where he lived the town council had planted a few acacias and some sober cypresses which grew by themselves, demanding nothing, dirtying nothing, putting up with both heat and cold thanks to their needles, simple and sharp like fishbones.

He put two logs in the chimney and lay down on the hammock. It was a cool day, though hardly cold enough for a fire. Still, he liked the feeling of warmth, the old, noble smell of wood and smoke, the playful lick of the flames. This was his only luxury. He'd been working for a few hours in the orchard that Aurora's parents had left them, which had vines, almond and orange trees. They also grew a few vegetables for their own use. With the water from a well he'd managed to create a small oasis at the foot of the dry surrounding hillsides, where only a few bushes grew with barely enough flowers to keep a dozen hives. At sunset he liked to lie down in the shed and watch the increasing darkness as he heard the sounds of nature. Those relaxing Sunday evenings in the secluded orchard, which was hidden near the river bend, and from which he had managed to chase away drought, thorny plants and poisonous animals, made it possible for him to return to work the following day in a calm mood.

He heard a noise through the open door and looked outside. Brindle was peering inside, with an expression of enormous love. The dog's slate-coloured eyes were asking his permission to be let in and lie at his feet, in front of the fireplace, where he would look at the flames until the warmth numbed him and his eyelids fell. Then he would make strange noises and his cold, wet, rubber-like muzzle would wrinkle in an expression that could look like laughing or crying, or he would whimper as if having nightmares, and bark at the monsters born in his own dreams. He was a mongrel of unknown age, not very big, and Rosco had named him because of his coat, an indefinable mixture of grey, brown and yellow.

'Come, Brindle,' he said.

He extended his arm and the dog walked towards him, expecting to be patted on the head – Rosco's palm was even rougher than the hard, bristly fur – and the deteriorated rump. Then the dog stretched at his feet, looking at him.

Rosco liked dogs a lot. No other animal was as kind to him. They never barked at him, as they did to postmen or deliverymen. On the contrary, as he went by sweeping they would look at him and wag their tails from behind the fences, expecting a pat, as if they were grateful for the fact that he always spoke to them warmly, called each one by its name and picked their faeces off the pavement.

Brindle yawned with his jaws wide open, showing the holes where his canines should be.

Rosco had picked him from a municipal dog's home while looking for a dog to keep him company in the orchard and scare away the petty thieves who kept stealing fruit and green vegetables. Yet the dog didn't look like he might frighten anyone. He was cowering at the back of a kennel, and was the last one to approach to get some food. When Rosco asked about him, the carer repeated a story he'd been told and opened the dog's mouth to show the absence of canines: it had been a stray dog that had bitten a child in one of the impoverished areas of the city. The child's father had caught it and had had its fangs extracted.

Not that Rosco believed this story. It seemed to him so cruel to leave a dog unarmed against others, mutilated in the essence of its species, that he couldn't imagine anyone capable of doing such a thing. He made the dog climb into the car and took him to the small farm, even if he had begun to have doubts about it on the way over: what would a fangless dog do in the countryside, where there were so many things to bite?

But since then Brindle had never let him down. Somehow he had managed to keep thieves at a distance, and had become a warm, unconditional companion. Rosco liked his character. Brindle never barked, as if he were ashamed to open his mouth and show the holes in his jaws. He would follow him always two steps behind, loyal and calm, unlike those conceited dogs that run ahead to pee on every tree and at every corner, making a show of their virility and territory.

Now he stirred with pleasure and made himself comfortable on the floor, showing a small erection.

'You'd like a bitch, wouldn't you?' The dog opened his sweet, elderly eyes, and perked up. 'I might get one for you. Now we're going to get some money, we might go to one of those pet shops in the city centre where they show them in the windows. None of that business at the dog's house. You and me, we'll go and I'll get you a nice, clean, pretty bitch. You can choose it. Just bark. Then I'll bring her over and you both can do what you like. You'll see how good that feels. How's that for a plan?'

Brindle looked at him, understanding not a word but understanding the friendly tone. He stirred again and placed his head over his front paws.

The mention of a companion made him think of his wife, Aurora, an affectionate, calm person, who was used to working for others without asking much in return, who caused no trouble and only raised her voice to complain of her own fatness. She was nimble, strong, capable of bending over to touch the floor with straight legs – but fat. And how could she not be? It was inevitable for poor women to get fat, he told himself; not so for the rich, who were elegant and thin, who dieted, went to the gym, applied tons of firming creams and wore gallons of perfume. And why should they eat if they did nothing all day, and barely knew how to handle a broom and a mop, or adjust a vacuum cleaner? They spent their days lying on the sofa, watching TV or in front of the computer, or driving around in their cars – in every house where she'd worked there were two cars parked in garages larger than her flat – to go shopping or have a coffee while they smoked those cigarettes whose butts they tossed onto the pavements. But Aurora could not afford not to eat and watch her figure. She worked tirelessly, running from one place to another, which built up her appetite so much that when she returned home she opened the fridge and started eating like a wolf. No wonder she was fat. She often complained of backache, and he then told her to lie down on the bed. He would sit on her thighs and give her a massage the best way he knew how, since no one had ever taught him. He would slide his fingers down her tired muscles and work down her vertebrae one by one, with the help of some cream so that his rough hands didn't trouble his wife's nice abundant flesh. She liked it so much that they always ended up making love.

He sometimes wondered what would happen if everyone in her line of work called a strike, how long would it take for the world to become flooded in shit. He imagined all cleaners, servants, maids, drudges, skivvies, organising themselves and going on strike to demand decent salaries and social security, like any other worker. In a few days, rubbish bins would overflow, floors would be dirty, furniture covered in dust, beds unmade, glassed smudged, clothes unironed, and every house sunk in chaos; their owners would not be able to take it anymore and they'd give in and grant them all they'd asked for.

Major Olmedo, however, had never been like that. He wasn't a demanding person, Aurora had told him, and so she made a point of doing good work for him and his daughter Marina. Olmedo had hired her to clean both flats even though he knew she'd been fired from the cleaning company when they found out she'd stolen a pair of earrings from one of the houses, whose owner had a jewellery box so full of them that one wouldn't have thought she'd miss a pair she never wore. Aurora had looked so beautiful when she showed up with them on! Too bad she could only keep them for a couple of days, before they threatened to report her to the police if the earrings hadn't turned up by the following day. Olmedo had known all that and yet he was the first one to hire her after she was fired. He gave her the keys to his flat and left her alone, and he never found anything missing, not a bit of soap, a yogurt, a handful of coffee, not even a few grains of salt or a miserable potato.

A short time later, one day as he was leaving the garage and Rosco was sweeping the street, Olmedo got out of the car.

'Rosco,' he said, in that calm tone of voice he had, perhaps because he was a soldier, and when he gave orders it didn't feel like he was doing so, 'I'm pleased with Aurora's work at my house and my daughter's. We trust her completely.'

Confused and surprised, he'd stammered out a few words thanking him and praising his wife. But Olmedo interrupted him. Having a cleaner, he then explained, can be the best or the worst investment one can make. The best if your employee is an honest person who, in exchange for a few bank notes, cleans the rubbish you produce and washes your clothes and irons your shirts and makes you feel comfortable at home. But it can turn into the worst investment if you let someone into your house who rummages through your personal things and does nothing when you're not there and steals your food and sleeps in your bed and tries on your clothes or your jewels and might spit on the food you eat.

Everything was clear after that conversation and later it all went well. Aurora cleaned his flat on Mondays and Thursdays. She barely saw the major, who left for work in the mornings before she arrived and, if anything in particular needed doing, left a note on the fridge. But Rosco did see him often, when he was sweeping the street and Olmedo greeted him, and made a comment about the weather or his work.

'Easy now, Brindle,' he said patting the dog on the flanks. His head had suddenly perked up. 'We'll go home in a minute, I know it's late.'

If they had asked him who, of all the people he knew, he thought would be the last person that might get killed, he wouldn't have hesitated to answer Olmedo. The man was always on the lookout, noticed any bag lying on the pavement or at the foot of a tree, any bicycle chained to a traffic light or any cardboard boxes sticking out of a bin. And on some occasions Rosco had seen, under his open jacket, the gun that he carried. Still, that was in the street. Perhaps he relaxed at home, and perhaps he'd been caught unawares the evening of his death after someone had rung his intercom and asked him for a word. The major had opened the door after a few seconds of silence.

Rosco was a few metres away, picking up some garbage, and heard it all. He didn't make much of it back then, or two days later, when Aurora told him she'd have to find a new place to work, because the major had committed suicide and, wherever the dead might be, they don't need anyone cleaning their flat. He only remembered it a few weeks later, when he saw the tall man return to the garage on Olmedo's bike. He was a detective hired by Marina, and he had asked Rosco about Olmedo. He wanted to know whether anyone had come to see the major on the evening of his death. Rosco had almost replied yes, but he'd had a brainwave and remained silent. What did those people think, that because he was a street sweeper he had to be at their beck and call on top of cleaning up their shit? He was a lot smarter than was necessary for his job, at least smart enough to understand that being honest is not enough to make money, to earn other people's respect, and not be cheated by tricksters and conmen. The detective's concern squared with what Aurora had told him: that Marina seemed very worried, that there was something strange about Olmedo's death, that she had even received an anonymous offensive letter, which Aurora had read with her own eyes.

Now, at last, all those hours working in the streets had paid off. A single phone call had been enough to make him feel in control of the situation. With the money he was going to get in exchange for his silence – he was waiting for the call to arrange the meeting place – he'd be able to finish a project he'd been dreaming of for a long time: he'd expand the well in the orchard and buy a better pump to extract water; he'd replace the reeds and rusty wires with a white fence to eliminate that look of poverty; he'd even have a doghouse built at the entrance for Brindle. He'd buy his children that computer they wanted so much. And he'd buy Aurora a big pair of gold earrings like the ones she'd stolen that had looked so good on her. A pity she'd only worn them once. After that she wouldn't need to look for another job and could take a rest. Her rest would be like the inheritance the major had left them.

'What is it, Brindle, why are you in such a hurry? Or do you smell a hare? But you can't catch them, can't you see you're missing your fangs,' he said kindly, almost fondly.

The dog stood up and looked alternately at him and towards the door, as if he wanted to go out and was waiting for his signal.

'Sit,' he said, pushing him to the floor and patting his neck. 'We'll leave in a minute, as soon as the fire dies down.'

Brindle lay down at his feet once again, no longer looking at the fireplace. He fixed his eyes on the door and pricked his ears. Yet Rosco didn't notice, as he'd closed his eyes and was relishing the warmth from the flames on his eyelids. It felt good to be there, surrounded by the night, in silence, and if it were not because Aurora and the boys were waiting at home he would dine by the fire, a tomato with a pinch of salt, a handful of almonds or dried figs and the juice of one lemon. Then he'd fall asleep on the hammock, alone in the countryside, even if the desert hills that surrounded the orchard were barely worthy of that name.

Without realising, he dozed off and when he opened his eyes the firewood was reduced to embers. Brindle was not inside, and he thought perhaps the dog had not gone after a hare but a stray bitch in heat. He stretched his legs, got up from the hammock and, with short, confident steps, walked to the door. From the doorway he looked at the deep darkness, a moonless sky, the stars shining bright and the trees stretching out as if to touch them, as if they were black hot-air balloons tied to the earth by their trunks.

'Brindle,' he called out. 'Brindle!'

The dog did not reply. Something, perhaps an insect attracted by the heat, flew by and brushed Rosco's forehead. Then, for no particular reason, he imagined a human presence, which instead of hiding in the dark wearing black clothes, appeared by a tree surrounded by a white halo. A light breeze brought to him the perfume of orange blossom, but this sweet smell was now drenched in disquiet, as if someone had scattered it about by shaking the leaves of the trees. He shivered and took a step back. Keeping a lookout, his hand fumbled for the hoe he kept by the door inside the house. His pulse settled down when he grasped the wooden handle. The tool was as sharp as a sword and as hard as a shield. Armed, his fear abated, and he thought that now he'd be able to confront anyone in that territory. He'd been born in the countryside and knew it well, knew how to move in the dark without making a noise. Walking in the country, he noticed at once who was from the city, because townies always looked at the ground, carefully placing one foot in front of the other as if they were afraid of stumbling or slipping on cow excrement or treading on a snake that would coil back to sink its poisonous fangs into their ankles.

He approached the orange trees in silence, alert, while he imagined a violent encounter and himself giving a blow, one strong ferocious blow to the head of the urban intruder. He heard a rustle at the same time he saw a shadow and raised the hoe, only to realise it was Brindle, who rather than protect him seemed to be approaching for protection. In spite of the darkness he saw that the dog had his tail between his legs and that his ears moved nervously from side to side. He patted him without looking down and, feeling that the animal had caught his own fear, whispered in a not very convincing voice:

'Easy, Brindle, easy. What did you see?'

He thought he heard a distant sound beyond the rusty wire fence, among the dry, thorny bushes where the darkness buried itself in more darkness. When he touched the dog again he noticed Brindle had calmed down and was no longer shaking. Still, his own hand was. For a few minutes he stayed under the orange trees, listening, looking for something that might explain what or who had been there, but the darkness made it impossible to identify any signs, any traces.

Constantly looking behind his back, he returned to the shed accompanied by the dog, locked the door and lit the gas lamp. Brindle was still looking from him to the door and back again. He barked nervously every so often and looked at him with his beautiful slate-coloured eyes which reflected two sparks of light. He looked as if he wanted to say something and couldn't, like a person who, instead of having had his fangs extracted, had had his tongue cut out.

'Where did you go?' asked Rosco putting down the hoe and preparing to leave. 'Don't do that again, don't leave me alone.'

15

Adolescence

'I found her,' said Alkalino. He walked into the kitchen and drank two glasses of water. Then he wiped his brow with a tissue.

'Was it difficult?' asked Cupido.

'It was. They act as though they've done something wrong and are in hiding.'

'Who?'

'Not just the girl, Violeta, but all of them. Teenagers! Grown-ups always want to know where their children are, and children do all they can to prevent them finding out,' Alkalino replied.

'What do you mean by something wrong?'

'Oh, nothing, nothing really. Violeta and her group of friends gather together at the end of the north beach, behind some sand dunes, not too near the water. They sit and talk, sing, crack jokes, push each another. They don't even drink. As innocent as doves, they are. And yet they don't look like it. Baggy clothes, shirts with drawings that a not even Malaysian pirate would tattoo on his skin, rags for trousers, as if deliberately ripped. And you should see the hair on some of them, all dishevelled, like they had just come out of a forest and their hair had caught on every branch!'

'Did you speak to Violeta?' Cupido cut him short.

'No, you'd better do it. I don't want her to think there's a strange guy stalking her,' he said with half a smile.

'Don't exaggerate.'

'She's very pretty,' he added seriously. 'I wouldn't be surprised if she was stalked. She's a beautiful girl.'

'At her age, no girl is ugly.'

'She's a brunette, short hair,' he continued without replying to his comment. 'I don't think you'll have trouble recognising her. It's like … she looks like a dead boy's girlfriend.'

'What do dead boy's girlfriends look like?'

'A little strange,' he replied after a few moments' thought. 'They seem to be longing for a change and at the same time fearing that it'll be a change for the worse,' he said. Then he looked at his watch and added. 'If you hurry, I think you may catch her now.'

Cupido stood up and grabbed his keys.

'Are you staying?'

'Yes, I'd better. Good luck.'

The detective went out into the street, took the first cab that came his way and approached the end of the north beach. Indeed, between the sea and a pinewood were a few dunes. He walked towards them, and in a small hollow, hidden from view, were a group of teenagers, looking strong, healthy, with well-defined physical traits yet something childish in their eyes and gestures, as if their bodies had grown faster than their minds and they were looking in surprise at the sudden manifestations of their species and their sex. They gave the impression of having had a long, happy childhood, filled with toys, care and protection. Seated on the sand, they chatted, listened to music and exchanged the head-phones of their MP3 players, commenting on the music.

As Alkalino had predicted, he had no trouble identifying Violeta among the four girls sitting cross-legged in a small circle, a little apart from the boys.

They saw him in turn and one of them must have made a comment, because they all fell silent as they watched him approach. Cupido stopped three metres away from them, so that his height did not intimidate a group who were seated.

'Are you Violeta?' he asked the short-haired girl.

'Yes,' she replied, although she couldn't have said otherwise, as on hearing her name several friends turned their heads towards her.

For a moment he thought of introducing himself: 'My name is

Ricardo Cupido, I'm a detective.' But she didn't know him and that would only make her suspicious. So he said in the kindest tone he was capable of:

'I'd like to talk to you for a moment about Manuel.'

Violeta tensed up and then, all of a sudden, blushed terribly and lowered her head to hide it.

'Gabriela spoke of you,' added Cupido as he wondered what else a private detective should say in order not to sound like a cop, not to sound authoritative to an adolescent's ears, as if demanding answers.

'Who are you?' put in one of the boys.

'A private detective,' he replied looking at Violeta. 'I'm investigating the death of Camilo Olmedo. The officer who was a friend of Gabriela's.'

No further explanations were needed. Violeta stood up, shook the sand off her trousers and walked towards him.

'All right,' she said. She turned her head and asked the group, who remained silent: 'You'll wait for me, right?'

They all nodded, and she and Cupido started walking towards the shore as if they had rehearsed the scene.

'I haven't seen Gabriela for some time. At first I used to visit her in the afternoons,' she said without waiting for a question. 'She had the hardest time. But then I stopped. She depressed me too much, even when she started seeing that officer. She's so unlucky!'

'Did you ever meet him?'

'The officer?'

'Yes.'

'Just once. One Sunday I went by her house as they were going out. They said they had errands to run. Gabriela told him who I was and then the officer put his hands on my shoulder and looked at me like … I don't know … like he was my father and he hadn't seen me for a long time. He also seemed to be thinking of Manuel. I mean, it was not like … like when a man looks at you and you want to cover yourself with a coat.'

Violeta stopped and turned towards Cupido to make sure he

was listening. Cupido nodded silently, thinking she was still stuck in that moment when nothing can touch a girl, neither facts nor looks nor words. Any obscene compliment or dirty proposition would wash over her, protected as she was by her blushes and her terse gracefulness. She too one day will be an adult and will meet men, and will bear children, and will be tired of work, and disappointed and sad. But not yet. There's still innocence in her eyes, still the belief that she'll never have to utter certain words, he thought.

'I think I know what you mean. Did you ever hear about him again?'

'No. Not until they told me he'd committed suicide. I found it hard to believe it, because that day I saw him he didn't look like he was depressed or sad, as Gabriela so often was. I remember wondering what might have happened, for him to make such a decision. Is that why you've come to talk to me?'

'Yes, because of his death,' he avoided the word suicide.

'But Manuel had nothing to do with him. They never met.'

'I just wanted to check. That was one of the things I came to find out. But you've answered it already.'

'What else?'

'Tell me about Manuel.'

Violeta stopped looking at him and started walking near the water's edge, where the wet sat mixed with the dry. At that moment she looked older than when sitting among her friends. She seemed almost as mature as an adult, as if conflicts had made her grow up.

'I don't know where to begin,' she whispered.

'Do you remember him well?' he asked tactfully.

'At times I remember him very well and at others I think he's slipping from memory,' she said, while Cupido thought of Alkalino's description of her: as if she wished for a change and feared it might be for the worse.

'How did you meet him?'

'That I remember well, although it's been a while, more than a year and a half. One day, a friend and I went to a cybercafé, where it was quieter than at home, to chat with some boys we'd met on the web the day before. We both took part in it, but she was doing the typing. And right beside me, on the next computer along, was this boy I didn't know, whom I'd seen on the street a few times. He was handsome, or looked handsome to me. He was leaning forward, very attentively, looking things up. Then I looked away, because my friend was talking to me. And the next time I glanced at him, I saw drops of blood falling on his keyboard. The blood was trickling from his nose, but he was so engrossed in what he was doing that he barely noticed it and wiped it casually with his left hand. It struck me as so odd that someone should bleed and not realise it, as if he didn't feel any pain or discomfort. 'You're bleeding,' I said. He looked at me for a second without understanding what I meant. But then he noticed a drop going down his nose and saw his bloodied left hand, as well as the keyboard. He fumbled for something in his pocket but didn't find it, and as I didn't have any tissues either, I took my scarf off and gave it to him to wipe himself and staunch the haemorrhage, well, not haemorrhage, just a few drops of blood trickling down one at a time. I helped him clean the keyboard, thinking that the owner might see the stains and make us pay for it. He closed down the page he'd been looking at and we went out, just the two of us, while my friend stayed inside, chatting. I asked him if he needed help. He was no longer bleeding, but his nose and T-shirt were stained. I dampened a tip of the scarf with saliva and helped him clean up. He thanked me again and, although I didn't mind, he insisted on keeping the scarf to clean it. He was about to leave without asking me for my number when I stopped him to ask when we'd meet again. He was always very absent-minded,' she said smiling, but with an air of sadness. 'He called me two days later. He brought me the scarf clean and ironed, and it smelled lovely. I asked him if he'd washed it himself and he said no, his mother had. Then we carried on talking. He told me he got them often enough, those nosebleeds. He'd had a vein in his nose cauterised and for a while he'd been fine, but then it'd happened again, as if he had so much excess blood that it had to issue from somewhere. "It's called epitaxis," he told me. "What?" I replied, not knowing what he was referring to. "Nosebleeds. It looks terrible, all the more so because you don't realise; it's not like you get hit or you bump against something. But it's not serious." I, however, thought it very strange and couldn't take it lightly. I didn't understand that you could bleed for no reason, without a wound, pain or anything. I asked him if it might happen when he was asleep and he said it might, although it always had happened when he was awake. "But then, if you don't realise, you could bleed to death during the night," I added, scared, and didn't understand why he was laughing. "It happens to you because you've got a very big heart," I told him. From that afternoon on we started seeing each other, going to the cinema, the beach, or just sitting on a bench in the park.'

'Seeing each other, does that mean you were an … item?'

Violeta fell silent for a few seconds. She seemed to be weighing up the word, doubting whether she should accept it, wondering if for the forty-year-old detective that word might have the same meaning it had for her.

'At first, no. At first we just went out together. We texted each other and chatted online. Then, one day, before a maths exam, he offered to help me with some stuff I didn't understand. I went round to his house for the first time and met his mum. Just for a few minutes, because Manuel said that she always wanted to control him and that, if he gave her the chance, she would never stop questioning me about myself and my family. So we went to his room and opened the books and he started explaining to me the things I didn't understand. We were in the same year, but in different schools. In fact, I was a year older, as I've repeated a year. I knew he was a straight-A student; someone had told me he was sort of gifted. But I don't think he was, just very smart. And very kind to me. I passed the exam and, from then on, we agreed we'd study together whenever I had difficulties. When he helped me it was all like a game. He didn't like to sit at a desk or on the sofa to study; he sat on the floor and put the notes or the books all around him. He'd pick a sheet of paper, read it for a few minutes and put it back where it was. Once he finished he would pick everything up and say he already knew it, that it wasn't difficult.'

Cupido remembered meeting people like that. He thought of gifted children who cannot find a happy middle and live peacefully: they either become prodigies dizzy with success, or they don't amount to anything and vanish with the feeling of being different, devastated by the gap between their intelligence and the world, incapable of facing up to the mob's contempt for whoever doesn't follow the flock.

'The first time I saw him do that I asked him who'd taught him to study in that way,' Violeta went on. 'He told me it was his mum who, ever since he was a child, gave him increasingly difficult puzzles and logical games. She would sit down next to him on the carpet and wouldn't let him go to bed until he solved them. That's what he said, and I thought of his mother, who at that moment might be in the living room, where the TV was on, but who also might be at the door, listening to us, because Manuel told me she watched over everything he did, where he went and with whom, who rang him and whom he rang, the pictures of his friends and which pages he looked up on the internet – which was why he sometimes went to a cybercafé … But she always treated me well, perhaps because I understood why she worried so much. It seems normal, if you've had a child on your own, without a father, without ever asking for help.'

She stopped again to look at the detective, as if she expected a reaction to her comments. Cupido mumbled a few words of agreement.

'And so, some time later I realised I liked him a lot. One day we agreed to meet up in a park, and when he arrived I saw he'd shaved the slight moustache that darkened his top lip, and I told him, laughing: "You've shaved." "Yes. I stole one of my mum's razors," he replied blushing a little. It must be something special for boys, shaving for the first time. Then I touched the skin over his lip and said, "How soft!" and then I took the plunge and touched his lips, which for the first time I felt like kissing – I hadn't seriously thought of that before. And from that moment on, yes, you could say we were boyfriend and girlfriend.'

Her mobile rang briefly, as a warning, and Violeta took it out of her pocket and checked the caller ID.

'I have to go back,' she said. 'My house is a bit far and ever since that thing happened to Manuel I'm afraid to go anywhere on my own.'

'You've been very kind,' said Cupido. He didn't have any further questions. 'Good luck.'

'You too.'

Violeta walked off towards the promenade where her friends were waiting for her, as if they hadn't trusted the detective and had followed them. Beyond the group of teens, the sun was beginning to drop behind the hills, a yellow, very deep sun, which seemed to push back the horizon. When Violeta reached her friends, they surrounded her, no doubt asking questions, and they all disappeared round a corner.

Cupido turned to look at the sea, which was growing dark and mysterious, and throwing his questions back at him. He had come this far in his investigation and found nothing. Violeta held no key. Cupido had confirmed that Olmedo and Manuel had never met, that all they had in common was their violent deaths. Dead men with women who mourned them. Gabriela was old enough to come through Olmedo's demise unscathed, but Violeta would always remember Manuel. And that might not be ideal, because no doubt boys her age looked for cheerful, outgoing companions, not someone already touched and indelibly marked by tragedy. For love to be eternal, it had to be tragic, he thought, his eyes lost in that watery horizon where shadows were drawing near. For love to remain intact in memory, it had to end before turning into routine, tedium and small unforgettable offences. Cupido saw himself a few months before with Lucía. No one had heard him talk about her or utter her name again, and now he wondered whether his stubborn silence did not reveal precisely how much he missed her.

He cast away those thoughts and concentrated on Olmedo. It was possibly the most complex case he'd ever encountered, because it had all the difficulties of several investigations rolled into one: the ambiguity of a death that he couldn't even say hadn't been suicide; a variation of the locked-room enigma; a hermetic environment for the prying detective; a client who regrets having hired him and fires him, further complicating matters; the lack of any certainties to rely on; the useless passage of time, while the likelihood of finding new information seems ever more remote.

Twice – before talking with Gabriela and Violeta – he'd decided to give up if he didn't find anything conclusive. He hadn't, so he should accept defeat and bow out. A detective hired to solve some- one's problem can be a great help; a detective fired that carries on with the investigation against his employer's wishes becomes an offence, giving rise to the same kind of suspicion as someone who tries to overhear a private conversation by standing too close. He was not disappointed in Marina; he understood her reasons. He'd believed her when she told him that her decision had nothing to do with his methods, but with a change of heart about the cause of death and her inability to withstand the emotional pressure. It wasn't, then, something personal, but in any case he didn't rent out his good manners – only his time, his work and his intelligence to solve enigmas. And also his honesty, even if at times some clients might not only not ask for it, but ask for the opposite of it. The fact that he hadn't managed to discern a solution might perhaps mean that the mystery didn't exist. In that case, the only decent thing to do was take a rest, without anxiety or guilt.

16

Vigour and Beauty

And yet, he couldn't do it. Every night in bed, the unfinished investigation came back to haunt him and remind him of his failure, lodging itself in his mind like a splinter under the skin. He would go over his hunches, build hypotheses that later would be toppled by some piece of information, examine again the words of everyone to whom Olmedo might have opened the door. But he never managed to put in order a coherent sequence – motive, opportunity and execution – that might account for a homicide. If that was what it was, someone was lying and he couldn't uncover the lie.

'Leave it,' said Alkalino one afternoon when, coming out of his room, he saw the detective sitting at the table, with a notebook and a pen in his hand, rereading his notes and disparate jottings. When he saw Cupido's gesture of disagreement, he added: 'If you still haven't found the answer, perhaps the questions doesn't exist.'

'And that question would be "Who killed Olmedo"?'

'Yes. Why not accept it was suicide and, therefore, that it's absurd to investigate what never happened?'

Cupido thought a few moments before answering.

'Apart from some details that don't fit together, the best reason is that the profile I've got of Olmedo is incompatible with that of a man who points a gun at his chest and pulls the trigger.'

'I don't think it's that strange. How else would an officer commit suicide if not by shooting himself? As you once said: no pills, ropes or jumping into the void. A military man has a gun and knows how to use it and where to point it so as not to miss.'

'I don't mean the *modus operandi*. I mean the act itself.'

'But why do you care so much about Olmedo? You didn't know him when he was alive,' he said, and Cupido guessed what he meant: *You've seen his picture but not the flesh of his face; you've heard the words others tell you he uttered, but not his real voice; you've read he died of a shot, but you haven't seen the weapon or his blood, not even the corpse.* 'Even if you managed to prove you're right, now you've been fired I don't even think his daughter would pay you what you agreed at the start.'

'It's not the money. At this point, the money is the least of my concerns. It's the need to know the answer to a question I've asked myself many times. Whether it was murder or suicide is incidental.'

'Incidental?'

'What matters is to know the truth,' he repeated a few seconds later, remembering that a few days before Alkalino had said something similar. He hadn't paid attention then, but now he saw that his friend's talk had not been in vain. 'Don't you mind leaving things unfinished?'

'I've left a lot of things unfinished … and sometimes I was glad to do so. I didn't like where some people ended up when they got to the end.'

Cupido knew what he meant: his dalliance with heroin back in the days when no one knew of the hell concealed in its dazzling mirages.

'You may be right, but …'

'You mean you'll carry on investigating?'

'Yes.'

'Even if you said you'd quit if nothing came of the talks with Gabriela and Violeta.'

'In spite of what I said back then. Sometimes it's not so bad to recognise one cannot keep one's promises.'

'If that's your decision, you can count on me.'

'Well, have a shave and put some new clothes on. We're going to the gym in a few minutes.'

Alkalino looked at him with a glint of alarm in his small dark eyes.

'To work out?'

'No, no, you won't have to lift any weights or pedal on an exercise bike.'

'Bramante?' he asked.

'Yes. Everyone who might be involved in the death of Olmedo said they were alone that evening. But he said he was at the gym. Vigour and Beauty,' he said. 'Let's check that out.'

The large premises of the gym were on a lower-ground floor. An inner wall with a swinging door split it into two areas. To one side was the office, as a sign over a door indicated. The exercise machines were situated here and there, in clusters, among the big columns of the building. In two rows of exercise bikes about twenty men and women pedalled in unison. Facing them on another bike – it all looked like a military formation – a trainer dressed in a tight T-shirt, leggings and legwarmers set the pace, which most cyclists struggled to follow, their tongues hanging out.

There were also weight-lifting machines, equipment to work on arms and legs, boards, rails attached to the walls and hanging from the ceiling, rings where the clients exercised, breathing strenuously after each series, and feeling their sweaty muscles to check their hardness or their excess fat to gauge whether they were burning enough calories. Some faced a large mirror that took up a whole wall, lending the place the appearance, emphasised by the leggings and shorts, of a ballroom.

There were clients of all ages, but most were between thirty and fifty: men and women who tried to maintain the muscle tone lost by age and improve their looks for the imminent summer, during which they might do what they hadn't dared do the one before. Among those who trained in groups or in pairs an obvious empathy existed born of common effort and the well-being brought about by active endorphins. But Cupido also noticed a kind of social awkwardness in the room: lads hardened by their job as deliverymen and bureaucrats alternated with rich women dressed in highly expensive designer clothes – hair bands, leotards, trainers. And yet, at both extremes of that mixture of society the same desire to improve one's looks showed through – a desire to temper one's muscles and tighten one's skin and offer one's body to the world free of fat and cellulite, apt for consumption.

Alkalino noticed a trainer who was placing weights on a machine as he asked the woman sitting on it:

'Is that okay?'

The woman tried to bring her arms together, but it was too heavy.

'A little less,' she asked.

They approached. The man was almost repellently muscular. His face and enormous naked arms conveyed no information other than the suggestion that they could do harm. Cupido asked to see the owner or the manager. The trainer glanced at him and pointed vaguely to the office, near the door to the second room, as he said:

'Galayo? I saw him leave a while ago. If he's come back he must be in there.'

He seemed too interested in his client to accompany them, and so they made their own way to the office. Cupido knocked on the door and, when nobody answered, opened it slightly. It was a medium-sized office, lit only by the light from the gym room coming in through the venetian blinds of a large window. The owner had decorated it in bad taste, with lots of pictures of bodybuilders and diplomas for his participation in conferences and courses. The furniture consisted of a filing cabinet, several chairs and a desk with a computer purring on top of it.

Cupido closed the door, and they went to look for the manager in the second room, where the fluorescent tubes gave off a harsher light. There were fewer clients, mostly men, who seemed to be training on their own without the need of advice. They looked with curiosity at Cupido and Alkalino's streetwear, which looked a little out of place. Everyone there was muscular, excessively so, and each exercise was as much a display of strength as a form of training, the ostentation of someone who knows that a muscle is always a deterrent, even in repose. Four men of about thirty were taking a break and, sitting on the carpet, spoke with low voices in a language that sounded like Russian. They had big tattoos in red and blue ink, and shaved heads. They looked as if they had just got out of prison. At the back, two young men had hitched their feet to a bar fixed to the ceiling and, hanging down, lifted their torsos to touch their feet in what appeared to be a competition to see who could do the most in the shortest space of time. The effort made their faces and ram-like necks red, and their muscles seemed to creak as they tensed up. Then they stopped and stretched, letting their overexerted hearts rest, their breathing stabilise, watching over their movements as methodically as if they were giving birth.

A sour smell of chemical sweat reached Cupid and Alkalino as a weightlifter started stretching near them. Cupido saw Alkalino's head rise a little as his nose tensed up and sniffed the air. He must have thought the same as Cupido, as he suddenly said:

'I can stand the smell of sweat, but this … It smells like we're in the back room of a pharmacy.'

They returned to the first room. The girl on the bike was still pushing the group, and the trainer, oblivious to them, was timing the woman's pulse with a chronometer.

'I'm going in,' said Cupido pointing to the office. 'I'll need three or four minutes.'

'I think I can create a diversion if need be,' replied Alkalino.

Alkalino wandered off among the machines. When no one was looking the detective slipped into the office and closed the door. He went over to the computer, moved the mouse and the screen came to life. On the logo of the gym, a V and B interwoven in a tacky design, he soon found the file with the attendance register. Standing over the keyboard, he clicked on it and a chart opened showing the hours of the day and the clients' names. An X in the box marked a member's attendance at a class. He searched for the 16th of April. The window took a moment to open, but he soon found the name: García Bramante, José. The slots corresponding to the evening Olmedo had died were empty, no X. He looked at the schedules for several days and saw that Bramante attended regularly on Mondays, Thursdays and Saturdays – yet on that occasion he'd been absent.

Two bells rang barely a second apart: first the phone, trilling on the desk, and then, louder, a second one in the room. Splitting apart two slats of the blinds he saw the trainer leave the client and start walking towards the office. Then, at the back of the room, he saw Alkalino bending down to pick up a bar with weights and, as if he didn't know what was behind him, turning around and crashing against a mirror, shattering it. All faces turned towards him and looked at the floor bestrewn with shards. The trainer stopped in his tracks, looked back and hesitated for a couple of seconds, long enough for the phone to stop ringing. Then he turned on his heels with an expression of annoyance on his face as Alkalino, who had bent down to put the bar on the floor, stood up and showed a bloodied hand. The trainer approached him and said a few angry words while pointing to the mirror, but then seemed to agree to take him to the restroom, where the first-aid kit must be. By then, Cupido had turned on the printer. As the page printed, he exited the attendance register and looked for Bramante's personal card, which confirmed he hadn't been at the gym at all on the 16th.

He picked up the sheet of paper, turned the printer off and shut down the programme. Through the blind, he checked no one was looking and he left the office. After closing the door he saw the trainer, back from the restroom, walking straight over to him, as if he had guessed the clumsy diversion Cupido and Alkalino had devised and was angry for not having dealt with it properly. His voice was clearly threatening when he asked, looking at the closed door of the office:

'Are you looking for something? Why don't you go and help your friend?'

Alkalino reappeared in the background, next to the cycle trainer, who was smiling at some of his comments as she picked up the shards. His hand was thickly bandaged.

'I think you're right,' replied Cupido. 'I'll take him to casualty to have that wound checked before he bleeds to death. I won't be able to wait for the manager.'

The trainer blocked his way.

'Hang on a minute. It's two hundred euros.'

'What?'

'The mirror. Your friend said you'd pay.'

'Oh, of course. It's not that much,' he accepted.

They left and Cupido inquired about Alkalino's wound, but it was just a superficial cut that required no further care. As they were going up the stairs to the street, he told him.

'Bramante didn't come to the gym that evening. He never misses a Monday, except that one.'

'And yet, he said he did. He must have felt pretty certain that the owner would back him up.'

'Did you notice the clients in the second room?'

'How could I not? Each of them takes up half a wall. And that smell …'

'Rivers of testosterone and steroids. Bramante cannot not know about that.'

'Do you mean that he too …?'

'From the way he looks, I'd say he does. And if he turns a blind eye, being in the military, why wouldn't he be able to ask the owner to back him up, no questions asked?'

'To say he was at the gym that evening?'

'At the very least, to forget he wasn't … It's just a hypothesis, but we can't rule it out until we find a better explanation. What's certain is that Bramante wasn't here when Olmedo died.'

García Bramante cut the engine, grabbed the key and leaned to the right to pick up the bag in which he carried his shoes and sportswear. At that moment, on the other side of the street, he saw the tall detective who had asked him questions about Olmedo on the day of the last pledge of allegiance. He was coming out of the gym, accompanied by a short dark man, who looked rather jumpy and had a bandaged hand. Neither was wearing sportswear or carrying anything in which to put it, so he understood they had not gone to the gym to do exercise. They walked down the street, chatting. Bramante felt apprehensive.

It wasn't fear. He was an army man, felt the support of the army behind him, and had nothing to fear from a private detective who did not belong to the State Security Forces and was not legally authorised to carry out an official investigation. That could only be decided by a judge faced with evidence of some sort. And there wouldn't be any. He trusted Galayo. Galayo had assured him he would change the attendance sheet, and that if anyone asked, he'd say Bramante had been at the gym on the evening of the 16th. I scratch your back and you scratch mine. So it wasn't fear. It was the apprehension of imagining that his posting to Afghanistan might be in any way delayed if he was obliged to answer the kinds of questions posed by people like the detective. At times, when he heard them utter those long sentences of theirs, he felt like cutting their tongues off!

He grabbed the bag, locked the car and made for the gym. He pushed the door open with the familiarity of regular customers, passed the electronic card over the turnstile and went in to look for Galayo. He wasn't in his office or in the second room, so Bramante returned and asked one of the trainers if he'd seen him.

'He should've been back by now. He said he was running an errand and would be back in half an hour. But with the boss you never know!' he added in a complicit tone.

Bramante was impatient to learn what the detective and his companion had been doing in there, whether they had asked about him and what had been said, but he didn't want the employee to notice his concern. After a few seconds he said:

'On the way in I crossed two guys I'd never seen before. New customers?'

'Those two? God, no,' he replied without concealing his scorn. 'They wanted to speak to the manager.'

'With Galayo?'

'They asked for the manager. They didn't know his name.'

'So, they're coming back?'

'No, I don't think so. Not after the mess they made.'

'What did they do?'

The trainer pointed to the back wall.

'Can't you tell?'

Bramante didn't like it when someone answered a question with a question, but he looked where he was pointing and, although he noticed something different, he couldn't say what. The customers carried on with their regular exercises.

'No.'

'The mirror that used to be on the wall.'

Bramante realised it was missing. A few times he too had looked in it as he exercised.

'He shattered it,' explained the trainer.

'The detective,' he was about to ask, but caught himself on time, the words almost formed in his mouth, when he realised that there was no reason for the employee to guess he knew Cupido. So he said:

'The tall guy?'

'No, the small one. He said he was trying to lift a bar with two ten-kilo weights and it slipped from his hands.'

'Galayo won't like it.'

'He won't, but at least I made them pay before they left.'

'Made *them* pay? So the other one was there too when it broke?'

'No, just the small one. Now that you mention it, I couldn't see the tall one anywhere when the mirror broke. But it was he who took out his wallet and paid without complaint.'

Bramante looked at the office door, which Galayo never locked. It wasn't difficult to imagine where the detective was while his assistant created a diversion by noisily breaking a mirror. He must have slipped into the office and checked the attendance register. If Galayo had done as he'd asked him, the detective couldn't have found anything. But he needed to make sure. He took two steps, opened the door with the confidence of those customers who were friends of the owner and told the employee:

'I'll wait for Galayo in here. I need a word with him.'

He turned the lights on and sat at the desk flicking through a magazine. A couple of minutes later he heard someone call the trainer from the second room. He stood up and pressed a key on Galayo's computer, which he always kept on. He checked the 16th. His name was there and alongside it the empty box showing he hadn't been in the gym. He heard the mouse creak between his fingers and released it on realising he was about to break it. Forgetting or ignoring his request, Galayo had not taken the trouble to fill it in. True, he had asked for it in a casual way, giving an excuse about being on duty at the base and without even mentioning Olmedo's death. But he had trusted his diligence.

It had been so easy for him to check that he had no doubts the detective had done the same.

He moved the cursor over to the box and filled it with an X, as he'd seen Galayo do when the automatic system failed. He looked up his own personal sheet and marked it too. Then he sat down again and went back to leafing through the magazine. Apart from the detective, no one could prove now that he hadn't been there.

He went out of the office and into the changing room. Ever since he had started weightlifting, he had noticed the resemblances between military instruction and physical exercise. The gym was a sort of civil instruction. In both you needed to repeat a series of movements until you gained full control of the instrument you worked with – pistol or bars, weights or rifle – and perfectly coordinated strength and motion. And then the physical discipline that both activities demanded was a branch of mental discipline – which was the capacity to make sacrifices and efforts and feel personal satisfaction, no matter what the actual reward was. He'd come to think that there was hardly any difference between being a good athlete and being a good soldier.

He himself set the pace, intensity and duration of the routines. He sat on an exercise bike and started pedalling energetically, hoping to relax with the effort and forget the anxiety caused by the reappearance of the detective. There was nothing like putting up a fight against the exercise machines to make tension go away, purging one's glands of the acid of stress by sweating, and making every muscle expel the detritus with which sedentary concerns tarnish the anatomy.

The problem of attendance solved, he had no reason to be anxious, he told himself. All evidence against him had disappeared and perhaps not even Galayo, after a couple of weeks, would remember his absence. And yet he couldn't be calm. He'd like to be far away, travelling in an armour-plated vehicle down a road in the Afghan mountains.

He got off the bike when the sweat was dripping down his chin and moved over to the benches. Finally he started to relax by the second series of fifty sit-ups, his anxiety dissolving among the sweat and effort.

He greeted the tattooed Russians, but he declined their invitation to train with them. Then he sat on the machine for exercising the trapezius and pectoral muscles, and from there he saw Galayo arrive and go into his office. He wondered whether he should go and talk to him, but decided to leave things as they were. To bring the matter to his attention again would mean underlining its importance. He pushed hard on the bars until they both met in front of his eyes, feeling his pectorals tense up. Although he was beginning to get tired, he didn't want to stop; he feared the anxiety would return. Those chatterboxes might ruin everything as in his worst nightmares: he'd be accused of murder and expelled from the army; he'd have to endure the degradation and humiliation of seeing a superior tear off his stripes and break his officer's sword in half on his knee.

The shower almost burned his skin when he finally went under it, but he stayed there several minutes soaping up and cleaning off the sweat. Then he left for home quickly.

Carmen was lying on the sofa, watching TV and smoking a cigarette, wrapped up in that indolence that was neither boredom nor tiredness, but a form of contempt: the certainty that nothing around her was worth moving for. Bramante looked at the ashtray full of cigarette butts. A few times he'd told himself that it didn't seem very reasonable to stop loving a woman because she smokes, that feelings should disappear for better reasons, if at all, but he couldn't deny that he'd thought about it and that that habit of hers intensely annoyed him. He walked over to the window and opened it to let some air into the room.

'It's really smoky in here! I don't know how you can breathe.'

Carmen took two drags in quick succession before putting the cigarette out in the ashtray. She looked at the sports bag he was still carrying. Was it his imagination or was there a hint of a sarcastic smile in her face when she saw him come in from the gym, as if she mocked his efforts to stay in shape, while she remained sunk in that state of inertia that, in spite of the smoke and the boredom, seemed to be more pleasant than his training? During the months in which he'd taken Dianabol he'd hidden the pills he'd bought from Galayo in a tool cabinet in the basement, convinced that Carmen would never open it. But one morning when he was not home she went down to look for a nail and a hammer to put up a picture and saw the jar. She read the label and guessed what it was for. When he came back home, she waited for him to undress and told him:

'I've seen those pills you take for your muscles.'

Then she looked at his forearms and biceps almost mockingly, as if implying they were fake and unnatural, implants alien to his nature.

Surprised, he tried to find an excuse.

'They gave it to me at the gym, just to try it.'

'Isn't that kind of thing illegal?'

'I don't know,' he lied.

Carmen looked at him, now without any sarcasm.

'Are you sure it's not bad for you?'

'Yes, I'm sure.'

But since that day he'd never taken another pill.

He put down the bag on the floor and sat across from her, on the armchair on the other side of the coffee table.

'I've asked for a new posting.'

Carmen turned down the volume and looked at him without any curiosity.

'Well, you'll get a new one even if you don't ask for it. The base is closing down.'

'No, not that. I've asked to go abroad.'

She sat up, suddenly alert to his words, she who hardly ever found anything he said interesting, who pretended to listen, nodding to everything, while she went on flicking through a magazine, or paying attention to the stupid, spiteful words on the TV.

'Where?'

'Afghanistan. Next month is the changing of troops.'

'Is this confirmed?'

'Yes. They accepted my application. I didn't mention it before because I wasn't sure I wouldn't back down at the last moment. But now it's confirmed,' he repeated.

'For how long?'

'To begin with, five months, with the possibility of extending it to double that.'

He saw her get another cigarette and light it slowly, taking one long drag at it, her face concentrated on the burning tip, so he couldn't know whether the news saddened or gladdened her.

'It might be good for you,' she said exhaling the grey, dense smoke. 'Ten months fly by and no doubt would help you get that promotion you've been expecting for so long.'

Despite his limited grasp of subtleties, it didn't escape him that she had automatically registered the longer period, and referred to 'you' rather than 'we' when speaking of his work prospects. Now she was taking a step back, as if everything concerning the army was his own business and she didn't want anything to do with it. However, a posting in a difficult territory was a serious matter, and he was hurt by the indifference with which she took the news, as if she didn't care that he was going away, that he was disappearing from her life for months. Perhaps, he suspected, she was glad to get some time on her own, to have the whole bed to herself, not to have to agree on mealtimes and work schedules, to smoke two packs a day without being reproached for the smell, the smoke and the ash falling on the table. She didn't even ask about the dangers involved in the mission: she'd been more interested, the year before, in what damage the Dianabol might cause him than now she was in the Taliban bombs.

How little he meant to her! She wouldn't suffer if he died, she wouldn't miss him if a bomb hidden on the side of a dirty Afghan road went off when his vehicle went by, blowing off his head. She would shed a tear or two, surely, when his colleagues lowered the coffin off the plane – and that would be the only time she'd cry for him – but before long she would be back attending cocktails and official functions, smiling a little flirtatiously, a young widow, sexy, attractive and free, without the ties imposed by children. Retired generals would slobber over her and his own comrades-in-arms would bare their fangs.

Well then, he would leave for Afghanistan and forget all about Olmedo, the closure of the San Marcial base, the detective's irritating curiosity and his wife's indifference. Far away, on the fierce Asian plains, in a place where action trumped words, where it was possible for a soldier to become a hero, he would fulfil his duty as a first-rate army man, with pride, without looking back, without fleeing risk, so that there might be a chance to earn a decoration and return with a medal on his chest and another stripe on his shoulders. It was possible that all the circumstances that now conspired to make him leave would contribute, in the course of a year, to his promotion, to earning the respect of his colleagues and having his picture printed in the newspapers. Maybe that old cliché wasn't true, he thought as he saw Carmen tip her cigarette over the full ashtray, but its opposite was: perhaps behind every great man there's a woman with whom he never has a moment's peace, from whom he escapes, compelled to do out in the world all the great things he cannot do at home. Bramante wondered whether it was not hurt, unhappy men who carried out heroic deeds, who drew from their malaise the necessary energy to take great leaps, who courted danger to ease their pain.

17

The Nights

His father had spent all morning making noises. Every ten minutes he flushed the toilet and, between visits to the bathroom, managed to knock things onto the floor, shout to Evangelina, bang doors, and drag around the chair next to the map showing terrorist attacks. So Ucha had barely had any sleep, which he badly needed after a bout of migraine.

In any case, he preferred working the night shift, and although this favoured most of his colleagues, who preferred the day, Castroviejo didn't always authorise it. When he did, Ucha had breakfast with his father on returning home and waited for Evangelina to arrive and take over. At eleven, without hurrying, not yet tired, he would go to bed after reading the paper and sleep for six or seven hours, until five or six in the afternoon. He would get up refreshed, do a few chores and keep his father company until half past ten, when it was time to return to the base.

Neither natural light nor the usual sounds of the day – the background noise of traffic, of the street, of Evangelina doing the household chores – bothered him or interrupted his sleep. But he was particularly sensitive to the noises his father made deliberately to awaken him for the slightest thing. His father didn't like his working at night. He reproached Ucha that he did it on purpose not to see him or talk to him, to leave him on his own: at night he was at the base, his father would say, and for most of the day he slept in his room, so there was no time left to look after him.

It was six o'clock. He put on his bathrobe, got some clean clothes and went into the bathroom to shower and shave. When he walked into the living room, his father was sitting in front of the map and seemed to be counting the number of tacks of different colours on it. No continent was tack-free: the Americas, Africa, Oceania and Asia were covered in circles, their size directly proportional to the number of deaths: New York, Beslan, Bali. But it was in Europe – Madrid and London – and the Middle East where the marks clustered together. In Iraq, Israel and Palestine there were so many yellow tacks that in some areas they overlapped to the point that they hid the place names underneath.

'A car bomb has just gone off in Istanbul. At least eight people dead,' his father informed him, before even greeting him.

Ucha shook his head and let out a grunt that could well mean resignation or anger, but which didn't encourage his father to launch into a more detailed explanation.

'When are you going to do something?'

'I've told you a thousand times, Dad, that the war against terror is not the duty of the army, but of each country's police.'

'And you see the results! In my time it was the duty of the army, and these things didn't happen.'

'Times have changed,' he replied patiently.

'And will change again … back to the way it was. You'll see. I'll die soon, but you'll live long enough and will see the old order again.'

Without warming it up, he ate a bit of what Evangelina had prepared, and drank a coffee filtered several hours earlier. He had nothing to do, so he decided to take the car to a garage to have it washed. And as he waited for it, he went for a stroll with his father.

On coming home, two hours later, his father seemed relaxed and grateful that he'd devoted some time to him, even though they hadn't walked around a nice area. That night he'd sleep better, he told his son.

They watched the news on TV – the images of the Istanbul attack that had already claimed eleven victims – dined on a reheated dish, and he waited until ten to leave for the base. He was going to be early, but he preferred this to staying at home with nothing to do.

The corporal on guard duty lifted the barrier to let him through and saluted him. He parked in front of the central pavilion and, when he got out of the car, saw that the lights were on in the colonel's office. What was the old man doing in there so late? He locked the door and went in to say hello to him. There might be good news.

The Colombian orderly – or was he Argentinian, or Ecuadorian? he couldn't remember – was sitting on a chair in the corridor, and stood to attention when he saw Ucha approach.

'Is the colonel inside?'

'Yes, captain.'

He knocked on the door and waited for a reply before trying the handle.

'May I, colonel?'

'Come in, Ucha, come in.'

The orderly closed the door at his back and Ucha walked along the long carpet that led to the desk. He thought that in the last two weeks Castroviejo had shrunk, not because his flesh was disappearing and ossifying as in so many older people, but rather because he seemed to have begun a retreat into extinction. Something in his attitude put Ucha in mind of a widower who had just lost his wife and has not yet come to terms with her absence and doesn't know how to organise his life.

'I wasn't expecting to find you still here. Is there anything you'd like me to do?'

'No thanks. There's nothing in particular that needs doing. I was just tidying some things,' he said, pointing to some piles of documents and folders on the desk, which was usually clear. 'Have you heard?'

'No, I haven't spoken with anyone today,' he replied, though he could guess what he meant.

'This morning we received official confirmation of the closure.'

'Is there a date?'

'Not yet. They'll tell us in due course, but I don't think it'll take long. Better be prepared. Have a seat, will you?' He pointed to the chair in front of the desk. 'Have you decided what to do?'

'I think I'll ask for early retirement.'

The colonel looked at him gravely. Ucha knew he didn't share that decision. He often heard the colonel speak badly of army men who hurried into retirement when they turned fifty.

'If I stayed on active service, I'd have to change houses and cities. And I don't think my father would welcome those changes,' he said, feeling the obligation to explain.

'I understand,' the colonel said in a calm, tired tone. 'The closure of San Marcial has upset our lives more than we can bear. Have you heard what Bramante has decided to do?'

'No.'

'He's going abroad, to Afghanistan. I myself submitted his application. Putting in a good word,' he added.

'This,' said Ucha, pointing at the office but also at the large windows behind which all was dark, 'will come to nothing.'

'Empty,' added the colonel. 'It's astonishing how quickly everything can empty out. To think of all the years it took to fill up!' he exclaimed in a low voice, without looking at him, as if he needed no interlocutor.

'We'll all miss it.'

'All? No, just a few of us. Make no mistake, Ucha, make no mistake. There's a world outside that doesn't even know we exist … or that regards us as a hindrance to the urban development of the city, as parasites with stale habits and ancient codes that no longer hold any value, as a group of fanatics. They think we'd be happy to die from a shot in the heart after planting the flag on a rock we'd just conquered. Would you believe it, in these last few days I've come to understand Olmedo?'

'Olmedo? Can't say that I have. I think he's mostly responsible for all that's happening to us.'

'No, captain. Without him the closure might have been put back, but it would have happened all the same. Olmedo was cleverer than us, he understood it first. Deep down, he may have done us a favour.'

'How?'

'By saving us from prolonging an agony that, like any agony, would have been painful.'

'That's called euthanasia, colonel. Professional euthanasia,' he dared to add.

Castroviejo looked fixedly at him, his blue eyes, slightly milky, filled with reproach, surprised at his comment.

'Well, we can only confront it with pride, captain, seeing that it's inevitable.'

'With pride?'

'The greater the failure, the greater the pride one must confront it with, whether one is a soldier or not,' he added fidgeting in his armchair.

Ucha smelled the mild aroma, at once sweet and foetid, of a fruit he couldn't identify. The colonel's voice sounded indomitable once again, disproportionate to his small body, as if it had been emitted by a younger self: the voice of someone who had done nothing but give orders and seen them carried out for two thirds of his life. But that was what was expected of him: he wouldn't leave his post with a fake smile, hanging his head, but would do it with his chin up and with as much pride as the defeated general – defeated, perhaps, but not conquered – who surrenders the keys to the city only when the gates are about to be pulled down.

'I'll bear it in mind, colonel. I'll bear it in mind,' he said before asking permission to leave to start his shift.

The changing of the guard took place a little early, and he went out into the esplanade. He looked up and saw the windows of the office: the lights were off now, Castroviejo must have left. A very thin crescent, tilted like a bowl pouring light into the darkness, hung in the sky. It was a mild dark night. He looked at his watch until the hand of the seconds marked exactly eleven o'clock. Then the clear, melancholy notes of the bugle punctually tore through the air, ordering absolute silence. As the last note froze, a distant cat meowed plangently.

Ucha walked towards the depopulated barracks. He liked the hours between sunset and sunrise, his night-time walks during which he watched over the place as everyone else slept. It seemed to him that, in those moments of freedom and deep silence, only altered by the gurgling of the city's entrails, he could hear the very breathing of the earth, the panting caused by its incessant spinning while carrying on its shoulder the increasingly heavy load of humanity.

He stopped and looked up at the sky, where the bowl of the moon did not cast enough light to dim the glow of the stars higher up – so far away, so immune to man's destructive impulses. They were an example for man; he'd always regarded them as more disciplined than the best elite corps: punctual, sleepless, hard, clean, always in the same harmonious and balanced position, always alert, always in their place, like tacks fixed in a place beyond the sky, holding up the dark, distressing cloth of the shadows, to stop it falling on the world and smothering it under its weight.

He was approaching one of the sentry boxes at the back when he discovered the shiny tip of a cigarette. He stopped for a couple of seconds, and continued in silence in order to catch the smoker unawares. When he got to the top of the high ladder he saw that the soldier had left his Cetme leaning on the wall of the sentry box, behind him, and was smoking with his back turned to it, blowing the smoke out of the window, in the direction of the headlights of the cars that went past on the distant road. He took a step in complete silence, raised his gun and pointed to the soldier's back. Only then did he say, in a threatening yet sarcastic whisper:

'One dead soldier.'

He gave the boy such a fright that he dropped the cigarette, which fell at his feet, the tip shining like incriminating evidence. The boy stood to attention, and Ucha waited for the cigarette to die out, without replying to the clumsy, stammered salute – 'At your service, captain' – which the boy barely managed to utter.

Only when the cigarette was extinguished did he say, without lowering his Cetme:

'If I were a terrorist, you would be dead, with a bullet in your chest. Don't you know that a guard must never abandon his weapon?'

'Yes, captain.'

'Don't you know that a soldier on guard duty mustn't smoke?'

'Yes, captain.'

'Don't you know that a soldier on guard duty mustn't get distracted?'

'Yes, captain.'

'Don't you know that a soldier on guard duty is the one who ensures their fellow soldiers' safety.'

'Yes, captain.'

Now he realised that the boy was only a child and that the fear of punishment had made his voice fainter with every reply. He slowly lowered the Cetme so that the barrel pointed to the floor, and for a moment wondered whether he should now give him a break. But he still added:

'Don't you know that a soldier on guard duty should never break down when he's surprised at fault.'

The boy was slow to reply, as he didn't seem to understand why, in spite of having lowered his gun, the captain was still angry. His voice sounded firmer when he said again:

'Yes, captain.'

'Then pick up your rifle,' ordered Ucha pointing at the Cetme, 'open your eyes, don't smoke, and be alert.'

'Yes, captain.'

'Return to you position. I'll talk to you later.'

'Yes, captain.'

He turned his back to him and went down the ladder without looking back. He decided not to punish the soldier, but he'd leave him to fear punishment all night. The San Marcial base was emptying, and a sort of abandon was contaminating all levels of the hierarchy, from the colonel down to the rank and file: that boy was behaving like a child who doesn't look after that which he's seen adults treat badly. He evidently thought that no one would be interested in entering there, a building about to be sold. Ucha thought at that moment of the detective and imagined him jumping over the wall in an area of darkness, out of the apathetic sentinels' sight, and slipping into the main building in order to break into Olmedo's office in search of some evidence that might prove there had been foul play.

The detective had found it strange that, even though no one believed it was suicide, nobody lifted a finger to disprove it. But why should it? Death by suicide simplified everything, suited everyone, no one would try to overturn it. Olmedo, who in life had been proud, fortunate, brilliant and successful, had had a painful, miserable death; no one could fix that. May he take with him to his grave his arrogance, his medals, his promotions, his prestige. May he rot with them, like the ancient dead who reserved their best jewellery for their last abode. And may he leave the living in peace.

18

The Old Garde

He started the old, trusty grey Mercedes, and slowly drove out of the base, giving the corporal on duty time to lift the barrier after hearing the familiar purring of the engine. That kind of recognition, in which man makes direct contact with the objects and machines at his service, would soon be a thing of the past. Technology, with its magnetic strips and electronic passwords, would replace the personal touch.

Fifty years before, when he was a young lieutenant just graduated from the Zaragoza Academy, any army man with accurate instructions and a few weeks' training could handle all the weapons, resources and instruments that military science had created in the last three thousand years for men to kill other men more efficiently. However, in the last couple of decades, the science of war had become so complex that the efficiency of an army depended entirely on its technological development. Concepts like personal courage, strategic intelligence, discipline, honour and acceptance of the rules of engagement – where were they now? It was no longer possible for an officer to be made general at a relatively young age by virtue of his bravery in battle. Those men who had lived by such codes of honour were now reduced to secondary roles. How far in the past was all that! How lost were the times in which young soldiers would march to the battle at dawn and gather together in the evening to share words of heroism, while their young, sweet brides embroidered mottos about loyalty, love and sacrifice in silk flags the colours of the regiment, kissing the cloth before rushing to volunteer as nurses in a hospital, to clean the blood and dirt of the wounded! How lost were those times of admiration, of bugles and ceremonies, when spurs clicked in the corridors of the base, and no officer could boast of being a good soldier if he was not a good horseman; when a parade demanded as much precision as a dance in which one holds a lady by the waist; when the barracks were held in as much esteem as the ballrooms of a palace! What nostalgia for a past in which one didn't have to hide one's uniform, which was a source of pride respected by all, from the highest civil servant to those orderlies who, with only a piece of cloth, made boots and buttons shine to perfection! All was behind him, and now the San Marcial base was the last thing to be liquidated. Bramante, Ucha and many others were young enough to adjust and move on. One was leaving for Afghanistan; the other retiring; others would adapt accordingly to their capacities. But he was too old and tired to feign enthusiasm and physical energy in each of his public appearances. He'd spent the best years of his life trying to build something that might endure when he was gone … and in the end he discovered that his efforts had been all in vain.

He arrived home and hung his jacket on the bare coat rack. His three daughters had left home and married, and since his wife had died he lived alone with Piedad, the nanny and maid who had looked after them and now looked after him: she washed his clothes, cleaned his house, prepared his meals.

The light on the answering machine in the living room was blinking. He listened to the messages from two of his daughters. They asked how he was and said they would call back later. It was now almost midnight, so he guessed they wouldn't ring before the following day. And yet, when he put the receiver down, he was surprised by the sound of the phone.

'Dad?' It was his youngest daughter, Loreto.

'Yes.'

'I called earlier and you didn't answer. Piedad wasn't in either.'

'She's at the cinema with some friends, like every week.'

'It was late and I didn't think you would be at the base, so I was worried. Is everything all right?'

'Yes. I had to catch up on some paperwork. I have to leave everything in order.'

'So it's true then, they're going to close the base down?'

'Yes, it's true. I told you.'

'But it's so unbelievable. And what are they going to do with it?'

'Flats.'

'Flats? You mean they're going to knock down everything you …? When?'

'When I am dead,' he was about to reply, but contained himself in time; his illness was still a secret.

'I can't believe they'll do that with the base … and with you.'

'They can do it with the base. They can close it down. They can't do anything to me,' he commented, with the firmness of someone who has always maintained and observed discipline: not even in front of family and friends would he ever blame a superior for giving an unjust order.

'Well, they're forcing you into retirement,' she replied.

Then he suspected, with a slight feeling of guilt, what it was that his daughters were really worried about. Had they talked amongst themselves about how difficult it would be to have him move in with them, to adjust to new routines; had they discussed with their husbands how long he would stay, what room he would be given? None of his daughters had married an army man, and, although he had no complaints about their husbands, they belonged to a civilian world which felt ill at ease with the rigid military milieu he represented. On occasion he had even wondered whether, deep down, the husbands did not belong to the kind of people who find anything a soldier says suspicious just because it is a soldier who says it.

No, he wouldn't move in with any of them, he would endure at home, with Piedad. The military club and those friends who were still alive would satisfy his needs for social life, and if there came a time when his legs were no longer able to carry him down the street, and his shaking hands no longer could hold a glass without spilling water or cut a piece of bread without hurting his fingers, and by midnight he didn't remember what he'd done in the morning ... if there came a day when his own decrepitude filled him with bitterness and there was nothing to hang on to, well, one didn't need much strength to put a gun to one's temple. In the past, life, the simple fact of living, had seemed to him a marvel. Misfortune, worries, disappointments had all been brief and manageable, and he had promptly reconciled himself with something like happiness. But life had lost its interest; the three or four things worth breathing for had disappeared. He listened admiringly to acquaintances who had overcome serious illnesses like cancer or pancreatitis: 'It happened three years ago, so I've defeated death for three years.' But he didn't share their enthusiasm. He didn't mind dying, so long as he was able to decide where and when. It wouldn't be long now. Ever since the doctors had told him that the hepatitis he'd had twenty years before was developing into a hepatic cirrhosis, he'd known that two years was the longest he had. Since then, that sweet smell of rotten apples had never left him: it pervaded his pillow, his clothes, the armchair where he watched TV, his breath and sweat.

Piedad, not knowing what it was, kept saying for a month:

'It smells of apples, how weird. I haven't bought any for months.'

But later she must have noticed it was him, that the hepatic foetor emanated from his body, and she made no further comments. She did something else, though: she started putting apples in the cupboards, among the clothes, in the fruit bowl, for him to think that she hadn't noticed. One morning, when he was looking for a shirt and an apple rolled out of his wardrobe, he smiled to himself, thanking her silently for her crude compassion, and let her believe that she could carry on deceiving him.

Both had fought a silent duel to see who better resisted ageing, but now that she had won, he found her sympathy touching and, on a couple of occasions, he had held back a tear, refusing to be a crying old man. All that remained was to live out whatever time he had in the best possible way before pain or anxiety became unbearable. In old age, the body just endures; only when one is young can it heal, he told himself as he pressed the palm of his hand on his belly, near his liver. He was a sick man who had no chance of recovering. The same illness that took away his appetite was weakening his legs; the same illness that had made his breasts grow was knitting a web of capillaries under the skin of his face which had scared his grandchildren the last time they'd visited.

He had often heard that a serious illness changes one's outlook on life. That values change and the ill person stops caring about some things and starts appreciating others. But he hadn't felt any substantial changes: he held the same beliefs and hated the same things as ever. His dislike of Olmedo had been the same before and after learning he was ill. Ever since Olmedo had arrived, the colonel had felt there would be trouble, because the provincial calm that he'd managed to establish in San Marcial did not square with Olmedo's fresh ideas. However, Castroviejo had never given in to the temptation of boycotting Olmedo's work, hiding information from him or putting obstacles in the way of his reports. He had played fair, observing the rules that he'd been taught to observe, and the military code he'd learned even before first putting on the uniform. That's why he thought Olmedo would not refuse the only favour that he had gone to ask of him: that, when the San Marcial base was turned into plots of land for flats, they did not demolish the main pavilion; that they at least leave standing that building that held so many memories of effort and sacrifice and pain, but also of honour and glory, being the oldest, most solid and most representative building in the compound. Castroviejo didn't want his grandchildren to have to ask him: 'Grandad, where was the base where you used to be a soldier?' No doubt, Olmedo could see to that, he had prestige and resources enough to come up with architectural, or heritage, or historical arguments to prevent it being knocked down and turned into a crowded block of flats or a public garden where dogs would shit. It was such an easy favour to grant!

A sudden need to go to the toilet made him stand up. He tried but didn't manage to empty his bladder. On coming back, he slumped on the armchair and closed his eyes, trying not to think of anything until Piedad came back from the cinema, but he felt a hint of fear at falling asleep and never waking up. Under his drooping eyelids small fleeting sparks went by like tiny ephemeral comets with a life of their own, independent from his will to see them or not. He opened his eyes, frightened, wondering whether that might be another symptom of his illness.

He was relieved to hear the key being introduced softly into the lock. He closed his eyes once again and called out:

'Piedad!'

19

Painted Nails

'Do you still trust Bramante will answer your questions without making up some new lie?'

'Yes, his previous alibi is useless now. And I don't mind if he does it willingly or unwillingly, so long as we can make progress.'

Perhaps it was arrogance that had made him list his address and full name – García Bramante, J. – in the telephone directory. He lived in a street in the centre of town, and Cupido and Alkalino walked over there unhurriedly, almost strolling along the wide pavements where the bars had put up tables for all the people who had gone out in the warm spring weather: it was one of those days when the street ceased to be a place of passage and became the scene of a chaotic, colourful spectacle. A radiant yellow sun was starting to tan winter's translucent skin, giving it a healthier look. And the bright sunlight sharpened people's eyes. All the girls seemed to have turned into women and decided to spill out into the street. Alkalino watched with admiration and astonishment life's organic plenitude, that fertile abundance, that whirlpool of curves which, with each movement, caused shakes and quakes of feminine flesh which seemed to reproduce the vibrations of the earth on which they walked.

They didn't know the exact floor on which Bramante lived, but on the third try someone told them. Cupido pressed the button and presently recognised his voice, too loud even on the intercom.

'Ricardo Cupido?' Bramante repeated when Cupido told him that he would like to have a word with him.

'Yes.'

'I've said all I have to say.'

'Of course you did,' Cupido replied. 'But other people talk too. There's someone who tells us you were not at the gym that evening.'

In the silence that followed they imagined Bramante behind the door, twelve or fifteen metres above them, with a serious, worried expression as he unnecessarily squeezed the receiver. Then they heard a feminine voice asking: 'Who is it? What – ' before his hand had time to cover the mouthpiece. Then, after another wait of several slow seconds, two simple words were heard, uttered in the same tone in which Bramante might have ordered a recruit to pick something up or run ten laps around the pitch:

'Come up.'

They pushed the door and took the lift. After ringing the bell they still had to wait a few seconds before Bramante opened and let them in.

'Good afternoon.'

The woman did not rise from the sofa, but only tilted her head to greet them with a curious, slightly sarcastic gesture. Cupido remembered her as part of a group of women who were laughing the day of the pledge of allegiance. She barely deigned to look at Alkalino's dark, badly shaven face, as if wondering why he didn't buy proper razor blades, but she stared at Cupido, whom she had seen just once before, at the party, as if she were surprised how accurately she remembered him.

'So you're still worrying about all that?' asked Bramante without making a single movement that might be construed as an invitation to sit down. 'I thought the case was closed.'

'I wish it was.'

'So?' He made a gesture of surprise opening his arms and showing his big, almost ostentatious, tense muscles – too tense for someone who's just at home – as though he were challenging him to a fight.

'We needed to check a few things, and we discovered you were not at the gym on that day.'

Even before he'd finished he noticed the spark of hot, hormonal anger that shook him and, at the same time, how the woman on the sofa, though still motionless, grew tense.

'Says who? A psychic that …'

'The attendance register at the gym,' interrupted Cupido, without giving any further details.

'I see,' he said, appearing relaxed. He crossed his arms, so that he no longer looked like he was threatening them but rather protecting himself. 'The attendance register. But machines often fail, and perhaps that day the box with my name on it was not ticked. A misunderstanding that can confuse any curious person who takes the trouble to check it.'

'Maybe that's what it was,' said Cupido. Now he knew that Bramante was aware he'd been at the gym, in the office, for a few minutes, time enough to see he'd been absent. And, by the same token, he guessed Bramante had solved the problem by ticking the box. 'A technical problem, easy to solve so long as …'

'As what?'

'As long as no one testifies that the machine didn't fail.'

Bramante looked at him for a couple of seconds in silence, concentrating, as if he was repeating to himself the last sentence to make sure he'd heard it right the first time.

'I see,' he said again. 'Someone … a psychic might guess … But I'd like to see a psychic try,' he stammered out the clumsy threat with difficulty, not sure he'd chosen the right words, perhaps wondering whether he was not making a second mistake.

Cupido saw his anger increase from one word to the next and thought of Olmedo, who was so different, who liked trim uniforms as much as a well turned phrase, a well constructed argument, a solid case. A hundred years earlier Bramante would have been a good soldier, someone who would never challenge an order even if it was unjust, so long as it was clear and brief; he was disciplined, coarse, severe, trustworthy, incapable of treason because he lacked initiative; he was passionate about the sound of swords clinking, barracks songs and the colours of the flag; he would never appreciate his soldiers less than his weapons.

'You mean my husband was seen outside the gym at that time?'

Cupido was not surprised that it was she who spoke. She had actually taken her time to come to his help.

'I mean someone saw your husband was not in the gym at that time,' he corrected.

'But, even if that were true, it doesn't mean anything. It doesn't mean at all that he was near Olmedo. The world is big enough, and there are plenty of places to go, you know,' she said, her voice filled with the same kind of gentle, self-confident sarcasm that shone in her eyes.

'Of course,' agreed Cupido. 'This is not substantial enough to be considered evidence. But it can complicate matters.'

The woman looked at her husband and then at the detective, gauging their strength and weapons.

'Better to avoid complications,' she suggested, as if she could foresee the outcome of the showdown.

'Yes,' said Cupido tersely. He guessed she would not carry on talking in front of her husband, and not out of fear or respect, but because of what she'd said a moment ago: to avoid complications, not to disturb that lazy, sensual comfort she inhabited.

'But even if those complications arose,' said Bramante, once again in a surly tone, breaking the pact of silence that seemed to have been made between his wife and the detective, 'even if they arose, there would always have to be some psychic who dared tell me that on that afternoon ...'

'José,' put in the woman, gently yet firmly.

'... I wasn't ...'

'José,' she interrupted again, wiser than him to realise that there are conflicts that not only cannot be solved through violence, but that violence makes worse. Or perhaps she just saw how ineffectual her husband's threats were to the tall detective, who listened calmly, as if the warning did not concern him, or was something trivial.

At that moment Bramante looked at her, and then seemed to give in, brooding in silence, even though he still exhibited his muscles, as if waiting for that psychic messenger he kept mentioning to arrive. There was nothing left to say. Cupido left them his phone number, and a little later Bramante walked them politely to the door.

Barely an hour and a quarter later, when Cupido and Alkalino returned back home after stopping for a bite to eat, the telephone rang, and the detective recognised the feminine voice who was asking to see him, because she had something important to tell him.

'When and where,' asked Cupido.

'Now, at your place. I'm out in the street, at a pay phone. Give me your address. I won't be long.'

They saw her get out of the cab and look up at the windows of the building, convinced that the two men were watching her. She rang the bell and pushed the door on hearing the buzz. Cupido was waiting for her at the door, and stepped to one side to let her in.

The woman walked without hesitating into the small living room and sat on one of the two armchairs. She opened her handbag and took out a pack of cigarettes and a flat golden lighter.

'Do you mind if I smoke?' she asked, already with a cigarette between her red lips, and without waiting for an answer she lit it. Then she blew the smoke directly in front of her and looked at the coffee table as if looking for an ashtray. There were none in the house, so Cupido fetched a small plate from the kitchen.

'What did you want to tell me?' he asked, thinking of Alkalino, who, sitting on his hard-backed chair behind the half open door of his dark room, would be listening intently not only to the woman's words but also to her tone for any hesitations, or a quickness or slowness to reply.

'It wasn't my husband,' she said. 'Maybe he did not go to the gym that evening. I guess you wouldn't claim that if you hadn't checked. But my husband didn't go to Olmedo's house and shoot him in the chest.'

'How can you be so sure?'

The woman smiled, impartial and kind, undisturbed by the detective's words.

'Don't you think I know him? Do you think that after twelve years of living with him, listening to his opinions, sleeping in the same bed as him, I still don't know him well enough?'

'Let's say there's always the possibility that there could be secrets in a marriage.'

'I guess so. But in this case José is not the one in possession of a secret.'

'Do you mean you are?'

She tipped the ash onto the plate with a deft movement of her index finger, which ended in a nail painted an intense red, not too short and not too sharp, but curved, hard and shiny enough to put one in mind of the paws of a powerful, amoral female feline.

'I'm not here to talk about myself, but to defend my husband. My secrets are mine. As for José's, he doesn't have any, he wouldn't be able to keep them. He's too naïve for intrigues, has never learned how to do that kind of thing. He thinks that in his profession being strong is enough.'

'And is that not the case? Isn't strength what matters most?'

'No,' she said firmly. 'One day, at the base, they were discussing that, and I heard Olmedo say that the result of a battle depends as much on the strength of the one giving the blows as on the resistance to pain and suffering of the one receiving them.'

'So you knew Olmedo?'

'Yes, he was the kind of man everyone criticised so much that your curiosity is awakened. Despite what my husband said of him, I think he was a very intelligent officer.'

Cupido found this declaration odd, almost astonishing.

'Are you surprised that I speak well of him?'

'Yes.'

'You shouldn't be. We speak well of the dead to make up for how badly we speak of the living – a matter of conscience. But I'll never praise him in front of my husband.'

'He didn't like him.'

'Like him? José hated him.'

'It would seem that what he had against Olmedo was more than professional rivalry.'

'My husband thought he was a traitor. And I've often heard him express his scorn of traitors. "A soldier will use everything you've taught him against you," he says. Anyway, I'm hoping you won't use this information against him.'

'You wouldn't be providing it if you didn't have some other information that makes it irrelevant. Right?'

'Right,' she smiled, and still took another drag at her cigarette, holding the toasted filter between her red-tipped middle and index fingers. 'Yes, because there was someone else who wasn't where they were supposed to be at the time Olmedo died.'

'Who?' asked Cupido steadily.

'Dr Lesmes Beltrán. We both work at the same hospital. Do you know of his troubles with Olmedo?'

'Yes.'

'He had serious reasons to hate him.'

'How do *you* know?'

'I'm a nurse. I work in the maternity ward. That evening we had a patient who asked for an epidural. It wasn't the moment to give the injection yet, but Dr Beltrán, who was meant to be on duty, went out for an hour. I happened to see him get in his car, drive out of the car park and head for the centre of town.'

'As in your husband's case, his absence does not prove that he went near Olmedo on that evening,' Cupido remarked.

'But it must have been an important matter. At least important enough for him to risk leaving when, if there had been any complications with the birth, anyone could have found out he wasn't there. Important enough for him to lie when he returned.'

'How so?'

'He'd been gone for almost an hour when the patient started complaining a bit. We nurses know what to do in those cases, how to calm them down, ask them to be patient. But I used that excuse to look for him. I called his house. He hadn't been there and his wife thought he was in the hospital. When he returned some ten minutes later I told him I'd been looking for him because the patient was complaining. He told me he'd been around the whole time, though he'd gone out to smoke a cigarette and had later popped by the pharmacy to collect some doses of anaesthetics and check on the stock. All lies of course. His car was not in the staff car park during all that time.'

As though it were planned, she finished her cigarette at the same time as her story. She stubbed it out on the plate as if sneering at the vulgar object. She put away the pack and lighter in her bag and made as if to rise from the armchair.

'Thank you for the information. It's important,' said the detective.

'Thank me by finding out the truth, so we can all sleep in peace.'

'May I ask you a question?'

'Sure, why not? You've barely asked me any.'

'He doesn't know, right?'

'That Beltrán left the hospital when …?'

'That you've come here to tell me,' he interrupted.

'No, he doesn't.'

Cupido nodded, as he did whenever he confirmed the unwelcome suspicion that his trade had altered his character, had turned him into a pessimist, always on the lookout for deceit and the basest motives.

'Say it,' she said in low voice, almost a whisper.

She was standing now and looking at him the way a calm, indolent, satisfied female feline would look at a male of the species that she has come across on her way to get some food – a male that may be bigger and stronger but does not unsettle her at all, as she's sure that there are only three things in life worth fighting for, food, pleasure and territory, and knows that she can get all three whenever she desires.

'What?' asked Cupido, disconcerted.

'That other question you asked before and you don't dare to repeat, however much you want me to answer it.'

'All right,' said the detective. 'All right. What are your secrets?'

'I want my husband to leave. I want him to leave not just the city but also the country for a while, even if he's going to fight in a war that's not rightfully his,' she explained. 'He's asked to be posted for five months in Afghanistan, with the same unit in which Olmedo served, as if he wanted to follow in his footsteps to learn what he knew … Colonel Castroviejo wrote a good report and they've accepted his application, but I'm anxious it might be turned down if he's implicated in an investigation. And I want him to be far enough away, so when he tells me he's coming back I'll have time to get the house ready, and when he comes home he can see that everything is the way it used to be, and he believes no one has used or moved anything. It will do us both good to be apart for a while.'

'There are other ways to achieve that.'

'Of course! But I don't want a divorce. Why complicate things, if complications can be avoided? It's been quite hard for me to get to the point where I have a comfortable life. Why would I want to undo all that if with a little tweak now and again it can be so pleasant?'

The woman looked at him expecting not an answer but con-firmation. Cupido was aware of her sensuality, of her grip on his desire. It wasn't just beauty or physical splendour. Among the fine, smooth wrinkles around her eyes, which were now fixed on him, one could see the tempting gold vein of experience. A handful of women had looked at him the way she did now, without any need for words, only standing still in front of him, not drawing near but neither retreating, and Cupido knew that if he reached out he'd find no resistance. The austere life of the last few months and his instinct – which was more powerful than the tacit laws that he upheld in his work – pushed him a few centimetres forward without the woman moving back or looking away but authoris-ing him to advance. It was only a moment. He then remembered the barely opened door and the room from which Alkalino was listening, and also remembered, still painfully, Lucía's body. He stopped, feeling like a stranger to himself as he replied:

'Of course. Why ask for complications?'

A smug, mocking smile quickly replaced her initial surprise at his rejection. Then her eyes registered not anger but disappointment as they seemed to say: 'Oh, you don't dare either. You haven't got the guts to fight for the sweet gift I'm offering you. Oh, you don't either. Get out of the way so I can leave.'

When Cupido returned to the living room after walking her to the lift, Alkalino was already sitting on the sofa, looking at the cigarette filter stained with lipstick.

'For a few seconds there, my real concern was how to close the door without attracting her attention.'

'You could have done it, her back was turned to you.'

'Do you think she didn't check which doors were open and which were closed when she came in?'

Cupido didn't answer the question. Instead he said:

'Were you so sure that I …?'

'Not you. Her! Her ability to … I don't know how she looked at you, but if her eyes suggested as much as her tone of voice …'

'You're exaggerating.'

'I'm just jealous,' he joked. 'To think that such opportunities are offered precisely to someone who can afford to turn them down because he knows another will come along soon enough!'

Cupido gave him a friendly look: a small man, dark and talkative, who lived without aspiring to be admired, or loved, or valued, who only had the ambition to make himself heard; a guy with his face bronzed as wood even in the coldest days of winter, not very attractive to women, who had not fucked enough, and yet who exhibited no rancour or bitter puritanism towards those who, like the detective, had.

He picked up the plate with the cigarette butt and was making his way to the kitchen when he heard Alkalino say:

'She's one of those women who always win, no matter what the relationship or with whom, whether it's with their husband, whom they will have chosen from the most docile and loyal suitors, or with a lover, who will be trivial and fun, and maybe a little difficult once she tires of him and tells him with tears in her eyes that they can no longer see each other, as the guilt is killing her. Who teaches them these things?'

'No one,' answered Cupido, although he knew Alkalino was not asking him but only expressing his astonishment and perplexity out loud.

'Who's taught them to look at people that way?' Alkalino went on. 'They know full well how to look past you as if they didn't see you, aware that the best way to prolong desire is to delay gratification. And they know when to look at you for only a second, which is enough for you never to forget them. How come they know what we take so long to learn, so long that when we find out we're too old for that knowledge to be of any use?'

The detective didn't answer. He went into the kitchen and dropped the ash into the bin.

20

The Pain

Before leaving the office he inhaled deeply, blew out the smoke and took another drag until the cigarette burned his lips. He threw the butt into the water-filled ashtray and put this away. With the window open, the smell would disappear by the time he returned from the delivery room.

He was tired; it had been a long night. The last operation had finished half an hour before: a teenager who had had his tongue pierced the day before. The pain had awakened him in the middle of the night, and his parents, who didn't know about the piercing, were terrified. They'd brought the boy in to casualty with his tongue so swollen that it barely fit in his mouth. He was very nervous and refused to open it for a local anaesthetic to be injected with a small syringe before the operation. It wasn't the first time a thing like that had happened, and Beltrán had learned how to deal with patients unable to conceal their panic when they saw him approach with a needle in his hand. He managed to persuade him and to calm his parents, who were more horrified about the child's decision to have his tongue pierced than by the consequences of the infection.

Carmen, the maternity ward nurse, approached him in the corridor:

'I was coming to get you. One of the patients is ready.'

'Let's go then.'

The girl, who was very young, was lying on the gurney, and when she saw him come in her swollen lips tightened into a smile of relief. She was very thin and her big round belly stood out as something alien to the rest of her body. Beside her, a corpulent, older man, waited with an expression of concern and fatigue.

As Beltrán put on his gloves he said to the man:

'I have to ask you to leave for a minute. Later, if you wish, you can come back in.'

The man did not need to have the instructions repeated. He gave the girl a quick kiss and left without saying anything.

'What's your name?' he asked.

'Perla.'

'First time?'

'Yes.'

'All right, Perla, don't worry. We're going to take away the pain. I'd like you to sit up, lift your robe up to your waist and bend forwards.'

Helped by Carmen, the girl obeyed silently and he prepared the catheter. When he turned round, she was already presenting her docile, naked back to him, bending forward as far as her belly permitted. Her vertebrae showed clearly under the thin, lean skin of the back. With great care, he located the right place between the lumbar vertebrae.

'Now be still, don't move.'

He gently inserted the needle and made sure it was secure before applying the first dose. The girl, after some initial fear caused by the cold drops, would start feeling better as the pain lifted. He made her lie back again while Carmen put a pair of thick woollen socks on her feet. A moment later, a new contraction tensed her whole body. He waited for it to pass and placed his hand on her sweaty forehead, while saying:

'The next one won't hurt. And the baby won't suffer,' he explained, smiling naturally.

'Thanks,' the girl replied, squeezing his hand.

He adjusted the catheter to let the right dose through, told Carmen he'd be back in a moment (she could call him if she needed him), and left the delivery room. The fat man was sitting outside on a chair, but didn't ask Beltrán if he could go in now.

Back in his office he lit another cigarette and watched the smoke quickly ascend as he thought, with something akin to tenderness, of the fragile, slender girl who was waiting to be dilated enough. A few times, with irascible or hostile patients, he could barely contain the temptation to reduce their dose as he thought: 'Let them suffer. They don't deserve for me to calm their pain, the resources we spend on them. If I reduce their dose a little, there's nothing wrong with that, I'm administering justice. Doctor God. Let them suffer a little for having gorged themselves on food and drink, producing so much fat, so much unnecessary flesh, for having forced their livers to filter all that shit they stuffed themselves with, for having tired out their hearts which pumped their soured blood through their veins hardened by cholesterol. Let them suffer now if they couldn't help themselves before.' He was of the opinion that, in a country so prone to hypochondria, it wouldn't be a bad idea to reduce the budget devoted to reducing pain. The number of ill people, operations and hospital beds would decrease in no time if a small wart was excised without anaesthetics and people had to pay for the prescription drugs they demanded, only to let them expire in a cabinet already full of medicine. If he were put in charge, they would soon see how the enormous public health deficit would decrease, how they would all disappear, those hypochondriacs who went for a check-up every month; who were admitted to casualty with symptoms they exaggerated so that their blood pressure would be taken, their cholesterol analysed, their blood sugar measured; who would familiarly lie down on gurneys and take off their contact lenses and dentures, as if preparing for a facelift; and who, after costly lab tests which were however free to them, demanded that their pain be taken away, without stopping to think that he, the man who controlled it, had his own reasons to suffer and yet no one cared about his affliction or offered consolation.

He would make all of them pay or go away, all the ones who had brought their illnesses on themselves – their emphysemas, cirrhoses, their beastly halitosis. He would only offer the miracle of anaesthetics to those who felt pain through no fault of their own: children, cancer patients and blameless accident victims, all the woman in labour like that thin girl who had squeezed his hand a few minutes before. He couldn't understand why it had taken so long for the widespread use of the epidural in childbirth, when no one had a cavity cleaned any more without a small injection. Perhaps it was because of blind obedience to the biblical injunction which punished with suffering an act that resulted from happiness and aimed at happiness.

When he heard the knock on his door, his instinct was to put out the cigarette at once and hide the ashtray, but he then refrained: after all, he was in his own office.

'Come in,' he said.

The door opened and he was surprised to see the detective who investigated Olmedo's death.

'Yes?'

He didn't ask him to sit down, but Cupido took one of the two chairs in front of the desk.

'Are you here to see a doctor?' Beltrán asked him, mustering all the strength of mind he was capable of. 'Because I thought I had answered all your questions.'

'In a way, I am.'

'I don't treat people. I only take the pain away. It's my colleagues who treat them.'

'They wouldn't be able to if you didn't do your job well.'

Beltrán twisted his mouth into a smile that didn't reach his murky brown eyes.

'In a way, it's not unlike what you try to do yourself, is it? Calm those who hire you and let others take action.'

'In a way,' agreed Cupido. 'But your job is no doubt a lot more important than mine.'

Beltrán looked at him distrustfully, as if seeing sarcasm where Cupido had not intended it.

'Few people have seen as much pain as I have,' he explained as he passed the tip of the cigarette along the border of the ashtray.

'And everyone tries to avoid it, even if that means harming others.'

'That's what you did, isn't it? You went to Olmedo's flat that evening to do exactly that, take away his pain.'

'Olmedo's flat?' he echoed, avoiding the question. He was sitting still, seemingly calm, though his feet moved under the table.

'Yes, you left the hospital for an hour. You were seen leaving, driving off in your car and returning an hour later. Enough time to do what you needed to do.'

'Who told you that?'

Cupido hesitated for a moment, but eventually said:

'One of the nurses.'

'Ah, one of the nurses. Carmen,' he guessed. 'I saw her spying on me through the window. Carmen! Doctors are taught to keep things from their patients, but none of us has ever managed to keep the slightest secret from our nurses,' he added with resigned sarcasm, as if given such a witness it was useless to keep denying anything.

'She doesn't remember the exact time, but she knows the patient gave birth at ten thirty and you left about two hours before that.'

'It's true, I went out. But that doesn't mean I went to Olmedo's.'

'No, it doesn't. But if so far you've claimed you'd been here all along, it's because outside you haven't got a better alibi. You'd get into trouble if they find you absented yourself from work when there was a patient who might need your help at any moment. A woman about to give birth. A baby. You know how touchy people are about that subject … And what with your track record!'

'I didn't see him,' he said after a while, in the same hoarse, restrained monotone as before, trying to conceal that his breathing had not become shallower, that he did not fear the threat. 'Didn't manage to,' he qualified. 'I went to his house and parked the car in the street, near the entrance. I lit a cigarette as I turned over in my mind the words I wanted to say to him.'

'What words?'

'About pain. Deep down, it's always about pain.'

'And did you find them?'

'What?'

'The right words.'

'No. You don't ever find the ones you're looking for,' he said as he put out the butt that had burned down to the filter. He appeared to be lamenting the fact that it had consumed itself too soon. Then he added: 'The perfect words that will silence your enemy.'

'What were you planning to tell Olmedo?'

Beltrán looked at him for a couple of seconds, his lustreless eyes fixed beyond Cupido's face, like those of a blind man.

'I was going to beg him to leave me in peace,' he explained in a slower, hoarser voice than before, the voice not only of a lifelong smoker but of someone who knows he'll never quit.

'Had he threatened you again?'

'Again? No. Olmedo did not need to renew a threat for anyone to feel it was still valid. He'd made it four years ago and nothing had changed.'

'And so, why were you there to remind him?'

'Remind him? No, that would be like reminding a wolf or a snake that they need to bite an enemy when they come across it. He had reminded *me* a few days before. I almost bumped into him in the canteen of the hospital. I was wearing my white coat. He stood still, staring at me for a few seconds, first in the eyes, and then at my badge, as if he couldn't believe what he was seeing and needed to confirm I had gone back to work.'

'And?'

'Four years ago he swore he'd never allow it.'

'But time passed, and you served your sentence.'

'That meant nothing to Olmedo. The day of the ruling he called me at home to tell me that, whatever the judge said, he would make it his personal mission to ensure I never worked again as a doctor. I chose to interpret it as a furious reaction in a moment of sorrow, it was still soon after the accident. But I never forgot his threat. And that day, when I saw him there …'

'But, legally,' insisted Cupido, 'you had nothing to be afraid of. You'd paid for all that.'

'More than my fair share. And I was legally protected, true, but not professionally. Do you know how difficult it is to bounce back in this profession? Almost impossible. Everyone points the finger at you at the slightest problem, and everyone will remember that, once, someone who went into the operating theatre thinking they would come out healthier, or more beautiful, or in less pain, left as a … as a … Olmedo could perfectly stir things up, go to the newspapers, write letters to the director of the hospital … Precisely now, when things are starting to go well.'

'Is that what you were going to explain to him?'

'Yes. When we met at the canteen he was not alone. He was with a woman and the way he acted, pulling back her chair, ordering for her, seemed to indicate they were a couple … or at least that he would like for them to be a couple. I even thought that if he was with her perhaps he'd started to forget, though I only thought about that later, when I came back home that night. At the canteen, Olmedo looked at me with the same spite as ever.'

'Did he say anything to you?'

'No, but neither was it necessary. The way he looked at me was enough.'

'So why did you go to see him the following day?' insisted Cupido. 'Why repeat something that …?'

'The woman intervened,' said Beltrán.

He opened the top drawer of the desk, took out the pack of cigarettes, got one out and left the pack in front of him, as if he reckoned there was no point in putting it away, as he'd need it in a few minutes. He brought the cigarette to his lips, lit it and blew the smoke through his teeth.

'"Camilo" was the only word the woman said, placing a hand on his forearm.

'To calm him?'

'To calm, with just one word, a man who wasn't easy to calm. I guess she understood who I was by reading my badge. Olmedo must have told her he'd been married, and that a doctor, during a simple procedure …' he went quiet and looked towards the window, almost oblivious to the detective, blowing out bluish-grey smoke. 'That night I thought things over and came to the conclusion that the woman, whoever she was, might be of help to me.'

'What made you think that?'

'The way she looked ... her attitude. A woman in her early fifties, tall, still beautiful, whom a man would like to hold in his arms if it wasn't because he would fear that ... that ...'

'What?'

'That perhaps she wouldn't even notice you were holding her. I observed her during those minutes at the canteen. She seemed to be lost in her own world, in which there didn't seem to be many pleasant things. Olmedo had his back turned, but I could tell he was talking about me, because she looked at me several times as she gently shook her head.'

'And because of her attitude you went to see Olmedo?'

'Yes, because there was no hatred in her eyes but a kind of curiosity which I'd call, I don't know, compassionate. And I didn't want to carry on feeling anxious about the possibility that Olmedo might come and harass me. If I had to confront him, the sooner the better. And so I remembered the woman's gaze, mustered all the courage I had and decided to go and see him to beg him for a little peace. I didn't expect him to accept that his wife's death had been a fortuitous accident. I didn't expect him to tell me: "All right, you've made a mistake, but you've paid for it. It's over now, it's been forgotten. No hard feelings." I was only going to beg him not to stop me being a doctor after all these years.'

'And how did he react?'

'I didn't get a chance. As I said, I lit up a cigarette in the car while I searched for the right words. And when I was about to go out – not that I'd found them, mind you – I saw someone stop at the door of his building.'

'Was it a strong-looking middle-aged man?' asked Cupido, but before he finished Beltrán's expression told him he was wrong.

'A strong-looking man? No. It was her, the tall woman that was with him at the canteen in the hospital.'

Cupido looked at him without saying a word, alert, serene, without showing any surprise.

'I remember thinking that, if they were a couple, they could not be very far along in the relationship, because she didn't have the keys to his flat. Still, she rang the intercom and immediately took a step towards the door, like someone who's confident she'll be let in. So I stayed in the car, wondering if it might be a good idea to ring right then, while the woman was in. But then I decided against it and came back to the hospital. I'd been out long enough.'

'What time was it?'

'Eight twenty.'

He picked up the pack of cigarettes and put it away in the drawer, as if he no longer needed it.

'Why have you kept it to yourself until now?' asked the detective.

'Why not? Why should I reveal it? For Olmedo's sake? I don't care which way this is solved. I don't care why a man who despised me is dead. I won't put my work on the line by saying I absented myself during a shift. And if that nurse insists, it'll be her word against mine.'

21

The Plants

Like all gardeners he disliked animals, which he regarded as an uncontrollable, often aggressive and always dangerous force that contributed nothing but manure to the vegetable kingdom. In his garden, animals were an unceasing source of trouble. His friends' dogs, and some cats that jumped over the fence, scrabbled in the earth and dug up seeds, broke stalks when they lay on them, and left their acid faeces on the soil poisoning the plants; once a stray cat had vomited in a pot and a rose bush had dried up and died. Birds pecked at the fruit, rejecting the cores. Snails and slugs bit the most tender stems under cover of darkness. And insects had the irrepressible tendency of turning into a plague.

He dissolved the poison in the water of the gas cylinder, closed it and injected air until he obtained the right pressure. He slung it on his back, and started fumigating systematically and energetically, missing none of the affected plants. He felt an unknown joy at seeing the ants flee the acid rain, fall onto the ground more heavily than their small bodies would make you think they were capable of, and retreat to the anthill to raise the alarm. The chemical dew covered the wisteria that took up the back wall, the rose bushes in the borders and pots, the hydrangeas and the azaleas. He treated the bellflowers and the ivy on the fence, whose most tender shoots were crawling with parasites; then he injected more pressure in the gas cylinder in order to be able to reach the highest branches of the fruit trees. While taking a rest, he looked at the cherry tree, which was the hardest hit. Ants – indomitable, frenetic, crazy

– went up and down the trunk from the nests hidden in between the bricks, where the poison wouldn't reach, towards the shoots, which were like grazing fields for them. Up there they shepherded plant lice, milking them and transporting them on their backs to the spot where they did the most harm: the spring leaf buds and the new leaves which, deprived of the sap the parasites sucked, could not grow and ended up shrinking into dark, sickly green balls.

He sprayed the poison from top to bottom, without missing one branch, persisting until the drops slid off the crinkled leaves while ants went up and down at a desperate speed.

Suddenly he wondered whether he was not feeling more joy at the death of the parasites than at seeing the plants rid of them. He'd fumigated other times, but he used poison with displeasure. He'd never stopped to watch the carnage caused by the chemical weapon, had never felt good about seeing its devastating efficiency. Nervous and ill at ease, he finished the task without observing its effects. He tried to ignore the uncomfortable feeling that sometimes it was necessary to shed some blood so that the rest remained in harmony. 'Although Camilo's death affects all of us, the most important things are fine,' he told himself. 'Marina is with me and she loves me. Now, here in the garden, in spite of the plague, insects buzz and flowers bloom and trees grow … I think I'll have to get used to this strange way of being happy.'

He put away the gas cylinder in the tool shed and kept some of the liquid, which he poured into a small spray gun. Later in the afternoon he'd treat the plants at Gabriela's, which also had some parasites.

An hour and a half later, he returned to the garden after a shower and a shave. There were no ants in sight. They were not dead but only hiding while the effects of the disinfectant lasted; they would return a few days later. He'd have to keep them away from their food, so in a week he'd repeat the process.

The plants shone in the spring sun and the garden was looking better and better. A blackbird flew in from the street and alighted on the cherry tree, looking at him with curiosity as it produced its ornate song of clicks and whistling. Samuel scared it away lest it ate anything while the drops of pesticide were still drying.

It was still early to go and see Marina, and so he bided his time enjoying the garden. The plants were in bloom but the trees had not given fruit yet. The brown monotony of winter was gone, and everything was in flower: the refined fragrance of the buttercups; the artichoke-shaped flowers of the rhododendrons that grew fat before exploding with colour; the pink stars of the honeysuckle; the nervous wisteria always wanting affection, stretching its branches to caress any nearby plant; the delicate lilac tree always putting out flowers in pairs, as if they were afraid of loneliness or the shadows, and so closed their petals when night fell. Samuel was interested in the way the camellias died, so like the way Olmedo had died: all of a sudden the whole flower comes off the stalk without having time to shed its petals.

In spite of his experience, every spring he was surprised at the beauty of his plants. Every year he followed the variations in tone and growth, the changes with which nature seemed to affirm its freedom to create, and he respected that, no matter what the trend. He thought it ridiculous that fashion should have reached the world of gardening. Magazines spoke of plants and flowers that were passé while others were in vogue, as if a garden had to change clothes with the seasons. A lilac bush is a lilac bush, and a rose is a rose, and it's neither less fragrant nor less beautiful because this or that garden designer prefers the former to the latter.

It was time to go. He picked up the small spray gun, locked his front door and walked over to Marina's place. He let himself in. From the living room he heard her voice speaking to the elder child – 'Stay still now, don't move as I comb your hair' – while the little one, on seeing him, dropped his toy, stood up in his playpen, and lifted his arms towards him.

'Hi,' he called out.

Before Marina replied he had picked up the small child and was walking with him in his arms towards the bathroom.

'How are you?' Marina asked. She kissed him and said: 'Jaime will be here any minute. Can you give me a hand dressing him? The clothes are on his bed.'

He went into the bedroom and started changing him, almost surprised at finding himself there, bending over and dressing a child who was about to be picked up by his father.

The intercom rang and he buzzed the person in without asking who it was. He felt awkward letting in the previous owner of the flat, who had lived there for longer than he knew Marina. Still now, when he was in the presence of Jaime, the word 'usurper' popped into his mind without the need for Jaime to utter it, as if it simply emanated from the ex-husband whenever he saw a change in the decoration that eliminated traces of him in what used to be his princedom. A minute later Samuel saw him appear at the door (he'd left it ajar), as elegant and attractive as ever, with that air of being single he had always had, even when he was married to Marina.

Marina, who was carrying the child in her arms, sat him in the stroller.

'That's great,' said Jaime. 'I'm in a bit of rush. Someone's waiting for me downstairs.'

'Someone?'

'A friend,' he said casually.

Samuel could not fail to see Marina's expression, the way she forced a smile and raised her eyebrows questioningly, looking at him with interest, when she never looked at him for more than two or three seconds. Up until then, Samuel was so happy to be with her that he'd never imagined he would find the presence of another man annoying, even if that man was her ex-husband. But that expression of concentrated interest made him think of the years in which they had lived together, a long time before he, Samuel, had even seen her at the school bus stop. The trellis of their shared memories was dense enough for him to be unable to penetrate it.

Marina saw Jaime to the door and came back to the window

from where, a couple of minutes later, they saw him put the boys in the car. A woman got out to help him. Marina remarked on her blonde, youngish hair, the tight clothes that showed her sporty shoulders, the waist of someone who had not had children.

'Do you miss him?' he asked in a calm, kind, affectionate voice.

'No,' she replied, still looking at them, after a pause that he judged unnecessarily long. 'Jaime was fun when we were with people. He knew how to be the soul of the party. But then, when we were on our own, he was boring, he didn't have much to say. But with you,' she went on, 'it's the opposite – I feel very well when it's just the two of us. So I have no reason to miss him.'

'So, it's better this way for everyone.'

'How do you mean?'

'With Jaime dating that girl.'

'Yes … maybe,' said Marina after a few seconds, looking at the car as it drove away and disappeared round the corner. 'Yes. I'm not jealous, if that's what you were thinking, but it takes a bit of time not to feel a hint of annoyance … Like many other women I'd like to think there's no one else who can replace me. Anyway, I guess I'll have to get used to it.'

'I guess so.'

'You do? But what do you know about Jaime?' she asked, not so much asking him as taunting him.

'I know what you once told me – that he's very successful with women. So perhaps that girl won't be the last.'

'But she's so young,' she disagreed.

'I'd say he's the kind of man who's condemned to date younger and younger girls.'

Marina turned round and, without walking away from the window, held him in front of anyone who might see them. Neither did Samuel mind about the street or the inhabitants of the city. He shut his eyes and silenced his fears, freeing himself of disquiet, breathing with his mouth buried in her hair, which brought calm and security. Every embrace of hers was pleasant, but this one was like a landmark: so far she had barely talked about Jaime, and perhaps for that reason his shadow, like a ghost, had always been present between them. And a ghost, they said, can break chains, go through walls, break into a sleeping woman's room at night, sit at her bed, whisper a name in her ear and caress her face so she'll dream of him; ghosts can be hurt with neither knife nor bullet, cannot be banished or burned to the ground inside a castle. To convince himself that his fears were absurd, Samuel tried not to think of Marina's life before he met her, and more than once he'd told himself: 'One doesn't love a woman for her past, but in spite of her past.' But now, with her words and that embrace, Marina was dispelling his fears. And so he didn't care about the city. He was no longer Samuel Gibello, the son of a rag and bone man, spying on a woman from behind a curtain. Everything had changed so much that it didn't matter if someone spied on him from the darkness.

He wasn't even afraid of overdoing it. When he woke up, he stayed a few minutes in bed, planning his day so that he could spend a couple of hours with her. But at times he'd feared his presence might be a bit stifling. He'd heard that women feel put upon by men who are too attentive, who study their tastes to satisfy them and watch their schedule so they are never alone. Once, with the excuse that he had too much work, he let four days go by without visiting or calling her. The fifth morning, Marina rang him up to ask him what she should do about some black bugs that had appeared on the leaves of a plant. He sensed the question was an excuse to talk to him, to find out why he hadn't phoned her in the last few days.

'Is that why you were calling?' he asked, after promising he'd drop by her flat in the evening.

'Yes. Well, I also wanted a chat with you. I haven't heard from you in a few days.'

'I've been very busy,' he mumbled, and even he realised how unconvincing he sounded. And so he decided to be honest. 'Besides, I didn't want to tire you. I understand you have your own life, your kids, your friends, and that you might want to be alone at times.'

Marina did not protest too much, but later that day Samuel received a package from her by courier: a recent book about gardening featuring the latest varieties of genetically engineered flowers. A few days earlier he'd mentioned it and said he meant to buy it. He liked the gesture, but he liked the note that came with the book even more: 'I love having you around, you know.'

Now he thought that, if you could measure in seven or eight steps the distance a man must travel until he's finally close to a woman, that had been the third or fourth movement. And what had just happened was the penultimate, when the woman stretches her arms towards a man and holds him as she was holding him now. It was a wonderful feeling. How was it possible that, when he held her in his arms, she seemed lighter and more fragile than when he saw her walking down a street, or even naked in bed or in the shower. He did not let go but suggested, perhaps talking too fast:

'And if we moved in together?'

Marina raised her eyes and looked at him in surprise.

'We've been seeing each other for seven months. We could try … It'll be a lot easier in many ways,' he explained, and then understood that the thought had crossed her mind before, and that she was not so much surprised at his question as at the fact that he'd taken so long to ask it and had chosen precisely that moment to do so.

'Are you sure that's what you want?'

'Yes. It's been seven months since … since that day you lost your bracelet and …'

'You sure?'

'Yes. It doesn't have to be tomorrow. We can plan it well,' he said, because he hadn't forgotten that Camilo had died only a short time ago.

'You sure?' she said kissing him.

'Yes.'

'I've got two small children that …'

'Yes,' he interrupted her. 'And I think if we asked them they wouldn't have a problem.'

He knew she had accepted when she asked:

'Which house would we live in?'

'It doesn't matter so long as we're together. Although I think the kids would be fine in mine. It's big, there's plenty of room, and I can even put up a swing in the garden.'

'A swing?'

'Well, all kids like swings.'

'I think you're a little behind the times,' said Marina smiling. 'All kids like videogames.'

'More than a swing?'

'At least as much.'

'In that case we'll find a way of setting up some kind of techno-logical contraption that moves back and forth and up and down higher and higher, so that they can understand that there are things which are scary but worth doing.'

Having spoken more than was his habit, Samuel went quiet, but Marina pushed him to the sofa, lay on top of him and asked:

'Tell me more about what it's going to be like living together.'

He felt happy when he walked to Gabriela's, and was surprised that his life had also changed in that respect: a few months before he just went from home to work and back, and now he was asked round a couple of nearby houses where he was always welcome.

Gabriela was out, but she had left her keys with Marina, so that he could come round in the afternoon to cure and fertilise some plants he'd given her, which looked a bit sickly.

He'd never been in the flat before and, when he opened the door, he was shocked by its darkness and stuffiness. It smelled slightly of rot in there, of a dry, mineral something: it was not so much an unpleasant as a disquieting smell – the smell of the habitat of moles, spiders, crocodiles perhaps. Unlike his place or Marina's, where colours and furniture suggested light and open space, eve-rything was baroque, dark, oppressive. All the important objects were inside, which was the opposite of what he liked: a house with a nice view that let in the natural light.

No wonder the plants were ill. The place was only suitable for fungi. He pulled up the blinds, which creaked with mould, as if they hadn't been moved in a long time, and threw open the windows, marvelling at the fact that anyone – least of all a woman, given that feminine reflex of detecting stifling smells, of airing everything and chasing dust away – could live there without asphyxiating. Though it was light and air that was needed, at least Gabriela had taken care of watering the plants lest they dry up completely. The two pots in the laundry room had resisted better, and with a bit of pruning and some pesticide and fertiliser they would revive in no time. But the ones on the balcony looked bad, as well as the rubber plant by the door, with its long leaves drooping, covered in dust, dry at the tips.

He had given her a pot for the rubber plant with a water deposit and a gauge that indicated when it needed refilling. He bent down and checked it: not a drop of water left. He poured in three jars until it was full, and, after tearing off the dead bits, turned the pot a hundred and eighty degrees to correct the inclination of the tropism.

It was then that he saw a yellowish piece of paper stuck between the wall and the plant. It was a delivery notice – not a very old one, but judging from the layer of dust it must have been there several days, perhaps weeks. The deliveryman must have slipped it under the door when no one was in. A handwritten note read: 'You were out' and the times at which he had twice called. No doubt when Gabriela had opened the door the piece of paper had been pushed behind the pot.

He blew the dust from it and placed it on the coffee table, beside a framed picture of the dead child, where Gabriela would not miss it. Then, as if the notice had given him an idea, he tore a piece of paper from the notebook by the phone and scribbled a message: 'I've taken care of the plants, but don't forget to water them now and again. Samuel.'

He left the keys and note next to the delivery notice and, before getting the spray gun from the laundry room, stopped and went back to the coffee table, realising what it was he'd seen without understanding. He bent over the small yellowish piece of paper written by an unknown deliveryman and, without touching it, read the date and the two times he had called, the exact hour and minutes, while understanding gave way to surprise and surprise to suspicion because of what that might mean, not only for Gabriela, for also for himself. For himself and Marina, he concluded with a shudder. At that point suspicion turned to fear.

'It can't be!' he moaned, and reread the date and times he knew so well. And there they were, clearly written and perfectly legible although it was only a copy, with no margin for error.

He took his hands to the back of his head, his thoughts racing, resisting the impulse to run out of the house and leave the windows open so that the stuffiness would disappear and perhaps a gust of wind would take the notice far into the sea, as if it had never existed and he'd never seen it. 'I don't want to think about it,' he told himself. 'I don't want to imagine what I'm imagining, don't want to think that ...'

He picked up the piece of paper and put it in the pocket of his shirt. Now it was he who needed darkness and silence; it was as if, with the notice in his pocket, he had to hide from the city that had seen him and Marina a few hours before, holding each other at the window. He quickly lowered the blinds and, before leaving, took a look around and made sure that everything – except the plants, watered, treated and cleared of parasites and dead leaves – was exactly the way he'd found it, the same isolation, the same darkness and the same clutter of photographs and mementos. He was too impatient to wait for the lift and so he ran down the stairs, two steps at a time, making no noise, like a thief in flight. The notice burned like a live coal in his pocket, but he checked he still had it every minute.

He could tear it into pieces and get rid of it anywhere in the city. He could burn it or throw it down a drain or sink it under the tons of paper his company sent to the cellulose plant, so that no one would ever be able to tell that it had reached Gabriela's flat. Of course, an original still existed, but no one, not even the detective that Marina had first hired and then fired, would ever think of asking at the offices of a certain delivery company whether they had left a notice at such and such address.

He walked fast, fleeing the house, until he reached the waterfront promenade, and sat on the parapet to think. A day or two after Olmedo's death Gabriela had called him to ask for what she'd termed a small favour. She asked him where he'd been at the time Camilo had died, and when he said that he'd been at home on his own, and that he hadn't talked to anyone, she put the question to him:

'If they ask about me, could you say you had a coffee with me for about an hour? Not that it matters, and if you'd rather not do it, and anyone comes looking for that information, I'll tell the truth, that I was alone at home and no on can confirm it. But then they'll want to check it and they'll want to know more about my relationship with Camilo. And, to tell you the truth, I don't think I could take any unpleasant questions about my private life. I've suffered enough. And Camilo would not have liked me to talk about our private life – you knew him.'

'Don't worry,' he'd told her. 'I'll say I was with you.'

'That way they'll also leave you in peace,' she added.

'Don't worry.'

Because Olmedo had committed suicide. Later, when Marina began having doubts, it was impossible to imagine that Gabriela might have harmed the person who had loved her. Fragile, sweet, wounded Gabriela, whom tragedy had marked on the brow with the initial of her dead son's name. She and Marina were the victims in all this, and it was impossible to imagine that someone might be both victim and executioner.

But then, why lie? What was she hiding? Until he'd found the notice, nothing had seemed particularly ominous in her request. In the last few months, Gabriela had been a constant presence in Camilo's life, and therefore in Marina's. In fact, the day he died both women had been to Samuel's place to pick up some cuttings and plants he'd put aside for them. Marina had keys and both had taken their time. He imagined them taking a look around the rooms, tidying this or that, turning off lights and appliances that he might have left on, gently mocking the absent-mindedness, clumsiness and inability of men to run a house. Marina had even taken down his clothes from the line and ironed some shirts. Did something happen to changes things a few hours later?

There was a loose detail knocking about at the back of his mind, a fuzzy fragment, out of place in the pleasant texture of that day, which he wasn't able to bring into focus. In his mind he tried to put everything into chronological order: left for work at nine; Marina called him an hour later, saying they were going to his house now, while he was driving one of his vans collecting paper containers following a list … a list … a list … What was so peculiar about that list? The route? No … The fact that he'd had to print it quickly that morning at home before leaving, because the printer at work kept jamming. What with the rush, he'd left the computer on, but on coming back he'd found it off. What?

'No, no,' he moaned again, as he stood up with such violence that he almost knocked down an old man who happened by.

Blinded by urgency, he started walking home as he repeated:

'No! I don't want to think what I'm thinking! Because if that's the case, I'm to blame too, not from the moment I gave her that false alibi, but from earlier, from that morning when she must have checked my computer and seen those pictures. No! Not even from then, but from a lot earlier, from the moment I decided to keep the file instead of deleting it.'

Never had the computer seemed so slow to start up. He clicked on 'Pictures' and then on the file he shouldn't have kept, 'Dog'. Although he hadn't opened it again, the statistics revealed that it had been last modified on Monday, 16th April, the same day they had been at his house. But he knew it wasn't Marina who had opened it, not only because she barely knew how to use her own computer, but because she would have told him. No doubt she would have seen the file with her name and she would have said something about the fact that he had spied on her.

So it could only have been Gabriela who'd seen how the dog tore apart her son in those horrible images she didn't even suspect existed. Was there anything in them that had made her channel her pain in Olmedo's direction?

His hands were shaking so much that he could barely place the pointer over the pictures. He opened them one by one, in order, studying first the street with the children and their mothers, Marina appearing, the school bus arriving and leaving, everything accurately timed, one take every sixty seconds, until he came to the last ones, where the boys appeared kicking the ball around, in baggy clothes two sizes too big, taunting the dog that was poking its head over the fence, with ferocious teeth and furious eyes that proved that dogs and men are alike in that they defend their own territory much more ardently than they attack someone else's. And then the leap and the boy being bitten while his two friends ran off, not knowing what to do but horrified, along with other passers-by who flee, like the man who, at the back, with a hesitant look, glances at the scene ... What was that? Why did he look so familiar? He enlarged the picture expecting the detail to contradict what the whole suggested. He shook his head, incapable of admitting that chance or fate might have used him as their plaything. Because that was Olmedo's face, unwittingly photographed by Samuel before he knew him, captured as he fled, turning his head slightly backward. Samuel sank into his chair, still refusing to accept it, but now with a logical sequence in his mind in which everything fitted. Everyone knew that Camilo always carried a gun, even when wearing civilian clothes, because his name had appeared on a terrorist organisation's list. If Gabriela had concluded that at that moment he was carrying a gun and didn't use it ...

No, it couldn't be that simple, yet also that complex and painful. He took out the notice left by the delivery company and once again read the date and time, checking that Gabriela's absence corresponded with the day the file had been last modified, only a few hours later. Everything fitted, and even Olmedo's last words acquired a fuller meaning. Desolate, he closed every window and turned off the computer, whispering:

'If you had asked me I would have helped you. I don't know how, but I would have found a way for you not to …'

He went into the bedroom and slumped on the bed. With his eyes shut, he understood that horror occurs when one's fears are fully realised, as his now were. A few seconds later he got up and lowered the blinds for darkness to flood his house like it did at Gabriela's and cut himself off from the outside world. He went back to bed, once again closed his eyes and searched in vain for an honourable way out. There wasn't any. Disconcertingly, his confusion was born of knowledge, his doubts of lucidity. Two hours earlier, before he had read the notice, he was happy because Marina had agreed to move in with him; now everything was on the brink of collapsing.

'Unless …' he told himself, in such a state of excitement that he didn't at first realise he was speaking out loud.

Unless he tore the notice into pieces and never said a word, even if that meant breaking the rules he'd followed all his life, abandoning the conviction that there are ethical codes one has to comply with even if they are not written in the penal code. If he didn't talk, he would be committing a crime of omission, but everything would stay the same: Marina would stay with him, Gabriela would stay free and the detective would end up forgetting all about the enigma or, at least, accepting there was no chance of solving it. On the other hand, if he spoke … if he spoke it was likely that Marina would leave him, because he had triggered the chaos by spying on her. She would reproach him for the fact that everything, from the time he approached her to give her the bracelet, had been a lie, that their relationship was based on deceit.

He opened his eyes in the dark and decided that he wouldn't do anything. Just dispose of the notice and keep quiet. He tore the piece of paper slowly, down the middle, afraid of making too much noise, while he told himself that, from then on, he'd only need to be vigilant for the rest of his life, second after second, so that whenever he met Gabriela nothing would make her suspect that he knew her secret; so that when looking at Marina he didn't shake for fear of saying the wrong word; so that when he held her he didn't get restless at the idea that by laying her head on his chest she might hear the echo of the imposture beating within.

Because that was exactly it, being able to live with someone you're deceiving and look her in the eyes without blinking – without your voice shaking or your pulse quickening. Or not being able to, because decency, or dignity, courage, integrity, whatever one wanted to call it, stops you not so much from lying as from living a lie, firmly uttering the words you need to sound convincing.

'No!' he said decisively, because he knew what he couldn't do.

He rose from the bed, picked up the torn piece of paper and stuck it together with tape. He wasn't proud of what he was doing. On the contrary, it was with resigned exasperation, as he was aware of the burdens of his character, that he understood he wouldn't be able to live with Marina if this shadow got between them. However, neither did he know how to tell her or confront Gabriela with the notice and ask her why she had lied, where she had been when Olmedo died, what she had done during that hour she was supposed to have spent with him.

The only solution was to go to the detective. He was a quiet guy for his trade, and he had barely questioned him enough to confirm what Marina had said about him. But Samuel remembered him well, a tall calm person who waited patiently for his answers. Neither had Samuel forgotten his questions or the way he'd phrased them. Because he did not put you on the spot like a priest or a lawyer, but asked things in the manner of a doctor who won't give a diagnosis before he has all the information and cannot but sympathise with the patient. Perhaps the detective knew how to solve the conflict in such a way that not everything would be lost. Samuel must have his number somewhere.

It didn't take long to find it. He identified himself and asked if they could meet to have a word.

The detective received him in a flat that seemed to be both his house and his office. Samuel had crossed his assistant downstairs.

'Why are you coming to talk to me, when a few days ago you fired me?' the detective asked when they sat down. But he didn't sound anxious or hurt, and neither did he seem to be bracing himself for a lie; he simply showed the same curiosity Samuel had noticed the first time.

'Oh, it's not Marina who … She doesn't know I'm here.'

'And you?' he asked, but without curiosity, as if he knew what was coming, 'Why?'

'For the same reason she hired you.'

'You mean you don't believe it was suicide either. And you want me to find out who shot him.'

'Not exactly,' he replied. Then he thought for a few seconds before adding: 'To find out if one person in particular …'

'Gabriela, right?'

'How do you know?'

'Someone saw her go into Olmedo's flat that evening. At the time she'd said she was with you.'

'It was a lie.'

'But you backed her up.'

'It was a lie,' he repeated. 'Gabriela asked me to say that just in case the police wanted to know about her relationship with Camilo. She told me that, when someone commits suicide, everyone takes a good look around wondering who might have pushed him over the edge. She was alone at home and that might cause trouble. She told me she didn't have the strength to answer any questions, to explain. Because it wasn't only Camilo who had just died; her son had died a few months ago.'

'And you believed her.'

'Why not? There was no reason not to.'

'Of course not,' said Cupido. 'Until someone claimed they had seen her going into his place that evening.'

Samuel listened attentively, but no longer in surprise, as if his capacity for astonishment had been depleted when he'd discovered the notice.

'Then, there is no doubt, is there?'

'No. If she lied about her whereabouts, it's because she had good reason to lie.'

'You mean that even if I don't implicate her someone else might.'

'That person won't do it, unless they feel threatened or accused. But you … You haven't told me why you've changed your mind. Or what exactly you expect me to do.'

'Before I came here I didn't really know.'

'And now?'

'I have no doubts now. I'd like you to talk to her. I myself can't.'

He showed Cupido the delivery notice torn in half and stuck back together with tape and told him in detail everything that had happened: the computer, and before that the file with the photographs of the pit bull, and before that Marina bringing her child to the bus stop, and before that a lonely man who, from the darkness, watches a woman.

'I see. You don't know what to do. And you want her to know,' Cupido said, and didn't need to add: Because if you tell a judge, you will be doing the right thing, but that might mean losing Marina. On the other hand, if you remain silent, you'll have to live with a secret that won't let you breathe, and in that case you won't be able to live with her either. It's that, isn't it? That's what it is. 'And now you want me to …'

'I can't do it.'

'… to talk to her and let her decide, let her choose what's to be done.'

'Yes, it's her decision to make.'

Cupido looked at him with the slight surprise he always felt in the presence of people who were capable of such love that they wouldn't allow anything false or evil to tarnish their relationship with others. He realised Samuel belonged to that small, nearly extinct, group of men who would rather lose a woman than compromise her or harm her; who would rather leave for the end of the world and be called a coward than do something loathsome. The detective wished he could be like them.

'Leave the notice with me,' he said a bit brusquely.

'I'll pay you,' he said handing over the piece of paper.

'We'll talk about that later.'

'I'll pay you,' he insisted, 'whatever Marina had promised you if you finished the job.'

22

Locked In

Cupido wanted to check one more thing before talking to Gabriela. He got in the car and drove to the delivery company. An employee looked with suspicion at the notice torn in half and taped back together, but she agreed to check her records. Indeed, the notice had been dropped at that time.

'It's been over fifteen days. The parcel must have been sent back,' she said, typing the reference number on her computer. 'In any case, it's not under your name. It's addressed to a woman.'

'Yes.'

'Without written authorisation, I can only give it to the addressee.'

'Of course,' conceded Cupido, without insisting, as he already had the information he wanted.

He went back to the city and parked in front of Gabriela's house. He rang the intercom several times but there was no answer. The blinds were still down, as when he'd visited her, and he considered the possibility that she might be in and refused to come to the door.

From his mobile he rang the phone number Samuel had given him, but the line was busy. Perhaps she was talking to somebody or perhaps she had simply disconnected the phone.

In any case, he had to contact her. If she was in, sooner or later she'd have to come out, or come back if she was out. So Cupido went back to his car and waited, patiently, while he thought of how Alkalino might help him reach the woman who probably was upstairs, in the darkness, locked up with her son's ashes, as lonely as he was.

Suddenly he recognised the gentle yet bitter touch of pity. He thought of Gabriela's sorrow and thought about himself. Something reminded him of Gloria, a painter he'd never met, who had been brutally murdered at Paternoster nature reserve. There came a point, while he was investigating her death, when he knew so much about her – he had read her diary, seen pictures of her, had plunged into other people's memories of her – that he felt as though he was falling in love with a dead woman. Now he realised the boy torn apart by the dog could have been the son he had sometimes wanted, and he wondered what he might have felt in the face of such a loss.

It was true that there was no romanticism in crime: a thief steals for his own benefit, not to give to the poor, and a murderer kills out of revenge or hatred, not to free the world of a tyrant. But he'd also come across cases when it hadn't been evil that triggered tragedy. And in such cases he felt a sort of silent, strong, individual compassion, which had nothing to do with the resonant sentimentality that infects the media and the public and is so easily forgotten. He hoped he never lost that capacity to feel compassion for any kind of victim.

Although he had no one to make a promise to, as he watched Gabriela's windows from his car he told himself that, if he ever felt indifferent to other people's pain, he would instantly stop being a detective. He would never resign himself to being a simple problem-solver.

23

A Letter

Dear Marina,

Forgive me.

These were the first words in the note that your father started to write to me, and they are also my first words. Forgive me for all that I'm about to tell you. I want you to know only the essentials, so I won't dwell on superfluous details. I have no time. The detective you hired because you couldn't believe that Camilo committed suicide – how right you were! – is downstairs, in his car, waiting for me to come out. He's rung the bell and phoned a few times, but I haven't answered, because I need this time to tell you everything. Through the blinds I have seen him look up, as if he has guessed I'm in and don't want to talk to anyone. I suppose I never fooled him, but this time I will. Tell him, though, that he's a good detective, that he was always tactful and, in the end, he discovered the truth.

They've just rung me from a delivery company to tell me that they have located the parcel that a man – a tall, attractive man – went to claim on my behalf. They delivered it on the evening Camilo died, while I was out, and slipped a notice under the door. But I never saw it, because it was possibly blown behind the plant by the door. In the laundry room I've found Samuel's tin of pesticide, which he left behind when he came to treat the plants. And I've read a note he left me. From that and the telephone call I can only reach one conclusion: the truth is finally out, I have nothing to hide. But don't think I'm scared by this. On the contrary, right now I feel a kind of calm I don't remember feeling for a long, long time.

By the time the detective gets impatient and finds a way to get into my house, I will no longer be here. The first thing he'll see will be this letter. I'm sure he'll give it to you, and he'll tell you anything you don't understand or that I haven't managed to explain. That's what you hired him for. Even if you later dismissed him, he went on investigating on his own. Some people need to know the truth.

But before he talks to you, I'd like to tell you my version. I'm the only person who saw your father die. I killed him. There is no better witness, really.

Do you remember that morning when Samuel invited us to his house to pick up some plants and cuttings he had put aside for us, because he said our flats looked sad and needed the light, colour and perfume of a few flowers? Do you remember? He was at work and you suggested we stay there a while. What woman could resist looking around the house of the man she's seeing when he's away? A few things needed tidying. Not because the place was a mess, he's a very organised man, but because of those details they always miss. I thought it was then that you said, while laughing, that men are animals who are always happy with the way their lair looks. In the bedroom you opened his wardrobe and arranged a couple of shirts and trousers on their hangers, so that they wouldn't get all creased. I don't know if you remember that, on finding a few old clothes, you threatened to throw about half of them into the bin. Joking, you said it wouldn't be such a loss, because Samuel claimed, almost boasting, that he bought all his clothes in supermarkets, as if that were a good thing. You took down the clothes on the line and, since we were not in a hurry, you said you were going to iron them, because otherwise he would not only wear them all crumpled, but he wouldn't even notice.

As I had nothing in particular to do, I went upstairs to take a look at the bedrooms, that beautiful study he's got, with so much light. I was looking at the few photographs placed around it when I realised the computer was on; it gave off that faint smell of heated cables that sometimes emanates from appliances that have been on for a long time. The monitor was off but the processor was still buzzing. No doubt Samuel had forgotten to switch it off when he'd left for work.

I've always been scared of leaving electronics on when there's no one around to keep an eye on them, so I moved the mouse with the intention of turning it off if there was no programme running, and then the screen lit up. I guess you've seen the picture he has set as his screensaver. Your face, Marina, your face is the first thing Samuel sees when he turns the computer on, a close up of you smiling as if you were saying hello. Your calm, luminous, beautiful face, which in so many ways reminds me of your father's face.

Of course, it's very common to set the face of the person one loves as a screensaver, but I found it surprising and I liked it – I hadn't imagined Samuel would do a thing like that. You were still downstairs busy with the clothes, and I almost called you over to show you, in case you hadn't seen it, but then I thought you might accuse me of being nosy, because I had no reason to touch the computer. I then clicked to turn if off, but curiosity got the better of me, because that picture of you was one in a series he'd taken on a day I'd been with you, and he'd taken some of me that he'd never shown me. So I opened the "Pictures" folder and the subfolders embedded in it, "Marina", "Garden", "Company", "Various"… I felt I was prying too much and I was about to close everything down when I chanced on a folder simply called "Dog".

I wouldn't be able to explain why I clicked on it, what aftertaste of pain pushed me to open it. I didn't know what was in it, behind that word, and all of a sudden I saw my son there, first smiling with his two friends, kicking the ball around, no doubt all noisy and cocky, calling attention to themselves, because the last thing a teenager wants to be is invisible. I don't know if your children, when they grow up, will behave like this. He was a bit of a rebel, he couldn't help it, perhaps because he never had a father to banter with – a father who would counteract a teenager's inherent rebelliousness.

Sometimes I've thought that ours is an unlucky generation: as children we suffered the tyranny of our parents, their old-fashioned ideas about education, hierarchy and familial discipline, and now we suffer the tyranny of our children, who are excessively mollycoddled and at the same time very demanding. I don't know. Perhaps I was too lenient with him. In any case, I do know Manuel was often impulsive and pigheaded. He wasn't an easy child. I tried to play the double role of mother and father as best I could. Do you want to know what the worst part is? Motherly love is not enough to make your child happy. In fact, I sometimes got the impression that that was the least of his concerns, as if at his age what all kids wanted was to be loved by the world, by their peers, by this or that girl, in fact by anyone but their family. And I often asked myself: how else can I make my son happy? And I ended up admitting that I couldn't or didn't know how to do any different.

So it was logical that Manuel should provoke that dog the way he did. Since then I've thought about this so many times! When you're a teenager you believe life is long and you're the centre of the world; that you're essential to the world and must answer all the voices that talk to you and rise to all the challenges they set you. To grow up, on the other hand, means discovering that the world is indifferent to you, that no one hears you or listens to you, that you will die and nothing will stop because of that. That life flies by and everything ends before it's even started.

You, Marina, have not seen those pictures, but you can imagine them: the children fooling around, getting scared, laughing, taunting the dog; the dog barking and then jumping over the fence. I saw it all like a nightmare, it was so vivid that I could almost hear the barks, the cries of pain, the screams coming out of the screen. Only later, when I went over them in my mind, did I come to the conclusion that the images must have been taken when Samuel wasn't there, he must have programmed the camera, because each take had a time on it, and there was one for every minute, and the framing and the angle were exactly the same in each of them.

I barely had time to close the file when I heard you come up the stairs. You were carrying the clothes basket and you saw me so pale that you asked if I was feeling okay. Do you remember, Marina? I told you I was fine and went to the kitchen to fetch a glass of water. I could hardly breathe and barely managed to look you in the face, because in one of the pictures I had recognised your father. Yes, Camilo.

He doesn't appear in the foreground, and at first I was so astonished that I had to enlarge the picture to make sure it was him. Samuel couldn't have known who Camilo was back then; if he had realised I don't think he would have kept the picture. But when the photographs were taken he didn't even know you and, of course, didn't know Camilo. I remember the day you introduced him to your father and me.

But, without a doubt, it was your father who walked by at that moment. And if he never told you, it was because he couldn't have felt proud of his, I was about to write cowardice, but I don't think that's the right word, because he wasn't a coward. Let's say the right word is ambition. No doubt pride played a part too. I'll explain.

Your father appears in profile, with his back slightly turned, walking away from the dog that's already biting my son's arm. He doesn't look like he's escaping yet: it's the moment before. His right hand is inside his jacket, as when someone checks he hasn't lost his wallet. But it wasn't that which he was touching, but his gun.

You know as well as I do that he always carried a gun, that he never went out without one since his name had appeared on the list of a terrorist organisation. He used to say he felt naked without a gun. But those pictures were taken in mid October last year, a little after that accident during a shooting practice, when his regulation gun was taken from him. So he was carrying the illegal gun he kept at home. I asked him about this on that last evening, of course I did. He told me that his first impulse was to shoot the dog, but that, used as he was to making decisions in a split second, he realised that to use a gun when he'd been given express orders not to constituted a serious infringement of military law. So he simply walked away, thinking it wouldn't come to more than a couple of bites.

Camilo was your father, so I don't need to tell you how this decision came to torment him, once he knew how brutally it had all ended. I'll say more, I think that when we met, we started seeing each other not because he was attracted to me, but to comfort me for a tragedy he felt partly responsible for. I mean, there are men who smile cannily when they trick a creditor or postpone a payment, and others who cannot bear having debts; their honesty and sense of fairness make them feel they have received more than they have given back, and they are not at peace until they find a way to repay what they owe. So at first it was all about remorse and trying to alleviate my grief. Love, if I can say so, came later. But that's a private matter between him and me, which no one will ever have access to, to which there won't be any witnesses by the time you read this letter, when I am gone.

As I was saying, you father fled the scene, and I'll add that he shouldn't have. He should have known that a dog like that, a pit bull, doesn't let go once it bites. He should have shot it, even if that meant a stain on his immaculate service record or being removed from the decision-making process at such an important time, when his name was being considered in Madrid to study the viability of the San Marcial base. That's what I meant by ambition and pride.

'Fine,' you'll tell me, 'but the fact that he walked away doesn't make him a monster. Do you know anyone who is not ashamed of anything he either did or failed to do?' Is there anyone who doesn't conceal things that they'd rather not remember and who blushes when they are evoked? Of course not! I too understand why Camilo did what he did, but I don't condone it.

Like a good soldier, Camilo was farsighted and the following day he must have weighed up the risks of what had happened. It was impossible that anyone should implicate him if he kept silent. What he couldn't imagine was the evidence in the hands of a man who programmes a camera to photograph a woman. Who could imagine a thing like that?

I've never spoken about this to you, but the first few weeks after Manuel's death were unbearable. It took me a long time to believe that I'd be able to live in peace with my sorrow, as it couldn't have been greater, and that I wouldn't always be one of those women who, when they speak about their children, have to be told, 'don't cry, please don't cry'. How short-lived that belief turned out to be! Because that morning at Samuel's I realised that the man who was trying to console me for my loss was also the one who could have prevented it. Camilo, however, didn't know what I had discovered. I didn't answer the phone when he twice rang me that afternoon. The hours between the discovery of the pictures and his death were horrible, a hallucinatory maelstrom of hatred and confusion. I locked myself in at home with the blinds down, but I saw everything in searing white, as if my pupils had dilated to take in all the light and heat in the world. Almost suffocating, I went out for a walk and noticed I was sweating. I remember I saw a noticeboard indicating the temperature and it wasn't high, but I felt as if a terrible heat descended from the sky. I went back home soon afterwards, barely conscious of where I'd been, carrying that turbulent, fresh, free-floating pain. I think I went slightly crazy in those hours, sorrow took me to that mental state in which one kills another to relieve tension. Time and again I asked myself a question for which I had no answer. What to do about someone who has done something terrible to you and whom you love all the same?

I went to his flat to see if he could help me answer it. He confirmed everything I already knew. He didn't deny anything. He'd been carrying a gun, and he'd never thought the attack would end in tragedy. He thought the owner of the house would come out soon and stop it, and that it would all end in a couple of bites. He didn't even try to hold me as he told me this. He just looked at me with a calm, sad acceptance, as if he'd always known that his escape would eventually come out into the open. He asked me to forgive him, although he must have known I never would. In fact, forgiving no longer mattered, it was all over and the lights would go off soon.

I mumbled something about going to the toilet and went out of his study. I knew he kept that gun with a silencer in his night table: I'd seen it one day and told him he should find a better hiding place. I went back to the study with it. Your father was writing something on a piece of paper and didn't raise his head until I was in front of the desk.

It all happened very quickly, effortlessly; I felt weightless, unaffected by the law of gravity. But I needed to complete the other half of the job before anyone came in to stop me on hearing the shot, improbable though that was: it didn't make a loud pop as when you open a bottle of champagne, but a quiet one as when you open an old, tired wine, sour like the smell of powder. I put the barrel of the gun in my mouth, determined to end it all. It was burning hot, as if I had put a match in my mouth, and I think it was the instinctive reflex of taking it out of my mouth and waiting for a minute that brought on the fear and made me put off until today what should have ended right then. Because that's all it was, a fear of pain, as if I had used up all my courage in the first shot.

Your father had started writing something on one of his cards, perhaps believing that I'd leave without giving him a chance to speak, or perhaps searching for the right words. 'Forgive me.' I understood that the words gave me back my life, it was like a document that saved me, a safe-conduct; I didn't need to wait for the barrel to cool down, because he'd opened the door and was ordering me to leave. I only had to wipe off my fingerprints and put the gun in his hands for the meaning and the intended recipient of those two words to change in the eyes of whoever found the note.

I didn't touch it. I left it on the desk, in front of him, and a few minutes later I left in silence. No one saw me.

Later I waited and grew restless and you found the body. And later still appeared the detective who, I sensed, would end up finding out the truth: you cannot invite a country person to your country house and not expect him to feel the earth and notice what grows in it. But I wasn't particularly afraid of the detective; I was only curious to see how long he would take to reach the truth by firmly yet gently asking questions that a regular police officer would shout at you. I was not afraid of him, and neither was I scared when another source of irritation – I don't want to call it a problem – presented itself in the person of the street sweeper in Camilo's street, something that barely merits a mention. I was confident they would give me enough time to plan my departure.

I'd thought of swimming into the sea until I exhausted myself. The sea would give back my body. It had always seemed to me the proper place to die, and the agony is short-lived. Now, however, I've found a better way of disappearing forever, without photographs and witnesses. I don't feel like putting up with curious, hateful or pitiful gazes, and the thought of explaining to a police officer or a judge something they'd never understand feels infinitely boring. You, though, deserve an explanation, hence my writing to you. You, Samuel and perhaps the detective. To understand what I did and am about to do one needs a modicum of pity, and I hope that you have some left in you, in spite of the sorrow caused by your father's death.

Don't blame Samuel. If he's guilty of anything, it's of having liked you so much that it wasn't enough for him to see you a few minutes a day through a window; he wanted to have a picture of you. That's surely why he took those photographs. Or perhaps he was afraid you would disappear and nothing would remain of you. Find out, ask him before judging him. Perhaps now you don't realise it, but after all the terrible things you've had to go through, you may need him more than he needs you.

Don't hate me, please, although you have good reason to. Hatred will only make you suffer, and it cannot hurt me. I'm going to a place where I'll be immune to everything and where time doesn't count. Up here it's just me and my sorrows, and nothing can separate us. Only when I go down will my sorrow disappear. Down there I'll do no more harm. It won't take much of an effort. It's not hard to die when everyone you've loved is dead already.

I'll leave through the garage. The detective won't be able to stop me. When he grows impatient and finds a way in, I'll be gone.

Time to leave. Forgive me. I couldn't forgive your father in time. Goodbye,

Gabriela

24

End Without Ending

'You say you've read the letter?'

'Yes, Marina gave it to me.'

'She did? After dismissing you from the case?'

'Well, yes. First she listened to the whole story although she reproached me for it: "Why, why did you have to carry on when I told you I didn't want to know anything else? Why?"'

'I see her point,' said Alkalino. 'She'd hired you to find an answer, but this wasn't the answer she expected you to find.'

'No, she'd never imagined that precisely Gabriela … She repeated she would have preferred not to know, that sometimes ignorance is bliss.'

'And that's why she gave you the letter, so she cannot read it again.'

'That, and because Gabriela named me as its third reader, and because she's learned a lesson from Samuel.'

'What lesson?'

'That you should not keep anything that might do you harm. That it's best to delete all documents, souvenirs or images which make us feel unclean or stoke up hatred. It doesn't matter if they're on paper, on a computer or simply in our memory. Here,' he said. He took an envelope with Marina's name on it out of his pocket. Inside were five sheets of paper written on both sides in handwriting less unsteady than he would have thought. He gave the letter to Alkalino. 'The judge has seen it, and it's a closed case. Read it before I burn it.'

'No!' he shouted. With a collector's passion, he kept many documents from Cupido's investigations.

'I promised her.'

'To burn it?'

'Yes.'

'In that case …'

Alkalino started attentively, slowly reading the letter, as if he wanted to memorise it, moving his lips or raising his eyebrows when he was surprised by a comment or a thought.

'The poor, unhappy murderess!' he exclaimed after several minutes, when he finished reading and carefully folded the pages and put them back in the envelope. His hard, small dark eyes were wet with pity for the stupid, tragic human race. The passionate, alcoholic man of yesterday had turned into a moralist and a sceptic. 'The poor, unhappy murderess, who was so wrong that she thought her desire to die allowed her to kill!'

'Well, at least she was happy during those fifteen years when the boy was alive,' said Cupido.

'Fifteen years! But I don't know if so little time can make up for all the pain that came later,' he said.

'Maybe it can,' replied Cupido after thinking for a few seconds of his dead brother, who was always in his mother's thoughts. 'Perhaps a man would rather not have a child that will die at the age of fifteen, but maybe a woman's instinct is different.'

'Why did she write "up here"?' asked Alkalino.

'Because she had already decided how to disappear, at the bottom of the earth, sixty metres underground in a volframium mine. And her body, next to a broken urn and the ring that Olmedo had bought her, would never had been found if a hunter hadn't seen her throw herself in.'

'For once no one will be sentenced.'

'No, she sentenced herself. The note Olmedo had started writing only delayed the ruling a few weeks.'

'But Olmedo didn't write that to save her.'

'No, but he wasn't lying either. Someone writing his last word doesn't lie. He was sincerely sorry. But we'd wrongly interpreted what he was sorry about and who he was addressing,' Cupido explained. Then he went quiet for a few seconds, and doubted whether that was really the truth, so he added: 'Unless he heard her going into the bedroom, opening the drawer of the night table, and guessed what would happen and felt so much love and remorse that he wanted to fool everybody ...'

'But we'll never know that.'

'No, we'll never know.'

'Do you think Marina will ever forget Samuel's photos?'

'I think he'll try to have those photographs forgotten.'

'He'll manage. She'll end up ...'

'It'll be hard for him too.'

'Do you think?'

'Yes, he may find it harder than Marina to forget all the damage they've caused.'

'But it all ends peacefully.'

'Everyone will need some time,' said Cupido, who, as always at the end of an investigation, felt confused, exhausted, empty, and pessimistic. Once again he'd solved a difficult case, but once again he didn't have the impression that he'd achieved a complete, clean, benign victory. The bad thing about victory in his line of work was that he got it at the expense of someone else's pain. There was no sense of final triumph.

'The purpose of civilisation is to curb people's natural impulses,' he heard Alkalino say. 'We know there will always be someone who feels hatred, or spite, or a desire for revenge, but that won't amount to anything if they don't act on it. We know it and yet we are always too late to prevent it.'

'You're right. We're never on time. What did you call her before? Ah, yes, the poor unhappy murderess!'

'But there's nothing else you can do. You did your job even after they fired you. Your work is done.'

'Done? In this job, you're never done.'